The Darkest Hour

Also by Barbara Erskine

Barbara Erskine

The Darkest Hour

HarperCollins*Publishers*

HarperCollins*Publishers*
77–85 Fulham Palace Road,
Hammersmith, London W6 8JB

www.harpercollins.co.uk

Published by HarperCollins*Publishers* 2014
1

A catalogue record for this book is available
from the British Library

ISBN: 978-0-00-751312-3

This novel is entirely a work of fiction.
The names, characters and incidents portrayed in it are
the work of the author's imagination. Any resemblance to
actual persons, living or dead, events or localities is
entirely coincidental.

Set in Meridien by Palimpsest Book Production Limited,
Falkirk, Stirlingshire

Printed and bound in Great Britain by
Clays Ltd, St Ives plc

MIX
Paper from
responsible sources
FSC
www.fsc.org   **FSC° C007454**

For my Dad, with love
and
In memory of my darling Mummy
who had her own part in the origins
of this story, and who would have loved
to join in the adventure of writing it.

The Family Tree

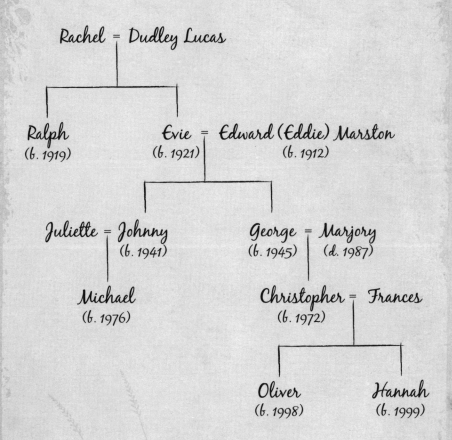

Rachel = Dudley Lucas

Ralph
(b. 1919)

Evie = Edward (Eddie) Marston
(b. 1921)   (b. 1912)

Juliette = Johnny
(b. 1941)

George = Marjory
(b. 1945)   (d. 1987)

Michael
(b. 1976)

Christopher = Frances
(b. 1972)

Oliver
(b. 1998)

Hannah
(b. 1999)

Prologue

March

Glancing into the driving mirror Laurence Standish frowned uneasily as he swung the old Citroën estate off the main road and headed into a side turning which wound down steeply through coppiced woods towards the valley bottom. The sleek black Ford which had been sitting on his tail for the last twenty miles or so had followed him and was drawing closer.

He had first noticed the car coming out of Chichester. It was close behind him. Too close, and he was growing increasingly irritated. Perhaps he shouldn't have turned off the main road. He was lost now, well off the beaten track, threading his way up and down winding lanes, ever mindful of the car still there in his rear view mirror.

He was approaching a crossroads now. On impulse he spun the Citroën's steering wheel to the left at the last moment without signalling, feeling the suspension sway and adjust as the road climbed steeply again, becoming narrower and more potholed as it crested the rise and plunged once more into the woods.

The black car followed him. If anything it had closed the gap between them slightly.

He didn't recognise the car and he couldn't make out the face of the driver but there was no doubt at all that he was being harassed in an increasingly dangerous fashion. He had no idea why. Was it road rage? Had he offended him by pulling out in front of him or something? He wasn't aware of doing anything which anyone could take offence at. Did the guy want to rob him? Did he want his car? He doubted it! He fumbled in his pocket for his mobile with the vague idea of calling the police and cursed, remembering that he had thrown it into the battered old briefcase which at this moment lay on the back seat with the surprise birthday present he had picked up for Lucy. A signpost flashed past. He couldn't see how far it was to the next village, but once there he resolved to pull up outside the first shop he reached and go inside.

The car was even closer now and it was flashing its lights.

Supposing there was something wrong. For a moment he hesitated, taking his foot off the accelerator and as though sensing his hesitation the driver behind him pulled out to try and overtake. Still flashing its lights the nose of the Ford drew level. The road was narrow and winding and there was a sharp left hand bend ahead.

'Oh shit!' Laurence stamped on his brake. The car behind him was trying to force its way past. It swerved towards him and there was a scrape of metal, followed by a louder grinding noise as the wheels of the two vehicles locked. Instinctively Laurence pulled his car towards the left, praying there was room for him to manoeuvre. His Citroën's wheels spun on the muddy verge, then gripped and flung the car into the dense hazel brake. Laurence was aware for a fraction of a second of the tangle of splintering branches thrashing against the windscreen, then beyond, a strip of woodland sloping steeply down towards a stream at the bottom of an area of rolling hillside.

The Citroën banked sharply, racing faster down the hill.

Laurence was stabbing frantically for the brake. Shocked and disorientated, he fought to hold the steering wheel. The last thing he saw was the huge oak tree heading straight for him.

The car reared up momentarily as it struck the oak, then it slid sideways in a cascade of shredded bark and started to roll. At the foot of the slope it hit another tree crushing the bonnet like a concertina as it came at last to a stop. There were several moments of silence as the ruptured fuel lines spilled their contents onto the hot exhaust, then with a roar the car burst into flames.

The driver of the Ford had pulled up at the roadside ten yards ahead. He climbed out and ran back, standing by the torn and broken trees, looking down at the burning wreck. That was not supposed to happen.

'Shit!'

Unknowingly repeating Laurence's last word he watched in horror as the car exploded, sending a ball of flame and smoke up into the windless air.

For a moment he stood completely still, then swiftly he turned away and ran back to the Ford. It was scraped and dented but still drivable. He climbed in. As he drove away from the scene he pulled the black balaclava off over his head and tucked it into the door pocket.

Nothing in the car would be recoverable.

But no one was going to survive that inferno.

Shit.

1

Three months later

Lucy Standish was in the kitchen of the small flat above the art gallery in Westgate, Chichester, an open letter in her hand. She had read it twice already, trying in her own mind to make sense of the contents.

Re: Your application for a grant to research the life of war artist and portraitist Evelyn Lucas, with a view to producing a biography and definitive history of her career:
    I am pleased to inform you that your application for a grant from the Women's Art Fund has been accepted . . .

She had been accepted. She had been given the grant. Lucy put down the letter and walked across to the window. The gallery was part of a terrace of narrow period houses, each one different, some two storey, some three. Hers was three, with a small attic floor under a roof of ancient tiles. From the kitchen, on the first floor, she could look down at the pocket handkerchief back garden she and Laurence had created together from the builders' rubble which had filled the small yard when they first took over the gallery four years before. The short paved path was lined with flowers now, the small lilac tree they had planted had blossomed. There were butterflies everywhere; she could see them hanging from her pots of lavender and from the clinging roses on the fence.

It was months since she had applied for the grant. She and Laurence had discussed the project endlessly, wondering how she could take time out from the gallery to research a book. It was their part-time assistant, Robin, who had suggested applying for some sort of bursary; Robin who had turned up the obscure organisation which had now come up trumps. Robin who had made it all seem possible. Then, before Larry died.

Now it was too late.

She glanced round. On one side of the first-floor kitchen was their living room, and on the far side behind a closed door was the studio where Laurence had worked. It was somewhere she could hardly bear to go, even now. It was in there they had discussed Evelyn Lucas with so much excitement when they had realised that for all her fame there were no books about her, very little research, hardly any information at all; it was there they stood together in front of Evelyn's self-portrait and it was there, in front of the painting, that Laurence had bent to take Lucy in his arms and kiss her hard on the mouth before running down the stairs and going out to the car.

It was the last time she had seen him. Taking a deep breath she walked across to the studio door and opened it. The portrait of Evelyn still stood on the easel where it had been on the day Laurence died. He had been about to start restoring it when he had had the notion, he hadn't told her why, that he would like a second opinion on its authenticity. He had contacted Professor David Solomon at the Royal Academy and arranged to take the picture up to London on that fateful day at the end of March. Two hours before he was due to leave the professor's secretary had phoned to say David Solomon had flu and they had postponed the meeting.

So why had he gone out anyway? She remembered his smile, his mysterious wink as he tapped his nose, his last words 'I won't be long'. He hadn't taken the painting with him after all, and obviously he wasn't going to meet David Solomon, so where was he going? The question had circled endlessly round in her head. For a while she had wondered if he had gone to buy her birthday present. That might have explained the wink. But that would have meant he had died on a trip to do something for her and she couldn't live with that thought. Her birthday had come and gone only days after the crash and she had tried to put the idea out of her head. She would never know now.

The professor had written to her several weeks later with his condolences and had suggested that one day, when she was ready, perhaps he could come down and view the portrait here at the gallery. She had not replied, though she suspected Robin had.

Dear Robin. She must start taking control of her life again. It had to go on. And she had to face the fact that almost certainly she could no longer afford him; probably no longer afford to go on running the gallery even with the bursary to back up her income. Glancing into the mirror on the wall by the door she sighed. She had lost a lot of weight over the last three months. Her face, always thin with high angular cheekbones, was positively haggard, her dark eyes enormous in contrast to her pale skin. She had raked her long straight dark brown hair back into an unflattering ponytail which Larry would have hated.

The studio was in darkness, the blinds pulled down over the north-facing skylight windows. The room ran the full depth of the house front to back and the front windows looked out over the street below. She pulled the blinds up allowing the clear north light to flood in at the back, and resolutely she faced the easel. Evelyn Lucas, if it was indeed her, had painted herself sitting perched on a farm gate. She was young, perhaps in her early twenties, and dressed in fawn jodhpurs with a blue sweater knotted round her shoulders over a blue and white gingham shirt, her honey-blond hair loose and wild in the wind. She had dark blue eyes which looked straight out of the portrait, eyes which were engaging, challenging even, daring the viewer to do, what?

At the corner of the painting, a patch of sky with torn grey clouds and fragments of blue behind her shoulder, there was a clean area where Laurence had started to remove some of the grime which covered the surface. Lucy moved closer and stared at the corner. There had to be something there he had spotted which had caught his attention and made him doubt the picture's provenance. But what?

'You OK?' Robin's voice behind her made her jump. He was standing in the doorway. She hadn't heard him let himself into the gallery below.

She nodded. 'Do you know what it was Larry saw here which made him think it wasn't an Evelyn Lucas after all?'

Robin came to stand beside her. 'No idea.'

They gazed at the painting in silence for several seconds. That it was of Evelyn had been almost beyond doubt. There were photos of her on the record and she certainly looked extraordinarily like them. Lawrence had picked up the painting at an auction only a few weeks before his death. It had been catalogued as 'Portrait of Unknown Woman', but when he brought it home in triumph he told Lucy that he suspected that it might be a missing Lucas from the early 1940s. It was being sold by the executors of an old lady who had died without close heirs and its past was, as far as he knew, a mystery. In Larry speak, he took a punt and bought it for a song.

Robin folded his arms and squinted at it. 'Whoever painted it, I think it's lovely.'

She smiled. 'So do I.'

Robin glanced at her. 'Sure you're OK?'

'Why go out if the professor has cancelled?' she had begged. *She hated it when he went away on his own. But he had insisted he had to go out. And he had refused to let her go with him.*

When the police knocked on the door a few hours after he had left

8

she didn't believe them. What was he doing on a remote lane on the way to Petersfield? Why had he turned off the main road? Where had he been going?

They never found out exactly what had happened. He had skidded, that much was clear from the tyre tracks, and there was evidence that another car had been in collision with his, but the fire damage had been too great to discover much more. He had probably been killed by the impact with the first tree. No other vehicle had shown up on the database with damage which would correlate to the paint marks which had survived. It was black, and probably a Ford. How many black Fords were there in the south of England? Lucy did not care. No amount of forensic evidence would bring Larry back, her perfect, adored, talented husband.

She turned away from the painting and looked at Robin. Short, plump, slightly balding and with the biggest and best smile of anyone she had ever known, Robin Cassell had been her mainstay and her rock for the last three months. When Larry was alive he had come in to run the gallery two or three mornings a week to allow them some time in the studio and the freedom to go to auctions and on buying trips around the country. When the gallery reopened three weeks after Larry's funeral it had been at Robin's suggestion, and he had started coming in every day. 'Just until you are back on your feet,' he had said, giving her a hug.

Guessing at her cash flow problem – neither her parents, nor Larry's were in a position to help her financially – and knowing Larry had made no will, he had refused to let her pay him. But that situation could not go on. However much he wanted to help her she could not let him continue to work for nothing. He didn't need the money; he was, as he mockingly put it, a trust fund kid, which meant he had inherited a large house from his parents which had been sold for development. Besides that, he worked on and off with his life partner, Phil, who ran a bookshop in the centre of town, but even so, her conscience had been beginning to worry her. Until now.

'I've got the grant, Robin,' she said quietly. She turned

back to the picture. 'I had the letter this morning. What am I going to do?'

'You are going to write the book, ducky.' Robin smiled. 'You owe that to Lol. And to our Evelyn here.'

'I don't know that I can. Not without him.' She blinked back the sudden tears so close all the time, so near the surface.

'You can. And you will. And it will be up to you to prove if this is a painting of her, by her, or not.'

'Professor Solomon would tell us that.'

'Maybe.' Robin stood back, still staring at the picture. 'Maybe not.'

'Did you tell him not to come, Robin?'

'I said we would be in touch when we were ready.'

'Thank you.'

'So, it's up to you, Luce. Take the money and start researching. Leave the gallery to me, at least for a while. You know I love looking after it.' Robin turned away and walked back into the kitchen. 'Did you have any breakfast this morning?' he called over his shoulder.

She followed him through and closed the door on the studio. 'I wasn't hungry.'

'Well I am, so I am going to make us some toast with lashings of marmalade and some coffee and then you are going to start planning how you are going to approach your research. OK?'

She gave a wan smile. 'Maybe,' she echoed.

'No maybe about it. You've got to start living again and this will gently lead you out into the world. You know Uncle Robin is right.'

She walked over and picked the letter up from the worktop where she had dropped it earlier. She read it through again and then she looked up at him. 'I'll think about it, OK?'

The evenings were the worst. When the sign on the gallery door had been turned over to read 'Closed' and Robin had gone home to Phil, and she was alone in the flat. At first there had been people around. Her family, friends, Larry's family, they had all been there for her, but slowly their visits had become fewer and further between. Neither she nor Larry had brothers or sisters; her parents and Larry's lived miles away and in some ways she had been glad of that. She needed time to be alone, to think and to grieve.

Tonight was different. She waved Robin out of the door and locked up behind him then she climbed the stairs back to the flat and went straight into the studio.

She stood for a long time staring at the picture, taking in the detail of the composition, the position of the young woman, just a girl, really, in the landscape, the detail of the countryside around her, then of Evelyn herself, if it was Evelyn, her clothes, her eyes and hair, her expression. It was strange. The more one looked at it, the more hostile that expression seemed to become. She was good-looking – beautiful even, but there was a rawness about her, a violence in the brushstrokes which was unsettling. Robin was right. The painting contained a mystery of some sort. And surely it was a mystery Larry would want her to solve. She shivered. Were it not for the fact that the professor in London had cancelled the meeting the painting would have been in the car with Larry. It would have been destroyed. Perhaps providence had saved it for a reason.

She moved over to the table and switched on the lamp. No doubt Larry had thousands of digital photos of the painting on line, but he had also made several prints, much enlarged, pinned to a board on the wall. She stared at the close-ups of the paint textures, then she turned back to the painting. Scrabbling round in the tray on the table beside the easel she picked up Larry's magnifying glass. Ignoring the sudden pain which swept over her as she took it in her hand and realised that he had been the last person to touch it, she held it up to the area of the picture which he had started to clean and scrutinised the paint. She could see nothing special. Just sky and clouds. Shaking her head she put down the magnifying glass and surveyed the selection of bottles of liquids and gels on his tray. Conservation liquids, solvents, acetone, turps, they were all there. Hesitantly she picked up one of the bottles of cleaning emulsion. Pulling up the high stool on which Larry perched when he was working at the easel, and reaching for a cotton bud, she dipped it into the fluid and gently stroked the edge of the clean patch where Larry had made his first tentative efforts. The cotton came away covered in dirt. And paint. She frowned. Paint? She felt a moment of panic. If this was an Evelyn Lucas it was potentially very valuable. Perhaps valuable enough to solve her money problems forever should she ever sell it. She must not damage it. She looked at the picture again and then she saw it, so obvious when you looked closely. A section of the sky had been over-painted. It had been done skilfully, but obviously at some point after the original paint had dried. She moved closer and worked on another small section, her tongue protruding slightly between her teeth, removing the newer paint, acutely aware that Larry would be furious with her; that working on the painting was something for a trained expert like him, not for a rank amateur, but she couldn't stop. The over-painting was resinous and smooth. It was coming off relatively easily leaving the texture beneath it untouched.

Suddenly she caught her breath in excitement. Something was emerging from the clouds. Behind Evelyn, if it was Evelyn, on the far side of the gate on which she was perched, there was another figure, a figure which had been completely obliterated, a figure in the uniform of the Royal Air Force, a young man with fair hair and bright blue eyes.

Lucy let out a whistle. 'So, Evelyn. You had an admirer.' She put down her swabs and the bottle and sat back, staring at the canvas. 'And you didn't want anyone to know about him.'

She had been sitting there working for two hours and she was stiff when at last she screwed the lids back on the bottles on the work table and stood up, pushing back the stool. The silence of the room had become oppressive and for the first time that evening she became aware once more of how empty the place was. The daylight had faded and beyond the circle of the spotlights the room was growing shadowy. Somewhere outside she heard a small aircraft flying low over the rooftops. The deep throb of its engine grew louder. She glanced towards the window, then back at the easel.

In the painting the figure of the young airman was clear now, standing behind Evelyn, his hand on her shoulder, his eyes gazing past her out of the picture. Who were they looking at? Not someone they welcomed, surely. Both looked angry and defensive. Only the touch of his fingers on her sweater was gentle. Lucy could sense the reassurance there. And the love.

By next morning her excitement had returned and she showed the painting to Robin.

'That is extraordinary,' he said. 'We had no idea he was there. Do you think Lol had spotted him? Do you know if he had the painting X-rayed?'

Lucy shook her head. 'I think that must be what he was going to discuss with Professor Solomon. He took lots of photos, some in close-up. He must have sensed something because there was no sign of it. None at all. I looked with the magnifying glass. It was only when I began to clean it that I spotted something underneath.' She turned to face him and for the first time in ages he saw the spark of excitement in her eyes.

'I've made my mind up, Robin. I'm going to try and find out more. I owe it to Larry, you're right, and I owe it to Evelyn as well. I want to know who this young man was and why he was painted out.'

2

Friday 28th June

The cottage where Evelyn Lucas had spent the last years of her life stood on a bank above a narrow lane. The hedges were thick and verdant, hazel and dogwoods threaded through with honeysuckle and wild roses. Lucy stood for a moment looking up at the front of the cottage. It was like a painting by Helen Allingham. The ancient peg-tiled roof was furred with moss and lichen above flint walls and windows with small diamond-shaped leaded panes; the wooden porch was covered with clematis. Pushing open the gate Lucy climbed the steps to the front door and reached for the bell pull. She heard a chime somewhere deep in the house.

Carrying on her shoulder a bag containing a notebook, a camera, and a small digital audio recorder, she had left her car in a lay-by just outside the village and walked down the lane, timing her arrival perfectly for four o'clock. It had taken quite a bit of detective work to find the location of the cottage and even more to trace a contact number but she had in the end managed to speak to Evelyn's former housekeeper. The cottage was to her delight still owned by a member of the family.

14

As she stood waiting for a response a thrush burst into song somewhere in the garden behind a lavender hedge to her right. To the left a sloping lawn led up towards a hedge of myrtle behind which she saw the roof of the building she was pretty certain must be the studio. Beyond the studio the Downs sloped up towards the intense blue of the sky. She could see the swallows darting and swooping over the fields.

At last she heard footsteps approaching. As the door opened she found herself momentarily thrown by the appearance not of the elderly woman she had been expecting, but of a tall man in his mid-thirties. His hair was a dark blond, severely brushed back from a deep forehead, his eyes a clear dusky blue, full of suspicion now, though they betrayed laughter lines at the outer corners. Most unexpectedly of all, given the rural location, he was formally dressed in a dark blue suit and a tie.

'I'm sorry.' She took a step back. 'Have I come to the wrong address? I was looking for Evelyn Lucas's cottage.' She knew it was the right address and now she guessed who this was.

'No, this is the right place.' He waited. 'How can I help you?' His tone was not encouraging.

'I spoke to a lady. Mrs Davis? She was expecting me.'

'Ah.' He gave her an austere smile. 'My housekeeper. She has gone home I'm afraid.'

Lucy could feel an overwhelming sense of disappointment beginning to drown her excitement. It had taken a lot of persuasion to get Mrs Davis to agree to let her come over and see the house. 'We are not open to the public, you know,' she had said down the phone, her soft Sussex accent gentle but nevertheless determined. 'The owner, he doesn't like people coming any more. I'm sorry.'

Sensing it was not the moment to talk about detailed research or the production of a book Lucy had merely described herself as an art student, deeply involved in studying Evelyn's work. 'I would so love to see where she painted,' she had said. 'I am sorry. I had understood you allowed people access to her studio.'

On the phone her conversation with Mrs Davis had ground to a halt at that point. And there had been a few moments silence. 'That was before Mr Michael moved in,' Dolly Davis had said at last. 'He doesn't want people poking around here. This is his home now, you see.'

'Mr Michael?' Lucy had felt at a sudden disadvantage. Should she know who he was?

Mrs Davis had provided the information without the need of further questioning. 'He is Evie Lucas's grandson. He inherited the cottage when his father died. Before that they did allow study groups here from time to time, you're right, but Mr Michael, he likes his privacy.'

'But surely, this is a place of national importance. He can't just refuse to let people see it,' Lucy said, with some indignation, perhaps betraying more vehemence than she realised.

They had talked for several minutes before at last Mrs Davis had agreed to allow her to visit the studio the following Friday afternoon. 'Only a quick peep, you understand,' she had said as they hung up. 'I wouldn't want Mr Michael to be upset.'

Mr Michael, it appeared, was only using the place at weekends. He lived and worked in London and should have returned there, but now here he was standing in front of her and he showed every sign of being if not upset then at least angry and intransigent.

She became aware suddenly that he was waiting for her to say something. This might be her last chance. On the other hand, she didn't want to antagonise him, or to get Mrs Davis into trouble. Playing for time she held out her hand. 'How do you do. I am Lucy Standish.'

Taken aback he hesitated for a moment before he took her hand and shook it. 'Michael Marston,' he said gravely. He had a strong handshake; he did not smile. Again he waited.

She found herself suddenly wishing she had taken more care with her appearance before leaving home. Her hair was scraped back as usual, held in an unsophisticated ponytail by a rubber band, she was wearing no make-up and she was dressed in a shirt and jeans. She gave a small audible sigh. 'OK, I give up. I am so sorry. I don't want to get your housekeeper into trouble. It's all my fault. I somehow managed to persuade her to let me have a quick look at Evelyn's, that is, your grandmother's, studio. I have been studying her work and it would mean so much to me. She, that is your housekeeper, explained that it is no longer open to the public and I can quite understand that. I am truly sorry.' She was rattling on and she knew it. Shaking her head she turned away. 'I am sorry. I will go. Of course, I will go. Please don't be angry with her. She is so proud of Evelyn and she understood how I felt. I didn't mean to intrude.'

'Stop!'

Michael Marston had folded his arms during her anguished soliloquy. He shook his head slowly. 'Do you ever let anyone else get a word in edgeways? No wonder you talked your way under Dolly's guard.'

Lucy bit her lip. 'I'm sorry.' He was making her feel like a small child.

'Stop apologising.' He smiled at last. It lit his face but it also betrayed how exhausted he looked. 'I am sure that just this once I could make an exception and allow you to come in as you've come all this way. I wasn't expecting I would be here this afternoon, and obviously neither was Dolly. No wonder she was so reluctant to leave me here and take the time off.' He stood back and beckoned her to follow him into the shadowy hallway. 'Please follow me. What did you say your name was?'

Repeating her name, Lucy followed him into a long low living room. With windows back and front open onto the garden the whole place smelled of newly cut grass and roses. She stared round in delight. 'This is lovely.'

'Indeed. She adored this place. She could never be persuaded to move once she found Rosebank Cottage.'

'She painted this room, didn't she? As a backdrop to some of her best portraits.'

He nodded. 'And got slated by the critics for it. Too chocolate box like some of her wartime pictures, but as you probably know, that wasn't really her style.' He made his way between an easy chair and a sofa, placed on either side of an open fireplace, heading towards the French doors which led out into the back garden. Lucy glanced at the hearth. It was empty now save for an arrangement of dried flowers.

He led the way outside and up some narrow mossy steps into the upper garden and towards the building which Lucy had already guessed was the studio. Built of timber framing, infilled with dark red brick, it was single storey but with a high-pitched roof, tiled like the house but with skylights on the north-facing pitch to add to the light from the large windows. The walls were curtained with wisteria and roses.

Groping in his pocket Michael Marston produced a key-ring and inserted one of the keys into the door. He moved aside and waved her in ahead of him. She stepped over the threshold with bated breath instantly forgetting him as she took in the large high-ceilinged room in which she found herself. Though Evelyn had been dead for many years it was as if she had just walked out for a few minutes. Her brushes and palette knives were lying on the table near her easel with a selection of squeezed tubes of oil paint. As Lucy took a step or two closer she saw that they were dried up and split, but she could still smell the linseed oil, the turpentine. She squinted at the painting on the easel and realised with sudden disappointment that it was a print of one of Evelyn's best-known works, the one which currently hung in Tate Britain. Slowly she began to walk round the room. On the large paint-stained wooden table several sketchbooks lay open. She went closer to look. Two of the walls were lined with shelves still laden with tins and boxes and rolls of paper. Several canvasses were stacked against one wall and more paintings hung on the other walls.

'None of them are originals, I'm afraid.' Michael Marston's

voice came from the doorway. She had actually forgotten he was there.

She turned towards him. 'It is wonderful. It still retains so much atmosphere. As if she had just this minute left.'

He gave a faint smile. He had loosened his tie, she noticed, and undone the top button of his shirt. It made him look marginally more relaxed. 'She was like that. She had a powerful personality.'

'Do you remember her?'

He nodded. 'Very well!'

'You must miss her.'

'It would be strange if I didn't. She was my grandmother.' He folded his arms. 'If you've seen enough –' He was clearly impatient for her to go.

She felt a pang of dismay. Not already. She hadn't seen nearly enough. She gave him a faint smile. 'Of course, I'm sorry. I'll leave now.' She paused for a moment, wondering if she dare ask if she could take some photos or even if she could come again. 'I don't suppose,' she hesitated again. 'I don't suppose I could come back some other time when it is more convenient?'

He was heading for the door. She had a fraction of a second to make up her mind, to tell him now honestly why she was there. She had to tell him something if she wanted his co-operation but was now, when he was tired and impatient, the time to speak to him? He had turned back and was watching her, she realised, a spark of interest in his gaze for the first time.

'Could I explain why I'm here?' she said at last. 'There is a specific reason for my interest. I know you want me out of your hair. It will only take a minute, I promise.' She hoped she didn't sound as though she was wheedling.

He leaned against the doorframe, his arms still folded. 'Go on.'

'I am an art historian by training. I am particularly interested in women war artists. People like Dame Laura Knight, Dorothy Coke, Mary Kessell and, of course, Evelyn Lucas. She was special because she came from Sussex and she was here during the

Battle of Britain, and of course most if not all of the artists who painted the action were men; I'm compiling a catalogue of her work and I would love to find out more about her. I want to write a book about her.' She fell silent, watching his face.

'You're working on your PhD?'

He sounded faintly patronising.

She smiled. 'I have my PhD.'

She felt an altogether unworthy flicker of triumph as he acknowledged his mistake with a slight nod of the head.

'This is a project for a full-length biography,' she added.

He said nothing for a while, frowning, then, 'My grandmother was a very private person. She didn't want people poking into her personal affairs.'

'I can understand that.' Lucy dropped her bag at her feet and perched on the edge of the table. She leaned forward slightly, unaware that the open-necked shirt with its rolled-up sleeves was alluring in its own understated way, as was the eagerness in her expression. 'But would she mind now? After all, your father opened this place to the public. He can't have thought she would object all that much or he wouldn't have done that, would he?'

'True.' He shifted slightly. 'I took the decision to close it because I valued my privacy. I'm more like her than my father was. Besides, he never lived here full time. That was why she left it to me. He kept an eye on it, and, yes, allowed people here, but after he died I decided to use it as a weekend cottage. I didn't want strangers here any more.'

'I wouldn't get in your way.'

He was watching her. He looked distinctly uncomfortable. 'Are you a painter yourself?' he asked eventually.

She shook her head. 'I'm a writer. A historian. My husband and I run, ran, an art gallery in Chichester.'

'Ran?' He had noticed the change of tense.

'I suppose I still do. He was killed in a car crash three months ago.'

20

She was surprised to find she could say it without faltering. 'I'm sorry.' He pushed himself away from the door and seizing his tie, pulled it off. 'So you haven't come a long way after all.'

'I didn't actually say I had,' she remonstrated gently.

He gave a wry smile. 'No, you didn't. Sorry. You had better come inside the house.' He was coiling the tie round his fist. Turning, he led the way out into the garden.

Picking up her bag she followed him and waited while he locked the door behind them. As they retraced their steps into the cottage and through the living room Lucy smiled at him uncomfortably.

'I am really sorry to have intruded on your afternoon off. I was going to write to you once I had spoken to Mrs Davis and seen the studio.'

He dumped the tie on the bookshelf. The room had a homely, old-fashioned feel; at a guess, there was no woman in his life apart from the doubty Mrs Davis.

'And you were hoping, presumably, that I will have lots of information about Evie to fill out your project for you.'

She pulled a face. 'I'm not asking you to write it for me, but obviously I would be very grateful for any pointers. As I said, apart from old exhibition catalogues there doesn't seem to be much out there. Even the Tate doesn't appear to know anything beyond her dates.'

'Perhaps it is a pointless exercise. Perhaps there is nothing.'

'There has to be something.' She heard a hint of desperation in her own voice. Its intensity surprised her. 'Her paintings must have a history behind them. The Battle of Britain series is iconic. The pictures of the airfield at Westhampnett, the Spitfires. Not really a woman's subject.'

'Ah well, that's easily explained. Her brother, Ralph,' he pronounced it Rafe, 'my great-uncle, was a fighter pilot in a Spitfire squadron.'

'I see. I didn't know even that.' Lucy felt a wave of disappointment. It was likely then, that the young man in the portrait was Evelyn's brother. Somehow, already in her own mind, he was her lover, a source of mystery and romance, just as in her own mind there was now no real doubt as to the picture's provenance. Evelyn's story had caught her imagination in a way it had failed to before. At the beginning it had been of more academic interest, now, since she had seen the young man with his hand on her shoulder, and since seeing her studio and her home, Evelyn had become real to her.

She still hadn't mentioned the portrait to Michael, she realised. The fact that she owned a possible Lucas original was crucial; it had been the reason behind the decision to research Evelyn's life, to find out where the picture fitted into her oeuvre, to date it and, since she had uncovered him, to identify the young man with his hand so affectionately on her shoulder.

'Did she live here during the war?' Lucy sat down uninvited on the arm of the sofa by the window. She felt more comfortable with her host now, more relaxed. His initial suspicion of her seemed to have lessened.

He shook his head. 'She still lived at home with her parents during the war. Her father was a farmer over near Goodwood. She inherited the farm after they died, then she sold up and bought this place. I can give you the address of the farm if you like, then you can go and pester them.' His smile compensated slightly for the harshness of the words. He glanced at his watch and gave an exclamation of dismay. 'I'm sorry. I do have to get on. I'm expecting someone. If you would like to give me your address and contact details I will get in touch with some suggestions about where you could start your research if I think of anything.'

'So, you don't mind my doing it?' She was disappointed at the sudden change of mood after he had seemed to be mellowing towards her, but at the same time elated that he appeared to be agreeing to help her with the project. She reached into her bag to find the gallery's card. 'You'll find my e-mail and phone number there.'

22

'And you are?' He was examining the card.

'Lucy Standish. I told you.' Twice to be precise.

He grinned, acknowledging the slight tetchiness of her tone. 'I'm sorry. I didn't take it in.'

And then she was outside and he had shut the door behind her.

Walking slowly back up the lane she noticed a car parked in the lay-by behind her own. A woman climbed out, locked it and turned towards her. They approached one another, exchanged the rather awkward smiles of strangers in a situation where they cannot avoid acknowledging each other, and passed. The woman was tall, slim and elegant in a pale silk shift dress. There was a large designer tote on her arm. Her car, Lucy couldn't help noticing as she pulled out her car keys was a BMW Z4. She couldn't resist a glance behind her. The woman was climbing the steps to Rosebank Cottage.

So there was someone in his life after all.

3

August 6th 1940

'Evie?' Ralph found his sister in the dairy. At twenty-one, he was two years older than Evelyn and had always enjoyed his role as her big brother. 'I've asked my station commander and he says he can fix it for you to go and sketch over at Westhampnett. I know it's not Tangmere as you asked, but it's a satellite field and only a couple of miles away. He reckons if you come to Tangmere people might ask why a squit of a girl like you was there. There are too many big brass there with it being the local sector control. He suggested that Westhampnett might be less conspicuous and a bit safer as a place to draw. There is a Hurricane squadron based there.'

'I don't want a safer place, Rafie!' She glared at him.

'I'm only obeying orders!' He held up his hands in mock surrender.

'I know.' She swallowed her indignation and dropping the empty bucket she was holding threw her arms round his neck. 'Thank you, thank you, thank you for arranging it!'

'Get off!' He pushed her away good-naturedly. 'You smell of

cow. Don't say anything to Dad. I'm not sure he would approve and I know he will worry. You'll have to find an excuse to leave the farm for the afternoon.'

'That will be easy.' She was glowing with excitement, her golden-blond hair mostly hidden by the scarf knotted round her head. 'I'll think of something. There are loads of things I need to collect in Chichester. I can do that first to justify using the petrol. It will give me an excuse to be out for a bit. Once I know where to go I can bike over there.' She reached up and ruffled his hair. 'How's it going? We see the enemy planes, watch the fights. There are so many of them, Rafie. I can't bear to think of you up there. Dad was listening to the wireless last night –'

'I've got a few hours off, Evie.' Ralph spoke sharply. 'Leave it. I don't need the official commentary.'

'Sorry.'

He shook his head. She could see the exhaustion in his face now she looked more closely, the strain in his eyes. As always when she felt a strong emotion she found her fingers itching to pick up a pencil; it had always been her way of dealing with things, even when she was a small child. Sternly she pushed the longing aside.

'I've finished here. I'll go and wash. Come into the kitchen and we'll see where Mum is.' She stacked the dropped bucket by the door and headed out into the yard. Tearing off her scarf she shook out her hair in the sunshine. 'I've had a letter from an art student friend, Sarah Besant,' she said over her shoulder. 'They are talking about evacuating the Royal College of Art for the duration. They are tired of having their windows blown out! She thinks they are going to go up to the Lake District.'

Ralph gave a sharp laugh. 'That will shake up the locals a bit, won't it?'

'Students and locals, both.' Evie smiled.

He glanced at her fondly. 'Are you sure you don't want to

go back and finish the course? I had thought it meant everything to you, getting into the RCA.'

She folded her arms. 'I'm needed here. I can always go back
after the war.'

He sighed. She was needed on the farm because he wasn't
there. It was that simple. But he couldn't be in two places at
once. He was no longer a farmer, he was a pilot now, first and
foremost. His father had resumed the running of the farm and
he needed Evie to help him. Even so, Ralph couldn't bear to
think of her stuck here when she could be back in the college,
studying the painting she loved so much.

'Mum and Dad would feel much better if you were out of it
all. If they are going to evacuate the college it would be so
much safer,' he persisted.

'No, Rafie. You are not going to change my mind. It wouldn't
feel right, leaving Daddy running the farm alone. I can paint
as well as helping him. I'll find a way.' She glanced up. He
followed her gaze and for a moment neither spoke. Small white
summer clouds dotted the clear blue of the empty sky.

Ralph had joined up in 1938, much to his father's disgust.
His only son had turned down the opportunity to go to university after he took his Highers and had instead immersed himself
in the farm, but suddenly he was turning his back on his destiny
for the sake of a bit of excitement in the RAF. Father and son
had not always seen eye to eye – Dudley preferred the old ways
on the farm – if it was good enough for your grandfather it is
good enough for us – and Ralph wanted to study new theories
and import new machinery and so, yet again, they were at
loggerheads. Then war was declared and Dudley's view changed
overnight. Suddenly he was proud of his son and silently he
took back the reins of the farm after clapping Ralph on the
back. It was all Ralph needed to know his father supported him.
The two men had called a truce.

'I need to get back,' he said suddenly. He bent and kissed his
sister on the top of her head. 'Don't worry the parents. I'll see

them tomorrow, God willing.' He grinned. They had both had the same thought. A beautiful peaceful afternoon. It was too good to last. It was only a question of time before the distant drone of engines heralded the next wave of enemy aircraft appearing from the south.

28th June, late afternoon

Michael Marston was in a thoughtful mood when Charlotte Ponsonby arrived at Rosebank Cottage. Her sudden phone call the night before, when she found she had two unexpected days off, and his spontaneous agreement to stay at Rosebank so they could spend them together was the reason he had thrown Dolly and therefore Lucy into disaray. After their initial hug Charlotte followed him through the house and out into the garden.

'So, are you going to tell me who your visitor was?'

He roused himself from his reverie. 'Who?'

'The woman I saw leaving here not ten minutes ago.'

'Oh, her.'

She narrowed her eyes. 'Yes, her. Who was she, Mike?' She herself was as far as she knew Mike's only girlfriend, his official partner to dates and parties, included automatically by his friends in conversation and future plans, but still she felt insecure; there was a reserve on Mike's side which she couldn't quite work out. Was it his natural way with women or was it just her? Was he as yet undecided? Had he in his own mind still to make a commitment? His next question did not reassure her.

'Why so interested?'

'Because I am.'

'Jealous?'

'No! Of course not. Hardly.' She gave a little snort as she tossed her head. Her hair swung in a glossy curtain round her face and for a moment hid her expression. She had narrow intense eyes and sharp features which were undeniably beautiful in their bone structure but her face held a certain hardness of which she was acutely conscious. It made her smile too much.

'Actually, she is quite attractive, if you like that sort of thing.' Mike grinned as he lowered himself onto the rustic seat on the lawn and held out his hand to pull her down beside him. 'She is an interesting person. Her husband was killed in a car crash three months ago.' He paused, frowning slightly, wondering how on earth anyone could possibly cope with something like that. 'She wants to write a book about Evie.'

There was a long silence.

'And is that good?' She surveyed his face carefully.

'I don't know.' He sat forward on the bench, his hands hanging loosely between his knees. He closed his eyes against the sunlight and sighed, leaning back at last against the rough lichen-covered bench back.

'Well, she is really famous, isn't she? I am surprised no one has done it before,' Charlotte said cautiously.

'I suppose it was bound to happen one day. But she was always reluctant to talk about the past. I remember my parents saying they knew so little, even Pops, for goodness' sake. Broad brushstrokes, that's all.' Mike gave a snort of laughter at his choice of words.

Charlotte smiled. She kicked off her wedge-heeled sandals and leaned into him. 'We're a couple of idiots sitting here in our office uniform,' she whispered. 'Shall we go and slip into something more comfortable?'

He didn't answer for a moment. She gave him a sideways glance, wondering if he'd heard what she said.

'If she starts poking round we won't be able to stop her,' he said eventually. 'There is no knowing what can of worms she might dig up.'

'Why should there be a can of worms?' Charlotte was getting tired of this conversation already. She jumped to her feet and reached for his hand. 'In fact, surely the more worms the better.

It would make it all more exciting. Make her pictures more valuable.'

He looked up at her. He liked her hair free of the severe knot in which she kept it restrained during the working day. 'OK. I'm coming.' Reluctantly he stood up and allowed himself to be towed back towards the cottage.

Upstairs she looked round the small bedroom with its quaint windows and chintz curtains. Rosebank needed a clean blast of modernity and a damn good builder. There wasn't even a shower, for God's sake. She could hear the bath running and the slam of cupboards. Mike always forgot where he had put the bath gel; and everything else, for that matter. The trouble with this place was that it was nothing more than a weekend cottage. It was inconvenient, small and uncomfortable. It needed a clean sweep and then a designer with a good eye for modern comforts. With a clever conversion and a large extension it would make a nice home.

She hadn't known Mike that long and their relationship was mostly based in London where his garden flat in Bloomsbury met her every criterion of comfort and convenience, but there was a small part of her which was beginning to think about a future with him which was definitely longer term than any other she had so far experienced. Which brought her back to her niggling worry about the depth of his feelings for her. Had he ever thought about marriage? They had never discussed it, but supposing, just supposing they tied the knot, what then?

Mike was an advertising executive in a medium-sized but well regarded company with a broad portfolio of accounts. He was clever and attractive, confident and talented but in some areas of his life he was reserved. He enjoyed his own company and although he clearly enjoyed hers she wondered sometimes if he was one hundred per cent dedicated to her; or for that matter to his job and to London. She returned to her reverie about the future. Commuting was out of the question, it was from her point of view just too far, but once there were children she for one would be more than happy to spend at least part of each week in the country. Husband in town; wife in the country. Recipe for disaster, she knew that. But a garden, a local playgroup, good schools. It would make sense. It was a lifestyle some of her friends were opting for and she had to admit she was beguiled.

She tiptoed over to the large chest of drawers which dominated the room, perched as it was incongruously on the uneven floorboards, and she pulled open the top drawer. Surprise! It was stuffed full of dusty books. It was years since Evie Lucas had died and the house was still full of her stuff like some goddamn shrine. Well, now there was a solution. She pictured her brief meeting in the lane with Mike's afternoon visitor. A tall slim woman, slightly sallow of complexion with dark straight hair; good features, large eyes – Charlotte always noticed other women's eyes – beautiful even, but not his type. Why not let her sort all this mess out?

When she and Mike had first met and she had realised he had a famous grandmother with a painting in the Tate Gallery Charlotte had excitedly imagined a house full of paintings worth millions. When, wide-eyed, she had said as much to Mike he had roared with laughter. 'If it was true I'd be a rich man! Sadly there are no paintings left. God knows where they all went. I suspect Evie sold some. I assume she was quite hard up in her old age. That often happened, didn't it? Artists were poor in their lifetime; only later was their stuff valuable. And to be honest I don't think she has ever been that popular as a painter. The others, the ones in the cottage, were left to my cousin.'

Charlotte found herself wandering round the room fingering the furnishings and picking up ornaments, deliberately putting them down in different places, well aware that next time Dolly came in she would return them to their original arrangements, exactly as Evie had left them years before. Bloody Evie! This could be such a pretty cottage without her malign influence hanging over everything. Ideally they should take everything out into the garden and burn it. Mike would never agree, of course.

She looked at the various bits of furniture. Perhaps instead she could persuade Mike to store it in the studio, to allow them to go and buy some really beautiful modern bits, choosing them together, changing the whole feel of the place. That would be a start. Who knew? Maybe that would be enough. He would begin to see the place as theirs rather than Evie's. She smiled. Maybe it was time to begin dropping hints that dusty chintz and threadbare rugs were not the way they wanted to start life together.

'Mike!' she called now. 'Mike, I've had an idea.' She went through to the bathroom and perched on the edge of the old chipped roll-top bath. Part of her made a mental note to find out about re-enamelling as she bent to drop a kiss on Mike's forehead as he lay, knees bent almost to his chin, eyes closed.

'I've had a wonderful idea. Why don't we do some sorting out? I'll help you. Go through the house and put all Evie's stuff out in the studio. Then you can get your widow woman to sort through it all. It will give her whatever it is she wants and give you some space to call your own. This is such a small house!'

She paused, holding her breath, trailing a finger through the foam on the bath water, then as the silence became intolerable she bent to kiss him on the mouth. With a shout of laughter he grabbed her and pulled her into the bath on top of him, slopping water all over the floor.

It was a long time later as they lay naked on the bed, watching the light leach out of the evening that he answered her question.

'You know, that might be a good idea. I do feel a bit over-powered by Evie when I'm here. It is still so much her house,' he said thoughtfully. 'She can keep the studio. That seems fair.

But you are right. She is swamping me. Why don't I ring Lucy Standish next weekend and tell her she can start as soon as she likes. If she is here during the week when we are in town we needn't see her or get in each other's hair.'

It was only later he wondered what Dolly Davis would think of the plan.

August 10th 1940

Enemy planes had been attacking since dawn. As Ralph's squadron scrambled for the third time in quick succession he felt his head throbbing with the strain. His stomach lurched as it always did with a lethal cocktail of excitement, adrenaline and good old-fashioned nerves. The ground crews had prepared the aircraft in record time, checking for damage, refuelling, rearming, restarting the engines ready to go. His own rigger and fitter were there, the men who kept his Spitfire flying. He acknowledged their smiles, their thumbs up; there was nothing for him to do but grab his Mae West and helmet, hop up onto the wing, slide into the seat, buckle up, and thrust the throttle forward as the planes swiftly taxied out, turned one after the other into wind, thundering across the airfield and up into the sky. He adored this moment, the feel of the joystick in his hands, the exhilaration of flying the small, fast, single-seater fighter, hearing the throaty roar of the powerful Rolls Royce Merlin engine. As always he felt a sudden expansive rush of joy as the wheels folded neatly into place and locked and the thrill as one after another the planes climbed swiftly up and away.

He heard the squadron leader's voice crackle in his ear. 'Squadron airborne.'

Concentrating on his place in the formation, he gently corrected his position every now and then, relaxing slightly, allowing himself to enjoy the skill and the plane. Another crackle and this time it was Control. 'One hundred and fifty plus bandits approaching at angels twelve, vector one twenty. Over.'

Angels. Ralph gave a grim smile. Every thousand feet an angel. Who thought that one up? He hoped he would not one day find out. He felt his stomach tighten. Higher and higher still. Time to turn on the oxygen. Ahead he could see them now, a cloud of black dots, getting ever larger, rank on rank of them, fighter aircraft escorting the serried lines of bombers. Mainly Dornier with Messerschmitt in attendance by the look of things and here was he, one of a squadron of only twelve planes. But they could do it. They would be joined by other squadrons from other airfields and they would chase the bastards away.

They would.

He was feeling cold now, and icily calm.

And then they were amongst the enemy.

'Break! Break!' The shouted order came over the RT. None of them needed telling. Forget the careful formation. From now on it was every man for himself. His thumb on the gun button, Ralph soared in pursuit of an enemy plane, aware only of his target as he threaded his way through the hundreds of speeding dodging spiralling aircraft, watching forward, port, starboard, above, below, behind.

Far below in the farmyard Rachel Lucas paused, as she pegged out her line of washing, gazing up into the distance. She could hear the bombs exploding over towards Southampton; the ack ack guns on the ground. Watching the sky she was aware of the scream of engines, the stuttering roar of machine guns, seeing tracer bullets streak across the sky, plumes of smoke. Men were dying up there. Boys, most of them. She saw a plane peel away from the action, trailing black smoke as it plummeted down, spinning out of control. Was it one of ours or one of theirs? Too far away to see. Either way she breathed a quiet prayer for a life snuffed out as the plane buried itself in a field somewhere in the Downs.

Please God, keep Rafie safe; don't let him die.

Her brother had died in another war twenty-three years before. He had died far away in France; now they were having to watch their young men die here, in the sky, over their heads. It wasn't fair. None of this was fair.

The airmen soon became used to the sight of the slim fair-haired girl in her slacks and linen shirt, a sweater hung around her neck or knotted round her waist. She had appeared two or three times now, leaving her old bicycle near one of the Nissen huts on the airfield which were used as crew rooms, or leaning against the wall of the old farmhouse, now the Officers' Mess. Leaving her gas mask dangling from the handlebars, she carried no more than a sketchbook and soft pencils and charcoal or coloured crayons to work with. She drew the planes, the ground crew, the pilots. She was friendly and exchanged some repartee with the men, but always she was drawing, not allowing herself to be distracted. The War Artists Advisory Committee was very strict about who it chose for its official team of war artists, and stricter still about women. She knew that to win her place on that coveted programme she should be painting in factories or depicting the brave men and women of the town streets and the people getting on with life under the threat of invasion; but it was the planes that fascinated her and to compete with the male artists, to get herself on the commission's list, she had to be twice as good as they were.

Since Ralph had got her permission to sketch at the airfield, she would repair to the farmhouse attic which she and Rafie and her father had turned into a studio for her when she had returned from art school. It gave her somewhere to paint; somewhere to be on her own and now somewhere to concentrate on her work away from the bustle of the farm. They had made a skylight which was blacked out now in the evening, but rigged up with electric lights hanging from the rafters, fed by the generator in the shed, there was just about enough light to transform her sketches into paint.

Her canvasses from college were stacked against the wall. Portraits mainly, though some were country scenes; some influenced by contemporary heroes of hers like John Nash and Graham Sutherland, others more strongly her own clearly emerging style. And there were the birds. Her first drawings had been of birds in flight, studied over the fields of the farm, over the woods and sea and over her beloved Downs. It was when she saw her first squadron of fighter planes wheeling in tight formation above the farm looking like so many swallows swooping after insects against the intense blue of the sky that she knew she had to paint them as well.

She was tired after the five-mile bike ride home from the airfield but that was no excuse. There was farm work to do. She ran up to the studio and left her sketchbooks there on the table before coming back down to the kitchen. Her mother was stirring a pot of soup over the range. She looked up.

'It sounded as though there was a bit of activity this afternoon,' she said with a thin smile.

Rachel Lucas was a tall strong-boned woman with a fierce loyalty and love of her husband and two children which she hid with a layer of gruff understatement and determination. She would never admit that she was worried about Ralph, or demand he somehow get her a message after a particularly fierce aerial battle or that she had any misgivings about Evie's excursions down to an airfield in the thick of the operations.

'Eddie phoned. He's back from London for a few days and he's coming to supper. Your dad has started the milking.'

Evie went over and gave her mother a light kiss on the top of her head. 'I'll go and see if he would like me to take over.' There were only two cows in milk now, much to her relief.

'Would you, dear? I know he denies it but he is finding it hard without Ralph and the men to help.'

'That's why I'm here, Mummy.' Evie reached for her overalls

from the back of the door and whistled to the two dogs lying on the flags. 'When will Eddie arrive?'

Rachel gave a rueful smile at the casualness of the question. 'You've got time to give your dad a hand.'

Eddie Marston was tall and slightly stooped with the mannerisms of a man far older than his twenty-eight years. He had dark straight hair and grey-green eyes, magnified by wire-rimmed spectacles. His parents were neighbours of the Lucases, his father's farm bordering theirs to the east. Eddie however had shown no interest in the farm, preferring to leave its running to his two sisters and a team of land girls. He had failed the medical to get into the forces after a childhood bout of measles had left him with poor eyesight and had been co-opted into the Ministry of Information. It was no secret that he had a soft spot for Evie, nearly ten years his junior. Her feelings for him were not so clear. She enjoyed his company and was flattered by his attention. She wasn't sure yet whether she felt any more deeply for him but in the meantime she enjoyed flirting with him.

Sitting next to her in the farmhouse kitchen he gazed round the table as they waited for Rachel to serve the soup, then he sprang his surprise. 'You know I took some of your sketches into Chichester to show to that friend I mentioned?'

Evie looked up quickly. She hadn't wanted to part with them but Eddie could be very persuasive.

'He likes them. He thinks he has a potential buyer. I have arranged to have them framed and the cost taken out of the proceeds.'

Evie's father narrowed his eyes slightly as he surveyed Eddie across the table. Their neighbour's son was becoming all too frequent a visitor in the house and treating it – and them – with just too much familiarity for his taste. 'I seem to recall Evie saying she would think about whether she wanted to sell those. Some of them were from her college portfolio if I remember right.'

'Daddy, I can speak for myself!' Evie retorted crossly.

Eddie scooped a piece of bread from the plate on the table between them and nodded nonchalantly. 'But remember, if you change your mind about selling them it will look bad. An introduction like this at this stage in your career is worth its weight in gold. She has talent, your daughter!' He smiled at Dudley Lucas. 'If she wants to go far in the world of art – and she could – she can't start soon enough.'

Rachel stood up, pushing her chair back on the flags with unnecessary force. 'I'm sure she does. She has enough ambition does our Evie, but Dudley is right. It has to be up to her.' The quick look she gave Eddie from under her lashes was less than friendly.

'I wish you wouldn't talk about me as though I wasn't here!' Evie said crossly. 'I can make my own decisions! Yes, Eddie. Please sell them.'

Eddie sat back in his chair with a smug smile. 'You won't regret it, sweetheart.' There was a touch of triumph in his expression as he gave a sideways glance at Dudley.

It was as he was leaving he took the chance to have a quiet word with Evie in the hall. 'Have you got your paintings of the airfield ready yet?'

She shook her head. 'I'm working on them.'

'When can I have them?'

'I'm not sure.' She hesitated. 'The thing is, the squadron CO at Westhampnett said I ought to be careful. I'm not really authorised to do this even though I have his permission. It is not quite the same.'

'Like when we kiss, eh?' Eddie put his hands on her shoulders and pulled her to him.

Evie submitted without demur. In fact she quite liked it when Eddie kissed her. It felt exciting and slightly risqué. He was quite a bit older than she was and no doubt a lot more experienced. Her inexpert fumblings as an art student, even going 'all the way' as one lad had put it, had been profoundly disappointing and she had not had enough relationships to realise that being in the arms of someone who, though enthusiastic and energetic, was profoundly unattractive to her, did not turn the right switches. Eddie was a solid, good-looking young man. He carried himself well and, with his even features, good skin and a small neat moustache he had a sophisticated air which radiated confidence. Sometimes she wondered how he squared this with his claims to have fragile health and poor eyesight – although he wore glasses most of the time he didn't always and even without them he seemed to miss nothing – but presumably the medics knew what they were doing and he would no doubt be an asset to whatever department he worked for in the Ministry.

'Evie!' Her father's peremptory call made her pull away from him.

'See you tomorrow,' she whispered.

Eddie grinned. Reaching across he gave her hair a little tug. 'Cheerio, sweetheart.'

She watched, a speculative look in her eye, as he climbed into his smart little Wolseley and drove out of the farmyard. She knew exactly what he was up to. He wanted her in bed and even more he wanted to lay his hands on more of her drawings. Both ideas had a certain appeal. She wasn't sure yet what she was going to do about either proposition.

4

Sunday 30th June

Lucy woke suddenly and lay staring up at the ceiling, her heart thudding with fright. The dream, if there had been a dream, had gone. She groped in the foggy emptiness of her memory and found nothing there. Reaching out for the clock on the bedside table she turned it to face her. It was two forty-five a.m. The room, on the second floor, under the eaves, was hot, the night very still. Outside a car drove down the street, the rattle of tyres, the sound of the engine, dying away into the distance. With a sigh she climbed out of bed and went to the window. The street two storeys below, even here near the centre of the city, was very quiet

She heard a creak in the room behind her and she turned round, her eyes wide in the darkness. There was nothing there. The floor-boards creaked all the time in this old building and she smiled wryly. In the silence of the night a dog barked far away somewhere towards the Bishop's Palace Gardens.

And suddenly she knew she was not alone in the bedroom. She was aware of a movement on the periphery of her vision.

She glanced round again, holding her breath as a shadowy, almost transparent figure slowly appeared on the far side of the bed. Her mouth went dry.

'Larry?' she whispered.

The room was very still.

'Larry, darling?'

But it wasn't Larry. For a moment in the half-light from the landing she glimpsed a thin angular face, the grey-blue uniform of the Royal Air Force, then he was gone.

She groped frantically for the light switches and, half-blinded as they came on, stared round wildly. 'Idiot!' she whispered. 'You're imagining things.' Her hands, she realised, had started to shake.

Her eyes filled with tears and she found she had started to shiver uncontrollably in spite of the warmth of the night. 'Larry?' Her voice broke into a sob.

Padding down the narrow stairs from the pretty attic bedroom which she and Larry had had so much fun designing and which they had shared with such joy, she went into the first-floor kitchen at the back of the flat and turned on the lights. She stood still, confronting the studio door which was closed. The figure had been part of her dream, of course he had. She had been becoming obsessed with the identity of the young man in the portrait and had gone to sleep thinking about him, of course she had dreamed about him.

Heading determinedly for the door before she could change her mind she pushed it open, reached up and groped for the light switches. Evie was staring at her from the easel with an expression of quizzical amusement. The young man behind her was interested only in the woman sitting on the gate so close in front of him. He had no time for anyone outside the picture.

Lucy glanced round, almost afraid that the shadowy figure from her bedroom would be there, but the studio was empty. Her eyes drifted back to the young man with the bright blue eyes and she swallowed hard, trying to gather her wits. This boy was fair-haired, his face square, his figure stocky. The man she had seen standing in her bedroom had darker hair and eyes and he was tall and slim. She had only had time to see him for a fraction of a second, but it had been enough to see that he was not the young man in the picture. Nor was it Larry.

She felt a sudden tremor of fear. The figure must have been part of her dream but he had seemed so real for a moment. She backed out of the studio into the kitchen and grabbed a glass of water. As she drank it she turned and looked back through the door into the studio. She took a deep breath, trying to steady her nerves and, putting down the glass she cautiously retraced her steps. The studio was still empty. Evie was still looking back at her from the canvas, her eyes once more enigmatic. And hostile? Maybe. And the young man behind her? It was almost as though Evie didn't know he was there.

So, who was the dark-haired young man, the other man, the man in her bedroom?

Acutely aware once more of how empty the flat was without Larry there at her side Lucy found herself suddenly over-whelmed with panic. The phone was in her hand before she could stop herself.

'Robin, I'm frightened. Can you come over?'

'Luce? What's wrong?' His voice was muffled. Sleepy.

'Please.' She was behaving irrationally. She knew it with some part of her mind, but the terror was in control.

As soon as she had put down the phone she regretted ringing him. She had forgotten what the time was. She was being a selfish cow.

Robin let himself in ten minutes later. 'What is it, Luce?' He ran up the stairs from the gallery followed by his partner, Phil.

She was standing in the middle of the kitchen, still shivering. 'I am such a fool. I shouldn't have rung you.'

'You said you were frightened. What happened?' Robin put his arms round her. 'Come on. Uncle Robin is here now.'

41

'I had a nightmare. A stupid nightmare,' she stammered. 'I woke up suddenly and I thought I saw a man standing in my room. He disappeared and I thought he must have been a ghost.' She buried her face in his shoulder for a moment. It was comforting to be near another human being; reassuring and for a moment she wanted to stay like that. It felt safe. She pulled herself together with an effort and stood back, aware that they were both staring at her.

'Lol's ghost?' Robin whispered.

She shook her head. She had confided in him once, on one of her bad days, how much she longed to see Larry again, how she was sure he would come back to her, how he would tell her what had happened and how much he still loved her. But he hadn't.

She saw Robin and Phil glance at each other.

'I'm mad. I know I'm mad. It was a dream. It must have been. I didn't realise what the time was. I shouldn't have rung you, I'm sorry.'

'I'm glad you did. What else are friends for?' Robin said gently.

'What did he look like, this figure?' Phil pulled out a chair and sat down at the table near her. He leaned forward on his elbows studying her face. He was a broad-shouldered man, reassuringly well built with wavy golden hair. Sensible. Down to earth. 'Can you remember?' Neither he nor Robin was laughing at her.

She explained again what had happened as Robin went over to the kettle. He switched it on and collected three mugs from the cupboard. Turning back towards them he glanced towards the studio. The door was shut.

'OK,' he said as he passed her a mug of tea. 'Why don't Phil and I go in and have a look, just to be sure everything is OK and put your mind at rest.'

She gave a weak smile. 'He was in my bedroom.'

'Then we'll look there first.' Phil stood up.

She had left the lights on upstairs. The room was empty, her bed in disarray but there was nothing there to frighten her. After looking round, searching the second bedroom and the bathroom they turned and trooped down to the first floor again. Then they went into the studio. In the beamed roof the areas of glass reflected back the spotlights against the black of the night outside, the painting a silent witness on its easel.

'So, if he didn't look like this chap or Lol, what did he look like?' Robin glanced at her.

'He was someone else. Not this man in Evie's picture. Same uniform. Completely different face.'

'Did he try and speak to you?'

There was a moment's silence.

'You think he was a ghost?' she whispered.

Robin put his head on one side for a moment, considering. 'I'm not sure what I think. Most likely you are right and he came from your dream, but dreams are supposed to carry messages sometimes, aren't they?'

She was feeling confused. 'He didn't say anything. I was in such a state of shock. I was sure he was my imagination. It was only when I came back in here and looked at the picture again that I realised that it was a different man and I started to panic.'

'Intriguing.' Phil took a slow thoughtful sip from his mug. 'Is he somewhere else in the picture, do you think? Behind her other shoulder?'

Robin frowned doubtfully. 'There is no room. Look at the composition of the painting. This was how it was supposed to be when she painted it. Without him there she is standing too far to the left. There is a huge empty space behind her. I'll bet that is what Lol noticed. It would have looked wrong to him. He had a fantastic eye. He would have seen that something was off balance. Perhaps that's why he thought that it wasn't a Lucas after all. She must have changed her mind after painting him there. Perhaps they had a row.' He reached over and caught Lucy's hand. 'You know what this means, Luce, don't you? You have to find out the whole story. Who were these men and what did they mean to Evie? Perhaps this guy wants you to write your book.'

Glancing at her sideways, noting her white face, he gave her a reassuring grin. 'Are you going to be OK here on your own tonight? Why don't you come back with us?' He had only just stopped himself from saying, 'Perhaps he doesn't want you to write it.'

Lucy shook her head. 'I can't leave the place, Robin. You know I can't.'

'Then we'll stay here.' Ever practical, Phil reached over with the kettle and topped up Robin's mug. 'Kip down in the living room.'

'Would you?' She didn't mean to say it. It had slipped out before she could stop it. She didn't like to admit how rattled she still felt by what had happened. Standing there with them in the room with her was one thing. Being alone in the house with its flights of creaky stairs and squeaking floorboards was quite another.

'Of course we would. If your boy in blue tries anything we'll give him a surprise.' Phil gave a small snort of laughter.

She smiled. 'You are incorrigible.'

'Always.'

'But thank you.'

August 13th 1940

On June 18th Churchill had made his speech informing the country that the Battle of France was over and that the Battle of Britain was about to begin. For weeks the country waited, then, on August 13th the first massed attacks began. Huge formations of German fighters and bombers started to thunder remorselessly in over the Channel, some bound for London, some for Dover, Southampton and Portsmouth, but most, specifically and unerringly, for the chain of airfields defending southern England, and Ralph was in the front line.

Evie was sitting outside A Flight hut on an empty oil drum when the phone rang in the hut. All round her men paused in what they were doing. She stopped drawing, her hand poised above the paper, counting under her breath.

She could hear the mumble of the voice in the dispersal hut then the phone slammed down and the single-word shout. 'Scramble!'

It was the third that day.

She swallowed hard, trying to keep her hand steady on the paper as she went on with her sketch. These lads had become familiar to her; they smiled at her and exchanged jokes as they waited between sorties. They were friends. And some of them were almost certainly not going to come back. In the previous three days eleven of the pilots had been killed and the majority of the planes damaged or destroyed. The surviving men were exhausted. The ground crew had barely finished refuelling the surviving planes, rearming the guns. The pilots had scarcely had time for a cup of tea. She sharpened her pencil and turned the page, forcing herself to concentrate on what she was doing, not letting the adrenaline get to her. She must not show her fear for them. Her job was to be invisible; to be utterly professional. Lightning charcoal sketches, a man pulling on his flying helmet, another knotting a scarf round his neck. The tractor dragging the refuelling bowser out of the way. Engines starting, the chocks being snatched from the wheels, the blur of propellers, as they gained speed and then they were gone, the remaining flight of Hurricanes, not even a full squadron now, swooping up into the air as in the distance she heard the air raid sirens start to wail.

Behind her, one of the riggers stopped to look at her page of drawings. 'There is a new squadron coming in this afternoon. 911 Squadron. Did you see the two big Harrows that flew in this morning with the advance ground troops and all their gear?' he said. He waved and she glanced at the two large planes parked side by side near the line of trees. 'It's a Spitfire squadron, like your brother's. Something new here for you to draw. Our chaps will be glad of a break, poor bastards. Jerry has really been going for us these last few days.'

She looked up at him and managed a smile. 'Our boys will cope.'

'Yeah. Sure.' The man pulled an oily rag out of a pocket in his battledress and wiped his hands. He looked up at the sky where already they could see the approaching attack. As they watched, the neat formations of fighters heading in from Tangmere to join their own boys began to break up and within seconds the sky was full of action.

'Suppose we'd better get ourselves ready for them when they come back,' he said with a sigh.

Evie watched him depart, sharing his anxiety; within seconds she had sketched the man's retreating form, the slump of his shoulders, the angle of his head as once again he glanced up at the sky. Evie followed his gaze, aware for the first time of the swallows which swooped and dived over the airfield, oblivious of the drama in the sky far above, and in the corner of the page she drew a small bird.

Only moments later two planes broke free of the mêlée and Evie was aware of men appearing from the various huts staring upward as the dogfight swooped low overhead. The guns rattled as the two planes dodged and wove around one another, the RAF roundel and the square black crosses clear; a Hurricane versus a Messerschmitt 109. Evie found she was holding her breath. They were so close now she thought she could see the men inside, then they soared upwards on and on up towards the sun. A final blast of firing and suddenly it was over. The German plane veered away and down, flames pouring from the fuselage. It was heading straight for them. She watched, her mouth dry, unable to move, only faintly aware of the shouts near her, of men running, of the tortured scream of the engine and then the plane was down, crashing in flames barely fifty yards away on the far side of the hedge. For several seconds she was paralysed with terror. She found she had dropped her sketchbook and pencil; she had forgotten to breathe. Men ran across the field towards the wreck but there was nothing they could do. The man inside had never stood a chance. Taking a long deep breath she dashed the tears from her eyes angrily. He was the enemy; she shouldn't be upset.

Only five of their own planes returned from the sortie, one ending up spectacularly on its back in the field almost in front of her. Evie jumped to her feet, heart in mouth, watching as the medics ran out with a stretcher, only to see the pilot extricate himself from his straps without help. He staggered from the plane, clutching at his arm, which hung uselessly at his side. He ran several steps, then stopped, swaying slightly, obviously disorientated, as the men with the stretcher reached him.

It was several seconds before, automatically, she reached again for her sketchbook. But her hand was shaking too much to draw.

She was still sitting there, stunned, when the promised new squadron appeared, circling the airfield in formation, their engines thundering deafeningly overhead. Fifteen Spitfires landed one after the other, coming to rest at last under the trees near the Nissen huts. The engines cut out, leaving the airfield eerily silent but for the distant song of a skylark.

Friday 5th July

The nights after her strange experience were hard for Lucy. Robin suggested he and Phil come and stay with her again but she refused. 'I have to learn to be here on my own,' she said stubbornly. 'If you come again I will want you here every night. I have to face it. I was scared, but nothing happened. He was just a shadow. He wasn't threatening. He was probably a dream or just my imagination.' She looked straight at Robin and gave a faint smile.

Noticing the defiant challenge in her eyes he said nothing to contradict her. 'Brave girl!' he said.

What she hadn't told him was that she couldn't get the man's face out of her head. His shadowy presence was in a way more real to her than the solid cheery figure in the painting. He had appeared for a reason. He was a link to Evelyn and he must have been trying to tell her something. Surely, if he had failed to get his message across wasn't he likely to come again?

The gallery had been busy but she used the occasional pauses between customers to rough out the outline of the book she was going to write about Evelyn, filling in the very few details she had been able to scrounge from the information that was out there in catalogues and on the Net. A whole week had gone by since she had seen Michael Marston and still she had heard nothing from him. At first optimistic that he would get in touch she wondered now if he ever would. Had he promised to help just to get her out of the door? It increasingly felt as though that was exactly what he had done. But if he didn't intend to help her, where did she go from here?

Putting her ghostly visitor firmly out of her mind she went over her meeting with Michael one more time in her head.

Had he given her any material she could work with, at least as a start? She went into the studio and stood in front of the picture. Michael had mentioned a farm where Evelyn had spent her childhood and he had implied that he would give her the address. There had to be some way of finding that out herself, but in the meantime, was there some way that she could identify it from the painting?

She dragged her eyes away from the faces in the portrait and this time concentrated instead on the landscape. The gate, the sky, the skyline. Was there a clue there which she could unravel, assuming it been painted on Evelyn's parents' farm? There was nothing to distinguish the gate. It was a five-barred wooden farm gate shaded with grey lichen and a mound of soft pale moss. No clue there. Nothing special. But the skyline? The silhouette of the Downs. Would she be able to find someone who recognised that? If it was a favourite place, a real place, then possibly; if it was imaginary then obviously it would mean nothing. But Evelyn painted real places. She painted the Downs she loved and the landscape around her home, that much one could tell from the paintings Lucy had seen in the catalogues, so there was a possibility that the place was identifiable.

What else had Michael said? He had mentioned Evelyn's brother, Ralph, who was a fighter pilot.

She looked back at the face of the young man behind Evelyn in the portrait. She was sure her initial impression must be right, that this young man was a lover. The touch of his hand on the shoulder, the expression in his eyes, both were too tender, too intimate to be the love of a brother and sister. She squinted at the painting again. It was strange how the expressions of the two faces seemed to change from one moment to the next. Perhaps that was the sign of a great portrait. Or was it just the change of light?

Whoever it was, at least she had one name. Ralph Lucas. So she would start with Ralph.

August 13th 1940

Tony Anderson had finished training in June. After the fall of France, Churchill had ordered that all trainee pilots be sent straight to squadrons and Tony found himself heading back to Edinburgh where until very recently he had been a law student in his third year. His first posting was, to his great delight, a Spitfire squadron based at Drem, some dozen or so miles from the city, and there he spent another two months training on active duty and getting to know the men who soon became his friends. On August 12th, the squadron discovered that it had been posted. They were to go to Sussex where the Battle of Britain was under way.

There was heavy cloud over most of the country and they flew well above it, stopping only once to refuel. As they neared the south coast the cloud began to break up at last and sunlight illuminated the landscape beneath them. Tony felt his heart lift. The most surreal moment had come as they approached London, seeing nothing of the city but an enormous number of barrage balloons poking up out of the heavy cloud.

'Something going on over to our left, chaps.' Tony heard the CO's voice crackle in his ear as they began to lose height. Tony squinted round and saw the planes in the distance. Dozens of them all over the place, criss-crossing the sky. 'No chance for us to have a crack at them this time. We're too low on fuel. Let's just get there safely for now; we'll soon get our chance.'

From the air he could see the Sector Airbase at Tangmere and then Westhampnett, so close it was almost next door. The latter seemed to be no more than a large field, without any runways. He could see a couple of Nissen huts, a windsock, a bowser and a few concrete hard standings around the perimeter and a line of trees. In the middle of the airfield a Hurricane lay on its back; behind the hedge he could see the wreckage of another plane amidst a heavy pall of black smoke. He felt a little kick of excitement under his ribs. This was it. They were now in the thick of the action.

He took his turn to land, taxiing in towards the trees and came to a standstill. As he pulled off his helmet and slid back the cockpit's canopy the last thing he had expected to see was a beautiful girl standing in front of him, sketchbook in one hand, pencil in the other, and a ferocious scowl on her face.

Friday 5th July, late

Downstairs in the gallery Lucy made her way to the back of the long narrow ground floor room which was their exhibition space. The gallery area had two windows, at the rear a tall narrow casement overlooking the small garden and at the front a bowed picture window onto the street which at present was lit by two spotlights focused on a bronze heron standing on a black dais. There was still light in the sky outside, late though it was, but the room itself was dark. She turned the lamp on in the small office area at the back, where an antique desk sat on an oriental rug between two comfortable leather armchairs. Sitting down at the desk she fired up the computer.

Threading her way through the usual entries offering to find Ralph Lucas on Facebook, to contact Ralph Lucases on several different continents, to establish their position in a dozen Lucas family trees, none of them relevant, to sell to them and to buy from them and even to provide their phone number, she found the right one at last. The entry was pitifully short.

Ralph James Lucas, Fighter Pilot (260 squadron, Spitfires) born 1919, died 1940

Lucy sat back. Twenty-one. Evelyn's brother had only been twenty-one when he died.

There was no other information that she could find.

Taking a deep breath she turned off the computer and the light and went slowly upstairs.

Pushing the studio door open, she stood there, staring at the painting once more.

'Ralph?'

Her voice sounded hollow and hesitant. It held no conviction.

There was no reply.

So, since Ralph was not the fair-haired young man in the painting, was he her dream, her ghost, the shadowed, enigmatic figure she had seen in her bedroom, not a part of this composition at all, but still around, off stage, an *éminence grise*, a restless spirit? The man in the shadows? And if that was true, why had he appeared now? What was it he wanted to say? And was he haunting her, or was he haunting Evelyn?

She found herself wishing desperately yet again that Larry was there, that she could talk to him, discuss the painting with him, share her compulsion to find out who this man was and how he fitted into Evelyn's life, and above all to feel safe, nestled in her husband's strong arms. She glanced back at the painting one last time, then, shivering, she turned off the lights and closed the door on the studio. That night she slept on the sofa in the living room, wrapped in Larry's old red dressing gown.

August 13th 1940

'But why are you so cross?' Eddie seemed to find Evie's fury funny. 'There's no harm done. You were going to work up the picture on canvas anyway. It was only a bit of dust.'

'He headed towards me deliberately. Nobody else came near me.'

'Maybe he was just the last one in and had to leave his plane at the end of the line.' He laughed again, putting his arm round her shoulder and giving her a quick hug. 'You said he apologised.'

'He thought it was a joke. Some of these boys are so arrogant!' She almost stamped her foot.

'They are fighting a war, Evie,' he said gently. 'I think they are entitled to be a little arrogant sometimes. Maybe he just didn't see you sitting there on your little oil drum.'

'That's what he said.'

'Well then.'

She wriggled free of his arm and went over to the table, studying her sketchbook with a concentrated frown. 'I saw a plane crash today. It went down in flames right there on the edge of the airfield. The pilot was killed. He had no chance to bail out.'

Eddie sighed. 'It's happening everywhere, Evie. You know that.'

'But there, right in front of me.' She looked up at him. 'It was an enemy plane. I should be pleased.'

He pushed his hands into his pockets. 'He's still a human being. You wouldn't be you, Evie, if you were dancing with glee. But if it hadn't been him, he would have shot down one of our boys, we both know that. Maybe more than one. Your young friend from this afternoon perhaps.'

She glared at him. 'I suppose so.' She looked back at her sketchbook. 'You'd better go, Eddie. I've got to help Mummy downstairs and then if I've got time I'll come up and do some more work here.'

'If?' he said, with not altogether mock indignation. 'You'd better find some time. I've got an investment in these pictures, don't forget.'

It was dark outside by the time she returned to her makeshift studio. She made sure the blackout was secure then switched on the lights, flooding the table with cold white light.

She reached for her pencil. Since the incident on the airfield with the young pilot she had been itching to draw him, but she wasn't going to give him the satisfaction of knowing that she had even noticed his golden good looks. The sketchbook lay open at her drawings of the crashed Hurricane in the middle of the airfield, the smoking shell of the Messerschmitt beyond the hedge. She folded the page back and looked down at the clean new sheet in front of her. They had started limiting the size of newspapers the year before, but so far there had been no more mention of paper rationing. Even so, she was going to have to be careful not to waste a single piece.

His insolence, that was what she remembered most clearly, his cheeky smile, the sparkling blue eyes, the wild hair springing up as he pulled off his helmet and goggles.

'Hello, gorgeous,' he had said and she had let fly. Instead of smiling and welcoming him to Sussex she had called him a selfish inconsiderate clod and probably more besides. She couldn't remember.

Her hand hesitated over the paper as she ran through in her head the things she had said and she blushed; here alone in the empty studio, she blushed at the memory. Why? Why had she been so angry and why so rude when for all she knew, as Eddie had just reminded her so sanctimoniously, the young man was quite possibly about to die for his country.

Tony. She remembered his name too. 'Hi, I'm Tony.' And he had held out his hand.

'Thanks a lot, Tony. You've ruined a day's work, Tony. Why did you have to taxi up here instead of down to the other end of the line, Tony?'

She had seen his face fall. He had been the one to blush. Then mercifully for them both someone had yelled his name from the Nissen hut behind them and he had raised his shoulders, then his hands, in a gesture of surrender. 'Sorry,' he had said and he had turned away.

And now she could picture every detail of his face in her mind, every freckle, every stray corkscrew spring of his curly hair, every quirk of his mouth.

With an exclamation of impatience she leaned forward over the table, her elbow on the page itself as if to hold it in place and she began to draw with swift sure strokes of the soft pencil.

Sunday 7th July

'I can't find her card.' Mike Marston was rummaging through the pile of post and papers on the kitchen table at Rosebank Cottage.

'Whose?' Charlotte was arranging some flowers in a blue pottery vase.

'The woman who wants to write about Evie. She gave me her card. God, what was her name? Why do I keep forgetting it?' He lifted a pile of magazines off a chair and looked under it. 'I hope Dolly hasn't thrown it out.'

'Dolly never throws anything out,' Charlotte commented tartly. 'If she did we might have a bit more room.' She rammed a vivid blue stem of delphinium into the vase.

Mike stood up and watched her for a moment, amused. 'You don't have to attack the poor flowers. You'll find they surrender quite easily if you push them in gently.'

She swore under her breath. 'They might surrender to you. They are out to get me! I am not the domesticated type, or hadn't you noticed?'

'I'd noticed.' He laughed.

She glanced up at him suspiciously. 'You sounded as though you meant that.'

'I did.'

There was a split second's silence. He reached over and touched her hand. 'I don't go out with you for your domestic skills, Charley, and you know it!' He caught her fingers as she reached for a rose and swore. 'You can snip off the thorns, you know. Then you won't get pricked.'

She sighed. 'So, who taught you that? I know. Don't tell me. Evie. Right?'

He gave a rueful nod. 'She loved flowers.'

She found the card on the dresser propped against a jar of peppercorns and for a moment she held it in her hand, staring down at it, studying the small sketch of the shop front, the elegant italic script, the name *The Standish Gallery*, and on the back the name, hand-scrawled in ballpoint. Lucy Standish. Her brow was furrowed in thought. He was looking the other way. She could drop it down the back of the line of old cookery books and it would be gone forever. She pictured the woman's shadowed, melancholy face and straight dark hair and gave a small satisfied smile. Was there any danger? None at all.

'Mike.'

He looked up and she held out her hand. He grinned and took the card. 'Glad one of us is organised.' He reached for the phone. She watched as he waited for the call to connect and registered by the slight slump of his shoulders that it had gone to voicemail.

'Hello Mrs –' He paused and looked at the card. Then he

turned it over to where she had written her name on the back. 'Mrs Standish, this is Mike Marston. I've been thinking about our discussion the other day and I was wondering if you would like to come over here again so we can work out some *modus operandi*. I'm sorry for the delay in contacting you. I've been rather busy.' He looked at Charlotte and winked. 'Give me a call. You have my number here.' He hung up.

'Have you given her your mobile number as well?' Charlotte queried.

'No. She rang the house when she first got in touch. Better that way, then she can speak to Dolly.' He stood for a moment looking round the kitchen. 'Your idea of putting Evie's stuff in the studio will take an awful long time. Hadn't we better make a start?'

He walked through into the sitting room and surveyed it rather hopelessly. 'There is such a lot. I don't know where to begin.'

'Why not leave it to Dolly and me?' Charlotte brought in her vase of flowers and put them down on a side table. She stood back to admire the effect. 'We could go to the supermarket now and collect some cardboard boxes. In fact, after this weekend, why don't we leave the whole thing to Dolly, then as you suggested Mrs Standish can come over during the week when we're not here? We don't want to waste our precious weekends.' She pulled a tissue out of her pocket and carefully blotted a drop of water which had fallen onto the table from the rose petals. 'You have told Dolly what you plan to do?'

'Well,' he hesitated.

'Oh, Mike!'

'I did hint at it, just to test out her reaction.'

'And what did she say?'

Mike gave a rueful smile. 'Quite a lot, actually.'

5

August 22nd 1940

It was Ralph who introduced them properly. He finally persuaded Evie to go with him to the pub.

'Eddie is more like a slave driver than a –' he was saying as they climbed into his car. He drove an ancient cream three-wheeler Morgan which was his pride and joy. He stopped suddenly mid-sentence and she looked at him quizzically.

'Than a – ?' she echoed.

'I was going to say boyfriend,' he said at last.

'Is he my boyfriend?' she repeated softly. 'Yes, I suppose he is. I'm sorry. I know you don't like him.'

'I never said that.'

'You don't have to.' She grinned mischievously. 'Dear Rafie, I can read you like a book. Daddy doesn't like him either. Not really. And you're right, he does make me work hard and just occasionally, yes, I do feel a bit put upon, and yes, I would like to go to the pub with my big brother.'

It had been a hard week. Tangmere had been targeted and it had received several direct hits. Parts of the aerodrome had been reduced to a mass of rubble. Many planes had been lost when the hangars were destroyed. There had been nonstop sorties as the waves of attack came over, but a blessed interval of quiet followed. It had been a baptism of fire for the new squadron at Westhampnett. There had been no night raids here, however, although everyone expected them soon, and a night off for a jar and some female company seemed like a really good idea for the exhausted pilots and ground crew alike.

Ralph took her to The Unicorn in Eastgate Square, a favourite with the pilots. The pub was noisy and very crowded. It was stuffy and hot inside and the air was thick with cigarette smoke. He bought Evie a drink, then they ducked out through the blackout curtains which hung over the door of the lobby and went to stand on the pavement outside. Within minutes a group of young men in RAF uniform had joined them.

'So, Ralph,' the voice behind Evie was cheery, the accent Scots, 'are you going to introduce me to the lady?'

Evie turned, the half-pint glass in her hand slopping shandy over her shoes.

'Hi, Tony.' Ralph slapped him on the back. 'Evie, this is Tony Anderson. One of the boys from Westhampnett. Tony, my sister, Evelyn.'

'Your sister!' Tony echoed with a huge grin. 'Wow!'

Ralph smiled happily.

Evie scowled. 'What he means is, we have met before. Flying Officer Anderson ruined one of my pictures.'

'Oh, come off it. It was hardly ruined,' Tony exclaimed. 'A wee bit of dust, that's all.'

'A wee bit of dust, as you called it,' Evie repeated, repressively, 'can destroy a picture if the paint is still wet.'

'True.' Tony nodded thoughtfully with a wink at the bemused Ralph, 'but you were only doing some quick pencil sketches. I remember most particularly.'

Evie gaped at him. 'You noticed?'

'Of course I noticed. To make amends, I will buy you a drink.

But that is all,' he added severely. 'I will not grovel for the rest of my life.'

Evie stared after him as he headed towards the door and vanished into the smoky interior of the pub.

Ralph laughed. 'So, you two have met before.'

Evie nodded. 'But I am not going to let it spoil my evening.'

'Glad to hear it.' Ralph raised his glass as another group of RAF officers headed their way. 'Let's see if we have more success here. Have you met my flight commander?'

By the time Tony threaded his way back through the crowds with Evie's glass in his hand she was engaged in animated conversation with Alan Reid. Tony elbowed his way to her side and pushed the glass towards her. 'Thanks.' She took it and turned back to Al with a smile.

'Evelyn!' Tony called out. He had to raise his voice to make himself heard.

She glanced back at him.

'If I concede that a small amount of dust from the airfield may have sullied your pristine sketches will it appease you if I allow you to draw my picture?'

Her eyebrows shot up as she stared at him.

'Go on,' he grinned. 'This is not an offer you can afford to turn down.'

She tried not to smile. 'What if I told you I had already done it?'

He gave Ralph and Al a sidelong look. 'Ah, well, I suppose I am irresistible. I shouldn't really be surprised if you have.'

Ralph gave a snort of laughter. 'Give up, Evie. I think you've finally met your match!'

Monday 8th July

Lucy waved the customer out of the gallery with a smile. He had been uncertain and unhappy, dithering between two pictures, not sure if the recipient of his gift would like it, angling to have her promise to give his money back if he had to return it. Which she would do, of course, but she would far rather he didn't feel he had that easy option. The small watercolour under his arm was one of several Larry had picked up at the last auction he had attended before his death. She looked at the empty space on the wall where it had hung and sighed. She had to get in some new stock and soon. At the end of the week perhaps she would go to the country house sale she had spotted in the paper only that morning. Friday, the announcement had said and it specifically mentioned pictures. A good call perhaps.

She tucked the cheque the man had given her into the little cash box in the drawer in the desk. Robin would be furious with her for letting him take the painting without clearing the cheque first. Larry would have been too. The purchaser had looked honest but neither of the men would have taken him at face value. Not these days. Well, she had.

She noticed suddenly that the light was winking on the answer phone and she leaned across to press the button. It was Michael Marston. She rang back at once but there was no reply. It wasn't until the next morning that she managed to get through to Dolly Davis. Mr Michael, she was told, would be in London for the next two weeks, but he had left instructions that Lucy was to be given access to the studio in the garden. She arranged to go the next afternoon.

'He's got this idea in his head that you can sort through all her stuff,' Dolly said with a look of sour incomprehension as she opened the studio door and pushed it back against the wall. It was raining gently and the garden smelled of fresh grass and roses and honeysuckle. She reached up to turn on the lights and ushered Lucy in. The huge table which before had borne only an open empty sketchbook and some tubes of paint was now laden with dusty boxes and piles of books. More boxes lined the walls, accompanied by suitcases and even a couple of hat boxes.

'You can look through everything but you mustn't take anything away,' Dolly went on, and by the set of her jaw Lucy could tell she intended to enforce that instruction personally. She wondered in sudden amusement if the old lady intended to search her before she left each day. She watched as Dolly turned and went out, closing the door behind her. Through the window she could see her stooped figure tramping across the wet grass towards the kitchen door.

Lucy stared round in awe. She had moved from having virtually no information about Evelyn Lucas at all to being given access to possibly the entire archive still in existence.

When Dolly returned after an hour or so with a cup of tea and a slice of lemon drizzle cake Lucy wondered if she had passed some kind of test. She had stacked the books on one side – very few novels, she noticed, mostly books on art, some technical manuals, exhibition catalogues, some brochures, biographies of famous artists – and she had shifted most of the cardboard boxes and baskets and bags either to the top of the bookcase or onto the floor in front of it. In this way she had managed to clear the table again, leaving it free to examine each item in turn. There appeared to be hundreds if not thousands of letters, not from Evelyn herself sadly, as far as she could see at first glance, but replies from other people, which was almost as good; bills, bank statements, most of which seemed to demonstrate a distinct paucity of funds and all kinds of other remnants of a busy life. The two portfolios, stacked against the wall behind the door had proved, to her intense disappointment, to be empty.

Lucy looked up as the door opened. Dolly set down her tray in the middle of the newly cleared space. There were two cups and two slices of cake.

Lucy smiled. 'I'm amazed that Mr Marston has trusted me with all this. And truly honoured.'

'He must have liked the look of you.' Dolly slumped down on one of the two straight-backed chairs near the paint-splashed deal desk. She was in her eighties, Lucy guessed, but energetic and fit enough to keep the cottage spick and span. 'It's been something he's put off doing again and again. And if it hadn't been for that woman he'd have gone on putting it off.'

Lucy frowned, puzzled. 'That woman?'

'Charlotte Thingy.' Dolly grimaced. 'She's behind this. Hard as nails, she is. She's not interested in poor Evie. She just wants the space cleared so she can makeover the cottage. She's even emptied the upstairs drawers.' She pointed to the two suitcases under the table. 'Poor Evie's personal things. Can't wait to get shot of them. Not that it didn't need doing, you understand. Of course it did. But she should have left it to someone who cared. I offered, but oh no, she had already done it. Shoved it all in a great heap. No doubt next time she comes the rest of Evie's things will all be pushed out here as well.'

Lucy thought it best not to comment. She reached for her cup. 'I'm not sure where to start. There is so much more than I expected. This will take me weeks, months, to go through.'

Dolly nodded. 'As I said, it's time someone did it. She deserves some recognition. I was with her here for the last forty years of her life, you know. I looked after her so she could paint. Right up to the end she was working. Her eyes were as good as someone half her age.'

Lucy looked down at the slice of cake on her plate with an absent frown. 'I didn't realise she was still painting. There are so few of her works on the record. What happened to them, do you know?'

'Christopher took them.' Dolly grimaced.

'Christopher?'

'Christopher Marston. Her other grandson. Mr Michael's cousin.'

Lucy gave a secret smile. Christopher obviously did not merit that honorarium of Mr.

'He took the paintings,' Dolly went on. 'Mr Michael got the cottage. That was the arrangement.' She pursed her lips.

Lucy digested that piece of news with disappointment. So, that explained the lack of paintings and sketches in the house.

'He took her diaries too. Everything he could lay his hands on that wasn't screwed down,' Dolly went on. 'I told Mr Mike but he wasn't interested. He said Christopher was welcome to them. He said it was what Evie wanted. He said it was the cottage itself that mattered to him because that was where she had been happy. Christopher would have sold it.'

Lucy was studying her face, noting the anger and frustration there.

'Did Christopher sell the paintings, then?' she asked quietly.

Dolly shook her head doubtfully. 'I suppose so. I don't know. They were never mentioned again. But I'll bet madam there,' she gestured over her shoulder towards the cottage, 'will want to know where they are once she realises how valuable they were.'

By 'madam' Lucy assumed she meant Charlotte Thingy. She hid a smile.

When Dolly had removed the tray she worked on for several hours, sorting through the different boxes. The suitcases poignantly contained a selection of clothes, underwear, nightgowns. Lucy could understand Charlotte's indignation if these were still in place in what must have been the main bedroom in the cottage. She hadn't been upstairs but it looked as if there wouldn't be more than two rooms up there. She pushed the cases against the wall. Somehow touching Evie's clothes was unbearably sad, but it brought her closer. She reached for another box. This seemed to contain the contents of a desk, perhaps the desk she had seen in the sitting room of the cottage. Stationery: unused notepaper and envelopes, cards, ancient fountain pens, old keys, stamps, a clip containing bills and receipts, all dating – Lucy turned them over carefully – from the summer before Evie died. And there was a tin box. She opened it and found it full of black-and-white photos of a young man. The top two snaps were of him in RAF uniform.

In one he was leaning against a small three-wheeler car, in the other standing beside a single-seater aircraft, painted in the familiar brown and green camouflage with the RAF roundel and a large number painted on the side. A Spitfire. She stared at him for a long time, gently running her finger over his face, then with shaking hands she turned the pictures over and looked at the back. Only one was labelled. *Rafie*, it said and *Summer 1940*.

When she looked up her eyes were full of tears. She had recognised him at once. 'Ralph?' she whispered.

There was no reply.

She had been right in her guess. The shadowy figure she had seen in her bedroom was Evie's brother.

She looked at the pictures again and picked up the others with unsteady fingers. There he was as a baby, a child, and as a boy in school uniform. Always the same wistful smile, the hair flopping in his eyes, the affectionate gaze directed at whoever was taking the picture.

She hadn't realised that Dolly had come back in until the woman approached the table.

'Sorry.' Lucy brushed the tears away.

Dolly looked down at the photos. 'Are those of Mr Ralph?'

Lucy nodded.

'He was killed in the war,' Dolly shook her head again. 'Evie never talked about him, you know.' She gave Lucy another curious glance.

Lucy gave an apologetic smile, aware suddenly of the tears on her cheeks and how odd they must look. 'It seemed so sad. This picture must have been taken just before he died. He looks so happy.' Or did he? Was that wistfulness there because he had a premonition of the future? She bit her lip.

'Where did you find them?' Dolly was frowning.

Lucy pointed at a cardboard box.

'So, she's been through the desk as well.' Dolly glared at the box.

'I'm sorry. Was it private?'

'Not from you.'

They looked at each other in silence for a moment and Lucy realised that her tears had unlocked something in Dolly's reserved manner. They were allies now, against Charlotte Thingy.

As though sensing she had unbent too far Dolly straightened her back. 'I'm afraid you are going to have to leave,' she said. 'I'm going home now and I need to lock up.'

Lucy's heart sank. 'Of course.' She glanced round the studio. 'I haven't really started,' she said helplessly.

'I usually come in on Tuesdays and Fridays,' Dolly stated firmly. 'You're welcome while I'm here. I arrive at nine and leave at four thirty.'

Friday. The day of the auction.

With Robin's co-operation, she had planned to set blocks of time aside, a week or two at a time, to go through the archive. If she could only come once or twice a week it would take forever.

'I'll do my best to be here,' Lucy said. 'If I can't make Friday I'm afraid it will have to be next week.'

August 24th 1940

Eddie counted out four crisp white fivers and folded them into her hand. 'More where that came from, Evie. Keep up the good work, sweetheart.' He drew her into his arms again and pulled her against him. 'They'll take as many of those small paintings as you can produce.'

Evie pulled away. He smelled of cigarettes and there was a taint of stale alcohol on his breath even though it wasn't yet five o'clock.

'That's great Eddie, thanks.' She tucked the notes into the pocket of her dungarees. 'Are you staying for supper?' She had just finished milking when he had arrived.

He shook his head. 'Best get home.' He paused for a fraction of a second. 'You haven't been down to the airfield for a couple of days.' He glanced down at her shrewdly. 'Is there a problem?'

She shook her head. 'There is so much to do here. There are only so many hours in the day, Eddie.'

'Yes, well, there is a lot to do there as well. Don't forget, I'm going to need a portfolio to put in front of Sir Kenneth Clark at the WAAC.'

'Don't worry. I'm working on it.' She gave him a playful push. 'Go on. Go home. I'll do some more work once I've scrubbed the dairy.'

Did he not realise, she wondered as she waved him away just how hard she worked on this bloody farm, doing the work of at least two land girls, and how hard it was to build up a portfolio if he kept selling her paintings as fast as she produced them?

It was nearly dark when at last she wandered, exhausted, back towards the farmhouse and pushed open the door.

Tony Anderson was sitting at the kitchen table drinking tea with her mother. She stopped dead, staring at him. 'What are you doing here?'

'I came to have my portrait painted.'

'You can't just turn up!'

He looked at Rachel. 'Tell her. What else can I do? We're on call nearly all the time. I've done five sorties today. We've only been stood down tonight because the battle was so fierce this afternoon the Hun have gone home to lick their wounds. But if you're not willing –' He stood up.

'Evie,' Rachel cried. 'Tell him you'll do it. The poor boy has been waiting hours. You can draw him down here in the kitchen while I heat up some soup for you both. I know you can sketch while you eat, I've seen you do it before.'

'You haven't been over to the airfield,' Tony interrupted accusingly before Evie could reply. He held her gaze steadily. 'I thought under the circumstances you might come to me.'

'What circumstances?' Rachel put in sharply. She had stepped into the larder and reappeared with a large earthenware pot of soup covered with a muslin cloth.

'I promised him I would draw him,' Evie snapped at her mother. She turned to Tony. 'I couldn't leave the farm. I've been so busy.' She was feeling unaccountably under siege, embarrassed and angry at his attentions and feeling worse because of her mother's amused gaze. She gave an exaggerated sigh. 'All right, I'll sketch you now, late as it is.' She heaved another sigh, this one even louder.

'Thanks.' He was trying to look humble now, a smile trembling behind his eyes.

There was a sketchbook on the dresser. She grabbed it and opened it at a clean page. 'Sit down. Here, under the lamp.'

He sat down obediently, an elbow on the table, chin on hand, profile raised to the lamplight. 'Will I do?'

'You'll do.' Now suddenly she was trying not to laugh, her irritation evaporating. She couldn't work out how she felt about this man. She had never met anyone like him before. His merry blue eyes, his sense of fun, his soft Scots accent, his stunning good looks and his cheeriness in the face of threat all intrigued her. Was he so stupid that he didn't understand the danger all round him? Wasn't he afraid? She knew Ralph was afraid. That was why he was so brave.

Then she realised what it was that was different about Tony. Eddie and Ralph were men. Tony was still a boy.

'Go to bed, Mummy!' It was midnight. They had finished their soup ages ago and Rachel was still sitting over her book in the corner. For the hundredth time her eyes had closed and she was nodding closer and closer to the volume in her lap. She hadn't turned a page in half an hour.

Tony glanced over his shoulder quickly then resumed his pose. 'I don't need a chaperone, Mrs Lucas, honestly. I'm sure I could fight her off.'

'Tony!' Evie was squinting down at the page. 'Stop wriggling.'

He gave her a broad smile. 'Can I look yet?'

'Yes.' She sighed and dropped the pencil. 'Yes, you can look.'

He stood up and walked round the table as with a groan Rachel closed her book and levered herself out of her chair. They both stood staring down at the sketch.

'That's brilliant!' Tony exclaimed. 'Almost as handsome as the real me. Not quite, that's not possible, but it will do. When will you paint it?'

Evie was staring up at him, blinking. 'When will I paint it?'

'Aye. Fill in the colours.'

Just in time she saw the twinkle, the twitch of his mouth. Reaching over she slapped his hand. 'I'll paint you when I think you deserve it. Until then you have a finished pencil sketch by the soon to be famous Evelyn Lucas, which will one day probably be worth hundreds of pounds. Here. Take it with you and get back to the base. I'm sure you should have been in hours ago.'

'Just like in school. You're right.' He nodded vigorously. 'But I'll show matron the picture then she'll promise not to beat me with her slipper.' He took the sheet of paper from her. 'I'm sorry to have kept you up so late, Mrs Lucas, I really am.' He grinned mischievously. 'But it was worth it. I'll send this to my parents and they will treasure it.' For a second he was serious. 'If anything happens to me –' He paused and left the rest of the sentence unfinished.

Evie walked with him to the door. The two dogs appeared from one of the sheds and she sent them back with a click of the fingers. By the light of the faint moonlight in the yard she could see a small open-topped car parked near the barn. He followed her gaze.

'I borrowed it. Brilliant little runabout. 1927 Morris Cowley. Chap at the base wants six quid for her. If I buy her I'll take you for a ride. If you're good.' He sighed. 'So, I'd best be going. The last couple of mornings they've been calling us at four a.m. Thanks, Evie.' He put his hands on her shoulders. Before she could turn away he had bent to kiss her lightly on the lips, then he was sprinting towards the car. She saw him pack the drawing away carefully then he made his way to the front and bent to the starting handle. The engine caught almost at once and he vaulted into the driving seat.

The blacked out headlights barely gave him any light to see by at all as he reversed and turned before heading down the lane.

She put her fingers to her mouth, staring after him. The touch of his lips had sent a shockwave through her system which had for a moment left her incapable of coherent thought.

6

Friday 12th July

'I thought you weren't coming down this weekend.' Dolly had opened the door to Mike with a duster still in her hand. It was four o'clock on Friday afternoon.

'Charlotte had to cancel our trip abroad. She was summoned to some sort of conference she couldn't get out of. It's a shame but we're rescheduling our break.' Mike dropped his briefcase and holdall and looked round. 'Is Lucy Standish here? I didn't see her car in the lane. I thought this would be a good chance to talk to her and see how she is getting on.'

Dolly frowned. 'She couldn't come today. There was some auction she had to go to, apparently.'

'Ah.' Mike couldn't hide his disappointment. 'So, what do you think of her so far?'

'She seemed nice enough.' Dolly was guarded. 'All she did was rearrange the boxes and poke around in some of them.'

'I don't suppose she had time to do much.'

Dolly sucked her teeth. 'Maybe she saw enough to realise there is not much of value here.'

Mike looked at her sharply. 'What do you mean?'

'Just that you mustn't forget that she is a dealer.'

'You don't believe she is writing a book? You think she had an ulterior motive?'

'I don't know.' Dolly gave an expressive sigh. 'She didn't bring anything to write on, as far as I could see.'

Mike studied her face for a moment. 'Maybe I should ring her.'

He waited until Dolly had gone home then pulled Lucy's card out of his wallet and reached for his mobile as he wandered out into the garden.

'I was sorry to miss seeing you,' he said when she answered at last. 'My housekeeper said you had to go to an auction today.'

'Yes. Such a nuisance. There was nothing I could do.' Lucy sounded flustered. She was in fact juggling her phone as she tried to unlock her car door, three carefully wrapped paintings one of which was quite large, under her arm. With relief she got the door open and slid the pictures behind the seat, dropping her bag into the footwell. 'Sorry. That's better. I hadn't realised I would only be able to come on Tuesdays and Fridays. That is going to slow up my research quite a bit.'

'I don't suppose you would have time to come over tomorrow?' Mike was grinning to himself. So Dolly planned to keep an eye on everything personally. He had never said that Lucy couldn't come on any other days. He grimaced. Was that naïve of him? Perhaps Dolly was right and he shouldn't be so trusting. Before tomorrow he would do what he should have done in the first place when she first got in touch. He would do some research of his own on line and find out some more about Mrs Lucy Standish. He brought his attention back to what she was saying.

'I'll come early, if that's all right.'

It was only when he had switched off the phone that he wondered how early early was.

She was there just before nine. She was still wearing jeans but this time she had on a pretty deep red blouse and her hair

71

was loose on her shoulders. She followed him into the kitchen and sat down obediently at the table while he made coffee.

'I must apologise for not being here on Tuesday,' he said. 'As I told you, I work most of the time in London. I left it to Dolly to make you welcome. I hope she wasn't too ferocious?' He pushed a mug towards her and sat down on the other side of the small table. His eyes, she noticed, were shrewd and steady as they focused on her face. This time he was dressed informally in jeans and a black T-shirt. The clothes suited him much better, she decided. He looked less intimidating and more approachable.

'I don't think she entirely trusts me,' she said ruefully. 'She kept popping back to check what I was up to. And fair enough. She cares a great deal about Evelyn.'

'She felt that as a writer you should have brought writing materials. It caused some suspicion that you were not laden with notebooks and a quill pen.' Her gallery was well respected, he had discovered. She had a degree in art history and her husband had been killed in an horrendous car crash nearly four months before.

She gave a snort of laughter. 'That never occurred to me. True, but not quite accurate. In there,' she indicated the tote she had dropped beside her on the floor, 'I have a laptop. I didn't get round to taking it out on Tuesday. I had just about sorted out how I was going to start categorising stuff when she said I had to go.'

'She chased you out?'

'Only because she was leaving herself.' Lucy laughed again. 'I suspect she thought I was after the family silver. Is that why she sent for you?'

He shook his head. He liked the way she laughed. Her face mobile, humorous, not classically beautiful like Charlotte, but elegant, her cheekbones emphasised by the way she tucked her hair back behind her ears as though she wasn't used to wearing it loose. She didn't look so exhausted and sad today; her eyes were brighter.

'You were at an auction yesterday, I gather.'

She nodded. 'Guilty as charged, but I promise I wasn't fencing stolen goods. I was buying for my gallery.'

'Did you find anything?'

She nodded. 'It was hard enough to find time to hunt for stock when Larry was alive. Larry was my husband.' Her eyes dimmed as he saw the sadness cross her face. 'Robin doesn't know enough to be a buyer,' she went on. 'Robin Cassell, he is my assistant. He's looking after the place today so I can come here. Opening on Saturdays is another problem for us but it is often our best day so we have to manage somehow.'

'Ah.'

'No.' The gurgle of laughter again. 'Whatever Mrs Davis thinks, I am not here to beg, borrow, buy or steal any of Evelyn's work. Far from it. The gallery was Larry's. I am not even sure I want to keep it going.' She stopped as though surprised by what she had said.

Mike was still watching her steadily and she was beginning to find it a bit disconcerting. She was talking too much but somehow she couldn't stop. 'My dream was to be a writer; a biographer and we both had this interest in Evelyn as a Sussex painter. I abandoned the idea after he died but then the grant came through and I felt I had to honour our dream.' Her voice faded and she sat staring down into the coffee mug. 'Maybe I can't do both. I don't know.' She looked up and saw he was still watching her. 'Sorry. Not your problem.'

'Unless you give up on Evie,' he said gently.

'I won't give up on Evie.' She picked up the mug. 'Or Ralph.' The name seemed to hang in the air for a moment longer than necessary.

She sipped the coffee then glanced at him over the rim of the mug. 'I don't suppose either of them haunt this place?'

It was his turn to laugh. 'Well, Ralph never came here, so I doubt if he would. But Evie?' He wrinkled his brow. 'She has certainly left a strong presence here, let's put it that way.'

She looked thoughtful for a moment and he put down his mug. 'You weren't being serious?'

'No, of course not,' she said quickly, 'but, as you say, she has left a strong presence here. One would have to be very insensi- tive not to feel it.'

'She loved this place. It feels a bit like a betrayal to be moving her stuff out, if I'm honest.'

'That's how Mrs Davis feels. But I can understand your fiancée wanting to –'

'She's not my fiancée,' he interrupted sharply.

'Sorry. Partner, then. Whatever.' She changed the subject hurriedly. 'It is helpful for me to have it all out there, then I can sort through it more easily.' She hesitated. 'I gather from Mrs Davis that any diaries there may have been were inherited by your cousin?'

He frowned. 'I don't think Evie kept any diaries.'

She looked puzzled. 'I must have misunderstood. No matter. There seem to be a great many letters from her friends. I am sure I can find material there. She was obviously a hoarder!' She smiled.

'Indeed.' He stood up suddenly. 'Shall we go to the studio and take a look?'

She followed him into the lush garden with its kaleidoscope of flowers, the grass perhaps a little too long now. It showed a trail of damp footprints behind them and she felt her feet grow wet in her sandals. Did he have a gardener, she wondered, or did he do it himself at weekends? She felt a pang of guilt. Their precious little garden behind the gallery was overgrown. It looked unloved. Neither she nor Robin had the time to look after it any more.

Mike produced a key and opened the door to the studio. He went in and looked round. 'You seem to have tidied up. Or was that Dolly?'

'Me!' Lucy moved over to the table. 'I needed space to work and make notes. There is a tremendous amount of stuff here. Even her clothes.' She moved over to a couple of large card- board boxes. 'Shoes. Hats. Handbags.'

'Ah.' For a moment he looked uncomfortable. 'Charlotte may have misunderstood when I said we should put her papers out here. She seems to have brought everything.'

'It's a small house,' Lucy said sympathetically. 'I'm sure you both need the space. I'll go through it all and then perhaps you can decide what should be kept. For the archive,' she added hastily, afraid she might have overstepped the mark.

'Good idea.' He glanced round helplessly. 'There seems to be an awful lot more stuff than I expected. How on earth are you going to find time to go through everything?'

'With great difficulty if I can only come once or twice a week.' She glanced up at him frankly.

He shook his head. 'I can see that. Perhaps we can find a way of circumventing Dolly's surveillance.'

For a moment she was speechless. 'Does she give the orders round here then?' she said at last.

He screwed up his face quizzically. 'Pretty much. I rely on her such a lot. You can see why. I'm away most of the time and she has been coming here for more than forty years. The house and garden wouldn't survive without her.'

'I see.' Lucy sighed. 'Sorry. It's not my business anyway. It won't be hard obviously to sort out the paperwork from the other stuff.' She gave a reluctant smile. 'Then I'll try and roughly put it into some kind of chronological order. I hope she won't mind me using a computer?'

'Now. Now.' The reprimand was gentle. 'I'm sure it will be fine. We are going to help you as much as we can.'

She felt very small suddenly. 'Sorry. It's frustration. I can't wait to start.'

'Then why not start now? I won't get in your way. Perhaps we can adjourn to the pub at lunchtime to compare notes?' He paused. 'I don't know how to tell you this but I'm afraid there is still much more in the house.'

She made a face. 'It is her whole life, Michael. May I call you Michael? Mrs Davis, Dolly, is always so formal. But as long as there is room in the studio we can go on bringing it over here. It is all stacking away quite neatly.' She hesitated for a moment. 'I take it you have no reservations about all this. You haven't changed your mind about me working here?'

He shook his head. 'I don't think we've got anything to hide. If I had the slightest inkling that there was I wouldn't let you within a mile of it all. Please don't let Dolly put you off. And it's Mike. Please.'

She watched as he strode back across the lawn towards the shed in the far corner. Ah, her question about lawn mowing was about to be answered. She saw him bend to pick up a red fuel can from just inside the door. He shook it experimentally, nodded as though satisfied there was enough fuel for his enterprise and then dragged the mower out into the sunshine.

Leaving the door open to let in the sunlight she turned back to the boxes. Almost at once she struck gold. A small battered attaché case had been pushed into one of the large cardboard cartons, together with several shabby leather handbags. Lucy was about to push the whole lot to one side when she saw the locks on the case. One of them had flipped open. She pulled the case out of the box and set it on the table. The other lock was stiff but after some tugging it reluctantly sprang back as well, releasing a musty smell of old leather. Inside the lid there were several suede pockets, ragged now and full of small holes as though they had been nibbled by some insect, one full of unused envelopes, the others stuffed with sheets of paper closely covered in small scrawled writing, much crossed out and rewritten. Pulling out a handful she stared down at them. Was this Evie's handwriting? She set the sheets down on the table and selected one, trying to decipher the words. *It has come to my notice that* . . . then a bit that was crossed out. Lucy squinted at it . . . *you have been less than honest*, then another bit more clear this time. *How could you do this to me?* Lucy hooked her foot around the leg of the stool behind her, pulling it closer and she sat down, her eyes glued to the sheet of paper. It was the rough draft of a letter. Carefully she read it through. There was much in the same vein – recriminations, anger, frustration – the strongest passages crossed and recrossed out, softened, reworded. She turned over the last sheet. Nothing. She sorted through all the sheets. Of this particular letter there was no beginning and no ending. To her enormous frustration there was no way of telling who it had been addressed to or the date.

The other fragments of paper she pulled out were varied and torn but some, to her great delight, were actually about Evie's painting.

'Yes!' Lucy murmured. This was what she wanted. She glanced over her shoulder towards the door. Mike was moving steadily behind the mower in the distance, partially hidden behind a couple of ancient apple trees. Her first instinct had been to call him and show him what she had found but something made her pause. In spite of what he had said she still wasn't a hundred per cent convinced that he was wholly on side about the biography. *If I had the slightest inkling that there was anything to hide I wouldn't let you within a mile.* The words echoed in her head for a moment. There was a warning there; a threat even. If she uncovered more personal stuff was he likely to confiscate it or worse, burn it? She had heard of families reacting like that before. She hesitated, tempted to stuff the contentious pages into her bag. No, that would be unforgivable, stealing. But perhaps just for now she would quietly put them safely to one side and wait to see what else turned up.

It was after one o'clock when Mike stuck his head round the door. 'Would this be a good moment to stroll up to the pub?' He stepped into the studio and fished in his pocket for a piece of paper. 'Put this somewhere safe before I forget. The address of the farm where Evie was brought up. I don't have the phone number, I'm afraid, but it is owned by some people called Chappell.'

She tucked the scrap of paper into her tote then she grabbed her purse out of the bag and followed him. They made their way up the lane towards the village. A cluster of houses, most built of flint like Rosebank, some old red brick and some timber framed, clustered around a small green, next to which was the village church. The thatched, picture-book country inn, the upper storey covered in hung tiles, was a few minutes' walk further on up the lane.

'So, have you found anything useful?' He introduced her to the couple who ran the pub and they had ordered at the bar before finding themselves a table on the terrace at the back.

'I'm still sorting stuff out.' Lucy sat down in the shade of a pergola covered with yet more roses. 'It seems to me she kept every single bill and bank statement and receipt she ever had.'

He laughed. 'That will make for a singularly dull biography.'

'It will if that's all I can find.' She reached up to her dark glasses tucked on top of her head and slid them down onto her nose. 'I hope you have lots of anecdotes you can tell me to fill out the gaps between her visits to the bank. Gossip, scandal, family rows. That sort of thing.'

She was watching him from behind the glasses and she saw him look away suddenly. He was quite handsome, she decided, in an unorthodox kind of way. 'All families have secrets,' she went on gently, 'and sometimes there is no reason for them to be secret any more. Times passes. The people involved have died.' She paused hopefully, taking a sip from her wine glass.

Mike sat back in his rustic chair with a sigh. Beneath him the wood creaked in sympathy. 'I think there were family rows. The trouble is they would have been when I was too young to understand them and once I had my own life, you know how kids are, I wasn't really interested. I loved my grandmother, but I'm afraid I was more interested in me. And so was she. She was fantastically modern in her outlook. She never talked about the past.' He looked up sharply. 'If I'm honest, I'd rather you stuck to the subject of her painting. You know she went to the Royal College of Art before she became a war artist? Now that is a topic people would find intriguing. She never completed the course because of the war. Instead she worked on the family farm. That is how she gained access to the airfields. Through her brother, Ralph, sketching between her stints milking cows.'

August 27th 1940

It had been a peaceful day compared to the last two; Tony had sat longer than usual over his lunch listening to the general discussion in the Mess about the reason for the lull. Were the Germans licking their wounds or were they planning an even more lethal raid? The consensus seemed to be with the latter view but in the meantime some of the men were planning an evening around supper at The Dolphin in Chichester. Tony found his thoughts wandering. To Evie. Again. He hadn't been able to get her out of his head. That kiss, three days before, so spontaneous, so electrifying, had burned its way into his very being. This had never happened to him before. He was used to girls falling at his feet, metaphorically at least, and her chippy reaction to him had fascinated him. She was sparky, intriguing, vivacious. Nothing like anyone he had ever met before and he wanted to see her again, badly.

'You coming down to The Dolphin tonight, Tony?' One of his friends clapped him on the shoulder.

He shook his head. 'There is someone I want to see.'

There was an appreciative groan across the room. 'I thought so. The laddie is smitten!' A voice called from the sofa by the window. 'Money on the fact that it is our little artist!'

Tony grinned. He tapped the side of his nose. 'State secret.'

'You'll be wanting to buy Esmeralda then.' Another voice. David Brownlow. From whom he had borrowed the car.

He still hadn't made up his mind about the little Morris, but suddenly it made sense.

'A fiver, I think you said?'

'Six was the deal.'

Tony grimaced. 'You want my shirt as well?'

'Go on. You've got a rich daddy.' The banter was good-natured. The men were climbing to their feet. Time to go out to the Flight hut. 'The lady will love it.'

Tony smiled. 'The lady loves me!'

Another general groan. 'Don't count your chickens,' David advised gravely. 'Even you can't have wooed her so quickly.' He reached into his pocket for the car key and dangled it in front of Tony's nose. 'Let's see the colour of your money.'

Tony reached into the pocket of his battledress. 'I trust there is petrol in it?'

It was David's turn to look shifty. 'Enough to get you there. Wherever there is!' He let out a whoop of laughter. 'I might have to ask you for a lift into Chi tonight, of course. On your way to the little lady's farm.'

They flew two patrols that morning; the skies were empty. When Tony set off for the farm he was in high good spirits, a bunch of flowers on the seat beside him. Evie hadn't been down to the airfield that day but it never occurred to him that she wouldn't be at home either. Rachel was walking across the yard, a jug of milk in her hand when he drove in and drew to a halt by the stable wall.

'I'm sorry, Tony. She's not here. She's gone with her father to Southampton.' Rachel waved an inquisitive fly away from her jug. 'She wanted to do some sketching over there and grabbed the chance of the lift.' She waited, smiling at him, seeing the boy's face fall. There was nothing for it. Tony had to turn the car and go back to the airfield.

September 1st 1940

Eddie had a letter in his hand. He caught Evie's wrist and pulled her across to the kitchen table. 'Sit.'

Taken by surprise, she sat. 'What is it?'

'I've had a letter from Sir Kenneth Clark's office.'

80

'About me?' Her eyes sparkled.

He nodded. 'The War Artists Advisory Committee wants to see more of your work. But –' he raised his hand as she jumped up ecstatically, 'it has to be the kind of work that they are approving for women artists.'

She sat down again with an angry pout. 'I am not going to paint women in aprons.'

'They don't like the thought of you painting on an airfield, especially one that may be bombed and strafed regularly. It is too close to the action. There are male artists painting the flyboys and that is enough. I explained that you live near the airfield and technically are in just as much danger at home, and that you go to Westhampnett with your brother and are chaperoned and in no danger whatsoever, but –'

'You said what?' Now she was blazing with anger. 'How dare you!'

'It's true, Evie. Well, more or less. They all look out for you, you know they do.' He folded his arms. 'It's up to you. I can't do any more.' For a moment they glared at each other, then at last she looked away. 'Don't they want to see any more pictures of the planes and pilots then?'

He chewed his lip for a moment. 'I think it's worth trying again with a new portfolio. We were stupid; we should have got you to sign the pictures with your initials. Then the issue of you being a woman might not have come up at all or not until it was too late and they had accepted you. I think the best chance now is to win them over with your sheer brilliance.' He grinned at her. 'So, sweetheart, have you anything new to show me?' He stood up and wandered over to the dresser where her sketchbook lay. Picking it up he opened it and began to turn the pages. 'You've torn some out.'

'So?' She was still fuming.

'So, you can't afford to waste paper. Have you anything upstairs in the studio?' He glanced up at her. 'Evie, you can't afford to slack. If you want to be taken seriously, you have to work.'

'I have worked!'

'Show me then.' He strode towards the staircase.

On the easel was a half-finished painting. Eddie studied it in silence for several seconds.

'It's good isn't it?' she said, standing behind him.

'Who is it?' He stepped closer, examining it more closely. The figure in the RAF battledress was standing in the middle of the airfield, a Spitfire pulled up on the grass in the distance, his helmet and goggles under his arm, the boyish grin and wind-swept hair immediately engaging and carefree.

'Tony Anderson. He's with the squadron at Westhampnett.' Her mother had told her of his visit, of the wilting flowers on the seat in the car. His wistful remark about his parents had touched her deeply; she hadn't been able to get it out of her head and almost without intending to do it she had begun the portrait for his mother. She thought back to his kiss and felt a jolt of excitement at the memory. She had hoped he would repeat his visit but there had been no sign of him.

'It is good, you're right.' Eddie moved away from the painting. 'Excellent, that can go in the portfolio. It's not an action painting, and it is a good portrait with lots of warmth and enthusiasm. It would appeal to them.'

'No.' Evie folded her arms and stood in front of the painting. 'This one is not for sale.'

'What do you mean?' Eddie frowned at her.

'What I say. It is not for sale and it is not for the portfolio.'

'Everything you paint is for sale, Evie.' Eddie's voice was suddenly harsh. 'That is our agreement.'

'That is not our agreement, Eddie. We have no formal agree-ment.' She glared at him. 'This picture is for Tony's parents. My gift.'

She held his gaze for several seconds and it was Eddie who looked away first. 'I'm astonished you think you can afford to be so generous,' he said coldly. 'Both with your time and the mat-erials. Which I obtained for you, I may add. If you are giving it away then you will have to reimburse me for the paint and canvas.'

Evie's mouth dropped open in astonishment. 'I don't believe I heard you say that,' she hissed at him. 'Of all the callous, hardhearted, mean-spirited –'

'That is enough, Evie,' he shouted. 'This is not a game!'

'No,' she said, 'It's not.' Her voice was bleak. She turned to walk out of the room.

He sighed. 'No, come back, Evie. I'm sorry. You are right. I shouldn't have said that. Of course you can give the picture away. It is just that we can't afford to squander materials. But you know that.' He hurried after her and caught her in his arms. 'Sweetheart. Wait. Don't be cross. Forgive me.'

She gave him a weak smile. 'Of course I forgive you. I'll paint lots more pictures, I promise.'

He followed her downstairs to the kitchen. Rachel had just come in from feeding the hens and she had a bowl of eggs in her hand. 'Can I give you some, Eddie? I think your mother said you don't have hens any more.' She glanced from one to the other. 'Is everything all right?'

'It's fine, Mummy,' Evie said impatiently. 'Eddie is just going and I have to get out to my chores.' She glanced at her watch. 'I'll see you next week, Eddie.'

'Next week?' he echoed. There was no mistaking the anger in his voice.

'You said you had to go to London first. And as you say, I have to get down to the airfield and make some more sketches. I mustn't shirk my duties,' she said coldly. She pushed past him and walked out into the yard.

He glanced at Rachel. 'She can be a bit touchy, your Evie,' he said with an uncomfortable laugh. 'I think I've upset her.'

Rachel gave him a cool glance. 'I'm sorry to hear that, Eddie.' She put three eggs in an old brown paper bag and handed them to him. 'Give my best wishes to your mother.'

She watched through the window as he walked across the

yard to his car and climbed in. As soon as he had gone she threw on her cardigan and went to find her husband in the barn.

The more she saw of Eddie Marston the more she found herself beginning to dislike him. Oh, he was good-looking enough, and had a certain charm but there was something about him which put her teeth on edge. She had known him since he was a child, of course, but this new, confident, older Eddie was beginning to grate on her nerves.

'Hopefully the honeymoon period is coming to an end,' she said to Dudley as he straightened his back with a groan. He had been working on the engine of the tractor, the tractor that Ralph had persuaded him to buy. 'They've had a row.' She put her hand down to the dogs as they milled round her.

'Do you know what about?'

'He's trying to exploit her again. She finally stood up to him. I could hear them shouting at each other upstairs.'

Dudley grimaced. 'He's too sharp for his own good, that one. Let's hope she stays seeing sense. The trouble is he is dangling some tempting ideas in front of her, to say nothing of the money. He's got the contacts. She thinks he can make her dreams come true.'

They were both silent for a minute and into the silence came the unmistakable drone of distant aircraft engines. They walked to the door of the barn and looked up.

'They're ours,' Dudley said quietly as he shaded his eyes against the glare of the sky. 'Spits. I wonder if our Rafie is up there with them.'

Saturday 13th July

As they stood up to leave the pub Mike paused thoughtfully. 'You know, there is one way I can help you sort out the research. Why don't I ask Dolly to go through the stuff that's in the studio and weed out all the shoes and hats and handbags and things? I'll tell her she can keep what she wants and pack up the rest to go to the charity shop. Some of that stuff probably counts as vintage. They would make some money out of it.'

Lucy froze. 'I suppose that would be all right.' She swung round to face him. 'The only thing is, there may be letters and papers in the bags. People often leave that sort of thing – I know my own grandmother did. Dolly might not recognise what is important.'

'We can tell her not to touch anything that looks like a letter. I'll make sure she understands that. I'll ask her to put anything she spots which might be significant into a box file or something and keep it safe until you have had a chance to look at it.' He led the way across the terrace and back into the bar, heading through it towards the front door. It was dark in there after the sunlight and Lucy found herself squinting to see where she was going, threading her way between tables as she hurried after him. When they were once more outside and heading back down the lane she caught up with him.

'You know, I think I would rather she didn't poke around in the studio, Mike.' She gave an awkward smile as he glanced at her. 'I think Dolly has a bit of her own agenda as far as Evie is concerned. She is very protective, that's obvious. If she were to find something important, she might feel that it would be better if she quietly put it somewhere out of my reach.'

He stopped. 'What makes you think that?'

She sighed. 'Instinct?'

'Has she said anything?'

Lucy shook her head. 'It's more the way she looks at me; the constant checking up to see what I'm up to.'

He laughed. 'I'm afraid that is inevitable. Look, supposing I say you can come any day you like, even when she's not here? I'd rather you avoided the weekends, that's when Charlotte and I like to get a bit of time on our own, but any other day. I'll give you a key to the studio. How would that do?'

She felt the relief sweep over her. 'That would be a great help. Thank you.'

They reached the gate of the cottage and climbed the steps. 'So, are you going to do some more sorting this afternoon?' he asked as he opened the front door.

'I'll stay for a few hours if that is all right. Then I must get back.' She glanced up at the sky. 'It feels as though there is going to be a storm.' Black clouds were beginning to appear in the west.

'Well, lock up and keep the key when you go. I have a spare. And feel free to come whenever you like. I have to go out this afternoon, so I'll leave you to it.' He gave her a warm smile. 'Keep me in touch with anything interesting you find, and let me know how you are getting on.' He paused. 'Hang on; I'd better give you a key to the cottage as well, in case you need the loo or anything. Then you can make yourself tea if you need to. Just help yourself. I'm sure I don't need to ask you to make sure you lock everything up carefully after you.' He went into the hall and opening a drawer in the small oak side table at the foot of the stairs took out a spare set of keys.

She looked up as she took the keys. 'You are very trusting, Mike. Thank you. I won't let you down.'

'I'm sure you won't.' He grinned. 'I pride myself on being a good judge of character.'

'Unlike Dolly.'

'Oh, Dolly is shrewd enough in her way.' He held her gaze for a moment as though reassuring himself about what he had just said, then he turned to the front door. 'I'll see you soon, OK?'

For a moment she stood still in the silence of the hall, listening to his footsteps as he ran down towards the gate. Only when she heard it clang shut behind him did she head towards the studio.

The clouds had turned to brazen overcast and it was already beginning to rain when she started to pack up for the afternoon.

She tidied the table, picked up her laptop and her notebook – a real paper one which would, she hoped, reassure Dolly – and went over to turn off the lights. It was at the very last minute that she paused and looked back. Had they left it that Dolly would come in to take stuff away which she thought would not be needed? She wasn't quite sure now. She studied the cardboard box near the table thoughtfully. In the top sat the attaché case with the letter drafts. Surely it was legitimate to take them and scan them into the computer at home. Then she could return them. Mike hadn't actually told her not to remove anything. He trusted her to make her own judgements.

It took only a couple of minutes to open the case, remove the contents and then put it back, tucked into the bottom of the box.

September 3rd 1940

'Evie!' Eddie found her in the cowshed. She had finished evening milking and was tidying up.

She turned towards him with a smile and pulled the scarf off her head with a sigh. There was only one cow in milk now that Daisy was in calf, which eased her load, but even so she was exhausted. From the yard the sound of the generator filled the evening air.

'I thought you had gone to London,' she said. She pushed the milking stool into the corner with her foot.

'I changed my mind. Work to do down here.' As always he was vague about his duties with the Ministry. 'My God, I love the way you look in those dungarees!' He moved towards her and swept her into his arms. 'Irresistible.'

'Get off!' She tried to push him away.

'Why? You know you enjoy it.' He caught her hand and pulled her towards the hay store. 'Come on. What about a little snuggle? I bet you've been working all day.'

'I have, Eddie, and I'm tired.'

'Just five minutes, eh? I've got a present for you in the car. Wait till you see it.'

He pushed the door closed behind them and set to work undoing the straps of the dungarees and pulling them down. 'Your mum is out. I checked.' He nuzzled her neck, then her face as he began to unbutton her blouse.

At first she didn't resist; she enjoyed sex, except the whole silly business with the johnnies, which she hated but insisted on. She might have been an art student, but she was not naïve and she had no intention of getting pregnant. But now, suddenly she did not want Eddie to touch her. She pushed him away. 'Not now, Eddie!'

'Oh, go on, you know you want to.' He had his hand around her wrist and he pulled her against him.

'No, I do not!' Suddenly she was angry. She pushed him hard in the chest and surprised, he let her go.

'Evie!'

'No, Eddie! I am not in the mood!'

'What about your present?'

'You mean I don't get the present if I don't make love to you?' Her voice sank dangerously.

Eddie shook his head. 'Of course I don't mean that. Don't be silly.' He sounded hurt. He turned away and took a deep breath. 'I thought you wanted it as much as I did.'

She was rebuttoning her dungarees. 'Not now.'

He shrugged. 'All right. Have it your own way.' Somehow he managed to summon a smile. 'So come on out to the car and I'll show you.'

The present was a wooden box of oil paints. She stared at it wide-eyed. 'Where on earth did you get this? It's wonderful.'

'I did a favour for a friend,' he tapped his nose in the irritating way he had, 'and he asked me what I would like as a way of saying thank you. I knew he was going up to the Smoke and I asked him if he could lay his hands on some oil paints. I have

88

to say, I didn't expect something quite so splendid.' He leaned across and kissed her on the top of her head.

'Evie! Eddie!' Her mother's voice rang out sharply from the kitchen door. They were standing by Eddie's car and hadn't noticed that Rachel's bicycle was leaning against the wall. They jumped apart.

'Mummy, look at this fantastic box of paints,' Evie called out. She carried it over towards the house.

'Wonderful,' Rachel said. The look she gave Eddie belied the enthusiasm in her voice. 'Are you staying to supper, Eddie?'

'Best not. But thanks for the invitation.' He glanced at Evie. 'Enjoy the paints. I'll call in in a day or two and see how you're getting on with them. Don't waste them all on the Scots cherub, will you!'

Evie froze at the words and opened her mouth to protest, but he had already turned towards his car.

'Sounds as though he's jealous,' Rachel said tartly.

'He didn't like me painting Tony's portrait to give to his parents.'

'I bet he didn't.' Rachel looked at Evie with narrowed eyes. 'Judging by the hay in your hair and the fact that your dungarees are not properly fastened, young lady, I suspect Eddie has a more than artistic interest in you. Do be careful, won't you? I don't want you bringing disgrace on this family. That would kill your father.'

She turned back into the kitchen so she didn't see the flood of angry colour in her daughter's cheeks.

Saturday 13th July, evening

The sky was even darker than before and the thunder clouds were massing overhead as Lucy drove back from Rosebank Cottage towards Chichester. The air smelled metallic and large raindrops began to fall as she turned onto the main road, hitting the windscreen as she drove.

She found a parking space almost outside the gallery and let herself into the house just as the rain began in earnest. Robin had locked up and switched on the display lights in the window, setting the alarm before he left. She picked up the note he had left on the desk. *Good day! Oodles of dosh. I'll drop it into the bank on my way home. Come and have Sunday brunch tomorrow. I'm cooking. Sleep well, darling.*

She gave a quiet chuckle as she ran upstairs to the kitchen and she turned on the lights as the first rumble of thunder echoed round the streets outside.

The kitchen was hot and airless with the window closed. She opened it a crack and the room was at once filled with the smell of wet earth and pavements and the sound of the torrential rain cascading off the roof and bouncing on the paving slabs in the little garden below.

She wasn't sure what made her look at the studio door. It was ajar. Robin must have gone in there during the day. She walked towards it and raised her hand to push it open. At the last minute she hesitated.

Behind her the sound of the rain faded; in front of her, the studio was oppressively silent as she pushed open the door. She peered in, holding her breath. Something was wrong. She felt herself grow cold.

Somehow she forced herself to stand her ground and raised her hand to grope for the light switches to the left of the door. The room was shadowed by the rain clouds outside and the streams of water running down the glass of the skylights. She flipped the switches and flooded the studio with light. Moving to stand in front of the picture on the easel she gasped. Someone had painted out the figure behind Evie. It had gone.

'No, it can't be.' She raised her hand and touched the surface of the canvas with her fingertip. The paint was dry. She found she was breathing in short tight gasps as she stared round the room. The table full of paints and chemicals did not appear to have been touched. The brushes and palette knives and swabs were all neatly stowed and clean and dry. There was nothing there to show anyone had been in there. Robin? Would he have done it? She looked at the painting again. He didn't have the technical ability never mind the inclination to do something like this.

She turned round helplessly.

The skylights were illuminated suddenly by a brilliant flash of lightning and a loud crash of thunder reverberated round the room, and it was then she saw him. The tall young man she had seen in her bedroom. The blue uniform. The mournful eyes. He was looking directly at her.

'Ralph?' she whispered.

Another crash of thunder echoed up from the streets outside, more distant this time. The lights went off for a moment. When they came on again he had gone.

September 4th 1940

Tony arrived at the farm as Evie was coming in from the stables. She stopped and gazed at the little car as the engine stuttered to a halt. For a moment Tony sat without moving, his head bowed with exhaustion, then he looked up and saw her framed in the stable door. His face lit up. He climbed out of the car.

'Would you like to come out to supper?' He grinned at her. 'Please. I shall starve to death unless you do.'

Evie laughed. 'Why, do you plan on eating me?'

He nodded. 'If only.' He gave her a cheeky smile. 'No, I thought we would go down to the pub. It's been a gruelling day. We've been up for most of it. Jerry is still active now,' he glanced up, 'but we've not been called so we've got a couple of hours.'

As they stood there in the farmyard they could hear the distant thump of explosions over to the west. 'Portsmouth is taking a beating again tonight,' Tony commented sadly.

Evie scanned his face, noting how tired he was, how the circles under his eyes shadowed his smile. 'I'd love to come out with you,' she said. 'Wait, I'll tell my mother I won't be in for supper.'

They sat opposite each other at a table in the smoky dining room at The Victoria in Bognor.

'Tell me about yourself,' Evie said. She sipped her shandy, still studying his face. She ached to pull out her pencil and sketch him.

He smiled. 'Not much to tell. I am – I was – a law student. Only child. Doting parents.' He gave a little apologetic shake of the head.

She nodded. She hadn't mentioned the portrait. It was to be a surprise. She felt unaccountably shy suddenly, as he looked up and held her gaze. He smiled at her.

'You're beautiful.'

She laughed. 'Untidy. Farmer"s hands. Dreadful clothes sense. I don't think so.'

'You have a lovely clothes sense.' He glanced down at her frock. It was a deep blue, with a marcasite brooch at the neck. She had changed from her overalls while he turned the car in the yard. 'One day I will drape you with furs and diamonds!'

She giggled. 'That sounds wonderful. But not me. I am always covered in charcoal dust and paint stains.' She held out her hands to prove the point. They were sturdy hands, rough from the hard work around the farm and there were traces of bright blue around her nails. He caught hold of them and held them for a moment. She thought he was going to bend forward to kiss them but he sat still, staring at her face, his eyes dreamy, just holding them. She found she could hardly breathe suddenly. Her heart was thumping unsteadily in her chest as she lost herself in the blue of his eyes. It was several minutes before he looked away and at last he gave her fingers a squeeze and let them go. Far away they heard the sound of the air raid siren.

7

Sunday 14th July

'Why didn't you call us?' Phil pushed a glass of Pimm's into her hand as they stood round the cooker in his and Robin's kitchen next morning. 'You know we would have come.' Behind them the table was littered with Sunday papers and the room smelled deliciously of the major fry-up Robin was conjuring into existence in the huge pan.

'I can't keep calling you every time I think I have seen something which isn't there,' Lucy said crossly. 'I just can't.' She saw the two men exchange glances and she glared at them furiously. 'I'm beginning to think I'm going mad. I admit I am getting a bit obsessed with the picture and Evie and everything, but he was so real.' She hadn't mentioned the fact that she thought someone had painted out the figure behind Evie. This morning the picture was untouched, the young man once more grinning cheerfully over Evie's shoulder. 'Do you think he's a ghost?' She chewed her lip for a moment. 'No. The whole thing is getting ludicrous. It was probably the storm. I hate thunder, it always gives me a splitting headache and I was tired anyway. I was probably hallucinating, no more no less. And it wasn't as if the figure was frightening. Not really.' She paused thoughtfully.

'But you think it was Ralph. Did you try and speak to him?' Robin put down his spoon and grabbed his glass.

'I think I said his name.'

'And he didn't reply?'

'No, but.' She frowned uncertainly. 'I felt he wanted to. He looked straight at me.' She glanced at Robin, then at Phil. 'Have either of you ever seen a ghost?'

Both men shook their heads . 'My mum believed in ghosts,' Phil said after a moment. 'She saw them, but she was Irish.' He grinned.

'Do you have to be Irish?' Lucy smiled miserably.

'No, of course not.' Phil became serious. 'No, I think they could exist. A lot of people say they have seen them.'

'I don't know much about ghosts,' Lucy went on. 'He wasn't transparent or anything. But what else could he be? He looked like a real man and yet he wasn't.' She sighed. 'I can't explain it.'

'But it wasn't a hallucination, was it? However much you try and convince yourself.' Robin put down his glass and turned back to the pan. 'So, what we need is an expert on these things. An exorcist maybe?'

'No.' Lucy said sharply. 'I don't want him exorcised.' She sat down at the table and pushed aside the papers. 'If he is a ghost, I want to know what he wants.'

'Then you need a medium,' Phil put in. He reached for the jug of Pimm's and topped up her glass. 'Someone who can talk to him and ask him questions. My mum used to go and see a medium.' He sat down opposite her. 'So, what is wrong with that suggestion?'

'I think it is me he wants to talk to. It's to do with the picture, isn't it? Even if he's not in it.'

'Did you tell the guy at Rosebank what you had seen?'

She shook her head. 'It wasn't the right moment.'

'Why not? Presumably Ralph was his uncle.'

'Great-uncle.' Lucy nodded.

'For all you know he haunts him as well.'

'No. I asked him that.'

The two men looked at each other again. 'Ah, so it is just you he haunts?' Phil said.

'Looks like it.' She gave a weak smile. 'Great, isn't it?'

'He's not trying to scare you, though. He definitely wants to tell you something.'

'That's if you assume "he",' Robin hooked his two forefingers in the air to convey the inverted commas, 'is anything at all.'

Phil and Lucy turned towards him. He bent over the cooker and flipped a rasher of bacon over in the pan. 'Lucy was the one who said she was hallucinating,' Robin protested. 'This does all seem a bit far-fetched, you must admit.'

'Lucy thinks he's real,' Phil said.

'No I don't,' Lucy wailed. 'Or at least, yes I do. What does real mean, anyway?'

'OK. Stop the conversation right there.' Robin put down the spoon and clapped his hands. 'Food is ready. This, Lucy, is our once a month treat, a reward for all that healthy porridge we have for breakfast the rest of the time, so I want no arguments. You eat what is put in front of you, right, my darling? Sit down guys and girls and let us eat. Our brains will work much better on full tummies!'

Lucy laughed. 'We are sitting down. Hadn't you noticed?'

'Good.' Robin hefted the pan onto the table. 'Help yourselves. Bacon, egg, sausage, mushrooms, tomatoes, toast is on its way. Coffee, more Pimm's.' He sat down opposite them. 'Three cheers for the cook?'

'Definitely.' Phil loaded a plate from the pan and put it down in front of Lucy. 'I bet you didn't have any supper last night.'

'No, as a matter of fact.' She had said he wasn't frightening, and he wasn't. But something was. She thought back for a moment to the cold terror which had gripped her as she closed the door on the studio. She had gone through into the living room and huddled on the sofa hugging a cushion until she had fallen into an uneasy sleep.

'There is one thing, though,' she picked up her knife and fork, 'he never moves. He doesn't smile. He is just – there. I feel he can see me, but thinking about it, I wonder if he can. I think I am just someone in front of him. I tried to convince myself last night that, even if he is not in it, he is a part of the portrait. Like the smell of oil and turpentine would be if it was new. Did he attach himself to it in some way when it was being painted? Is he no more than a shadow stuck on the paint before it dried?'

There was a long moment of silence. 'That sounds desperately sad,' Robin said at last. 'I think I would rather he was a proper ghost.'

'But you don't have to live with him,' she retorted tartly.

'True.' Robin climbed to his feet as the toaster on the worktop regurgitated four slices of toast, evenly browned. He juggled one onto each of their plates and tossed the spare piece into the pan.

'I still think you need to see someone about this,' Phil said. He reached for the marmalade and spread a large spoonful on his toast.

The other two stared aghast. 'You can't have marmalade with bacon,' Robin said after another second's pause.

'Why not? The Americans do. It's fantastic. Try it.' Phil dug the spoon into the jar and homed in on Robin's plate.

'No way!' Robin pulled it out of the way. 'That is grounds for divorce.'

Phil laughed. 'Fair enough.' He dropped the spoon back in the jar and glanced at Lucy. 'Honestly. I think you need to talk this through with someone who knows about this sort of thing. For all sorts of reasons.'

She reached for the coffee pot. 'Because of Larry, you mean? But it isn't Larry, is it? I wish so much it was.' She poured herself a cup of coffee and sipped it slowly, her face suddenly once more a picture of misery.

Robin leaned forward and touched the back of her hand lightly. 'He's at peace now, Luce. Let it be. This other guy isn't. Presumably. If he is a ghost.' He leaned over and turned on the radio. 'Right, change of subject. I want to see that food eaten after all my hard work. I don't want to see you languishing away into nothing.' He gave Phil a wink. 'And that goes for you, too.'

It was after four when Lucy finally returned to the gallery. It had been hard leaving the warmth and friendship of the little house in Lion Street. She felt secure there and cosseted, but she had to get back. She walked upstairs and went straight to the studio door, pushing it open. The room was full of sunlight, the painting as she had left it, Evie and the young man behind her untouched. There was no sign of Ralph. She stood for a moment, waiting, before turning her back and walking through into the living room leaving the door open behind her.

The sheaf of papers she had smuggled out of Rosebank Cottage lay on the table by the window. Drawing up a chair she sat down and began to read through Evie's notes again, slowly and carefully this time, scrutinising every word.

Almost every page seemed to be the core of a separate letter. Lucy suspected Evie found letter writing difficult. She was anxious to get the wording right, often feeling she had committed herself to something she had not intended and reworking the letter until it became bland and characterless. The only one that spread to more than a page was the first she had looked at, which she found, once she had sorted them, extended over nearly three pages of foolscap. It was infuriating not to know who Evie was writing to. She sat back and sighed. Perhaps there were more letters like this one back at the studio waiting to be unearthed.

It took an hour to scan all the pages into the computer downstairs, before placing them in a brown envelope ready to return them to Rosebank. She wondered how she was going to categorise everything she found. It had been stupid to worry about taking the papers away. How else was she going to sort them and write a book? Dolly Davis might not trust her but obviously Mike did.

Switching off the scanner she stood up, the envelope in her hand, deep in thought. Liaising with Mike wasn't quite that easy, though, was it? However friendly he had been yesterday at the studio and over lunch, which he had paid for, not allowing her to contribute anything, she had the feeling he was holding her at arm's length. He was charming and attractive, no doubt about that, but there was something reserved about him. Her instincts were usually fairly good about people and she kept coming back to the unease she had felt when they had said goodbye. He had said he would be back in time for supper and asked her to stay but she had the feeling he didn't mean it. He had expressed worry about her driving through the storm, but she was sure he didn't actually want her to stay too long. Was it that he was afraid of what his girlfriend would say when she heard he had been spending time with another woman? Hardly. Surely it was obvious to everyone she was not, never would be, in the market for a relationship. Not after losing Larry. So it had to be to do with the research into Evie. But if he didn't want her to do it all he had to do was say so. Again the words of his caveat came into her head:

If we had anything to hide . . . I wouldn't let you within a mile.

Did what she had just read hint at some kind of secret or was it merely a spat with a local tradesman?

But then again, Mike had invited her to use the cottage. He had given her a key. She could go there whenever she wanted. Not the actions of a man with something to hide.

She put the envelope down on the table.

Before she left Lion Street, Robin had taken her hands in his. 'Listen. We've talked, and we agree. Starting tomorrow I am going to come up to take care of the gallery every day to give you the chance to get this Evie stuff sorted. We think it's weighing on you, the research, and we think you need to get it all sorted as soon as possible. So, OK? No argument. It is settled.'

And so it was. Tomorrow she would go back and take the

chance to walk round the cottage alone, to get a real feel of the place and to look through Evie's more personal belongings before Dolly came and took them away.

September 5th 1940

Rachel was out when Tony Anderson came up to the farm the next day. 'I've been given a few hours off.' He leaped out of the car, having drawn up near the kitchen door.

Evie had just been going out to feed the hens. She stopped, a bowl of scraps in her hand. The dogs were up in the fields with her father.

'Sorry,' he went on, seeing the flash of irritation on her face. 'Is it not convenient?'

She shook her head. 'It's never convenient!' She sighed. She hesitated. 'I didn't mean that. I meant I am always busy. There is always something to do on the farm. Tony,' she smiled at him. 'I had such a good time last night. Thank you for the meal.' He had brought her back about ten p.m., dropping her off in the yard after a quick almost apologetic kiss. For a second they had both hesitated, both thinking of the last time, when he had kissed her. But the moment passed. She opened the door and climbed out.

'Thank you, Tony,' she had whispered. 'Will I see you again?'

She thought he nodded and for another second they looked at each other, silent in the darkness, then he had put his foot on the throttle and the little car had roared away down the drive.

She looked at him now, overwhelmed by the urge to reach up and touch his face. She pushed the feeling away sternly.

'Now you're here I've something to show you.'

She turned back into the house and put the bowl down on the table. 'Follow me.'

He was hard on her heels as she ran up the two flights to the attic studio and opened the door.

'My goodness, this is fabulous,' he exclaimed as they walked in. The room was flooded with light from the skylight windows, and warm from the summer sun outside. It smelled of the wood of the old twisted roof frame, and of paint and turpentine. He stared round. 'Oh wow! Look at your paintings, and there –' He stopped in his tracks. 'That's me!'

'It certainly is.' She laughed. 'It's for your mum and dad. I thought they would like it. It is a present.'

'Oh, Evie!' He stood staring in front of the easel. 'Oh, Evie!'

'You just said that.' Suddenly she was worried. 'You do like it?'

'Oh, yes.' He turned to her and put out his arms. 'Oh yes, yes, yes!'

She stepped towards him and he enveloped her in a huge bear hug.

There was a split second when she could have moved back. Could have laughed. Could have turned to run down the stairs but she didn't. She shut her eyes as his arms closed round her and she knew that she was lost. As though magnetised she raised her face to his.

Their kiss lasted for what seemed like an eternity. When at last they drew apart neither of them spoke. He took her hand and led her back to stand in front of the picture.

'You've painted the man you are going to marry,' he whispered.

Her eyes widened. He was joking. But for once he looked serious. For a moment she felt a wave of panic, then almost reluctantly she nodded.

'I think I knew it from the first moment I set eyes on you.'

'When you swore at me?'

'When I swore at you.' She smiled. She turned to look at him again, her whole body flooded with sudden anxiety. 'You are joking?'

'No, I don't think I am,' he said slowly. But the sparkle was back in his eyes.

'Have you felt like this before?' she asked.

He shook his head. 'Never.' He put his arms round her again and buried his face in her hair. 'You smell nice. Sort of like paint and hay and straw, oh, and cows.'

'Thank you!' She pushed him away and smacked his arm.

'No.' He caught her arms and pulled her back. 'It is the nicest thing I have ever smelled. Shall I ask your dad for his permission to marry his daughter?'

She giggled. 'You can't.'

'Why? I'm sure he would expect it.'

'After one kiss?'

'Two.'

'Tony. We don't know each other.'

'That's perfect. We will explore everything there is to explore. We will go together into the mysteries. You shall be my America, my New-found-land. Do you read John Donne? You need to know all about me. And I need to know all about you.' He paused and to her horror she saw sudden tears in his eyes. 'There is so little time, Evie. Who knows what will happen? I'm so scared.'

They clung together for a long time. Outside the sun went behind a cloud and the studio grew dim. It was very quiet. The scent of the warmed oak beams was heavy in the air.

At last he drew away. 'I want you to come to a dance with me tonight. In Chichester. At the squash club. Please.'

'All right.' She laughed. 'I'd love to.'

She washed her hair and changed into a dress while he waited in the kitchen, drinking tea. When she appeared he sat gazing at her, speechless. Her hair was still damp, still irrepressibly wild even where she had tried to tame the curls into fashionable sausage-shaped loops to bounce on her shoulders. Her dress was brightly coloured in blue and white, the padded shoulders and swirling skirt emphasising her narrow waist. She giggled when she saw his face. 'Will I do?'

'You'll do.'

She followed him out to the car. 'This will blow my hair everywhere,' she said as he helped her into the narrow front seat.

He laughed. 'You will look gorgeous whatever it does. At least it will be dry.' He raised an eyebrow as he touched it gently and brought his hand away dripping.

The room was decorated with flowers and flags, the band sitting on a dais at the back. It was crowded already when they arrived. 'Can you dance?' He caught her hand and pulled her onto the floor to find a small space to themselves.

She laughed and nodded. 'Can you?'

'Oh, yes.'

Tony was a brilliant dancer. The band was fantastic and Evie was in seventh heaven. They jived, they danced to the latest big band tunes, they paused to drink luke-warm fruit juice and they danced again, throwing themselves into the swing, the boogie, and then at last, they waltzed. As he put his arms around her he looked down into her eyes.

'Still going to marry me?'

She laughed. 'I think I just might.'

'Good.' He bent and kissed her on the lips. Evie closed her eyes. She rested her head against his shoulder and lost herself in the dream of his embrace. She felt safe there, and warm and happy. She wanted the dance to last forever but all too soon the exhausted band was striking up the National Anthem. Tony and the other servicemen stood to attention and his arms fell away. She leaned against him gently.

Outside in the street it was very dark. He caught her hand. 'Come on. Let's find the car. I'll run you home, then I have to go back.'

She nodded. 'I know.'

'The next time I get an hour or two off I will come to see you, but you can come to us. Draw me in my Spitfire. Show posterity what good-looking pilots there are in my squadron. Give me a reason to come back safe.'

'I'll do that. I'll come tomorrow.' She managed a smile. For a moment neither of them was capable of saying anything more. He opened the little door for her to slide into the car and they drove back through the dark lanes, the blacked out headlights barely showing up the narrow road and overhanging hedges. At the farm he pulled up outside the back door. They could hear the dogs barking from the kitchen. 'Mummy is still up,' she whispered. He nodded. She turned to him. 'Thank you for a perfect evening. Don't get out. I don't want to say goodbye.' She leaned across and kissed him lightly on the forehead then she slipped out of the car and ran towards the door without looking back.

Monday 15th July

Rosebank Cottage was bleak in the rain. Inserting the key into the lock and letting herself into the hall, Lucy stood for a moment looking round.

'Hello?' she called nervously. 'Is there anyone there?'

She had half expected Dolly to be there but the house was empty. The lights were off, the doors and windows shut, the only sign of life a fly buzzing angrily against a window pane.

She walked into the kitchen. The silence was broken by the sound of a tap dripping slowly into the sink. Lucy stepped forward and turned it off with a shiver. It felt as though someone had just that minute walked out of the room. The atmosphere was tense, the room alive. She touched the kettle gently, anticipating it to be warm. It was stone cold. It wasn't Dolly she was expecting to find here, she realised suddenly. It was the former owner of the cottage.

'Evie?' She spoke out loud, questioning, waiting for an answer. There was none. And yet she had the feeling that Evie was there, somewhere, waiting to be summoned.

She went back through into the hall and stood at the bottom of the stairs looking up. The steps were narrow and uneven, polished oak, turning sharply halfway up so that she couldn't see the top. She took a deep breath and set her foot on the bottom step, wincing as it let out an agonised creak.

There were two small bedrooms opening off the landing at the top and a bathroom. She hesitated again, feeling intrusive, even a little prurient as she peered first into one room and then into the next. But then Mike had told her she could use the bathroom and there was nothing to see in the two bedrooms which spoke of the present-day occupants. The rooms were neat and tidy, impersonal. She wondered if that was because Evie's belongings were now stacked up in the studio and she felt a wave of sadness for having been the cause of her exile from her own home. She stood in the slightly larger of the two bedrooms and looked round. It was several seconds before, cautiously, she went over to the chest of drawers and pulled the top drawer open a crack. It was empty, as was the drawer below it. They smelled faintly musty. Obviously they had been recently emptied.

Lucy turned and looked at the pictures on the walls and felt an immediate pang of disappointment. There was nothing here by Evie herself. She peered at each in turn. There was one by the door, two on the opposite wall and a cluster of small prints near the window. She peered at them closely, noticing the fade marks on the wallpaper beneath them. They didn't match. There had been other pictures here but they had been moved and not all that long ago. Was this the mysterious Christopher's handiwork? If so he had obviously been very thorough. The pictures which had gone had been very small. She groaned quietly. She was going to have to ask Mike about his cousin and see if he would give her his address. There were obviously going to be pictures in his custody which had never been in the public domain at all and which would be crucial to include in a complete survey of Evie's work.

There was a creak on the staircase and she spun round.

'Hello?' she called nervously. She was overwhelmed with guilt again, horrified to have been caught poking round the house even though she had every right to be there. She tiptoed to the doorway and peered out. There was no one there. She went to the top of the stairs and looked down. From here she couldn't see the bottom because of the bend in the flight. The house was silent again.

'Is there anyone there,' she called. The sound of her voice was overloud and intrusive in the silence. There was no reply. Cautiously she set foot on the top step. Slowly she began to descend, wincing at the creaks and groans from the staircase beneath her. The cottage was empty.

She worked for two hours in the studio, then paused to make herself a cup of coffee in the kitchen. She had amassed a pile of papers and notebooks and was beginning to get a feel of what had gone on. Christopher – or whoever had done the preliminary sweep of Evie's belongings in the past – had, at least at first glance, taken everything that was obviously of potential value, that much was clear. As far as she could see, there were no sketchbooks or paintings, no drawings or note-books with what she would describe as painterly annotations, no small sketches, scraps or doodles. But there were other things which were of value, at least to her. Notes, more letter frag-ments and letters from other people including some from dealers, referring to paintings she had never heard of, sometimes with quite detailed descriptions. She began to put the papers into a series of cardboard files and to these she added those she had brought back from the gallery. She would take a few back each time to scan them so that she had the complete sequence on her computer at home. After a while she stopped and straight-ened her back, staring round. She had barely scratched the surface of the work to be done but at the same time she had achieved enough to feel she had made a proper start. Tomorrow she would attack the pile of boxes beside the far wall.

As she was tidying up, switching off the lights, she heard the sound of footsteps on the path outside. She paused, holding her breath, looking towards the door. The studio was silent. From somewhere in the distance she heard a blackbird's harsh alarm note echoing through the garden. On tiptoe she moved towards the door and took hold of the handle. She waited for a few seconds, listening, then she pulled open the door. There was no one there. Behind her, a jar of brushes, caught by the sudden draught, rocked for a moment and fell to the floor with a crash.

September 6th 1940

Ralph was standing in the kitchen looking from his father to his mother and back. 'We need to tell her. Eddie is cheating her out of a lot of money.'

He pulled up a chair and sitting down at the scrubbed deal table leaned forward earnestly on his elbows.

Dudley sat down opposite him. The dogs, Jez and Sal, threw themselves down at his feet. 'And how exactly do you know that, son?'

Ralph felt a quick surge of his old antagonism towards his father. Always the need to doubt him, to disbelieve. 'I was in Chi. I walked down Westgate and I saw a couple of her pictures in the window of a little gallery there. The price on them was astronomic. Far more than he is giving her.'

Rachel was leaning with her back to the sink. 'How do we know what he is giving her?'

'She told me. She was so pleased. He gave her two quid for her picture of the barn with the roses growing over it. It is there, in the window priced at five guineas.'

Dudley snorted. 'I always thought he was sharp enough to cut himself, that one.' He sighed.

'He has to make a turn on them, and so does the shop,' Rachel put in.

'That much?' Ralph looked at his mother in indignation. 'I would have gone in and talked to them about it but the place was closed. I will go though, another time, and find out just what is going on with Eddie. I don't want my baby sister being made a fool of. Where is she, anyway?'

'She biked down to the airfield. Eddie was complaining that

she wasn't producing enough for her portfolio for the War Artists Committee. You know how much she wants to be recognised by them.' Rachel paused thoughtfully. 'There weren't any pictures of the airfield in the shop, were there?'

Ralph shook his head. 'Just farm scenes. Chocolate box stuff.'

'Well, that's something I suppose.'

'I don't think she would be allowed to sell pictures of the airfield,' Ralph said thoughtfully. 'She's not even supposed to be there. Eddie seems convinced it's OK, and that he can convince the WAAC that she would be a credible witness, but they are not keen at all on women doing this sort of thing. They are supposed to be painting other women, not dogfights in the sky.'

Rachel sighed. 'She has set her sights on this. I don't think we can stop her. And she won't argue with Eddie. She doesn't want to put her chances of being accepted at risk. He does seem to have influence in a lot of places. I wish he didn't, but I don't think we should interfere. She'll sort it out.'

Ralph pushed back his chair and stood up. 'I'll speak to her when I have had the chance to go back and talk to them. Don't worry,' he added as his mother opened her mouth to argue. 'I will be tactful. Besides, I don't think Eddie is quite as high in favour as he once was. Our Evie has her eye on a new beau.' He smiled.

Dudley let out a guffaw of laughter. 'That blond Scots boy? I saw her ogling him the other day.'

'I'm not surprised,' Rachel said with a smile. 'He's a real charmer.' She went over and lifted the kettle off the hob. Carrying it back to the tap she half filled it and returned it to the stove. 'I wouldn't be sorry to see her distance herself a bit from Eddie but at the same time she needs to be careful. He could destroy her chances of a career in art with a snap of his fingers. He's only got to say something detrimental to the War Artists Advisory Committee, or in one of those reviews of his, or even to the local galleries, and it would all be over for her.

I know she is talented, and one day I am sure she would make her way in the art world, but at the moment she is young and inexperienced and she doesn't know people, at least not the way he does. As long as he thinks she respects him and is fond of him he will be a good friend to her.'

'Do you know what you are saying, Rachel!' Dudley burst out. 'Listen to yourself! Give her credit for a little pride. You seem to be telling her to sell herself to the man.'

Rachel tightened her lips. 'I am saying nothing of the sort. I am just worrying that she might spoil her chances of real success.' She turned to her son, a touch of heightened colour in her cheeks. 'How long have you got, Ralph? Do you want some tea?'

'Go on then.' He smiled at her affectionately. 'I have to be back soon enough. A cuppa with my mum and dad gets priority over Jerry and his attacks any day.' He pretended not to see when Rachel turned away to hide her face. 'They are giving Portsmouth a walloping at the moment but I am sure the boys can manage without me for a bit.' He saw his father's raised eyebrow. 'OK, I've been given a few hours off. We are getting leave in short bursts at the moment. Don't worry. I'm not playing hooky.' He paused. He would have to leave time for another visit though, a visit to a pretty young WAAF called Sylvie who he had met at a dance in Bognor. But time enough for Sylvie once he had drunk his cup of tea. He knew enough about his mother to realise if he mentioned a girlfriend he wouldn't get out of the door without the third degree. He sighed. 'You do realise I might get posted to another station one of these days, don't you?' he said to her gently. 'It was incredibly lucky my squadron getting posted to Tangmere. It could just as easily have been to any other station in England.'

Rachel nodded. 'We'll make the most of it while you're here,' she whispered. She cleared her throat and, turning away, walked stiffly across the kitchen. 'I've some fruit cake here in the pantry. I think you deserve a bit as it's tea-time.' There was a moment's

silence as she clattered about out of sight. When she reappeared
with a plate in her hand, her eyes were suspiciously bright.

Evie had spent the morning sketching the Nissen huts and the
ground crew. The squadron had taken off before she arrived and,
touching down swiftly to refuel and rearm, had taken off again
without her having the chance to see Tony. She had concentrated
on her job, sketching furiously, making notes, planning a series
of paintings which she could work on in her studio at home.
The flight commander of B flight had invited her into the Officers'
Mess for a snack lunch and the chance to admire the new china
someone had given them to add to the furniture which had been
donated to make life more comfortable. She had accepted in the
hope that Tony would appear at some point, but he had, she
was told at last, landed at Tangmere with a leak in a fuel line
after catching some shrapnel in the fuselage of his plane.

She didn't see him until late that afternoon when he arrived
at the farm with a bandage on his arm.

'It's nothing,' he said cheerily when Evie flew out to meet
him in the yard. 'A splinter, that's all.'

She flung her arms round his neck and he let out a yell.
'Ow! Careful!'

'Sorry, sorry!' She backed away horrified. 'Did I hurt you?
Oh, Tony, I'm sorry.'

His face was white. 'No, I'm fine.' He managed a grin. 'Patched
up by a local body snatcher. I'm healing already. But I'm not
allowed to fly for a couple of days in case I prang the old bus.
So, I am all yours.'

Evie gazed at him. 'My parents are up in the top field stooking
the last of the barley. They won't be home till dark. I should
be going up there too.' She smiled at him then she took his
hand. 'Let's go inside and I'll find you some beer. Then we
could go upstairs if you like.'

He caught her hand. 'Can we go for a walk first? Just stroll
about. Do you mind?'

She gazed at him, taken aback. 'You don't want a beer?'

He smiled, his eyes lighting up with a mischievous twinkle. 'Of course I do. And I want to be alone with you. You know I do. I just want to walk and talk first. It's all been a bit too exciting, the last few days.' He drew breath as though to say something else and changed his mind. 'If we were to –' he waved his good arm in the air as though unable to find the words to describe what was in his mind, 'you know, make love,' he paused again, then took a deep breath. 'I respect your parents, Evie. And you. I don't want us to, you know, do anything which would upset things. It's too important we get this right.'

She grinned. 'You old romantic! Nothing we do is going to upset things, Tony. I know I am young, but I was an art student,' she said gently. 'I was living in London before the war.'

For a moment he looked taken aback, then his face creased into its usual irrepressible grin. 'That was then,' he said. He leaned across and kissed her cheek. 'Come on.' He took her hand and pulled her towards the door.

They walked across the yard, down past the duck pond and then up the track towards the hillside where their flock of Southdown sheep were quietly grazing in the sunshine. Beyond, the South Downs stretched out from the farm east and west, whilst to the south the flat lands of Sussex spread out towards the English Channel. The farm lay in a fold of gentle hills and wooded slopes, the soft grasses spangled with wild flowers, the stubble of the fields lying gold in the afternoon sun. It was an idyllic setting, the setting Evie painted with such love in her pictures of England in happier times, England before the war. The England she no longer wanted to show.

'Right.' Tony stopped, faced her and put out his hand. 'Let's start from the beginning again. If we are going to marry, we have to be introduced properly, as if our parents were here. Pleased to meet you, Miss Lucas. Can I tell you something about myself?'

She giggled. Holding out her hand, she shook his. 'Pleased to meet you too. Tell me everything.'

'I am twenty-one years old, three-quarters of the way through my law degree at Edinburgh University. If I get out of this war alive,' he took a deep breath and went on, 'I want to go back and finish it. It was my dream, to be a lawyer. It still is.' He was silent for a moment. Evie said nothing. She was studying his face.

'I am the only child of Alistair and Betty Anderson who live near Wigtown in the south-west of Scotland. They are farmers a bit like your parents except they own mountainous land instead of downs. We have a lovely stone farmhouse which has been in our family for several generations,' he went on slowly, 'and they are heartbroken that I didn't want to be a farmer, but they have encouraged me to follow my heart.' He paused and took another deep breath. 'If I am going to be a lawyer I would have to go back to Scotland after the war, so you would have to come and live with me in Edinburgh.' He paused again. 'But you would love my parents, I know you would, and they would love you. We will go and see them often.'

'Tony, wait.' She put her finger against his lips to silence him. 'This is all getting a bit serious.'

'I am serious.' They reached a gate in the hedge and turned through it onto the grassy shoulder of the Down, skirting a hanger of hazel trees clinging to the steeper slopes and following a sheep track towards the summit, sewn with harebells and cat's-ears. He reached out for her hand so he could pull her behind him. 'Come on. I want to see the view from the top.'

They made love in a shallow hollow, sheltered from the wind, serenaded by the song of a skylark far overhead. Afterwards Evie lay on her back, her arm across her eyes, sleepy and content, inhaling the smell of the soft grass while Tony sat up staring into the distance. The sound of the binder, carried on the wind from the distance, where her parents were working in the barley field far below them, was clattery but monotonous, lulling them both in the gentle warmth. They kissed long and gently then they made love again, and it was only the sound of the distant throb of aircraft engines high in the south which made them draw apart and sit up. Evie reached for her blouse and pulled it on with a shiver. 'The first raid this afternoon.'

Tony dressed hurriedly and shaking his head sat down again beside her. 'I wish I was down at the airfield. I hate not being part of it all.'

'They'll manage without you, just this once.' She put her arm round his shoulders, avoiding his injured arm. 'I think I've fallen in love with you, Tony Anderson.'

He laughed. 'I should hope so after what we've been doing.'

He picked a small blue flower out of the grass and threaded it into her hair. 'I shall buy you a ring.'

'A flower will do.' She reached across and kissed his lips. 'Do you know what it is? It's called milkwort. It is an emblem of eternal love.'

'Not really?'

She smiled. 'No, not really. But it is for me. I shall press it and treasure it forever.' She fell silent as the planes approached, the specks in the sky growing larger in tight formation.

'Stukas and Messerschmitts. Where are our boys? What are they waiting for?' He rose to his knees.

Evie pulled him down. 'Careful. They might see us!'

He gave a humourless laugh. 'I think they have their eye on rather larger targets than a couple of small people in a field. Like Southampton. Ah,' he gave a satisfied exclamation as a formation of planes appeared high in the east. 'At last.' He narrowed his eyes in the glare. 'Is that our boys or are they from Tangmere? Both probably. There. More of them. At last!'

The squadrons peeling off high over the wood had split, one section taking on the bombers heading west, and the others cutting in amongst the escorting fighters. In seconds the sky was a mass of diving and wheeling planes, the sound of engines screaming through the silence of the afternoon.

They sat side by side watching in awed fascination at the battle being fought over their heads. 'The Battle of Britain,'

112

Tony said at last, his voice full of awe. 'Did you hear Churchill's speech on the wireless when he said that? It is in full swing and I am missing it!'

'You are not missing it, Tony. You have a ringside seat,' Evie said at last. 'Think of it as research. You are watching their manoeuvring and their tactics so that you will know how to react when you are up there too.'

They both felt the visceral excitement and the breathless tension of the encounter going on over their heads. And then as suddenly as it had started it was over. The German planes one by one turned and headed south, two trailing black smoke, one spinning at last out of sight in the far distance, presumably plunging into the sea. Two of the Spitfires followed the stragglers, harrying to the last, the others, probably out of ammunition and rapidly running out of fuel, were returning to base. For a long minute the sky was empty, then a pair of swallows swooped low over the field.

Evie turned to Tony and snuggled into his arms. 'You will soon be back in action,' she said reassuringly. Her whole spirit was crying out in denial. She didn't want him to go, she wanted him to stay safe here with her on the ground, but she knew she couldn't keep him with her; he was not the sort of man to be tamed. She stood up at last and held out her hand to pull him to his feet. 'Let's go back to the farmhouse,' she whispered.

8

Tuesday 16th July

Dolly Davis was standing at her kitchen window at home, the drying up cloth in her hand, staring into space. In ten minutes she would need to leave her small terraced cottage in Midhurst to walk up to the bus stop at the end of the street, ready for the long tour of local villages which would at last drop her off near Rosebank Cottage.

She had been thinking hard all night and was still turning her dilemma over in her mind. Did she trust Lucy Standish? Obviously Mr Mike did. He had told her on the telephone that he had given Mrs Standish a key to the house and to the studio and had told her she could come any day she chose, every day if she wished. He had made it very plain that she, Dolly, was not to interfere or question anything the woman did and was to give her every bit of help she could. To that effect Dolly had written down some dates and facts for Lucy, sitting down the night before with an exercise book and carefully making a list in her best writing of all the dates she could remember, starting with the date Evie had bought Rosebank Cottage. She was to write down the names and addresses of anyone she thought could help with researching the book and any details of the family she knew. Mr Mike said he was going to do the same, but he knew she probably had the key to so much more knowledge about Evie than he did. She knew he was flattering her; she wasn't born yesterday. But on the other hand he obviously genuinely wanted her co-operation.

She had written down the names of Evie's parents and grandparents, the name of the street where she had lived in London before she came to Rosebank, she couldn't remember the number, the names of several of Evie's friends, the ones who used to come and visit her. She no longer knew their addresses, if she ever did, but it was something to put on the list. She omitted the address of Christopher Marston. It was up to Mr Mike if he wanted to tell her about that side of the family.

At last she had put aside the notebook and stood up. Painfully she made her way up the narrow staircase, cursing her rheumatism, and she walked into the small second bedroom at the top of the stairs. Since her husband, Ronald, had died she had gratefully expanded her life into this second room which had been his for so long. He had suffered privately, as he did everything, from the pain of his long illness and died quietly one night seven years ago. She had not found him, still and peaceful in his bed, till morning when he was already cold.

She had waited a year, that was only decent, then she had sorted all his belongings into bags for the charity shops or for the bin men and moved some of her own things into the room, taking time to lay it out as she liked it with a comfy chair, a table and her small electric sewing machine and cupboards and a light so she could sew in there in her own domain. In one of the cupboards was a large cardboard box. She hauled it out and sat down with it on her knee.

As soon as she had realised what Christopher Marston was up to, clearing all Evie's personal stuff out of Rosebank, she had saved what she could. It hadn't been much, the diaries, hidden in the chest of drawers in Evie's bedroom, two small sketchbooks and the old log book which had lain under the diaries. She had glanced at the log book and frowned in disappointment. She had thought it would be Ralph's but it belonged to some man she had never heard of. Nevertheless she tucked it into the box with the rest and that same night, quietly, after Christopher and his wife had left, their car stuffed with everything of value in the house, she carried it up the lane and lugged it home on the bus.

She chewed her lower lip thoughtfully. What to do? She didn't want to ask Mr Mike. He would be furious with her for taking it all in the first place but she was unrepentant about that. She did it for Evie. Instinctively she had known that Evie would hate to have anyone, never mind her difficult and rude grandson, poring over her diaries.

She glanced at her watch and pulled off her apron. Time to go. She would think about what to do during the day and make a judgement then.

Lucy was already at work when Dolly arrived at the cottage at exactly nine a.m. The old lady frowned a little, but glancing quickly round she was satisfied that Lucy hadn't touched anything or messed up the kitchen. She opened the door to the cupboard under the sink and pulled out her polish and dusters. At ten thirty she would go over to the studio and take her a cup of coffee. Until then it was up to Lucy. If she had the manners to come in and say good morning that would be a mark in her favour.

Lucy had pushed open the door of the studio with some trepidation when she arrived that morning after a sleepless night. She stood in the doorway and stared at the scattered brushes on the floor. When the jar fell she had not waited to pick them up. She had slammed the studio door and locked it. When she climbed into the car she was astonished to find that her hands were shaking.

Taking a deep breath she put down her bags and walked over to pick up the scattered contents of the jar. She put it back on the table and pushed it firmly to the centre, well away from the edge, then she glanced nervously round the room. Everything was as she had left it last night. Or was it? She looked at the pile of boxes against the wall. Had they been rearranged? She frowned. Perhaps Dolly had arrived early. Walking over to the wall she stooped and picked up the top box. She didn't remember seeing it before. Her heart thumping she put it down on the table and pulled open the flaps at the top. Within moments she was completely absorbed. Amongst the shabby cardboard files she found two or three that contained flimsy carbon copies of Evie's letters. They were smudged and faded and occasionally so faint as to be illegible. Obviously Evie went on using each sheet of carbon paper long after it was too worn to be of much use, but there was enough there to show that these were the letters she wrote to galleries and exhibition organisers about showing her work. Lucy felt a shot of adrenaline run through her as she saw the names of various paintings listed again and again, one or two of which she recognised, several which she did not. This must be an inventory of her basic exhibits, the ones she sent off round the country on tour. At the top of each letter was the name and address of the place to which they were going. She found a sequence of dates spanning some five years of Evie's main exhibitions. Perhaps elsewhere in the studio she would find the catalogues themselves. Dolly was forgotten. This was like striking gold.

An hour later Dolly arrived with a tea tray. Today there was one cup. 'I don't want to interrupt or get in your way,' the old lady said coolly.

Lucy looked up then she glanced at her watch. It was nearly ten o'clock. She should have gone over to the cottage to say good morning. Reluctantly she pushed the files to one side. 'You are not interrupting, I promise. You haven't brought a cup for yourself. Can I fetch one so we can have coffee together?'

Dolly looked at her suspiciously. 'I assumed you hadn't come in because you wanted to be left alone.'

Lucy shook her head. 'I'm sorry. It was me, not wanting to get in your way. I thought you must be so used to having the place to yourself that I would be under your feet, but I would love to talk to you, when you have some time. I so much want to hear your reminiscences about Evie. You and Mike are the only people I've met who remember her, and you both knew her so well.' She was cursing herself for putting Dolly's back up again. She slipped off her stool and stood up with a smile. 'Can I fetch that cup? There is enough in this cafetière for two and it smells so gorgeous.'

Dolly hesitated then she nodded. 'No, you stay here. I'll fetch it.'

When she came back she brought a plate of biscuits.

By the time she left that evening Lucy had filled several pages of her notebook with anecdotes and she was clutching Dolly's exercise book, but she did not know about the box of diaries. The old woman was still hedging her bets.

September 9th 1940

On September 7th Churchill believed that invasion was imminent. High Command at last used the codeword, 'Cromwell' and service personnel were issued with side arms and live ammunition. Roads in the south were blocked and guards on the south coast were reinforced. All temporary leave had been stopped. Ralph telephoned home once or twice to reassure his mother, but patrols were constant and the pilots were becoming increasingly exhausted. There was no word from Tony.

Since she was a child Evie had kept her diary under her mattress. She did not think her mother would snoop in her bedroom but she was not taking any chances, and especially not now with the new glorious secret which had overwhelmed her every waking second. She was in love, deeply and overwhelmingly in love. She could not get the thought of Tony out of her head. Everything she did on the farm, every moment she was awake she was thinking about him and at night she dreamed of him as well. And now, overwhelmed with worry, she hadn't seen him to speak to for three days even though she had biked down to Westhampnett early and spent the whole day loitering round the airfield under the pretence of making sketches. No, not pretence. She was sketching but she had been distracted every few minutes by the possibility that he would appear. He had been declared fit to fly by the local doctor and was once again on operational standby. The squadrons were in constant action, flying out on sortie after sortie. Their lunchbreak never happened and tea was being made for them out in the dispersal huts with the WVS ladies taking their van over to them as they waited for refuelling. She saw Tony in the distance twice and each time he grinned at her and waved, but he was with the other pilots and she knew better than to interrupt or draw attention to herself.

It was nearly six o'clock when Eddie drove down to the airfield, left his car by the gate and strolled in past the guard.

'Evie?' He stood beside her and looked over her shoulder at her sketch. It was rudimentary, concentrating on Tony, one face standing out amongst several others who were mere outlines. He made no comment. 'Your mother asked me to come and fetch you,' he said after a moment. She had not looked up to greet him 'You are late for milking and she said you hadn't done any of your chores today. She is worried.'

Evie scowled. 'I'll come back when I've finished this.'

'No, now, Evie. It's late.' Eddie saw the guard from the perimeter gate heading his way and groaned. 'Now they are going to tell me off for coming in here. The security is appalling on this airfield. I should make a complaint to higher authorities. Only that would stop you coming down here too.'

Evie looked up at the implied threat. 'You wouldn't.'

'I don't want to.' He sighed. There was no point in putting her back up even further by mentioning his feelings about her visits down here to sketch Tony. 'Come on, Evie.'

'I didn't realise the time. I'll collect my bike.'

'Leave it. It will be perfectly safe. I'll run you back to save time.'

'No!' Evie snapped. 'I'll come when I've finished.' She didn't want to speak to Eddie. She didn't want to see Eddie. She wished she had never made love to him. If it wasn't for his role in furthering her career, she would tell him to go away and never come back. Whatever she had felt for him in the past was nothing compared to what she felt for Tony. Her whole body yearned for the young airman in a way she had never experienced before. She was overwhelmed with longing. In contrast the thought of getting into the car with Eddie was suddenly repugnant to her.

Eddie leaned across her and took the sketchbook and pencil out of her hand. 'You will come now, Evie. I promised your mother.' He frowned at her as she rounded on him.

'No!'

He held up his hand before she could protest, his temper barely in check. 'Have you any idea just how worried she gets when you are down here? You are in danger every second you are here. The Germans aim for the airfields, you know. I am amazed the CO lets you come here at all. Your mother is frantic about your safety. She doesn't say anything because she knows you want to do your bit for the war effort, but you owe it to her to come home when you say you will. It is bad enough for her to have to worry about Ralph all day every day, up there.' He gestured towards the clouds where a dozen or so planes were circling ever higher, small black dots heading suddenly towards the horizon as a message from ground control sent them on the right vector to encounter the enemy.

She slumped back onto her seat on the old oil drum which

had become her favoured perch. 'I'm sorry. I didn't think.'

He smiled at her 'No, well, you have now. So let's get back and put her out of her misery at least as far as you are concerned, OK?'

Wednesday 17th July

Dolly had given Lucy the address of the Lucas farm and the following afternoon Lucy drove the half dozen or so miles to the village of Chilverly, taut with anticipation. Pausing in the village to squint at her road map she turned the car up a narrow lane on the far side of the village and drove the few hundred yards to the gate at the end. There she parked and climbed out. Box Wood Farm. Evie's parents' farm, the home Evie had known for so much of the early years of her life. And Ralph's home too. She shivered. She stood for a moment on the gravelled driveway studying the front of the building, aware of a sudden lump in her throat. It was a lovely traditional farmhouse, lying in the golden sunshine in a gentle basin in the Downs, the upper storeys white-painted and timber-framed, the ground floor a soft terracotta, built with ancient lichen-stained bricks. It had been separated from its land many years earlier, Mike had mentioned, and now boasted only an acre of beautiful gardens and an orchard, but, beyond the gardens, the downland fields were still populated with sheep as they must have been in Evie's day, the short-cropped grasses interspersed here and there with patches of woodland. The front of the house was curtained with wisteria and the door decorated with urns full of geraniums and variegated ivies. Overhead swallows were threading the air with high-pitched twitterings as they swooped overhead much as they had done in Evie's day.

The door opened and a tall, thin woman appeared on the steps. 'Lucy Standish?'

Lucy took a deep breath and smiled. She walked forward,

hand outstretched. 'Mrs Chappell? Thank you so much for agreeing to let me come.'

Elizabeth Chappell was older than she had first appeared, nearer seventy than fifty, Lucy guessed, but her fine bones and English rose complexion gave her a glow of youth which Lucy doubted she would lose even in her eighties or nineties. She followed her through into a large elegant kitchen and stared round.

Elizabeth smiled. 'A farmhouse kitchen, which it really was when we bought the house. The place was a tip. We didn't buy it from Evelyn Lucas of course. There had been at least two other owners in the intervening years, but I like to think she would recognise it again now.'

Lucy looked round at the butler's sink, the dark green, four-oven Aga, the handmade cabinets, and secretly doubted if Evie would have recognised it at all. She knew Evie's kitchen at Rosebank Cottage and she didn't think this elegance was Evie's thing. But then it would have been Evie's mother's kitchen in those days and she didn't know anything about Rachel. Not yet. There was no mention of her in the letters so far, no clues as to what Rachel was like at all. She had only discovered Evie's parents' names from an offhand remark of Mike's and then in Dolly's helpful little list.

It was rather like being shown round by a house agent. Elizabeth Chappell gave her the whole tour, room by room, finishing at last in the attic.

'I understand this was Evelyn's studio,' she said as they went in. It had been laid out as a children's playroom, complete with a model railway on the floor. 'The grandchildren,' Elizabeth said over her shoulder. 'They live in London but they love coming down here. It keeps them amused all day.'

Lucy smiled. 'I can imagine. It looks very inviting.'

Where was Evie? Where were the echoes, the memories, the hints of the room's artistic past? The beams were still there but the walls between the stud framing of the roof were a pale blue, the floor had been sanded and sealed to a golden tan and the windows and skylights had new wooden frames with locks on their elegant ironwork latches.

'I don't suppose Evie haunts this house?' Lucy asked tentatively. Or Ralph, she added silently. Why was it she felt compelled to ask that wherever she went? She softened the question with a rueful smile, implying that she was joking.

To her astonishment Elizabeth nodded, her face suddenly taut with anxiety. 'It is strange you should ask. We have often wondered. There are footsteps sometimes, you know, and Georgie, that's my eldest grandson, who was about seven at the time, said he could smell paint up here. Can you smell paint?' She held Lucy's gaze for a moment. 'No. Neither can I, but occasionally Georgie says it was very strong and oily. We took him to an art shop and he identified the smell as oil paint. None of us is artistic so he wouldn't have smelled it here, and the house itself was redecorated a while ago and anyway house paint smells nothing like oil paint.'

Lucy felt a jolt of unease deep in the pit of her stomach. 'No one is afraid, though?' she asked cautiously.

There was a moment's silence. 'Not of the smell, no.' Elizabeth put her hand up to the necklace she was wearing over her cotton sweater and twisted it nervously. She had moved away from her visitor and was standing by the train track staring down at it as if lost in thought. 'I'm often alone here,' Elizabeth went on at last. 'My husband travels a lot.' She paused, as if regretting that she had said too much.

Lucy hesitated. 'My husband died a few months ago,' she said at last. 'I know how it feels, being alone.'

'My dear, I'm sorry.' Elizabeth looked at her as if seeing her for the first time. 'So you understand. He's supposed to have retired but he runs a consultancy, advising people on buying overseas properties, and,' she hesitated for a moment, then continued softly, 'when I am here by myself, at night, sometimes I think I can hear people in the house. It is a big house for one person.' She gave an awkward smile. 'When it is full of family and children and my daughter's dogs it comes alive, then it belongs to us. But when I am by myself I am sure it still belongs to the Lucases. They were here for generations, you know.'

For a moment Lucy was stunned. 'But you said there were other families here in between,' she said at last.

'Yes. And of course it could have been them.' Elizabeth shook her head. 'But it isn't. Evie's brother was killed, you know, in the Battle of Britain. There's a memorial to him in the village church. I think his mother went mad with grief.'

Lucy held her breath, staring at her in horror, intensely aware of the silence around them.

'I hear her crying,' Elizabeth went on almost under her breath. 'I tell myself it's the wind in the chimneys, perhaps an owl screaming into the night, but it isn't. It's Rachel. I sometimes think I can't bear it.' She gave a small wistful smile. 'I'm sorry, my dear. You must think I'm ga-ga.'

'How do you know it's Rachel?' Lucy asked at last. Her voice was husky.

'I just know.' It was a whisper. She shuddered. 'Let's go downstairs. Do you mind? I'll make us some tea. Then you must see the outbuildings.' Suddenly her voice was stronger. 'They were all farm buildings in Evie's day and I think you'll see they have probably changed much less than the house has. In fact I doubt if they have changed in hundreds of years. The land itself is all owned by a huge company now. There is a farm manager who lives on an estate the other side of Chichester.'

Lucy followed Elizabeth down the two flights of stairs back into the kitchen. While they waited for the kettle to boil on the Aga Elizabeth disappeared into the old-style walk-in pantry to find some biscuits and Lucy stared round the room. With part of herself she was listening, afraid she was going to hear Rachel's cries.

The kitchen was immaculately tidy. There had only been one car outside, a smart new Mini. It was obvious that Elizabeth's

124

husband must be away on one of his trips. The woman was living alone in the house with nothing but the ghosts of the past for company.

She looked up as her hostess put the plate of biscuits in front of her. 'Do people in the village remember the Lucases?' she asked, trying to change the mood.

Elizabeth shook her head. 'I doubt it. I don't know. To be honest we don't mix with the village much any more.' She reached down the teapot from a shelf and set it on the hotplate to warm.

'But your family come down to see you?' As soon as she had said it Lucy regretted it. She had already guessed what the answer would be

'They used to. All the time. But they have other calls on their time now. The children have grown out of the countryside. They want to go abroad or spend the holidays with their friends. You know how it is.' Elizabeth helped herself to a biscuit and broke it in half, scattering crumbs on the pine table before putting it down without tasting it. She didn't seem to notice. 'There was a time when I could have offered you a homemade biscuit. Not any more. It's not worth making them just for me. I bake when there is something on in the village of course. I do my bit, but even that has been taken over now by young families. The mothers are very energetic, very bossy,' she laughed quietly. 'They like to do things their way.'

Lucy's heart went out to her.

Behind them the kettle began to whistle. Elizabeth stood up abruptly and went over to the Aga. She made the tea and came back to the table. 'There you are, my dear. I am so sorry; you must think I am pathetic. Drink that, and then we'll go outside. I love my garden. It's mine. Out there I have no sense of Rachel at all. Out there I feel as if I still have a use in the world. I'll show you.'

Rachel. Once more she was talking about Rachel. Only in the studio was there an echo of Evie left behind.

The garden, as Lucy had glimpsed when she first walked up the drive, was lovely. It was formal, carefully planned and obviously much loved. She looked round in delight. 'You make me feel so ashamed. Our, that is my, garden is so tiny.' When would she get used to talking in the first person singular. 'It was very precious to my husband and me, but since his death I have neglected it terribly, there seems to be so little time for it now.'

Elizabeth nodded. 'Being alone is very hard to bear.'

Lucy bit her lip. Without quite knowing why she recognised that she had been tactless. She wondered suddenly whether Elizabeth's husband was alone on his trips abroad and guessed immediately that he was not.

'Evie would have approved of this garden,' she said softly, trying to change the subject. 'She loved flowers. Her own garden at Rosebank Cottage is very pretty. Not formal like this. It is very much a classic cottage garden, but it shows the love and care she must have lavished on it for years.'

'You know her grandson, you say.' Elizabeth fished in her pocket and brought out a pair of secateurs. She must always have them with her, Lucy guessed, just in case something needed dead heading. 'He came here once. He wanted to know if we had any of her paintings.'

'Mike came to see you?' Lucy frowned. 'I'm sorry, I didn't realise you knew him.'

'Christopher Marston. A nice man. We keep in touch now and then.' Elizabeth leaned forward and snipped off the broken stem of a rose.

'Christopher,' Lucy echoed thoughtfully. 'Mike is his cousin. He owns Evie's cottage. I gather the arrangement was that Mike got the house and Christopher, the paintings.'

Elizabeth nodded. 'I think he mentioned something to that effect. He felt short-changed, I gather. He said a lot of the paintings were missing and he suspected they were stashed – I believe that was the word he used – here somewhere.' She gave a bleak smile. 'I am afraid I had to disappoint him. There was nothing

126

here when we bought the house. It was totally empty and nearly derelict.'

'Evie's paintings are very valuable,' Lucy said, 'perhaps the more so because so few seem to have survived.'

'And you too were hoping they might be hidden here?'

'No!' Lucy looked at her, aghast. 'Oh no! I'm not here because of that. I thought I explained. I am writing Evie's biography.'

'You did tell me that, yes. I'm sorry, my dear. Cynicism is one of my more disgusting failings.' Elizabeth sighed and reached out to clip off a shrivelled rosebud before determinedly pocketing her secateurs again. 'Come with me. We'll go and look in the barns. Then you will be able to describe them in your book.'

Lucy followed her across the lawn to a range of neat outbuildings around the back of the house. They were meticulously cared for, with clean windows, black boarded walls and peg-tiled roofs. Beside each door there was a tub of scarlet geraniums. Elizabeth pulled open the door of the first.

'I have been told this was probably a dairy. The actual barns were pulled down when the land was sold. They were too small for modern equipment apparently, but these, because they were all grouped round the back yard, were sold with the house, for which I am rather pleased. They are attractive buildings and as you can see very old.'

She gestured to Lucy to go in.

As she stepped inside the gravel of the yard outside gave way to rounded cobbles. There were broad low shelves around the walls and large nails protruding from the beams which had obviously been used in the past for hanging things on. The building was completely empty. Lucy took another hesitant step forward and stopped dead as she was enveloped in a wave of cold unhappiness. It seemed to leach from the walls on every side and cling to her skin like some kind of damp mildew. She shuddered. As she turned hastily towards the door she remembered her camera.

'May I take a photo?' she called out. There was no reply.

She took a couple of photos and hurriedly made her way back to the door. In the fresh sweet-scented air of the courtyard she took some deep breaths. To her surprise she found that her hands, as she returned the camera to her pocket, were shaking.

'You felt it, didn't you?' Elizabeth had been leaning against the wall a few feet away staring down at the tub of plants at her feet. She had glanced up as Lucy appeared.

Lucy gulped in another breath, trying to steady herself. 'What happened in there?'

Elizabeth shrugged her shoulders. 'Most people say there is nothing there. You seem to be sensitive.'

'Is it Rachel?'

'I assume so. I imagine she had to go on running the farm. It was the war. Every drop of milk would have had to be accounted for. Butter. Cheese. I expect they made it all here.'

'Would you mind if I made some notes about all this?' Lucy asked suddenly. 'You have a far better grip about the family than I have. I started from a baseline of nothing. Mike is telling me some stuff, but he is, to be honest, not all that interested in the family history. He comes up with afterthoughts every now and then. I am being allowed to look through what are left of her papers but there is very little there that is personal. It is mainly bank statements and stuff like that.'

'So, was she very rich?'

'Ah, from the statements, you mean. No. As far as I can see she was actually quite poor. Artists often were, weren't they, in their own time?'

They had begun to walk slowly down the line of buildings. There were several looseboxes, all equally neat and empty, another couple of larger outbuildings, one of which contained a ride-on mower and a wheelbarrow, with rakes and spades and forks hanging on the wall, obviously the heart of the gardening empire, and there was an open-fronted cart shed with wonderfully twisted beams. In the distance Lucy could see a small pond, carefully fenced. On it a pair of moorhens swam anxiously back and forth uttering little calls of alarm.

'Well, that's it.' Elizabeth drew to a halt.

'It's very kind of you to have shown me everything.'

'Please, don't go. Not yet.' For a moment Elizabeth seemed quite panic-stricken. 'You wanted to make some notes and take some pictures. You ought to snap the studio. Please, why don't you stay and have some supper? You can wander round on your own as much as you like.'

For a moment Lucy was hesitant; the atmosphere of Box Wood Farm was getting to her, as was Elizabeth's neediness, but it was, she realised, too good an offer to turn down.

After a moment she nodded. 'I would love to. Thank you.'

She took dozens of pictures and made notes in almost every room of the house, lingering in the studio wondering if she could smell the taint of oil and turpentine in the air as she had at Rosebank. There was nothing. It was almost sterile up there save for an almost imperceptible smell of dried wood from the beams.

They ate in the kitchen. Elizabeth produced a chicken casserole from the freezer which they ate with fresh bread and salad from the garden accompanied by a glass of sauvignon blanc. Lucy had her notebook on the table beside her plate and from time to time made notes as Elizabeth talked.

'I never knew them, of course, but when we first moved here people in the village used to talk about the Lucases a lot. I was so intrigued. I had never had anything to do with someone famous before, and occasionally people would come and knock on the door and ask about her.'

'When did she move?'

Elizabeth thought for a moment. 'After her father died her mother stayed here alone. They had sold off the sheep and horses – I think they still used horses on the farm after the war. And, of course, they had some cows. Then at some point Rachel sold the land. That was sad. It probably wasn't worth all that much then. After she died Evie sold what was left. She didn't come back here at all as far as I know. Someone in the village told me she sent someone to pack everything up. They were very disappointed. The word was that she was too grand for the place by then. She was living in London, I think. There was a lot of resentment locally.'

Lucy was scribbling hard. 'How strange. I had somehow formed the impression that she was very low key. Certainly not a snob.'

Elizabeth sighed. 'Who knows what makes people do things? Perhaps it was just too painful for her to come back here. I am afraid I was told all this a long time ago, when we first moved here. I don't think anyone is left who actually knew them.'

Lucy watched as Elizabeth made coffee and then followed her through into the room she described as the snug. Double doors opened out onto the lawn and they sat side by side staring out into the garden.

'This is a magical place,' Lucy said after a while.

'It is, isn't it.'

Somewhere outside a blackbird was singing and Lucy found herself listening so intently she hardly registered the distant cry from somewhere in the house. She took another sip from her cup and then saw Elizabeth lean forward suddenly, her face white, her hands shaking.

'What is it?'

'Listen.' Elizabeth held up her hand. 'It's Rachel.' She swallowed hard, turning to look towards the door. 'She's here.'

Lucy felt her stomach turn over. Setting down her coffee cup with a deliberate effort to keep it steady she sat forward on the sofa listening hard.

Elizabeth took a deep breath, standing up. 'She'll cry again. She always does.'

Lucy found her mouth had gone dry.

'Shall we go outside?' Lucy glanced at the garden doors which were standing open only feet away from her. She was really scared now.

Elizabeth clenched her fists. 'This is my house now. I am not going to let her chase me away!' she said stubbornly. 'You go if you want to.'

Lucy was tempted. Beneath the bravado, Elizabeth's fear was visceral and infectious. She found she was using every ounce of willpower she possessed to stand her ground.

And then the sound came again. Distant, eerie, but recognisably a woman's voice, and it was a woman in agony. The sound echoed down the stairwell and round the hallway outside the door of the snug. There was another moment's silence and then it came again, more distant this time. And this time it sounded not unlike the soughing of the wind in the eaves. Then there was silence.

Lucy couldn't bear it. Her own eyes were full of tears as she glanced helplessly at Elizabeth, who seemed rooted to the spot. Without knowing where she found the courage to do it she stepped forward and eased the door open, looking out into the hall. There was no one there.

'Hello?' she called, her voice shaking. 'Where are you?'

Elizabeth stared at her, her clenched fist pressed tightly against her mouth.

Lucy stepped out of the doorway and stood at the bottom of the stairs, looking up. 'Rachel?' Her voice sounded odd even to her own ears as it echoed up towards the first floor. 'Rachel!' she repeated. 'Can we help you?'

There was no response. The two women waited for several minutes, then at last Elizabeth shook her head. 'She's gone.'

Lucy went back into the snug and sat down abruptly. Without thinking what she was doing she picked up her cup of coffee and drank it all in one go. Her hands were shaking so much the cup was rattling against her teeth.

Elizabeth came and sat down beside her. 'You were very brave to do that.'

Lucy groped in her pocket for a tissue. 'How can you live here?'

The other woman was silent for a moment. 'I've got used to it. It happens very seldom. I think –' She paused, then went on, 'I think I guessed it would happen tonight.'

'Because of me?'

She nodded.

'Oh God, I am sorry. I had no idea –'

'Of course you didn't.'

For a moment both women were quiet, then Lucy got to her feet and went back into the hall. Something was wrong. It had all happened too much to order. Could the whole thing be some awful vicious hoax? If it was, it was a hoax played on Elizabeth, not her. The woman's fear had been too real, too gut-wrenching to be a pretence. She glanced up the stairs and, not giving herself time to think, ran up the first flight.

'Rachel!' she called again. 'Are you there?'

Her voice sounded flat; the place was empty. She looked around for several minutes, aware that her own fear was contained only just below the surface, that she was waiting to hear the cry again. But it didn't come. The rooms were silent. All she could hear was the distant cooing of a turtle dove from the trees around the lawn.

Thoughtfully she made her way downstairs again. She gave her hostess an apologetic smile. 'I'm sorry. I suddenly wondered if –' She paused. 'Oh God, Elizabeth I am sorry, but I wondered if it was a hoax.'

'A hoax?' Elizabeth stared at her and after a few seconds she began to laugh. It was a shaky, half-hearted laugh but nevertheless it was real. 'You mean you thought it was Dennis, trying to drive me insane? Shades of *Fanny by Gaslight*. He and his girlfriend trying to get rid of me so they can pursue their sordid little affair in peace? I wish it was, in a way. No, Dennis wouldn't do that. He knows I know about the girl and he knows I would give him a divorce if that is what he would like. He is free to indulge in whatever he wants. The truth is he wouldn't want to marry her. I am his get-out-free card. He uses me as an excuse to refuse her and keep her hanging on. In exchange I get the house. It is a mutually convenient arrangement. He wouldn't want me to go.'

'You get the house, but it's a haunted house.'

'She doesn't hurt me. And I never see her.' Elizabeth sounded stronger suddenly as though the challenge of the real-life woman was enough to give her the strength to face out any ghostly challenge.

Lucy perched nervously on the edge of the sofa. 'You are a very brave woman.'

'So are you, my dear. You were prepared to take on a hypothetical murderous husband, with the option being that it is a deranged spectre. I am impressed.'

For a moment they smiled at each other.

'I have a ghost of my own. In the gallery.' It slipped out before Lucy had time to think. 'He doesn't make a sound. He just stands looking at me.' She managed to stop herself revealing who the ghost was. Maybe in time, but not now. Not here. That would be unfair to Elizabeth and maybe upset Rachel all over again. Now, all she wanted to do was go home as soon as possible and ponder the extraordinary happenings of the day.

'So, you are a bit of an expert on ghosts,' Elizabeth nodded. Her face was wan.

'Far from it.' Lucy lapsed into silence again. 'I don't like to go and leave you here after this,' she said at last.

Elizabeth smiled. 'My dear, Rachel and I have been living together for twenty years perfectly amicably. Don't worry about me. I feel scared at the time, but then it is over and I know that when she has gone there is nothing left to fear. There is just a feeling of cleansing, like after a thunderstorm. She is just a woman like me. A mother who is still in terrible pain. I understand that. She has cried again and she has accepted what happened again and she can rest again.' She hesitated. 'If we talk about the family in future perhaps we can meet in town and discuss it there so as not to upset her. I thought maybe I could ask around the village for you. See if there is anyone alive who remembers the stories about the war years. It would give me something to do.'

They left it like that. Elizabeth had Lucy's mobile number. They would be in touch. As she left, Lucy glanced at Elizabeth's car, parked outside on the gravelled drive, as she left. An unusual choice for a woman like Elizabeth, she thought as she climbed into her own dusty and battered hatchback, or was this souped-up bright red convertible Mini a further sign of her husband's guilt?

As she drove away from the house down the narrow lane Lucy glanced into the rear view mirror. Was that a figure leaning on the gate? After they had kissed, strangers who had become if not friends then at least allies and exchanged a wry handclasp by way of farewell, Elizabeth had closed the front door behind her and Lucy had heard her footsteps as she walked slowly away towards the kitchen.

If there was a figure there, perhaps it was Rachel staring out into the lonely dusk waiting in vain for her son to come home.

9

September 12th 1940

Rachel followed Evie upstairs as her daughter raced ahead of her and slammed the door of the studio in her face.

'Evie! Evelyn! Open this door at once!' Rachel banged on it with her fist as Evie thrust the bolt home on the other side. 'Evie, what is happening? What is wrong?'

There was no reply though Rachel could hear the sound of sobbing.

'Evie.' She was more persuasive this time, her voice gentle. 'Please, darling. Let me in. If something has happened maybe I can help.' She subsided on the top step of the stairs, trying to regain her breath.

Evie had come into the kitchen that evening closely followed by Eddie. Rachel could see at once that they had had a quarrel. Evie's face was taut with anger, her eyes full of tears. She had thrown her bag down on the kitchen table with considerable force and raced for the door. Her only comment as she ran for the stairs was, 'Ask him!'

With a sigh Rachel climbed to her feet and made her way

downstairs again. Eddie was standing in the kitchen looking out into the yard. Dudley, followed by the two dogs, had just brought Bella, their old black cart horse, in from the fields and had unharnessed her from the binder. One of the two land girls they had been allocated, Patsy, was stroking the horse's nose and laughing as Dudley made some comment as he pulled the traces free. She led the horse forward clear of the shafts and began to unbuckle the harness. The sound of the generator in the shed drowned out their conversation.

'Eddie?' Rachel said. Eddie's shoulders were rigid, and when he turned his face was white with anger. 'What has happened?'

'I went to the airfield to fetch her. Again!' He emphasised the word bitterly. 'She was drawing, of course, but not what I had told her.'

Rachel frowned. 'Does she have to draw what you tell her?'

'If she wants to sell her work, if she wants to be accepted by the War Artists Advisory Committee, yes she does.'

'And what was she drawing?' She had already guessed the answer.

'That boy Tony. Again and again. On every page.' His tone was repressive.

Rachel glanced down at the sketchbook lying on the table. She stepped forward and opened it. On the first page was a watercolour sketch of the old farmhouse on the edge of the airfield that the officers were using as their Mess. She turned over. There was nothing else in the book. The next few pages had been torn out.

Quietly Rachel closed the book. 'You tore up her drawings?' It wasn't really a question.

Eddie didn't answer.

'Eddie, look at me please when I am talking to you,' she said sharply.

He turned round at last and she was shaken by the fury she saw in his face. 'She has to be stopped,' he said at last. 'They were worthless anyway.' His voice was tight. 'Nothing more than doodles.'

'I see.' She closed her eyes for a moment. 'You did know that his parents live in Scotland. He is their only son. He asked her to do some drawings for them so they had something to remember him by if he is killed.' She managed to keep her voice steady with difficulty. Evie was drawing this boy for his parents, but as far as she knew she had never painted Ralph for her. Never even sketched him.

'She has already painted a portrait of him for his parents,' Eddie said so quietly that his words were barely audible. 'I said I would arrange to have it delivered to them.'

'But she still draws him,' Rachel said. She turned away and went over to the sideboard. Her basket lay there with her shopping still packed from her visit to the shop in the village. The weekly ration of bacon, butter and sugar. They were so lucky living on a farm; milk, eggs, vegetables were plentiful and soon they would make their own butter and cheese again. Methodically she started to unpack. 'I know it's hard, Eddie, but you must remember how young she is. This is no more than a passing infatuation. Wait. She will come to her senses.' Privately she could understand perfectly why Evie would prefer the handsome young RAF officer with his charm and his humour and his glamour.

'No, she won't. She has told me she wants nothing to do with me any more.' Eddie rammed his fists into his pockets. 'Oh, she wants me to help her place her paintings, of course she does. But she can never love me. "Sorry, Eddie, but it was never really like that between us, was it?' He mimicked her voice with cruel coldness.

Obviously Evie's infatuation was so strong she found it impossible to hide it. Rachel felt a moment's sympathy for Eddie. She didn't doubt that in his own way he was every bit as hurt and jealous as any other man would be. She just hoped that the money Evie was making for him would safeguard his interest in her art. That way they could at least keep a working relationship.

Over the last few days she had been thinking a lot about her daughter, who had sacrificed so much to come home and live on the farm. History had repeated itself in uncanny fashion, but Evie's reaction to the circumstances was very different from her own. She too had been an art student; she too had exciting memories. She had had lovers long ago, and she was realistic about the time Evie had spent at college in London. Dudley had never known of course. Old-fashioned, strait-laced, possessive, he had assumed his wife would be a virgin and idolised her from the first day of their marriage. In due time he had idolised his little girl as well, as all fathers did. Or should, she corrected herself, lost in her thoughts. He would not be so sanguine if he suspected that Evie had had boyfriends before. And it would never have occurred to him that Evie had slept with anyone, be it a fellow student, Eddie or Tony. He trusted her absolutely. To him she was as pure as the driven snow. If he ever found out otherwise she doubted if any of them would weather the storm that would ensue and she doubted if the young man in question would survive. She sighed with a sad retrospective glance back at the excited, optimistic, talented Rachel of the past. She was never quite sure why she had come back to Sussex, turned her back on the excitement of London and the world of art, accepted the proposal of a solid down-to-earth farmer and settled into the role of a farmer's wife. It had had something to do with the death of her brother of course and the need to reassure her parents that their surviving child would be safe. She had never allowed herself time for regrets, but when Evie made the choice to follow her dream of going to art college Rachel had been uncharacteristically firm in overruling Dudley's initial opposition to the scheme. Her daughter would succeed where she hadn't.

'So, what should I do?'

She realised suddenly that Eddie was talking to her.

'Leave her alone for a bit, Eddie.' Rachel managed a sympathetic smile. 'It may not last. She's been overwhelmed a bit by the glamour of the boys down there. They are heroes at the moment, don't forget.' She saw him wince and could have kicked herself. A man with damaged eyesight and a boring job in the Ministry of Information could not be regarded as glamorous. 'She will come back to her senses. I'm sure she will.'

Eddie nodded. He rammed his hands into his pockets and walked slowly towards the door. She watched him go without a word. What else could she say? She glanced back at the defaced sketchbook and sighed. Poor children. What a world they were all having to live in.

As if on cue she heard a plane fly overhead, closely followed by two others. Was Ralph up there even now, defending his country? Or Tony? She gave a sad smile. She could easily grow to love Tony and she was sure that Dudley could as well. But how would that help Evie, caught as she was between the man she loved and the man who could secure her a career in the world of art she so adored, a man who, if her instincts were right, could be dangerous.

Wednesday 17th July

It was late when Lucy got home from Box Wood Farm. She let herself into the gallery and closed the door quietly behind her, listening. There was no sound. The room was dark save for the spotlit bird on the dais in the window. She tiptoed across to the foot of the stairs and paused, looking up. The flat upstairs was in darkness. Taking a deep breath she switched on the lights and put her foot on the bottom step.

The flat was as she had left it that morning save that there was a note from Robin on the kitchen worktop informing her that he had made two sales, he had asked someone to come in the following weekend with some paintings they wanted to sell, and he made a note of the telephone number of a local artist who wanted to discuss holding an exhibition in the autumn. After those bits of good news he reminded her to keep her chin up and signed off with three kisses. She smiled, cheered as much by his scrawled optimism as by the news it contained, and glanced at the studio door. She did not go in.

As soon as she climbed into bed she found herself reliving the anguish she had felt and heard at Box Wood Farm, thinking about Elizabeth and wondering if Ralph, like his mother, would be called back by the mention of his name. The harder she tried to put him out of her head, the more insistent his memory became. On the way back from the farm, still stunned by the events of the evening, she realised she had forgotten to visit the church at Chilverly. Not forgotten actually, just not found time for it. Not found time to go and look at Ralph's memorial. Not wanted to. Maybe. 'If I go tomorrow, will you let me sleep?' she murmured into the pillow.

She left the following morning half an hour before Robin was due. Heading east through the centre of Chichester she drove through a light mist of warm rain towards the airfield at Westhampnett and up past Goodwood on the road which presumably Evie had taken to and from the farm when she was sketching the airfield. It was a pretty route, taking her through woods past the racecourse and then across the Downs, climbing steeply then heading down again with stunning views across the valley, towards Chilverly. St Margaret's was a lovely old Norman church, nestling in a small churchyard thickly sewn with lichen-covered gravestones. Under the gentle summer rain it smelled of grass and roses and wet moss.

The ancient oak door was locked. It was a moment before she spotted the note on the board in the porch directing her to a house in the village if she wanted the key. She wandered up the village street through the rain rather hoping she would not run into Elizabeth again; she wanted some space to assimilate everything that had happened the day before.

She collected the key from an elderly woman in a row of almshouses near the pub and, promising to lock up and return it when she had finished, made her way slowly back down the quiet street.

The cottages and houses which lined it were all old and mostly in perfect condition. The whole place seemed oddly quiet and she found herself wondering if this was a commuter area, or maybe a haven for holiday cottage owners. Perhaps these people like Mike Marston spent most of their lives in London leaving a ghost community behind them to struggle on during the week.

The door of the church creaked as she pushed it open. She closed it behind her and stood looking round in the dim light filtering through the windows. It was a small narrow building with no side aisles or pews. A few lines of chairs had been arranged haphazardly on either side of the aisle and if their number was anything to go by there was a very small congregation. There were no guide books or postcards on the table near the door and only a box of slightly mildewed hymn books on the one remaining pew, against the wall, at the back. In spite of this, perhaps because of it, the church felt overwhelmingly peaceful and she found herself slowly relaxing as she wandered towards the back and began to look at the memorial stones and brasses on the walls.

The whole history of the community was here. As far as she could see, the earliest memorial, a carving on a stone tablet, dated from the late fifteenth century. Most of them were from the nineteenth. It was several minutes before she found Ralph. She stood looking up at the simple stone slab on the wall for a long time.

In loving memory
of
Ralph James Lucas
1919-1940
who gave his life for his country

✝

greater love hath no man

Evie would have come here. Evie would have stood on this precise spot, gazing at her brother's memorial with tears in her eyes. Evie would have come here for his funeral, and probably for her own wedding. This place was part of her history and her life.

As Lucy stood staring up at the memorial, lost in thought, she heard the door open behind her but she took no notice. Whoever had come in did not approach her and she barely heard the soft footsteps making their way up the aisle towards the chancel.

She only realised there were tears on her cheeks when she heard someone clear their throat immediately behind her. 'A very brave young man.' The man's voice was soft and tactfully noncommittal. 'Was he a relative of yours?'

She turned and found herself face to face with the vicar, a man in his late sixties, she guessed, with a thatch of white hair and brilliant green eyes. He wore his dog collar with a dark blue sweater and jeans which strangely seemed to suit him very well.

'No he's not a relative,' Lucy answered. She took a deep breath, trying to rid herself of the terrible sadness which had swept over her, and to remember why she was here. 'Were you here when the Lucases lived in the village?'

He gave an unexpected hoot of laughter. 'Good Lord no. I may have white hair but I'm not that old.' He paused. 'I'm sorry. That was crass but I've been here only eighteen months. I am only just beginning to feel my way round all the ins and outs of this place. The house where the Lucases lived was up a lane off the Goodwood road. The couple who live there now are not part of my flock sadly.' He glanced round. 'As you can see not many people are, though I'm working on it.' He paused. 'Are you from round here?'

Lucy shook her head. 'I live in Chichester. I'm working on a biography of Ralph's sister, Evelyn.' She glanced at the memorial again and then back at the vicar to see if there was any sign of recognition at the name. There wasn't. 'She was a war artist and went on to be quite well known in her day. Sadly there isn't that much biographical information around so I am trying to find as much as I can from scratch. I went to Box Wood Farm yesterday and met Mrs Chappell. She very kindly showed me round. Evie Lucas was born there and lived there until she married.' She paused. Was that true? She didn't even know that much for certain. 'The family had been there for generations, I gather, but when her parents died and Evie inherited the place she sold it without ever coming back here to live.'

'The world was a very different place after the war.' The vicar nodded slowly. 'I'm Huw Redwood, by the way.' He held out his hand.

She shook it. 'Lucy. Lucy Standish.'

'So, did you see the ghost at Box Wood Farm?' His eyes twinkled mischievously.

She stared at him. 'You know about the ghost?'

'Everyone knows about the ghost. Besides, ghosts are part of my job. In theory anyway.'

'So you believe in them. You think they are real?' She heard the anxiety in her voice.

He nodded. 'I do, yes.' He eyed her curiously.

Lucy walked a few steps away from him and threw herself down on one of the chairs.

'I heard it,' she said. She found her hands were shaking again at the thought. 'I stayed to have supper with Elizabeth last night and we heard it. Her. It was awful, frightening, sad.'

He studied her face for a few seconds and silently came to sit beside her leaving an empty chair between them. 'Tell me about it,' he said quietly.

She described what had happened.

'Poor woman.' She wasn't sure if he meant Rachel or Elizabeth. 'Several people told me about it when I first came here. I think it is one of the ways that congregations assess a new pastor – how will he deal with the local legends and will he feel compelled to exorcise any ghosts still knocking around in the old buildings? There are, of course, said to be several ghosts in the village but this one is the most tragic. No one has asked me to do any exorcising I am glad to say. I'm not allowed to anyway. There is a special department in the bishop's office that deals with that sort of thing, but stories of ghosts always intrigue me. They usually betray so much unhappiness which has remained unresolved.'

'Elizabeth isn't one of your congregation, you said,' Lucy reminded him.

He shook his head. 'I went and introduced myself, of course, when I arrived in the parish but I wasn't asked in.'

Lucy gave a rueful smile. 'I'm afraid I'm not a churchgoer either.' She hesitated and he waited, patiently. 'My husband died nearly four months ago,' she said at last. 'We had a church funeral because his parents wanted it and I couldn't think of anything else. Laurence, that's my husband, would have laughed and said he wanted a blazing pyre on the beach, or a rocket to the moon or something, but I knew he would want to comfort his mother as well. She was inconsolable.'

Huw slowly nodded. 'And so were you,' he said gently.

She sighed. 'I wanted him to be a ghost. I wanted him to come and speak to me and explain what happened. I needed him so much.' Suddenly she was crying properly, unable to stem the tears running down her face.

Huw reached into the pocket of his jeans and produced a pack of tissues. 'How did he die?' he asked at last.

'A car crash. The police think someone ran him off the road, but they never found anyone. It was all so pointless.' She was sobbing out loud, unable to stop. 'I'm sorry. This is silly. I'm over it. It's just I miss him so much.'

'We never get over the loss of the ones we love,' Huw said after another long silence. 'We learn to live with our pain, that's all.'

'Rachel Lucas never learned to live with the pain of losing her son,' Lucy whispered. 'She is still crying.'

'It must have been a horrific experience for you both to hear

144

her like that.' Huw sighed. 'Poor Elizabeth. It would be very hard for her and her husband to live with that.'

'I don't think her husband is there much.' Lucy blew her nose. 'I think he has other interests.'

'Ah, I see. Then I am even more sorry for her.'

'Rachel is not the only ghost in this story,' Lucy blurted out suddenly. Everywhere she was looking for Evie, and everywhere she was finding Evie's family. 'Ralph, that's the guy on your memorial there, Rachel's son, Evie's brother, has been haunting me. At home.' He wasn't a nightmare; he wasn't a construct of her imagination; however much Robin tried to hint that he might be, Phil was right. Such things existed and Ralph was one of them.

There was another silence and she looked at him anxiously. 'You do believe me?'

'I do believe you, yes,' he said. 'There is obviously a desperately sad story here. But I am interested in why he is haunting you. Is there a family connection to the house you live in? You said you weren't a relative.'

'No, but I'm writing about his family and he comes into the story. I'm thinking about them, I'm already so involved with them.' She scrubbed at her eyes with the tissue. 'I was scared of him at first but he never does anything. He never says anything. He is just a shadow, standing there, in the studio.' And suddenly she was telling told him the whole story. When she had at last finished she gave a weak smile. 'You must be very good at your job. You know how to wheedle secrets of the confessional out of people.'

He laughed quietly. 'That wasn't part of my training, I assure you. I just know how to listen. And,' he added, suddenly serious again, 'I know how to keep my counsel.'

'Would you do something for me?' Lucy asked after another moment's pause. She liked this man and instinctively she trusted him. 'Would you come and talk to him? I don't want to have him exorcised. I don't want anything to do with your

145

bishop, I just want someone to talk to him and ask him what he wants.'

'Why don't you ask him yourself?'

She shook her head. 'I don't think I could. Or, at least, I have asked him if he is Ralph – when he didn't answer I assumed that was it, he was just a shadow standing there, and I would never know for sure who he was. But now I have seen photos of him. I recognised him. I know it is Ralph, but I still don't know why he is there.'

'And so you came to find his memorial. If I came, would I be allowed to pray?' Huw looked at her seriously. 'I don't try and force people into my church or railroad them into my beliefs, but God is what I do. If I come I would have to pray for Ralph and for his family.'

'And you think that works?' She couldn't hide her scepticism.

'Oh, yes, it works.'

'And you think no one else has prayed for them in all these years?'

'Ah, that is a good point.' He shook his head. 'I am sure they have, but maybe not properly. Maybe there was too much sadness, too much anger. Maybe too much bitterness. Without forgiveness and love and understanding people get stuck.'

She stood up and walked slowly up towards the altar. It was modern, in some ways out of keeping with the rest of the church, but somehow it fitted. A huge raw chunk of pale wood with a plain wooden cross and two small vases of flowers on it.

'I wish I knew how to pray,' she said sadly. 'I know it means a lot to some people but to me it means nothing. It would be hypocrisy to speak to a God I don't believe in.'

'He wouldn't mind.' He followed her and stopped several paces away from her. 'He would be pleased that you were trying it out, giving him the benefit of the doubt.'

'Really?' she turned to face him.

'Try it one day when no one is looking.' He smiled. 'Now,

my dear, I am afraid I do have to go. I only came in to collect some notes I had left in here. I need to get to the hospital. If I give you my card – I know that seems unexpectedly business-like for an otherworldly guy like me but that's the way we work these days – will you ring me if you would like me to come over and talk to Ralph? I would like to meet him, and if you don't object too violently I will in the meantime pray for you and for the Lucas family.'

He took her hand in his for a moment, then he turned and headed for the door.

September 14th 1940

'Speak to her, Ralph.' Rachel clung onto her son's arm for a moment. 'She is so angry with everyone. Your father is furious. Eddie is behaving like a jealous spoilt child. I just can't cope with them all.'

Ralph smiled. 'I doubt if she will listen to me, but I'll have a go. Is she upstairs?'

His mother nodded. 'She won't come out.'

Ralph dropped a kiss on the top of his mother's head and turned towards the hall. He ran up the two flights of stairs two at a time and knocked on the studio door.

'Evie? It's me. Can I come in?'

There was a moment of silence then he heard a movement behind the door. Evie pulled it open and ushered him in, then she bolted it again behind him. 'I suppose Mummy sent you.'

'She certainly did. She is frantic. What on earth is going on?'

'They won't let me see Tony.'

'Who won't? Not Mummy and Daddy surely. They like him.'

'Eddie has spoken to the CO at the airfield and told him that they are so worried it is making them ill. Eddie has asked him to ban me from going down there. He has arranged for me to go to Shippams meat paste factory in Chichester instead to sketch the women working there. He says that is what the WAAC want and so that is what I have to paint.' Her eyes were red and swollen with crying. 'Tony sent me a letter via one of the land girls. Patsy. He was waiting at the end of the lane and she said he was distraught and begged her to give it to me. He didn't dare come up here, and Daddy had to go down to the airfield to collect my bike and the CO had a word with him. He said he would rather I didn't go down there any more if it was making the whole family upset, and the CO said anyway my presence was distracting Tony and affecting the other pilots.'

Ralph gave a low whistle. 'My goodness. What a mess.'

'Tony wants to marry me, Rafie.'

Ralph smiled doubtfully. 'That's a bit fast, isn't it, even for you, little sister?'

'It isn't fast for wartime, you know that.' She threw him a stormy look.

He sighed. 'I suppose not. He's a nice chap. I like him. I take it you want to marry him too?'

She nodded vigorously. 'Look. They tried to stop me drawing him so I've been working on another portrait secretly. We went for a walk last week. Here.' The canvas, covered by a sheet, was facing the wall behind the cupboard. She pulled it out and swung it round to face him. She had painted herself, sitting on a gate, her hair blowing in the wind with Tony standing behind her, his hand on her shoulder. Ralph studied it for a long time. Her face in the picture reflected her mood today; it was stormy, suspicious, accusing. Tony's expression was one of pure adoration. 'After this, I'm not doing any more painting,' Evie said crossly. 'I've told Eddie he can kiss goodbye to the pictures I've been doing for him. And the WAAC, I'm not painting any more for them either.' She pushed the picture back into its hiding place. 'Will you take Tony a message from me? Please. I'm practically a prisoner now. Daddy says Eddie is right and I am making Mummy ill with worry and he is so angry I've made trouble for everyone at the airfield. He's forbidden me to go down there and I don't want Tony to get into trouble with his CO. That would be awful. And I don't want to embarrass you! It's all Eddie, stirring things up. Making trouble for us. It's not fair! But I want Tony to know I still love him. Please, tell him, Rafie. And make Mummy and Daddy understand. I don't know why they are being like this. I'm not in any danger. Not any more than I am here. And I thought they liked Tony.'

Ralph sighed. He wondered if he would ever pluck up the courage to tell this wayward family of his that he had a girl-friend. That he was in love too. That his Sylvie was a beautiful, gentle, quiet, uncomplicated girl whom he loved to bits. This was all getting too complicated for him. He wasn't even sure himself why his father had agreed with Evie and put his foot down in the way he had. 'They do like Tony, Evie,' he ploughed on. 'But neither of them likes the trouble that's going on, you know that. You've just been too indiscreet. You've upset Eddie a lot. Talk about tactless. Your endless visits and drawings were so obvious, throwing it in his face. You must know how he feels about you! You've made him really angry.'

She bit her lip. 'I hate Eddie!'

'No, you don't. He's not been very fair to you, we know, and I think he's been exploiting you, but at the same time, if you want to further your career and be accepted by the WAAC people, you need him. You're a woman, which is hard enough, and you're very young. And he has put himself on the line for you. Think about it, Evie, for goodness' sake. It will all work out OK, Sis. You just have to learn to be patient and a bit more tactful.'

She gave him a glimmer of her old smile. 'I am not a patient tactful person, you know that.' She was serious again at once. 'And there is no time to be patient. Any day Tony could be posted somewhere else.' She paused. 'Or worse. Please, Rafie, help us.'

'I'll do my best.' He gave her a quick kiss on the cheek. 'Just play the part for a while, Evie, there's a dear. Think of what Mummy and Daddy are going through. Help them as much as you can. They are truly frightened for you. I can't help being in the firing line,' he grimaced, 'but you can, sweetheart. Forget Eddie if you want to – carefully, but don't be angry with the parents. They are only doing what they think is best in telling you not to go down there. They are frightened for you and they are frightened you are going to have your heart broken if anything happens to Tony. After all, you've only known him for ten minutes. Give it a little bit of time. Let everyone, especially Eddie, get used to the idea of you and Tony together and I'll have a word with Al, ask him to speak to Tony's CO. I'm sure I can smooth things out for you so you can go back and do some more sketching, as long as you are sketching the airfield, not just lover boy. All right? And in the meantime go and paint the meat paste factory! Please.'

She nodded. 'All right.'

'Good girl. It will all come right in the end, I promise.'

Friday 19th July

There was too much to think about after the meeting with Huw, too many notes to make to try and make sense of the emerging story of life at Box Wood Farm to face Evie's studio and the probability of finding yet more material that afternoon. Instead Lucy set off the following morning, let herself into the studio about ten and set about lining up the day's quota of boxes. At once she realised that the box of handbags was missing. She looked round, puzzled, then she realised. It was Friday. Dolly had already been into the studio doing a bit of sorting of her own. Damn! She had meant to check them before Dolly had the chance to remove them. She hurried out of the studio and across the grass to the kitchen.

Dolly was sitting at the kitchen table polishing silver. She looked up over her spectacles and gave Lucy a quizzical look. 'Can I help?'

'Would you mind if I made some coffee?' It seemed a good excuse to come in. 'Can I make you some too? I don't want to interrupt what you're doing.' She hesitated for a moment, wondering whether to tell Dolly about her latest discoveries. There seemed no reason not to. 'Yesterday I went to look at St Margaret's Church where the memorial to Ralph is.' Her eyes were darting round the kitchen. There was no sign of the box of bags.

'Coffee would be nice, thank you.' Dolly put down the cloth and sat back in her chair. 'I had a call from Mr Michael last night. He wondered how you were getting on. He said you could come tomorrow if you liked even though it's a weekend. He'll be here alone. Charlotte Thingy isn't coming.'

Lucy felt her spirits lift. 'That would be nice. Then I can ask him some more questions about Evie. You don't think he'll get fed up with talking about her, do you?'

Dolly laughed. 'I doubt it.'

'All the stuff you gave me was really useful.' Lucy looked out of the kitchen window while she waited for the kettle to boil. A wren was sitting flirting its tail on the ivy near the washing line. 'I'm beginning to work everything into some kind of time-line. I'm hoping to find some addresses in amongst her papers. Where she lived after the war before she came here, for instance. You've given me the name of the road but I really need the number as well.'

'That I can't help you with. Doesn't Mr Mike know?'

Lucy shook her head. She reached for the jar of ground coffee and measured some into the coffee pot. 'Would his cousin Christopher know, do you suppose? I will need to speak to him soon.'

'No!' Dolly looked shocked. 'You don't want to talk to him.'

'Why on earth not?' Lucy's hand paused as she stirred the coffee.

'It's not for me to say. You just need to know that Mr Mike and he don't get on.'

Lucy put down the spoon. She was not entirely surprised. She had sensed an undertone when Mike had mentioned his cousin before. Hardly surprising if he had made off with all Evie's paintings. At a guess, put together, they must be worth considerably more than the cottage.

'I have been to see Box Wood Farm as well,' she said. 'Mrs Chappell showed me round.' She poured out their coffee. 'It is a lovely house.' She decided not to mention the ghost. 'She told me about the memorial they had put up to Ralph in the church. So sad. His mother and father are buried in the church-yard there.'

She had found the graves in a secluded corner under a gnarled oak tree before she walked up to the village to return the key and she had promised herself that she would come back soon with some flowers. Both graves looked untended. From the weathered stone she had garnered the dates of Rachel and Dudley Lucas. Ralph and Evie's father had died in 1950; their mother in 1959. It was only ten months after that that Evie had sold the farm and moved from London to Rosebank. There was no sign of Ralph's grave nearby. She wondered where he was buried. 'It's a tragic story, isn't it?' She brought their coffee cups over to the table and sat down opposite Dolly. 'What is really worrying me is that there is so much stuff over there in the studio, but it is all impersonal. I haven't found anything which relates to her private life. Do you think Christopher took things like that as well?'

Dolly's face soured. 'He went through the whole cottage. He sent me away and told me not to come back until he had finished here. I expect he took everything. He only left these bits of silver because they were damaged.' Her fingers gently sought out a dent in one of the candlesticks on the table. She glanced up at Lucy, paused for a moment and suddenly she seemed to make up her mind. 'I did save a few things.' She hesitated again and then she went on. 'When I saw which way the wind was blowing I took the two diaries she kept in her bedroom home with me when I left. I was going to tell Mr Mike and see if he minded, then I realised that there was no love lost between them and I didn't want him to get into trouble with the will and everything, so I just kept quiet. But I think you should have them. I think that is what Evie would have wanted.'

Lucy felt a flash of excitement.

'She didn't leave me anything at all, according to Christopher,' Dolly went on concentrating on the piece of silver she was polishing. 'That wasn't right. Evie told me she had left me two small paintings and a little money which would come to me each year. I had been with her so long. Then I was told that wasn't true and she had left me nothing. Mr Mike made up for it. He said he couldn't believe it, and he gave me some money of his own, but I think Christopher lied about it. He is not a nice man.'

Lucy was shocked. How could anyone begrudge a small bequest to a faithful old retainer like Dolly?

'That all seems very unfair,' she said quietly. 'I would very, very much like to see the diaries. I only need to read them, and then I would give them back to you. I would be very careful with them, I promise.' She couldn't hide her excitement.

Dolly nodded. She still did not look up. 'I trust you,' she said. 'I've been thinking about it and I think it is time Evie got the recognition that is her due. She is a famous person and yet no one knows about her.'

Lucy smiled. 'I know what you mean, and I agree.'

'I thought I had better look through her bags and things,' Dolly went on, 'in case you didn't think of it, and I've found one or two letters you might want to see, but her large handbag, the one that held all her treasures, the one she used right up to the end, that was empty. You could ask Mr Mike, but I suspect Christopher went through it and took everything, even her powder compact, which was gold.' Suddenly her eyes flooded with tears. 'Her key-ring had a St Christopher medal on it, which went with her everywhere. She told me that belonged to her brother. They gave it to her after – after he died. She had wanted me to take it and give it to my grandson. He is in the RAF.'

Even admitting that he had probably been entitled to take whatever he liked from Evie's belongings, Lucy found herself quietly resolving to make a point of meeting Christopher Marston as soon as possible. He sounded a greedy and unpleasant man. She had been planning to visit him anyway. As Evie's only other living descendant apart from Mike it would be inconceivable not to have him on her list of interviewees, but it was becoming more and more obvious that the apparent dearth of information about Evie led directly back to this one man.

'I'll bring the diaries back next week,' Dolly said. She looked up at last.

'Have you read them yourself?' Lucy asked gently.

Dolly shook her head. 'I couldn't. They were private. But you didn't know her so it is different for you. She was still keeping a diary when she died so one of them contains the last things she ever wrote. The other goes back to the war. I don't know why she kept it in her bedroom. It must have meant something very special to her. All the others, the ones in between, they have all gone. She kept them in her desk in the sitting room there, so I suppose Christopher took them all.'

10

September 16th 1940

Ralph picked Tony up in the Morgan at the gates to the airfield at dusk and they drove up into the Downs to The Fox and Hounds for a quiet pint. Tony looked at Ralph over the rim of his glass and grinned.

'Is this where the brotherly chat comes in? I am really sorry this has all blown up the way it has. I wouldn't have had Evie get into trouble for the world.'

Ralph looked at him steadily for a moment then turned his attention to his drink. 'Evie is quite capable of getting into trouble herself without anyone else's help,' he said fondly. 'What we have to do is to get her out of it.'

'I love her very much,' Tony said solemnly. 'I want you to know that. And I want to marry her. My intentions are totally honourable.'

'You haven't known her very long,' Ralph put in. 'Are you sure you really want to make a commitment like that so quickly?'

Tony nodded. 'She's a lovely girl. She's the right one for me.'

He put his tankard down and met Ralph's gaze. 'I know I'm probably not a good bet at the moment, any more than you are,' he said slowly. 'But we've both survived so far. If I make it through to the other end of the war I will have a good career as a lawyer. I will be able to support her. I wanted to speak to your father but she wouldn't let me, not yet.'

Ralph laughed. 'That all sounds too proper for our Evie. She's a bit wild sometimes.'

'Even so, I would want to do things by the book. My parents would want that too.' Tony looked wistful for a moment. 'I wish they could meet her. They will as soon as we can arrange it.'

'She was very insistent that she paint a picture for them. I saw it up in her studio. Not the one she did of you; this is one of you both.'

Tony smiled sadly. 'I haven't seen that one. I've been banned from the house.' He shook his head. 'I'm not sure what we've done wrong, to be honest.'

'You've displaced Eddie for a start. He is not a happy man.'

'He's not the right man for Evie,' Tony retorted sharply.

Ralph glanced at him. 'No. I agree with you there, and so if I am honest do my parents. They've never trusted him entirely. But he has a bit of a hold on Evie because of his contacts in the art world. Don't underestimate that, old bean. It means a lot to her. And Eddie is quite a forceful character. I sometimes wonder if he might have some sort of a hold over the parents as well. I'm not sure what, but it is not like my dad to cave in to bullying and Eddie is definitely bullying everyone. They've known him and his family a long time – since before Evie and I were born. I suppose they might feel some sort of misguided loyaltly to the Marstons. I don't know.'

'So I will have to fight for her.'

'Not literally, but yes, I think you will.' Ralph drained the dregs in his glass. 'Sorry, but I have to get back. We've a pre-dawn start, trying to intercept their recce planes. Jerry never lets up, does he?'

Tony shook his head. He emptied his own glass and stood up. 'You'll back me, Ralph?'

'With Evie? Of course I will. I think you're made for each other.' He slapped Tony on the back. 'Come on, I'll drop you back at the airfield.'

Saturday 20th July

'It would NOT be a good idea to meet Christopher, believe me,' Mike said firmly next morning. He was standing looking down at the table where she had separated out several piles of papers. 'For some reason he is very protective of Evie's memory. He rang me yesterday. Someone has told him you are poking around doing research into the family and he is very angry.'

Lucy stared at him, shocked. 'Who on earth would know I was researching the subject apart from you and Dolly?'

'I'll tell you. Mrs Chappell.'

Lucy stared at him. 'Elizabeth?' She sighed. 'Of course. She told me he had been over there looking for paintings. And she said she was still in touch with him. I must speak to him, Mike, and explain that I am no threat. He's got the wrong end of the stick, and as he seems to have the monopoly on Evie's surviving paintings, I can't progress without his co-operation.'

Mike sighed. He hitched himself up to sit on the table next to her. 'It didn't sound to me as if he had any intention of co-operating with you, I'm afraid. I don't know what to suggest.'

'What did he say when he rang you?'

'He made various accusations. He said you were a money grubbing, dishonest imposter with no academic credentials who was out to try and milk Evie's reputation, to puff your own name and that of your gallery. Just a few choice epithets like that.' He softened the words with a grin. 'Sorry, but you did ask.'

'Elizabeth Chappell told him that?' She was aghast.

'Is that what you told her?'

'No, of course not.' She was indignant. She paused. 'I thought we had become friends,' she went on sadly. She looked up at Mike. 'Something awful happened when I went to see her. The house is haunted. By your great-grandmother, Rachel.'

Mike stared at her. 'You are kidding me.'

'No. I heard her crying in the distance. It was dreadful. So sad. I didn't believe it when Elizabeth told me about it. She is a sad, lonely woman but I got on with her quite well. I stayed and had supper with her and as it got dark we heard this terrible sobbing.'

'And it wasn't some sort of scam?'

'No.' Lucy shook her head adamantly. 'I spoke to the local vicar the next day and he knew all about it. The house is known for being haunted. It is Rachel, crying for Ralph after he was killed. I'm sorry. This is your family.' She put her hand over his on the table, and gave it a gentle squeeze. 'This must be very painful for you to talk about.'

He sighed. 'It is sad, but it was all a long time ago.' He didn't move his hand.

She waited several seconds then she quietly sat back in her chair, folding her arms. Touching his hand had seemed suddenly too intimate a gesture.

'I drove past your gallery on the way here last night.' The abrupt change of subject took her by surprise.

She frowned uncomfortably. 'Checking up on me?'

'Yes, I suppose I was.' He had never told her that he had looked her up on Google.

She felt a shiver of apprehension run down her spine. 'Why?'

'Because of Christopher's call. He seemed to know a lot more about you than I did. So I thought I would do a bit of research myself. I asked myself if I had been a bit too trusting.'

Lucy stared at him, speechless. 'And what did you decide?' she whispered at last.

'That it would probably take a further in-depth interview over lunch before I could be sure.'

She felt the colour flare into her cheeks. 'I don't like being interrogated!'

'That was a joke.'

'Was it?'

He nodded. 'I would have thought that by now you would understand that my cousin and I do not get on. He is stirring things for some reason of his own and I am quite keen to find out why. So,' he slid off the table and held out his hand, 'as it is after twelve and I for one am quite hungry I suggest we go up to the pub and have a drink and a sandwich and try and work out exactly what it is that Christopher is so frightened of.'

'I would have thought that was obvious.' She stood up and, ignoring the proffered hand, grabbed her bag. She was suddenly not certain of her ground.

'Not to me.' He stood still. 'Well? Tell me.'

She headed past him towards the door. 'Your relationship with your cousin is not really any of my business.'

He caught her wrist and pulled her to a standstill. 'I think you have made it your business. If you want to write about my family, then you need to know the truth and if I am going to help you, so do I. So tell me.'

'OK. He seems to have acquired all Evie's paintings. Every one. Even two little ones which apparently she had promised to Dolly. He has taken her sketchbooks and her diaries. Everything. According to Dolly he took far more than he was entitled to.'

'But those were the terms of the will,' he said, his voice more gentle now. 'He got the paintings and I got the cottage. That seemed fair. I would have liked a painting or two and I was angry that Evie seemed to have forgotten Dolly after promising her those pictures and a small annuity as well, but we had to stand by the will.'

'Then maybe he feels guilty that he has taken more than he should.' she said. 'There is nothing like guilt to put people on the defensive. After all, the paintings are probably worth a fortune. I know houses in this part of the world are expensive, but maybe not quite as expensive as the Lucas collection. He must realise that. Evie's paintings are an unknown factor, I admit, because they don't have an auction record and there are too few of them around, but believe me, they are really valuable.'

Not for the first time she felt a pang of guilt of her own at not telling him about the portrait in the studio at home. Especially if Christopher was accusing her of wanting to make money out of Evie. After all, why else had Larry bought the picture in the first place?

She was silent for a while, deep in thought, unaware of Mike's pensive gaze fixed on her face. Both Evie's grandsons were inextricably bound into her story and Christopher was someone she was going to have to face. He held the key to much of Evie's life. Even if he hadn't known her well himself, he now possessed her surviving diaries and somehow Lucy had to get hold of them.

'What does Christopher do for a living?' she asked at last.

'He is some sort of banker. He lives in Midhurst.' He grinned. 'And that is all I am telling you except that to go and see him would be inviting trouble. Please think very hard before you consider going there.'

She nodded. 'I have to meet him, Mike. Surely you see that. He has her diaries; the best part of her archive. Perhaps I can convince him I am not the criminal mastermind he seems to think I am.'

'A criminal mastermind,' Mike echoed. 'That would seem to be an excellent place to start our lunchtime discussion.'

This time they found a table in the corner of the bar. They ordered two ploughman's lunches and a couple of glasses of red wine.

'OK. Assume I am your defending counsel,' Mike said as they sat down.

The room was already noisy and he leaned across towards

her to make himself heard. It was a small table and she could feel the brush of his leg near hers. She tried to ignore it.

'What am I defending myself against exactly?'

'The aforesaid accusation that you are money grubbing, dishonest and have no credentials. I think that was the gist of what he said.'

She took a deep breath, fighting back her wave of indignation. 'OK. Money grubbing. That is a hard one, but I doubt if I will make money from this enterprise unless the book is a bestseller. Of course I live in hope but it would be foolish to bank on it.' She gave a wistful smile. 'If he is accusing me of trying to steal Evie's belongings, I think it is fair to say that he has left nothing worth stealing.' She looked up and held Mike's gaze.

'Ouch,' he said. 'All right. Go on.'

'The accusation of dishonesty is harder to defend, except that I have no criminal record and I have never been accused of being dishonest in my life –' she paused, thinking of the portrait at home – 'and all I can say is you will have to trust me on that one.'

'And your credentials?'

'Ah, I'm on firmer ground there. I have a master's degree in art history and a doctorate in eighteenth-century decorative architecture. I am also the recipient of a prestigious grant to pursue my research, which must mean something. Your cousin has clearly not done a huge amount of digging into my background or he would have known that. He could have Googled me.'

'Indeed he could.'

'As could you.' She took a sip from her glass. 'Or have you?'

He didn't answer.

She looked down, not wanting to meet his eye. 'I see.' She waited for a few seconds but he still said nothing. 'Did Christopher mention the haunting at Box Wood Farm?' she said at last, changing the subject.

'No.'

'I wonder if Elizabeth told him.'

'I doubt it. Christopher is not the type you confide that sort of thing to.'

'So how well do you know him?'

'He is my cousin.'

'I know, but that doesn't mean you know him. I have a cousin who lives in Australia. We've never met.'

'Ah.' He rubbed his chin thoughtfully. 'Well, he's four years older than me. We used to meet when we were children at family parties at Rosebank. The age gap was a bit too big for us to ever play together or be friends, but we knew each other. We got on fairly well as we grew older but we had nothing in common after Evie died and we've grown apart since then. I don't think I've seen him more than twice since the funeral. And before you ask, I kept away when he came to Rosebank to take the pictures.'

'As did Dolly. So you both let him take what he wanted.'

'I suppose I did, yes.'

'You obviously trust him.'

'Of course.'

'But not with me.'

'Oh, I see.' He smiled at her. 'I just don't want to see you chewed up and spat out. He has a reputation for plain speaking, shall we say, and he clearly has you in his sights already.'

'And you don't think I would be able to stand up to him?'

'I am sure you could, but who needs that kind of hassle?' He smiled. 'Besides, you have more chance of persuading him to show you her diaries by gentle methods than by having a flaming row with him and believe me, if you go there, you will have a flaming row.'

They both looked up as the landlord's wife appeared with their plates.

'I shall consider your advice,' Lucy said as they contemplated crusty chunks of warm bread surrounded with wedges of local cheese and salad and farmhouse pickle. They began to unwrap the paper napkins from around their knives and forks. 'I shall consider it very carefully,' she repeated. 'I appreciate the warning.'

'Then you will ignore everything I have said,' he commented with a grin.

'Probably. But I do take your point. If I quarrel with him he will never show me the diaries. But then he seems to have made up his mind anyway.'

'Think about it at least.'

'One thing,' she raised a finger, 'before we change the subject. You said Christopher is very protective of Evie's memory. Does that imply that he thinks there are events in Evie's life that need to be kept hidden?'

He frowned. 'Not as far as I know. I'm not sure what I meant. I think it was a phrase he used.'

'From what you've said of him I would have thought that he would welcome anything that would boost the value of her work, as he seems to have cornered the market.'

'You would think so.'

'Curiouser and curiouser.'

'Indeed.' He smiled at her again and held out his glass to clink against hers before taking his first sip.

September 19th 1940

It did not take long for Evie to complete two watercolours of the airfield, working them up from earlier sketches, one of a group of three Spitfires drawn up together to form an inverted C with, between them some of the pilots. She called it *Waiting to Scramble*. It showed the young men already wearing their Mae Wests with helmets and goggles at the ready, relaxed and laughing. Near them on an orange box stood a gramophone and on a folding chair she had put a pile of books and newspapers. Beneath the chair was a box of records. The second painting was of the ground crew, fitters, riggers and armourers, clustered round the Nissen hut which was dispersal for B flight. They too looked relaxed and happy, the job done, nothing more to worry about until the planes came home. She passed the paintings over to Eddie who scrutinised them carefully and nodded with a satisfied smile.

'Good. We'll put these in your portfolio with the factory painting. You're nearly there, Evie. If you could see your way to including a few women, that would be good.'

'To do that I would have to go back to the airfield,' she said. She scrutinised his face closely and saw him hesitate and then at last nod.

'Mummy and Daddy needn't know,' she said quietly. 'Need they?'

'No.'

'Because it was Daddy who made sure I wasn't allowed to go down there any more, wasn't it?' She tried to keep the suspicion out of her voice. She was watching him intently.

'You know how they worry about you.' He said it blandly, refusing to meet her eye.

'Indeed,' she replied quietly. She left it at that.

So she went back to the airfield at Westhampnett and painted the WVS mobile canteen which had just arrived, much to the delight of the airmen. She had met the two nice ladies who ran it before and liked them, drawing as they opened up the flap on the side of the van and let it down to make a counter behind which they poured tea from their great big teapots for the men. They chatted cheerfully as they worked and kept everyone's spirits up. Just what the War Artists Advisory Committee wanted to see, she thought ruefully. On neither of her next two visits did she see Tony or ask about him; on the first occasion his plane was absent and she heard later that he had landed at another airfield and after a couple of hours she meekly climbed on her bike and began the long ride home in time for afternoon milking. On the visit after that the boys were on standby and although she thought she saw Tony in the distance and half-heartedly raised a hand to wave, none of them seemed to notice her and she turned away. Later, as she rounded the corner away from the airfield on her bike she heard the flight take off and almost at the same moment the distant bray of the air raid sirens. Groping in the basket for her sketchbook she dropped the bicycle into the hedge and crouched there to draw. Almost at once the planes had climbed to thousands of feet, too high to see. Up there somewhere were her lover and her brother. Heart in mouth she recorded the spiralling smoke trails, trying to keep her fears at bay with the sheer speed of her drawing.

Eddie was waiting for her at home. He gave her a perfunctory kiss on the cheek and took the sketchbook out of her hand. 'Good. If you could do me a couple of small watercolours for the gallery before you start on something bigger for your portfolio that would be helpful. I have a buyer who is very keen to build up a collection of local artists' work.'

She wheeled her bike into the shed and then followed him into the kitchen. She was tired and disheartened after missing Tony, and growing ever more resentful of Eddie's constant presence at the farm when she was not allowed to see the man she loved. She threw herself down at the kitchen table and ran her fingers through her wind-tangled hair. 'I should grab a cup of tea before I go out,' she said wearily.

'Don't make yourself so tired that you can't paint tonight,' he said sharply.

She looked up and glared at him. 'Have you any idea at all how hard everyone works on this farm? Mummy and Daddy are dropping every night. I've seen Mummy go to bed without any supper because she was too tired to eat. The land girls are brilliant. They do far more than they need. I never do as much as I should because of painting. It is not,' she added, narrowing her eyes as she looked at him, 'as though it makes enough money to make it worth my while.'

Did Eddie look taken aback? She wasn't sure. When Ralph had first told her that Eddie was not giving her the full amount of money her pictures earned she realised she had always suspected as much. He had pretty much told her he expected to take a cut from everything he placed for her. But part of her hadn't wanted to acknowledge that he was cheating her so she had said nothing. So far.

'I'll see if I can get a bit more for the pictures,' he said after a second's hesitation. 'No one has much money these days, Evie. You know they don't. It will be different after the war. And if you become an official artist, then you will be paid a retainer specifically so that you don't need to work on the farm. Your parents will probably be able to get another land girl to help.' He walked over and put his hand on her shoulder. 'It won't be long now. I'm sure you are going to be accepted. You would have been by now if you had been a chap!' He gave a quiet chuckle.

She moved away sharply. 'So you keep telling me. Well, I sketched two WVS women today down at the airfield. That should please them. And there are some women pilots ferrying the planes around between the bases. I am going over to meet one of them I hope in the next week or so. Ralph said he would let me know if there is a chance of my running into them somewhere. It's hard to know what's going on.' She pushed the chair back and stood up. 'Do you want something to eat?'

He shook his head. 'You go on and have some supper. Your mother said she had left a slice of pie in the pantry for you. I'll get out of your way.' He headed for the door, then he stopped and looked back. 'I'm glad to see you've forgotten about that Anderson boy. He was distracting you unnecessarily.' If he was testing her she rose to the bait instantly.

She turned on him. 'What did you say?' Her voice dropped dangerously.

'I said that young man was a distraction.' He saw the expression on her face and stood his ground 'I am sorry, Evie, but you know it is true. You have to concentrate on the painting.'

'As you well know, I haven't spoken to him for days.' She spoke very quietly.

He wasn't sure if it was because she was sad or furious. 'Which is a good thing.' He tried for a reasonable tone. Perhaps he had let her go back too soon. 'Think about it, Evie. They are expecting an invasion any day. The boys are on standby all the time. Don't you listen to the wireless?'

'Of course I do!' She looked cross.

'Then leave him alone. He is the one who will get into trouble. He doesn't need the distraction. Neither of you do.'

'I would never distract him,' she said icily. 'Please go, Eddie. As you say, I need to have time to paint and I have a cow to milk.'

'Do you love him?' He turned back, his hand on the door knob.

'You know I do.' She held his gaze defiantly.

For a moment he said nothing, then he shrugged his shoulders. 'More fool you.'

'What do you mean by that?'

'Nothing.'

'Yes, you do. You and I had a good time together, Eddie,' she said defiantly. 'But it was never going to be forever, was it?'

'Wasn't it?' He gave a grim smile. 'Whereas this boy, who you have known all of five minutes, would have been forever, would he?'

She sat still for several minutes after he walked out. She was trying to analyse what he had said. Had there been a threat there? She wasn't sure but something in his tone had filled her with foreboding.

Two days later Evie had a phone call from the WAAC to say that they wanted to buy two of her paintings. They were also prepared to commission her to paint a series of four more of a subject to be decided later. She sat by the telephone in the hall for several minutes after she had hung up, staring into space.

'Evie?' Rachel had been listening from the kitchen. She stood in the doorway and stared at her daughter, who was sitting on the bottom step of the stairs, glaring down at the receiver in her hand. It was dusky in the hall without the lights on and the phone was purring disconsolately. Rachel took the receiver, straightened the tangled plaited cord and put it back on its bracket with a clatter.

'They want to buy two of my paintings,' Evie whispered. 'And they want me to paint some more.'

Rachel stared at her. 'Evie!' she said, in awe. 'Oh, darling, that is wonderful.'

'Eddie must have had a word with someone,' Evie went on, suddenly bitter. 'He wants to make sure I have no time to see Tony.'

Rachel pulled up the chair by the hall table and sat down. She leaned forward earnestly. 'Evie, you know Eddie has contacts in the Ministry. If he has used them on your behalf, that is wonderful. There are hundreds of painters trying to become war artists. You know that's why he has been asking you to create a portfolio for him to take in to show them.'

Evie nodded. 'But they are not going to give me a full-time job.'

'Not yet perhaps.' Rachel sighed in exasperation. 'For goodness' sake, Evie. Be pleased with what you have got! It is a tremendous honour to be chosen to help the war effort.'

'They want propaganda, not reality.'

'Did they say that?'

Evie shook her head. 'But you know as well as I do that is what they are doing. Someone has to show women doing their bit. There are plenty of male artists to paint the boys in the air force. Men should go and paint the soldiers.' She sounded petulant. 'I can see the air force in action. Here. Above our heads.'

'As can everyone else. No one sees the women slogging away in the factories.' Rachel was beginning to sound irritated. 'Does it matter, darling? There is a war on. We all want to do our bit.' She stood up wearily. 'I must get on. Be glad for what you have, Evie. I am sure you will get more chances. It will all come right in the end.'

Evie stared after her as her mother walked back into the kitchen. If there hadn't been a war on she would never have met Tony. Her mother was right. She was being ungrateful and selfish. Pulling herself to her feet she turned and, climbing the stairs to her studio, she pulled her painting from its hiding place against the wall behind the old sofa. She stared long and hard at Tony's face. She was missing him desperately. She needed to be with him. Somehow she had to find a way for them to meet without them getting into trouble.

Monday 22nd July

Huw Redwood arrived at the Standish Gallery at about eight o'clock in the evening. He was dressed in a navy open-necked shirt and shabby cords. There was no sign of the dog collar this time. Lucy let him in and locked the street door behind them before leading the way up to the flat. She was feeling very nervous. She took him into the sitting room and sat down, indicating that he should do the same.

'Have you done this sort of thing before?' she asked.

He nodded. 'I am not making any promises, Lucy. It may not be appropriate that I become involved in this matter at all. All I can do is be here.'

She was knotting her fingers together. 'I don't want Ralph to think we are trying to get rid of him. Does that sound stupid? I want to know if we can help him. Find out why he's here. There must be something wrong, mustn't there? Otherwise why would he be haunting me?'

'Is he haunting you?'

'Me, or the painting. Not the gallery. Why would he haunt the gallery?'

'Well, let's see if we can find out.' Huw looked at her from under his eyelashes and smiled gently. 'Would you show me the painting if that is where you usually see him, then you can stay or go away, whichever you like.'

'It's in Larry's studio.' She stood up and led the way into the kitchen. She could feel her mouth dry and her hands were shaking as she pushed open the studio door and flipped on the lights. Outside the sky was overcast above the skylights and the room was dull. The sudden flare of the bright spot-lights illuminated the easel with a cold precision.

Huw walked over to it and stood in front of it for a long time. 'She was a wonderful painter.'

'She was.'

'But this is not Ralph?'

She shook her head. 'I don't know who this chap was yet. Maybe a boyfriend.'

Huw nodded thoughtfully.

Lucy walked over to the table and picked up a photograph. 'This is Ralph. I found this snap amongst Evie's stuff at Rosebank Cottage.' She handed it to him and retreated to the doorway.

Huw spent a long time looking at the photograph, turning it over to read the name and the date on the back, then he put it down on the table. He closed his eyes for a few seconds and Lucy wondered if he was praying.

'Ralph.' Huw spoke out softly at last. 'You have visited this studio and shown yourself to Lucy for a reason and we would like to help you. If it is in your power would you show your-self now so that we can try and understand your needs?'

He paused. Lucy held her breath, her eyes wide. Nothing moved. It was hot and airless. Outside, a car drove down the street, the sound of the tyres on the road fading into the distance; from far away they heard the chime of the clock on the bell tower beside the cathedral.

'Ralph,' Huw went on at last. 'Please let us help you. May I pray for you and for your family, to help bring them peace?'

He paused again. Lucy could feel the perspiration running down her back. She clenched her fists, forcing herself to breathe calmly.

Huw took a couple of steps forward and placed his hand lightly on the top of the painting. 'Ralph, we think that this painting bothers you. Your sister looks so happy here. Is that how you remember her? Happy?'

Lucy found she was shaking her head. Happy? Was she happy? Evie's expression had seemed to change every time she looked at her. It was challenging, wistful, enigmatic. But happy? Is that how Huw saw it? She focused on Evie's eyes, concentrating, then shifted her gaze to the young man standing behind her.

She shivered suddenly and took a step back in surprise. Moments earlier she had been too hot, now a freezing draught seemed to be chilling her spine. She looked at Huw and saw that he had closed his eyes. His lips were moving. He was praying. She watched, half embarrassed, feeling intrusive, half curious as to what effect his prayers were having. It was presumably making him feel better, but what about Ralph? Her eyes drifted away from the canvas and from Huw and she slowly scanned the room, searching the darker corners, the shelves, the walls, but there was no sign of anything out of the ordinary.

Huw finished his prayer, opened his eyes and smiled at her. 'Shall we go next door?' he whispered. He turned and led the way out of the room, pausing to close the door behind them. He walked through the kitchen across the small hallway at the top of the stairs and into the sitting room.

Lucy followed, overcome with disappointment. There had been no sign of Ralph. Nothing had happened. She sat down in the armchair near the window and closed her eyes for a moment, marshalling her thoughts. When she opened them Huw was standing near her, gazing out of the window down into the street. He was looking thoughtful. Obviously aware that she was at last looking at him, he turned towards her.

'Are you all right?' His voice was gentle.

She nodded. 'Disappointed. I was so hoping he would appear.'

'He was there.'

Her eyes widened in astonishment. 'You saw him?'

'No, but I could sense him.'

For a moment she was speechless, then slowly she nodded. 'When it got cold?'

'So you did feel him.' He sat down on the edge of the sofa, frowning. 'I need to think about this and pray more.' He gave her an apologetic grin. 'You are uncomfortable with prayer, Lucy. I am sorry, but Ralph was eased by it. I am sure he was.'

'Did you get a sense of what he wants?' Lucy's mouth was drier than ever.

He gave a small sigh. 'No. You felt he was trying to say something when you saw him?'

'I am not sure. Yes, I suppose I did.'

'He will try again until he has succeeded in communicating with us,' Huw said after a moment. 'I am sure he will.'

Lucy blanched.

'I am sorry. That idea frightens you. I don't sense that he is in any way a threat, my dear, I really don't. He's unhappy and wants to tell us something. Or you. It is probably you specifically he wants to contact. Maybe it is because you are so involved with his sister. You have forged a link.' He sat forward, gazing at her intently. 'If he returns, talk to him as you would to a friend, but allow space for him to answer. His words may come to you in the silence, not through your auditory channels but telepathically. To speak out loud would be too much effort for him.' He paused as though trying to gather his thoughts. 'The reason people say the temperature drops when ghosts appear is, I'm told, that they need so much energy to show themselves to us that they take a living force from the air around them and even from the people they are trying to contact. I am no scientist, I don't know if that is true but it makes sense. And I am not an exorcist. As I told you I am not even part of the bishop's team. By rights I shouldn't be doing this at all, but it interests me so much. I feel for these poor lost souls. They are coming from another dimension to speak to us and that takes determination and effort and I want to help –'

'So he is not in heaven,' Lucy interrupted. She was surprised at the hostility in her own voice.

He gave a half-smile. 'If he was, he has come back over the threshold to speak to us.'

She stood up restlessly and paced up and down the floor. 'Would you like a drink?'

He shook his head. 'I think I should go and leave you to think this through.'

'And you're not worried that I am going to run away screaming after all this?'

'No, I'm not. You seem remarkably calm. You didn't run away before and now you are more informed about what is happening and you know he is no danger to you you should be even more so.'

'But that's the point. I don't know, do I? *You* think I am in no danger, but you can't be sure.' She was lacing her fingers together as she walked up and down the carpet. 'You say I have forged a link with him through Evie.' She swallowed. 'Perhaps he wants to stop me writing about Evie. Perhaps he wants to silence me.' She faced him suddenly. 'You hadn't thought of that, had you?'

He shook his head. 'No, because that is not what I think. I have a strong sense that he is trying to communicate with you and my gut feeling is that that is because there is something he wants you to know. He has information.'

'Perhaps he could write it down for me.' She gave a half-hearted little laugh.

'It has been known.'

She stared. 'Seriously?'

He nodded. 'Ask him.' He stood up. 'I am going to go now, Lucy. Can I come again? Please. To pray, yes, and to see if I can communicate better with Ralph. It may be that we can forge that link more successfully if we go on trying together. Do not become obsessive about it.' He paused as though considering the word he had used and then nodded. 'Please go on living in peace here. Joke about him with your friends if it helps you come to terms with his presence, he will understand. But allow him the space to come to you.' He held out his hand. She shook it, taken aback by the gesture as he put his other hand over hers and stood for a second, looking at her before smiling and turning away. 'Ring me at any time, Lucy, if you want me to come, and if I don't hear from you I will be in touch next week anyway to see how you are and if you would like me to return. Stay here now. I will see myself out.'

She didn't follow him down to the front door. She heard his steps moving steadily down the old uncarpeted staircase, then nothing as he walked across the gallery with its sisal matting. After a couple of minutes she heard the latch click back, followed by the bell on the front door, then the slam as he pulled it closed behind him.

She walked slowly back into the studio and stood looking round. 'He thinks I should talk to you, Ralph,' she whispered into the silence. She paused, half expecting a response. None came.

11

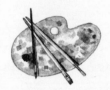

Tuesday 23rd July, 2 a.m.

Branches were rushing towards her and she heard the crack and agonising scrape of undergrowth against the windscreen. All was a chaotic whirl of green, spinning over and over. She was part of the violence, the thundering, bumping, uncontrolled horror as the speed increased; she could smell petrol, felt the shriek of jagged, torn projectiles, metal against metal, the rain of shattered glass on her face and she flailed out wildly, trying to brace herself as the tree approached, the great trunk standing upright, ancient and solid, moving towards her so fast it was hard to see at all. The impact when it came was sudden and overwhelming. She saw for an instant a sheet of flame then all was black and she was lying sobbing in her bed, the sheet tangled over her, her pillow soaked in sweat and tears.

Lucy threw herself out of bed before she was properly awake, tore open the bedroom door and staggered downstairs to the kitchen. Switching on the lights she grabbed a glass and filled it with water from the tap. She was shaking all over, aware that tears were still pouring down her cheeks. Larry. Poor, darling

Larry. She had tried to convince herself that he had known nothing about the horrors of the crash, that he had been knocked out before the car had hit the tree and burst into flame. The coroner had said that almost certainly he would have known nothing about it, but in the nightmare she had felt his fear and his pain and his panic as he tried to grab the wheel, tried to steady himself in the spinning, flying car. Oh God! She put down the glass with trembling hands and leaned against the sink, trying to steady the pounding of her heart in her chest. 'Oh Larry,' she was sobbing out loud. 'Darling Larry. Why? Why did it happen? I can't bear it!'

She was tempted for a moment to call Huw. Was this what he meant by 'ring any time'? Surely not in the middle of the night, or had he expected this to happen? Had he realised she would have nightmares?

No, poor man, she would let him sleep. Larry was not part of the deal. Larry was her problem. Huw had been here for Ralph.

Hardly aware of what she was doing she headed downstairs and walked through the gallery to the back. She groped blindly for the keys to the security locks and opened the French doors which led out into the little walled garden. It was totally dark outside. She had no idea what time it was. She stepped out barefoot onto the weed-covered terrace, desperate to feel the cool presence of the flowers. Making her way to the small wrought iron table under the pergola she sat down. This had been one of Larry's favourite places. In the summer, after they had closed up the gallery for the evening, they would come out here with a glass of wine and sit quietly talking over the day's business and planning – planning for a future which now would never come. Her tears started to flow again and she heard herself sobbing out loud.

It was a long time before her tears subsided at last. She sat very still, listening to the night noises of the sleeping city. She suppressed another sob with a shiver. It was chilly, she realised suddenly and her bare feet were like ice. With an effort she pulled herself up and made her way back in through the open doors. The gallery was cold and as she pulled them closed behind her she realised the place smelled of flowers from the garden. It was a long time since she had put any cut flowers in here. Tomorrow, no, today, she would do it, find Larry's favourite white porcelain vase, the one they used to put on the central table and she would fill it with roses for him.

Upstairs she ran a bath and lay in it for a while. She was exhausted by her crying. The awful reality of the dream had gone, leaving only shards of pain behind. Eventually she climbed out of the bath and dried herself. Wrapped in her bathrobe she went into the bedroom and remade her bed then she climbed in and within seconds she was fast asleep.

The next thing she knew Robin was knocking on the door of the bedroom. There was a cup of tea in his hand. 'Not like you to sleep in.' He put the cup down beside her.

'What time is it?' She sat up slowly, trying to clear her head.

'Half past nine.' He pulled a chair towards him and sat astride it, his elbows on the back studying her face. 'You look like hell,' he said conversationally. 'Are you going to tell me what happened when the exorcist came round?'

She gave a wry grimace and reaching for the cup took a sip of tea. 'Nothing. Not really. We both thought we sensed something, but there was no sign of Ralph – not the way I've seen him before.'

'And that is it? No drama. No screams. No ectoplasm?'

She shook her head. 'Nothing like that. It was a bit of an anti-climax, to be honest.'

'So why do you look as though you had been to hell and back?'

'I had a nightmare.'

'Ah.' He waited. 'Are you going to tell me about it?'

'Larry's crash.' She found she was breathing heavily suddenly. Her eyes were stinging and the cup rattled on its saucer as her hands began to tremble. Robin jumped to his feet and took the cup and saucer away from her. He put them down then he sat down on the edge of the bed.

'Tell me about it. Get it out of your system, Luce,' he said firmly.

'I was in the car with him. Not next to him, I was him. It was falling, rolling over and over. He knew about the crash. He was fighting to control it. He hadn't been knocked out. Then it hit the tree and there was fire everywhere.' Tears were rolling down her cheeks again. 'I've had nightmares about it before, but not like this.'

He nodded sadly. 'Poor Lol. He sighed. 'Poor Luce.' He stood up. 'I'll go and open up and let you get dressed then we'll have a really strong coffee to wake us both up. Good idea? I think you should give Rosebank Cottage a miss today, don't you?'

She nodded gratefully. 'You're a star, Robin.'

'I know, darling.' He beamed at her. Neither let on that his smile didn't – couldn't – quite reach his eyes.

September 23rd 1940

'I finished milking early, took my bicycle and peddaled down to Field End tonight. Tony was there waiting for me in the dark, his car tucked right into the hedge. It was so lovely to see him. We made love for a long time, then he said he had to go. His friends would cover for him if anyone noticed he was out but there might be an early morning call and he needed to be able to wake up. He said I had exhausted him!!'

As they lay in each other's arms they had heard the distant rumble of thunder. A flash of lightning lit up the horizon.

'For once it isn't guns,' she whispered, her lips against his neck. The first heavy drops of rain had started to fall, releasing the heavy scent of the dry earth beneath them and he had rolled over onto his back, opening his mouth to the rain. She laughed silently and kissed him again. 'Shall we walk up onto the top field?' she whispered.

'In the rain?'

'Of course in the rain. I adore thunder!' She climbed to her feet and pulled him up. Taking him by the hand she ran sure-footed up the lane and unlatched the gate into the field. The thunder was coming closer, slow heavy rumbles grumbling up from the coast. They ran out into the middle of the field.

'As a town boy, I can't help wondering if we'll be struck by lightning,' Tony shouted as the noise grew louder round them.

She laughed. 'It wouldn't dare!' She let go of his hand and raised her arms above her head, spinning slowly, her hair flying out, wet and irrepressible. 'I love the storm, I love the rain. I love you, Tony Anderson!'

A fork of lightning streaked across the sky behind the Downs and he made a grab for her. 'That's it. Get down. The storm gods will see you. They will claim you with a lightning shaft.'

They fell to their knees, soaked to the skin, laughing and kissed again. By the time they had returned to the yard they were shivering and drenched. She walked down the lane with him to his car and blew a kiss as he drove away into the night. Already the storm had moved on up the coast. The stars were coming out and the only sound now was the patter of raindrops falling from the hedgerows and trees onto the soft earth beneath.

Evie closed her diary and tucked it under the mattress, after which she lay back, a towel still round her wet hair, staring up at the ceiling in the dark. She couldn't stop smiling. This was the second time they had managed an illicit meeting. It had been so easy. No one noticed her absence. All was peaceful at home in contrast to the escalation of the number of attacks by the Luftwaffe over southern England. Her parents were too tired to notice when she came and went as long as she completed her chores. There had been no new land girl to help, but the harvest was over now and safely in, and life on the farm was calming down a bit. She just prayed that the Germans didn't start night raids in this part of the country.

Tomorrow would see her first visit to the Woolston factory in Southampton to sketch the girls working on Spitfire parts. She had been given a special permit to go there. Inside she was fluttering with nerves. If she carried off this commission and pleased the Committee she would with luck be offered another assignment, but her dream was to be allowed to go officially to Westhampnett and paint the pilots and their planes. Until then she was going to have to make do with a few hasty visits now and then, never knowing if she was going to see Tony. To make up for the frequent disappointments of not being allowed officially to paint the men waiting with their planes for the call to take off for yet another sortie she made do with the excitement of painting the battles high above in the air. She drew them as a network of vapour trails and smoke and fire, high above the Sussex Downs. But now, with her own private assignations in the dark of the summer nights, that was enough. With a gleeful wriggle she snuggled down into her bed and closed her eyes. Her whole body was alive with the thrill of making love to Tony. At the moment her life was good.

Friday 26th July

Lucy was sitting at the table in the studio at Rosebank when Dolly came in. The latter stood for several seconds watching as Lucy tapped away at her laptop entering a sequence of dates. She stopped at last, saved her entries and looked up. 'I am beginning to work out a definite framework here.'

'That is good.' Dolly stood looking mesmerised. 'Do you think you will have enough to write a proper book about her?'

On Tuesday Dolly had waited in an agony of anticipation, for Lucy to appear, her shopping basket on the chair in the kitchen. In it the diaries and the old log book were almost burning a hole through the paper bag in which she had wrapped them. Her heart was thudding uncertainly. She had almost changed her mind about giving them to Lucy when there had been no sign of her earlier in the week and Dolly had lugged them all the way home on the bus rather than leave them in the cottage. And now Lucy was here but she had arrived late and in the interim there had been a phone call from Mr Michael announcing that he and Charlotte Thingy were on their way down and would be here by lunchtime.

Scrutinising Lucy's face, Dolly noted the exhaustion there and the sadness in Lucy's eyes and forgave her for not coming in on Tuesday, but her impatience and anguish were still very real.

Lucy looked up, suddenly aware of Dolly's distress. 'What is it? Is there something wrong?' Dolly was clutching a paper bag which looked as though it contained books.

Dolly put the bundle down in front of her. 'Evie's diaries. As I promised.'

Lucy stared down at the packet in sudden excitement. 'Oh, Dolly. You don't know what this means to me.' She reached for them and began to open the paper bag. 'You haven't read them I think you said?'

Dolly shook her head. 'It wasn't my place.'

In the bag were three hardback notebooks, one with a blue cover, one green and one red, all shabby and well thumbed, perhaps old-fashioned quarto in size. Lucy extricated them carefully from the wrapping and, pushing aside her laptop, laid them side by side on the table in front of her.

She reached for the red one and opened it carefully. The book was ruled with narrow lines but it was not printed up as a diary. Evie had entered her own dates at the head of each new entry. Her writing was free flowing, hasty, almost excited,

181

cramped in places, in others spilling over the constraint of the lines on which it was written as if impatient of the limitations put on it by the format of the page. In places there were little sketches. Lucy caught her breath hardly able to breathe for excitement. She turned towards the end of the book where the last few pages were blank. The last heading was 8th November 2000. The writing here was weaker. For the first time it seemed aimless and tired. 'Just a few days before she died,' she said gently as she looked up at Dolly.

Dolly nodded bleakly. 'I put it away for her in the chest of drawers in her bedroom with the other one. That is how I knew where they were. I tucked them under some of her clothes.'

Lucy turned back to the book and read. 'The weather is bad again. The light is still too bad to paint even if I had the energy. Johnny is coming tomorrow with Juliette and Michael. It will be good to see them. I hope I am strong enough to get up. This wretched cough is no better.'

That was it. Her last entry. Lucy looked up trying to hide the sudden rush of emotion which threatened to overwhelm her. 'Johnny was Michael's father, that's right isn't it?'

Dolly nodded. 'What does she say?' In spite of her resolution not to read the thing she was clearly dying of curiosity.

'She was waiting for a visit from Johnny and Juliette and Michael.'

Dolly nodded. 'Juliette is Mr Michael's mother. A wonderful lady. She and Evie were very fond of each other.' She sighed and sat down abruptly on the only other chair at the table. She took a deep breath. 'Evie died three days later, after I put the diary away for her. '

Lucy was silent for a few moments. She closed the diary, sitting for a while, lost in thought, with her hand on the cover. 'I don't think I realised Michael's mother was still alive?' she said cautiously at last.

'Oh, yes. His father died two years ago and she went to live in Brighton.'

Lucy frowned. There was so much of Evie's life still to catch up with. Neither Michael nor Dolly had thought to mention that Michael's mother was still around, a woman who must have known Evie well.

'Would I be able to go and see her?' she asked at last. Aware of their reaction to her suggestion that she meet Christopher she was careful to keep the urgency out of her voice.

'You would have to ask Mr Michael. I don't see why not. She married again, you know.'

No, I don't know! Lucy almost said it out loud. She hid her exasperation with an effort. 'I'll ask him when I see him next.'

Dolly's face darkened as she suddenly remembered the phone call. 'I forgot to say, he rang just now to say he is on his way back. He's taking the day off. With Charlotte Thingy. He'll be here by lunchtime.'

They looked at each other. Lucy made a sudden decision. 'I think if she is going to be here I might just take myself home. It won't be a good time to talk to him about Evie and I can just as easily enter this stuff there. Besides, I would love to read the diaries undisturbed.'

Dolly nodded. 'You don't want her to see them. If she realises how valuable they are she might just want to get her hands on them.'

Lucy looked up and held her gaze. The same thought had occurred to her, although she had been too tactful to say so. 'Would you like me to give you a lift home, Dolly?' she asked suddenly. 'We could leave the cottage to them.'

She could see the longing in Dolly's eyes but at last the old lady shook her head. 'He is expecting to see me. I had better wait and give them some lunch. It is kind of you to offer, but I wouldn't like them to think I had left early.'

Lucy nodded. She stood up and began to pack away the laptop and the diaries in her bag together with a couple of files of letters. She tidied the table and reached for her jacket.

'I'll see you on Tuesday then,' she smiled. 'And thank you, Dolly. This means a lot to me.'

They left the studio together. Dolly went back into the cottage and Lucy cut across the grass towards the front gate. As she ran down the steps Mike and Charlotte appeared in the distance at the top of the lane. She cursed under her breath. There was no way of avoiding them. Mike usually left his car, she had discovered, in an improvised parking place further up the lane. She walked towards them, her bag on her shoulder.

'Hello. I was afraid I was going to miss you,' she managed to greet them cheerfully.

Mike made the introductions. It turned out that Charlotte Thingy was called Ponsonby. Too posh for Dolly, obviously. Lucy suppressed a small smile. The two women eyed each other and Lucy felt a small lurch of envy as she took in Charlotte's elegant summer dress and designer sandals. Her hair was immaculate and her overnight bag expensive.

Charlotte inclined her head. 'So, you are the lady researcher I have heard so much about. We saw each other I think the first time you came to see Michael but since then you've become quite mysterious, flitting to and fro to the studio unseen.'

Lucy gave a cold smile. 'I've been here most days. It is a fascinating project. I am so grateful to Michael for helping me.'

'And I to you for encouraging him to clear this old place out.' Charlotte gave Mike an arch look, which, as far as Lucy could see, he did not altogether appreciate. She saw Charlotte eye her own bag curiously. She was probably making a fashion judgement. Shabby, cheap and serviceable, Lucy thought with a secret smile.

'Well, I must be on my way,' she said. 'I am sorry not to be able to stay and talk but this was just a lightning visit to pick up a couple of files.'

'We'll speak on the phone,' Mike said suddenly. It was as if he hadn't been there up to now and he wanted to remind her of his presence.

Lucy nodded. 'Of course. Dolly is inside waiting for you.' She raised her hand in farewell and set off up the lane, aware that they were both standing watching her. She hoped her anxiety to leave had not been too obvious. Hitching the bag with its precious cargo higher onto her shoulder she headed for her car.

On the way home she picked up some food for lunch from a deli near the Cross and she and Robin shared it at the table in the back garden. Twice the bell on the gallery door rang and Robin disappeared, wiping his fingers on a piece of torn off kitchen roll, to attend to a customer, one who merely wanted to ask directions to the cathedral, the other to buy a birthday card from their small rack of old master reproductions by the door. He looked heavenward after the second interruption, rolling his eyes theatrically. 'I wish they would go away. I am tempted to put the "Closed" sign up on the door.'

Lucy grinned. 'Don't you dare. Even two pounds fifty is worth having these days. And the lost tourist might have a rich aunt who is dying to buy a local watercolour.'

He laughed. 'Fair enough. I'll hold the fort while you get on with your research.'

She had forced herself to wait before unpacking the diaries when she got home, she wasn't sure why. It was like waiting to open her Christmas presents when she was a child. She had looked forward to the moment for so long, then at the last second she would sit staring at all the exciting packages putting off the actual act of opening as long as possible to prolong the anticipation.

She paused as she walked into the sitting room and listened. Silence. It was always there now, the slight frisson in the air, the feeling that she was not alone, that any minute someone would appear. She refused to let it get to her. She was not going to be chased out of her own home. Besides, Robin was down-stairs, sitting on the old leather chair at the back of the gallery, reading.

Carefully she pulled the paper bag out of her tote and laid

it on the table in front of the window. Her heart was thudding with excitement. All the notebooks were worn and faded, the red one she had already glanced at less so than the others. She pulled them gently out of the bag and lined them up in front of her. The green book was not a diary at all, she now realised. She had been looking at the back, which was a plain shabby green. She stared at the cover.

ROYAL AIR FORCE

VOL 1

PILOT'S FLYING
LOG BOOK

P/O
Name ~~SERGEANT~~ A. ANDERSON

Lucy frowned. She opened the book. Inside the cover someone had pasted a typewritten sheet of instructions, the first of which read: ALL ENTRIES ARE TO BE MADE IN BLOCK CAPITALS. On the opposite page the heading read CERTIFICATES OF QUALIFICATION AS FIRST PILOT. Underneath P/O A. Anderson had filled in his name, beneath which was a large question mark. She smiled and turned the page. Starting in March 1940, the book was a list of A. Anderson's training flights, his practices and, stamped and signed, his qualifications as he made his way through his training as a fighter pilot. Lucy frowned. So who was he? Why did Evie have his log book? Was he a friend of Ralph's? She flipped through the pages as day by day he progressed from an aircraft called a Cadet, which seemed apt, to a Hart, to a Hind. He was learning low flying, spinning, he recorded his first solo flight. She moved on. There it was. His first solo flight in a Spitfire. So he was a friend of Ralph's. She studied the details more closely. He was based in Drem. She frowned. Where was that? Turning over another page she saw the entry: *To Westhampnett* and suddenly the right-hand pages of the log book, which up to now had been more or less blank, were full of comments, scrawled in a large loopy hand, and definitely not in block capitals as instructed, detailing each day's activities. She squinted at the first entry.

Met lots of Me 110s over Dorset coast. One fired at, went down steeply with smoke from one engine. Tried to follow but too fast. (about 520 E.A.S) Turned and pulled out and saw red flash and explosion on ground. Think it was probably c/a crashing.

This was an actual blow by blow account of the Battle of Britain. Fascinated, she turned over page after page as he described sweeps and patrols, recording the heights he had flown, the weather and the encounters with the enemy: *the highest yet over Dungeness at 29,500 feet; half roll at 18,000 feet above Portsmouth and dived to sea level; circling 110s 10 miles south of Beachy Head pooping at intervals.* Lucy smiled. Presumably he meant shooting. *Got white smoke from one engine. Believe I damaged him a bit. 3 bullets collected here.* The record went on, day after day with as far as she could see very little let-up. At the end of each month the pages were stamped by the squadron leader and on the following pages the record went on.

There was nothing personal in the record beyond the occasional comment about his feelings during the action, lines of exclamation marks and underlinings. She smiled. She was getting the impression that P/O A. Anderson was an extrovert young man with a good sense of humour and, it almost went without saying, very, very brave. She closed the book to look at again later in more detail and reached for the blue-backed diary, recognising Evie's writing at once in the close packed pages. The first entry was dated August 22nd 1940. *Went with Ralph to The Unicorn this evening and met several young RAF officers*

187

including his CO. Nice boys. One <u>particularly</u> irritating chap called Tony Anderson.

Lucy stopped reading. A. Anderson. Anthony. Tony. Bingo. She found herself wondering suddenly if he was the young man in the portrait. It felt right. His face, his smile, his whole demeanour suited the exuberant loopy handwriting of the log book, and the underlining in Evie's entry, the selection of one man to mention by name, even if it was to be rude about him. That surely hinted at the fact that she was smitten.

Lucy turned the page and began to read on.

12

October 1st 1940

When Ralph next came up to the farm he found Evie in the dairy scouring the empty buckets

He stood watching her for a minute reluctant to interrupt. She looked preoccupied but content as she finished the job and dried her hands on a towel by the sink. She turned and saw him. 'Rafie!'

'Hi, Sis.'

Her smile of welcome faded as she studied his face. 'What is it?'

He said nothing for a moment then he held out his hand. 'Come for a walk. There is something I need to say.'

He saw her face grow pale as she followed him out into the yard and through the gate up to the fields. 'Is it Tony? Has something happened to him?'

'Nothing has happened to him,' he said calmly, 'but it is about Tony, yes.'

He wasn't sure about this at all. Eddie had singled him out in The Unicorn a couple of evenings before and sat him down at a table in the corner.

'This has to stop,' he had said. His face was hard. 'You realise that Tony Anderson is ruining your sister's life. She has this one chance to make a career as a painter and he is getting in the way. He will spoil everything for her.'

Ralph had been sceptical. 'Oh, come on, old boy,' he had blustered. 'That's a bit strong, surely. She's young. She is bound to have boyfriends.' And then he had seen his mistake. Eddie's face had darkened, his eyes narrowing as he surveyed Ralph's face.

'I warned her,' Eddie went on quietly. 'But she chose to ignore everything I said. She seems to take me for a fool.'

Ralph paused for a moment or two, studying Evie's face. 'Someone has reported Tony for being back after midnight several times after coming up here. The CO has had a word with him. It's not on. And it's not going to happen again.'

'Eddie!' she said. 'It was Eddie, wasn't it?' Her cheeks had blushed scarlet.

Ralph was going to deny it, but he could see she had already made up her mind. 'I don't know, Sis, but I suspect it might have been,' he said with a sigh. 'The CO says he doesn't want to see you down at the airfield again. I know things lightened up for a bit, but no more. They are expecting a huge attack any minute. They want all the boys there, on full alert. It's for Tony's own good, Evie, you know it is. If any of us loses concentration for even a minute it could be fatal. Leave it for now.' He thought back in anguish to the previous evening.

To his surprise he had found a message at the Mess from his father. Dudley had suggested that he and his son meet for a drink in Chichester when Ralph next had a few hours off. They were seated in the corner of the pub before two untouched tankards of beer when Dudley fixed Ralph with a miserable stare. 'I can't tell Evie this, Ralph. I can't tell either of them. Rachel would kill me.' He gave a sad smile. 'And Evie.' He paused for several seconds. 'Truth is, I had a spot of bother a while back.' He glanced up at his son. 'Didn't want to trouble you with it. The tractor and things. They cost a bit. I borrowed some money. Couldn't pay it back.' He reached for his glass and raised it with a shaking hand as he scanned Ralph's face and looked away. His son had gone white. 'Eddie knew about it. Don't know how, but he offered to lend me some money to get me out of hock. He,' he hesitated again, 'he wants the money back. He says he only lent it because he thought he and Evie would marry one day and he would have an interest in the farm. He is threatening to tell everyone about the debts. Destroy my good name.'

'Jesus Christ!' Ralph muttered. 'Why didn't you tell me we didn't have the money for the tractor?'

Dudley shook his head. 'Pride, I suppose. Eddie said there was no need to pay it back.' He shook his head. 'He wants Tony out of Evie's life. He will make trouble for the boy as well as us if we don't arrange it.'

There was a long silence. At last Ralph reached for his beer and took a long draught.

'Just tell her, son. Tell her Tony doesn't care for her. Anything. Just get her to end it.' Dudley sounded near to tears. 'I can't do it. I can't bear it. She loves the boy, anyone can see that.'

Ralph sat staring down into his glass for a moment. 'So, it's a trade-off. Your good name or your daughter's happiness,' he said softly.

His father looked up, his face crumpled with unhappiness. 'Tony's safety is at stake,' he whispered.

'Oh, come on.'

'Eddie has contacts. I believe him. He could make good his threats. Please, Ralph. Do this for Evie and the boy.'

There was another long pause, then at last Ralph reached forward and put his hand over his father's for a moment. 'I'll do what I can,' he murmured.

And now here he was facing Evie, about to tell the biggest lie of his life. 'Tony has told me he doesn't actually want to come up here any more anyway.'

'He said that?' She stared at him aghast.

Ralph bit his lip. Then he nodded. 'He said that.'

'Why didn't he say it to me? I'd have understood.'

Ralph was taken aback for a moment. 'Of course you would. Maybe he just couldn't bear to disappoint you. Or maybe,' he took a deep breath and plunged on, 'maybe he just isn't as keen as you are, sweetheart.'

There was a long silence. She turned away from him and when she spoke he could hear the tremor in her voice.

'Did he tell you that too?'

'Not in so many words, but underneath I think that is what he meant. He didn't want to hurt you, Evie.'

'How silly.' Her voice had grown thin and shrill. He could see her clenching her fists. 'As if I would be hurt. He was just a fling. A silly boy who was fun to be with.' She began to make her way back down the track.

'Evie –'

She ignored him, walking fast, her head high.

He stood still and watched as she pulled the headscarf off and shook her hair free in the wind. Her pace increased until she was running. He saw her reach the gate and drag it open. It swung shut behind her and she disappeared across the yard in the direction of the dairy.

'You shit, Ralph Lucas,' Ralph whispered to himself out loud. 'You have just broken your sister's heart.'

Saturday 3rd August

It turned out that Dolly had known Christopher Marston's address all the time. She was reluctant to pass it on, but in the end caved in to Lucy's persuasive argument that without it no progress could be made.

Lucy decided to risk calling in unannounced. If she telephoned and he hung up on her then short of climbing in through a window she would have shot herself in the foot with no fall-back plan. This way, at worst, she would at least see in through the front door, at best be invited in to talk, or given an appointment to return.

The house was close to Midhurst, about ten miles north of Chichester. Parking her car in a lay-by, next to a stile which looked as though it hadn't been used for many years, Lucy walked up the shadowy lane towards the substantial gates which led to Cornstone House. To her surprise they were open. Taking a deep breath she began to walk towards the house which was out of sight round a bend planted with evergreen shrubs. The house was smaller than she had expected but elegant and beautifully maintained, built of old red bricks and hung tiles beneath a mellow uneven roof.

The gardens on either side of the drive were carefully laid out and the lawns neatly mown. There were no cars outside and the place was very silent. Damn! She had chosen Saturday afternoon especially in the hope that the family would be at home, reasoning that if Christopher was a banker he would commute to London during the week. Of course the opposite might apply; perhaps they had all gone out together.

She didn't allow herself to hesitate. She mounted the steps to the door and tugged at the rustic bell pull. There was a faint chime from somewhere deep in the house followed by the sound of a dog barking.

She eased her bag on her shoulder uncomfortably trying to calm her nerves and was reaching for the bell a second time when she heard footsteps from behind the door. It was pulled open by a thin tall woman with elegantly styled hair and beautifully cut shirt and trousers. Behind her an elderly black Labrador wagged its tail slowly back and forth. Lucy found herself wondering if the dog was the only one who was going to welcome her.

She forced herself to smile, holding out her hand. 'Hello, I'm Lucy Standish. I wonder if I could have a word with Christopher. I'm sorry to drop in unannounced, but I was passing your door.' It could be possible she supposed. The road on which she had parked was fairly busy for a country lane.

If this was Christopher's wife she was obviously as hostile as he presumably was. The woman made no attempt to shake her hand. Her eyes were cold and hard as she surveyed Lucy.

193

'I suppose one of you was bound to turn up one day,' she said. 'Well, I'm sorry to disappoint you but he is out.'

The door was already closing in Lucy's face and reflexively she put her hand out to stop it. 'Please, give me a moment.'

To her surprise the woman didn't try and make it a trial of strength. She removed her hand from the door. 'What can you possibly have to say to me?' Her voice was quiet, well modulated, but flat.

'May I come in?' Lucy moved forward slightly. 'I think your husband may have got the wrong idea about me and I wanted to explain.' It was a guess that this was his wife but the woman didn't contradict her.

She narrowed her eyes. 'I doubt if he got the wrong idea about you at all, my dear,' she said grimly. 'He normally knows exactly what he is doing.'

'No, he doesn't.' Lucy edged forward again.

The woman's eyebrows shot up. 'I'm almost inclined to listen to you. You're certainly not his usual type,' she said. There was a slight curl to her lip which Lucy resented even more than her tone of voice.

'His usual type?' Lucy echoed. 'Oh Lord,' she gave an embarrassed giggle, 'I think we are talking at cross purposes. Please, can I start again? I have never met Christopher. I don't know him at all. I am a friend of his cousin, Mike. I am so sorry; I don't know your name.' She paused, hoping desperately that the woman would fill in the information, but her words were greeted with silence and Lucy suspected suddenly that Christopher's wife was as embarrassed as she was herself. 'I am writing a biography of their grandmother, Evelyn. '

Slowly the woman raised her hands to her face and rubbed them slowly over her cheeks.

'I am so sorry. I –' She broke off and turned away. 'I thought you were someone else.' She took a deep breath and faced Lucy again. 'What did you say your name was?'

'Lucy Standish.'

'Christopher hasn't mentioned you. He and Mike don't see much of each other these days.' She gave Lucy a long frank look and then seemed to make up her mind. 'You had better come in. Christopher is away for the weekend.'

She ushered Lucy in and closed the door behind her.

Lucy stood staring round. The hall was wood-panelled, the stone floor covered by a large Persian rug. Two oak chairs stood on either side of a small table near the foot of the staircase, but what she was looking at were the two paintings hung facing each other on the walls. They were unmistakably Evelyn Lucases and they were paintings she didn't recognise from any catalogue. She paused in front of one of them. It was one of Evie's later works, modernist, bright, full of the colours of summer.

She realised suddenly that Christopher's wife had stopped and was watching her. 'I like that one,' she said. 'It's one of my favourites. It lights up the hall.'

The painting opposite it was darker, a depiction of tangled branches and tortured cloud. Following Lucy's gaze as she turned to study it the woman shuddered. 'And I hate that one. I think it must have been painted when she was feeling very miserable.'

Lucy nodded. They could certainly agree on that point. She followed the woman through a door at the end of the hall, pleased to see sunlight pouring through the windows on that side of the house.

'I'm Frances, by the way.' Christopher's wife waved her towards a seat beside one of the windows. The room was comfortably but formally furnished with old oriental rugs on the ancient floorboards and expensive-looking matching armchairs and sofas casually arranged around a glass-topped coffee table stacked with magazines. The curtains were draped in pale green brocade which picked out the background colour of the fabric on the chairs. She sat down opposite Lucy, leaning forward anxiously.

'When you arrived you said that Christopher might have got the wrong idea about you,' she said. 'Why did you say that?'

Lucy was silent for a moment, wondering how frank she could

be with this woman who clearly had issues with her husband's fidelity if nothing else. 'I am not sure myself,' she said at last. 'I gather he contacted Mike and told him to warn me off. I think he must have heard about my project from Elizabeth Chappell who lives in Box Wood Farm where Evie's parents lived. I went to see her recently. I want to know why he should object to me writing about Evie. I need his help. I don't want him to get the wrong idea about me or my motives. I have a genuine interest in women war artists and I have been given a grant to pursue my research.'

Frances dropped her gaze to her own hands which were clasped in her lap. 'You will never get him to help you with a book about Evie,' she said after a long pause. She looked up at Lucy, her face suddenly compassionate. 'I am sorry. I'm not sure myself what went on in the family but I think there were some terrible rows. The brothers didn't get on. Christopher's father and Michael's – Evie's sons – they couldn't stand each other. But,' she stopped for a moment, 'that doesn't explain why Chris would object. You say Mike knows all about it?'

Lucy nodded. 'He is giving me as much help as he can, but I understand that Christopher inherited all her diaries and working notes. I would dearly love to be able to read them.'

Frances's mouth turned down. It was an enormously eloquent expression which made Lucy's heart sink. 'I shouldn't think he would let you do that,' Frances went on. 'As I said, I don't know what lies behind his suspicions but he is very possessive about his grandmother.'

Lucy sighed.

'I would show them to you if I knew where they were, but I think he put them in the bank,' Frances went on. 'He probably thinks they will be worth a fortune one day.'

'Then you would think he would foster any publicity which might accrue through my book,' Lucy said bitterly.

'You would, wouldn't you?' Frances leaned forward. 'Have you got a camera?' She looked suddenly eager.

Lucy nodded. 'In my bag.'

'You could take some pictures of the paintings at least. Would that help? He'd kill me if he found out, but he won't, will he? Or at least, if he does it won't be for a long time. If you promise not to tell him, I'll take the dog in the garden for half an hour or so. We'll enjoy the sunshine and you can whizz round and take some snaps. Her pictures are all downstairs except for a couple of small ones in our bedroom. That's on the right at the top of the stairs.'

Lucy stared at her. 'Are you sure? I don't want you to get into trouble.'

Frances gave a grim smile. 'Maybe this is payback time. Christopher is a bully and a cheat. Don't quote me. One of these days I will pluck up enough courage to leave him. Doing something subversive like this will give me a few moments of intense pleasure.' Standing up, she called the dog and walked towards the French windows. Letting herself out, she strode across the lawn without a backward glance.

Lucy watched her for a moment, then she dived into her bag and brought out her small digital camera. Her hands were shaking with excitement.

There were six paintings in the room in which they had been sitting. She had been surreptitiously looking at them as they talked. Two large oils, a pair of small watercolours between the windows, and two gouache landscapes. She made her way back into the hall and studied the two large paintings there, then went on into the dining room which had a row of silverpoint etchings on one wall and two unframed oils on the opposite side of the room. There were more paintings in a second sitting room and two in the breakfast room which led off the large kitchen. Climbing the stairs, she found three more on the landing as well as the two Frances had mentioned in their bedroom. She paused for a moment there to look round at the neat formal room. It was elegant but impersonal. This was not a room where people left things lying about. There were no clothes on view, no books by the bed, no make-up scattered on the antique dressing table. She wondered if anyone slept there at all. She glanced into some of the other rooms but Frances was right, there was no sign of any more paintings.

That made about thirty, she reckoned. She could feel the excitement building inside her. That was twice as many as all the so-far recorded Lucases. There must be more. Portfolios, sketchbooks, notebooks. Perhaps they were with the diaries in the bank. But this was an amazing start. None of the paintings had attributions or titles on them, but Evie's style was so distinct she had no difficulty identifying them. Several were signed – she could see the famous scrawl – but the others might have labels or inscriptions on the back. She glanced at the two in the bedroom where she stood, longingly wondering if she had time to lift one off the wall and examine it more closely. It was more than half an hour since Frances had gone out. She went over to the door and listened for a moment. There was no sound from downstairs. Hurrying back to the wall, she lifted down one of the paintings and turned it over. There was a label on the back. In Evie's writing it said, *This picture is for Dolly, Thanks for taking care of me so selflessly over the years.* Lucy stared at it. So Christopher knew the paintings were for Dolly. He had had no excuse for taking them. Disgusted, she laid the picture on the bed and took a close-up photo of the instruction, then she carefully replaced the picture on its hook.

She heard a scrabbling sound from downstairs – the dog's claws on the stone floor of the hall – and she headed towards the door. Frances had walked back into the drawing room.

'Thank you so much –' Lucy began.

Frances raised her hand. 'I know nothing about it,' she said firmly. 'Please. Forget it. Now go, please. Christopher will be back soon.'

'But I thought you said –'

'I lied. I didn't know who you were.' Frances suddenly looked frightened.

Lucy nodded. She hurriedly slipped the camera back into her bag. 'I'll go at once. I'm sorry.'

Frances nodded. 'Yes, go. Now. Please don't come again. I won't recognise you if you do.'

Lucy bit back a protest. 'Of course. I understand. I am really grateful for everything.' She backed away towards the door, suddenly nervous that Christopher would appear from nowhere. There was no sign of anyone however as she made for the front door. Frances had not followed her so after a moment's hesitation and a final longing glance around the hall she let herself out and made her way quickly down the drive.

As she began to walk up the lane towards her car a large black Audi turned in to the gate behind her. It slowed to a halt and the driver lowered the window to stare after her, before driving on between the gate posts and up towards the house.

October 5th 1940

Ralph walked slowly towards the gallery and stopped, peering in the window. It was hard to see through the strips of anti-blast tape but there was a statuette on a table in the middle of the room and paintings all around the walls. His interest had been caught by the oil painting standing on an easel in the window. It was one of Evie's. And this time the gallery was open.

David Fuller, the owner, looked up from his desk, saw the RAF uniform and, visibly disappointed, gave him a less than enthusiastic nod. 'Can I help you, sir?'

Ralph smiled. 'I see you have correctly guessed I am not a customer.'

Fuller stood up looking slightly abashed. He was an elderly man, balding with grey eyes and round wire-framed spectacles. 'I am sorry. One should never make assumptions. You might be an art collector.'

Ralph shook his head. 'No, you are right. I am not an art collector. But I am the brother of an artist. Evelyn Lucas to be exact.'

Fuller's face lit up. 'In which case you are more than welcome.

Did you see her wonderful painting in the window? And there are some smaller ones over here.' He was already heading towards the far wall, indicating a group of pictures near the French doors at the back of the room. 'I had been hoping Evie would find the time to come in and see us.' The man was, Ralph now saw, in his late seventies at least. His eyes were twinkling with enthusiasm. 'I know the dear girl has been picked for the War Artists and I am so pleased for her. That of course is why her pictures command such a good price although she is so young. If Sir Kenneth Clark thinks she is good, then that is recommendation enough for the people of Chichester.'

Ralph had stopped in front of the line of small watercolours and stared at the price stickers. The bastard! Eddie was even now taking her for a ride. 'How much is the one in the window?' he asked.

His warm smile had visibly charmed the old gentleman. 'That is expensive. Ten guineas,' David Fuller said. 'But worth every penny. I do hope she is pleased with the amount she is making.'

Ralph was still getting over the shock of the price. 'And you think you will get that much?' he asked incredulously.

'Of course. We got more for her picture of the birds in the harbour at Bosham but that was a larger composition and birds are always a popular subject. Didn't she tell you?' He looked anxious suddenly, obviously wondering if he had betrayed her confidence.

'She probably did.' Ralph managed a grin. 'I've been a bit busy. I'm sure you can imagine. I promised her I would look in here and I haven't had the chance up to now, or at least not when you were open but finally I have a day's leave so I thought I would call in.' He was finding it hard to keep his smile in place. Eddie was a lying, thieving bastard! How much money had he conned Evie out of, exactly? He must take them all for a bunch of ignorant fools, watching Evie come in from milking, patronising her, encouraging her, seeing off poor old Tony. He knew he wouldn't be able to hide his fury much longer. He glanced at his wristwatch. 'I must go,' he said, managing another rueful smile. 'I'm on my way to see my parents and I promised my mother I would be home in time for a meal and I am on the slow ride today.' They both looked at the window where Ralph had left his borrowed bike defiantly leaning against the glass. His Morgan was back on the aerodrome with a puncture.

Outside he took a deep breath and he stood gazing up at the cathedral spire, trying to calm his anger. Next time he saw Eddie it would be very hard not to lose his temper.

Monday 5th August

'Huw!' Lucy was sitting by the table in her small upstairs sitting room. Beside her was Evie's diary, lying open beside the telephone. She had sat staring at the looped writing veering across the page for several minutes before reaching for her phone. 'I have discovered the connection between Ralph and this place. He did come here. It was an art gallery during the war. They sold Evie's paintings here. Isn't that the most incredible coincidence?'

Rafie had a day's leave today and Mummy made us a rabbit casserole. She was so looking forward to seeing him but it was all spoilt when he came in absolutely <u>furious</u>. He had been to the gallery in Chi and said that Eddie was <u>still robbing me</u>. They are charging a great deal of money for my paintings and Eddie hasn't passed it on to me. I have <u>never</u> seen R so angry. He said he was sorry for spoiling our day – Mummy and D were upset too – but he had to tell me. I don't know what to do. If I make Eddie too angry he will stop helping me get commissions.

'I wanted to tell you as soon as I read it,' Lucy went on. 'It explains why he is here, why he is haunting this place.'

'That is an amazing coincidence,' Huw said thoughtfully. 'Are you sure it is the same gallery?'

'Fuller. She mentions the name Fuller. I thought I remembered it and looked it up in the file. When we applied to turn this into an art gallery we were able to say it had been one before, during the war. It was a tea shop when we came here. I remembered the names. David and Vera Fuller; they were there in the papers we were sent when we bought it.'

'I see.' There was a pause. 'That could explain a lot, Lucy. It gives you another connection, although I have to say I still think the painting is the trigger point here.'

Lucy frowned. 'So you don't think it is important?' She could hear the disappointment in her own voice.

'I do, yes. As you say, it establishes a physical link. But there must be more to it than that. There must be a strong emotional reason for him haunting the place. I still think it is more likely to do with the painting you have. You haven't seen him again, I take it?'

Lucy shook her head then remembered she was on the phone. 'No. Nothing,' she said out loud. She hesitated, then took the plunge. 'Well, yes, actually. I had a dreadful nightmare. It was so real. It was about Larry, my husband, and his car crash. I wanted to ring you, but then I thought it wasn't anything to do with Ralph. But I think it was in some way.' She could hear herself talking faster and faster. 'It was as if the two were connected. But they're not. They can't be. I can't get the crash out of my head. These dreams go on and on, but this was the worst I've had.'

'Would you like me to come over so we can talk about it?' He sounded gentle now.

Trying to calm herself, she gave a wry little smile. His counselling side had kicked in. He was obviously good at it. 'I don't want to take up your time. It's not as though I am one of your parishioners.'

'No, but in a sense Ralph is.' She could hear the smile in his voice. 'I don't actually need you to be a parishioner, Lucy. If you need someone to talk to, then I will come.'

She hadn't realised he meant straightaway. Only an hour later he was seated opposite her and Evie's diary was lying open between them.

'I don't always come at once,' he said when she commented

on his speedy service. 'I am often so busy I think the Lord made the days at least a hundred per cent too short just to test us, but today you were lucky I am in flying vicar mode.'

She laughed. 'I'm impressed.'

Picking up the diary, he closed it and held it for a moment with both hands, his eyes shut. Her smile died on her lips as she watched him and she found herself feeling uncomfortable, sensing something was happening from which she was excluded, something she didn't, couldn't understand. She wanted to ask what he was doing, to take the book away from him, to turn and glance over her shoulder in case he was summoning Ralph back from the past but she didn't dare move. She hardly dared breathe. When at last he opened his eyes and put the book down she went on sitting without moving or speaking for several seconds. Then at last she took a deep breath.

'Were you praying?'

He smiled. 'In a way. I was waiting for a sense of the woman who wrote it.'

'And did you get it?' Her question was so quick and so needy she was embarrassed.

He nodded slowly. 'I think so, yes.'

'Tell me.'

He rested his hand back on the book, his palm flat. He was, she noticed for the first time, wearing a gold wedding ring. 'When she wrote this she was young, emotional, full of excitement and full of dread. I suspect you can tell that by reading what she has written, but I feel she turned to her diary when she was in trouble. I sense that years later she would take out this same diary and clutch it to her breast like a talisman, not opening it, not reading it, just holding it as though it contained the essence of something very precious which had been lost to her.'

'Ralph,' Lucy murmured.

'Maybe.'

'I haven't read it all yet,' she said. 'Tempting though it is, I didn't want to skip and see what happened at the end of the year so I am reading it carefully page by page, making notes as I go. It covers everything in her life. The Sussex cows she milked, the paintings she worked on, her mother and father, air raids and the Battle of Britain, her boyfriend, Eddie, and then the new one, the young man she met at the pub, Tony. I think he may be the RAF pilot in the picture.'

'And Ralph?'

'There isn't much about Ralph, to be honest. He was stationed at Tangmere and came home whenever he could. But then today I read this bit about Ralph having a day's leave and going to the gallery in Chichester – this gallery – and finding out that Eddie, that's her official boyfriend, was ripping her off. The paintings even then were fetching high prices and he was only giving her a fraction of the value.'

'Agent's commission, eh?'

'Something like that. He sounds a bit of a Flash Harry to me. He bullies her and blackmails her by reminding her that he is the one who introduced her to the War Artists Advisory Committee. She is ambitious and has plans to be a famous painter, even then, and he is the key to her fulfilling that dream.'

'And how does Ralph feel about her painting?'

She looked thoughtful. 'Up to now she hasn't mentioned him in that context. The entries only say that she is worried or that her parents are. Her mother was frantic, as every mother in the country must have been with their children in the forces. Reading this is bringing the war alive for me, Huw. They stood there in the garden or in the fields looking up and they could see people being killed above their heads. See planes spiralling down and crashing in flames, know there was no escape for the pilot –' She broke off trying to suppress a sob.

Huw reached across and put his hand over hers. 'Don't be afraid to cry, my dear. Cry for those boys, and most of them were only boys, who were killed, and for Ralph and for your Larry.'

'They're mixed up in my head,' she said slowly. 'The crashing planes and the crashing car.'

He nodded. 'Maybe.'

'And in the diary Ralph is going to crash. But she doesn't know it yet.'

Huw sighed. 'I fear so.'

'Aren't you going to tell me not to read any more?'

'No.'

'You think I should go on?'

'Of course you must go on. You are writing a book about Evie. However emotionally involved you are becoming, you are a professional writer. And your own nightmares have a message for you, unpleasant though it is. In my experience, once you face that message the dreams will stop.' He pushed the diary across the table away from him. 'I feel that Ralph and Larry both died with unfinished conversations. You are a strong woman, Lucy. You can be there for them.'

She shook her head. 'I don't think I can do that.'

'You are not alone. I am at the end of the phone and you told me you have a good friend who helps you run the gallery who is there for you as well. I suspect he would help you at any time and I will too. At any time. Ring in the middle of the night if you are afraid. But you needn't be afraid. These are people. One of them is the man you love, the other was loved by Evie. How could they be frightening?'

She leaned back against the chair in silence. 'It is all very well you saying that here with sunlight pouring through the window,' she whispered at last. 'But in the dark, at night when I have woken to the sound of tearing metal and breaking glass? Then it is frightening.'

13

October 10th 1940

Eddie pushed the door to the gallery open and walked in. He had a package under his arm and David Fuller stood up to welcome him with a feeling of excited anticipation.

'More of Evie's?' he asked after they had exchanged greetings.

Eddie nodded. 'She gave them to me a couple of weeks ago and it is the first time I've had the chance to pick them up from the framer and bring them over here. You've sold a couple since I was here last, I see.' His keen eye had at once spotted the gaps on the wall.

David nodded. 'I was hoping you would bring some more in, otherwise I was going to rearrange the display and put some others there.' He watched eagerly as Eddie laid the parcel on the desk and began to unwrap it. 'Evie's brother came in a few days ago. Nice young man.'

Eddie stopped fumbling with the string on his parcel and stared at him. 'Ralph?'

'He didn't tell me his name. He had a day's leave and he was going home for lunch. I gather he had promised her he would look in to see her pictures on display.' He noticed Eddie's expression and recoiled slightly. 'Is there something wrong?'

'No. Of course not.' Eddie pursed his lips. He resumed picking at the knot and managed to loosen it, remove the string and coiling it neatly put it into his pocket. 'Here. What do you think of these?'

He displayed the two paintings. Both were of the farm, both were more traditional in style than her usual exuberant bright brushstrokes.

David frowned. 'I prefer her more modern approach.'

Eddie's face darkened. He had been angry when Evie produced these for him. They were makeweights, hurriedly done and thrust at him angrily when he complained that she was forgetting her promise to give him pictures to sell as well as those for the WAAC.

'Do you think you can shift them?' He tried to keep the impatience out of his voice. He was on his way somewhere else and had no time to waste.

'I'm sure I can.' David instinctively spoke soothingly. 'My older customers like more traditional stuff, but I think she is doing herself a disservice with pictures like these. I won't be able to charge so much.' He glanced at Eddie, his eyes narrowed. 'Evie's brother seemed astonished that her pictures demanded such a high price. I presume she hasn't told the family how successful she is?'

'Probably not,' Eddie responded sharply. 'It's none of their business.'

'No. Quite.' David nodded thoughtfully.

'Has anyone else from the family come in?' Eddie asked after a moment.

'If they have they haven't introduced themselves.' The old man sighed. 'I would love to meet Evie at some point. She hasn't time to come into town, I think you said?'

Both men fell abruptly silent as the air raid siren began its caterwauling wail nearby.

'Are you going to the shelter?' Eddie asked when they could hear themselves think.

David shook his head. 'The gallery and I live and die together. They haven't bombed us yet, I doubt they will. They are aiming for Southampton or Portsmouth if our boys let them through. Leave the pictures. I will let you know when I have sold more.'

He stood at the door and watched as Eddie hurried down the street, turning away from the town centre and walking swiftly to the corner before he was lost to sight. Wherever he had gone it was not to one of the city shelters.

Tuesday 6th August

'I guessed you would probably go and see him whatever I said.' Mike had swung the chair in Evie's studio to face him and was sitting astride it, leaning his arms on the back. 'So, how did he react?' He did not look pleased.

'He wasn't there.' Lucy had been surprised to find Mike at Rosebank the following day. There was no sign of either Dolly or Charlotte.

'Ah.'

'No. Good. I spoke to his wife. She was nice. She asked me in.'

'Frances?' He sounded incredulous.

'Yes, Frances. Why, is she not usually hospitable?'

He gave a cynical laugh. 'Not particularly, no. But then I haven't been to see them in a long time. So, what happened?'

'She let me look at Evie's pictures, or at least the ones hanging on the walls.' Lucy didn't mention the fact that she had photographed them, partly out of a feeling of loyalty to Frances who would get into trouble with Christopher if that fact ever emerged, and partly because she wasn't sure how Mike would react to what he might see as a breach of trust. He did not look happy about her visit. She hadn't yet worked out what she would do if she needed to use her photos in the book. Which obviously she might. He would find out then, obviously. 'They have some wonderful stuff. Pictures I've never seen in any catalogue. She thinks he has put the notebooks and sketchbooks in the bank.'

'Ah. Tricky.' He looked thoughtful. 'Are you going back to beard the lion in his den another time?'

'That is tricky too. I got the feeling that there is a huge amount of baggage there. Family rows and stuff.' She looked up at him challengingly. 'You hinted as much. Though why that should stop him wanting his grandmother's story to be told I don't know.'

'I may have hinted, but I am not sure what I hinted at,' Mike said thoughtfully. 'I know my dad didn't get on with Christopher's dad particularly well, though they were brothers.' He paused as though searching his memory. 'But even if they didn't get on that doesn't seem to point to more than the fact that he and I saw little of each other and that he seems to avoid contact with me now.'

'Dolly thinks it's because he took more than his fair share of Evie's work.'

'She's probably right. But then he wanted it so badly and I wasn't particularly interested at the time.'

'It's probably worth a fortune, Mike.'

'He's not going to sell it. And he's got kids. I haven't.'

'Not yet.' She was indignant.

He laughed bitterly. 'Careful, you sound like Charlotte. '

She blushed. 'Sorry. None of my business. Where are Dolly and Charlotte?' She quickly changed the subject.

'Dolly had to go to the dentist. I told her to take the whole day off. And Charlotte is at a conference. As I was down here on my own over the weekend I thought I would take a day or two off and give you a hand if you were here. I wanted to see how you were getting on.'

'And I hit you with the Christopher update.' She smiled

anxiously. 'Well, apart from that, I've been doing a lot of research. Evie's letters and notes are packed with clues and I'm making good progress with the chronology of her life. I sketched out a family tree too last night. Will you look at it for me and see if I've made any mistakes? There are still gaps.' She was not going to tell him about her nightmares. That was definitely none of his business.

She fished in her bag and brought out an A4 pad. On it she had drawn a pencilled family tree starting at the top with Rachel and Dudley Lucas. On the next line down came Ralph and Evie. Evie's name was bracketed with Edward Marston and beneath them came the two boys, John and George, the brothers who had quarrelled. Beneath them came Mike, son of John, and Christopher, son of George.

'Well, you can put in Frances as Chris's wife, and their two children, Hannah and Ollie.'

'There was no sign of them on Saturday.'

'Boarding school.'

'Isn't it the holidays?'

'Ah, you are probably right. In which case they will have been packed off to somewhere by the sea, I expect. In Cornwall. Or Scotland.'

She smiled. 'Don't they like their children?'

'I think children were merely part of the designer lifestyle.'

'Ooh! That's cruel.' She grimaced. 'Have any of them inherited Evie's talent?'

'Not that I've heard.' He paused. 'To go on with your family tree, there is my mum, Juliette. She remarried after dad died, but that's probably not relevant.'

'She is still part of the story, though. Would you mind if I went to see her?' Lucy glanced at him cautiously. She had begun to realise that she could take nothing for granted in this family.

'No, of course not. Why should I?'

'Well, you were pretty sure you didn't want me to talk to

Christopher.' She smiled at him. 'I would love to talk to her about Evie. Get the woman's view. Dolly told me they were very close.'

'That's true. If Evie confided in anyone it would have been my mum.' He reached into his pocket for his phone. 'Why don't I ring her now? Fix something up for you. She lives in Brighton. In fact I could drive you there if you like. I have some things I need to drop off to her.

'There's no need,' Lucy returned sharply. 'I can go on my own.'

He gave a shrug. 'As you wish. I am not going to interfere. I thought it might make it easier.'

She hesitated, then she conceded the point. After all, why not go with him. It would give her more time to talk about Evie.

Two hours later they were driving along the sea front in Mike's Discovery and turning up into the maze of Regency terraces behind the Pavilion. Juliette Bell was waiting for them at the door of a classic white-painted house in a beautiful square. Mike performed brief introductions on the doorstep, then dived back into the car to go and find a parking place as Juliette led Lucy into the cool shadows of the hallway and through into the garden at the back.

'I am so pleased someone is writing about Evie at last,' she said over her shoulder. 'It's long overdue, if you ask me.' She waved Lucy towards a reclining chair on a terrace hung with roses and poured her a glass of fruit punch. Sitting down next to her, she studied Lucy for a moment and then nodded as though satisfied with what she saw. She herself was a powerfully built woman in her late sixties with short glossy white hair held in place by sunglasses, pushed up on top of her head. She was wearing a crimson dress and her arms were weighed down with bangles. Lucy found herself wondering if she too was a painter – something artistic anyway. 'The old man, who is of course my new man, is playing golf, which seems insane in this heat,' Juliette said with a chortle of laughter, 'so he won't interrupt us, and when Mike comes back I shall send him out shopping for our supper so you and I can have a nice gossip about Evie without interruption.' She paused for a moment. 'Have you met Charlotte?' She fired the question at Lucy without preamble.

Lucy nodded. 'Briefly. I don't really know her.'

'Hmm.' Juliette's response though monosyllabic spoke volumes. 'Well, we'll leave her out of the conversation. I gather she is trying to expunge Evie's memory from the cottage so I'm even more glad you are there as a counterweight. Right,' she took a sip of her punch, 'fire away. What would you like to ask me?'

'I met Frances Marston at the weekend,' Lucy started cautiously. 'She said she thought there had been a family row of some sort, or a division at least between your husband, John, and his brother and it is because of that row, she thinks, that Christopher doesn't want anything to do with me and my research. As he inherited most of Evie's papers and diaries that makes it very hard for me to proceed.'

'Ouch. In at the deep end.' Juliette leaned back and slid her dark glasses down over her eyes. 'I'm not sure I can help you over this one. Johnny and George were so different. They were never close. I don't remember them being enemies, though. I wouldn't have thought there was any deep-seated animosity. Have you asked George?'

Lucy stared at her open-mouthed. Here was another prime character in her saga who nobody had mentioned. 'I assumed he had died,' she stammered. 'Because Christopher had inherited everything. This is crazy. Mike never said.'

'He probably thought you knew.'

'Where is George? Why didn't he inherit the paintings? There is something odd there, isn't there?' Lucy wondered if she sounded as bewildered as she felt. Plunging into someone else's family had seemed so straightforward when she was planning to write about Evie. She had never given a second's thought to Evie's surviving family and their reactions.

'Yes, it is odd, come to think of it.' Juliette nodded. 'Evie left everything to Johnny. I don't mean she cut George off, but it was arranged that George would inherit Edward's fortune, and it was a large fortune, and Johnny would inherit Evie's which consisted of the cottage and the paintings. She had very little money as such and was always in debt, bless her.' She gave a fond smile. 'You knew Evie and Edward were divorced? It was about a year before Johnny and I married. It was very acrimonious and quite horrid. Johnny always said his father ripped her off. He never got on with his father and that was why his father to all intents and purposes disinherited him. Johnny didn't care. Darling man, he had no idea about money any more than his mother. You'd think as a solicitor he would have had more of a clue, but apart from our small house in Littlehampton, which was mortgaged up to the hilt, he left me more or less penniless, so when Rick asked me to marry him it wasn't a hard decision to make.' She gave a happy gurgling laugh. 'Johnny and I had known and loved Rick and his wife for years. She died about five years before Johnny and we drifted together. He was a great comfort when I was hurting a lot.' She paused for a moment. 'I don't regret it. I was determined I wasn't going to be a burden to Mike.' She reached for her glass. With every move her bangles rattled on her wrist.

Lucy was silent, trying to assimilate this torrent of information when she noticed Juliette's attention shift to the door behind them. 'Talk of the devil,' she said with a smile. 'Mike, darling, I want you to go out again and stay out for at least two hours so this delightful girl and I can gossip about your grandmother. If you can pick up something for supper that would be lovely. Take some money out of my bag, darling, it's in the hall.'

Mike had stepped out onto the shaded terrace and was standing there, the shadows of the overhanging roses playing over his face as he watched them. He threw a look of mock despair at Lucy. 'Is that all right with you? I don't think I warned you how bossy my mother is. Or of the fact that she still treats me as if I were about ten.'

Lucy laughed. 'It's very all right with me.'

As they settled back into their chairs Lucy looked at Juliette with a frown, determined not to let the interlude with Mike destroy her train of thought. 'When you were talking about the bequests just now you said Evie left the paintings to Johnny. So was he the one who decided to leave them to Christopher instead of to Mike?'

'You may well ask!' Juliette shook her head. 'No. Johnny left his share of everything to Mike. It was Christopher who came up with a codicil to Evie's original will saying she left everything to Johnny for his lifetime but then his effects should be divided between the grandsons. It was in a letter she had given him apparently. Personally I was in grave doubt that it was even legal but Mike wouldn't contest it.'

'And it cut out George?'

'George had his father's money. Still does.'

'And where does George live?' Lucy leaned down to her bag, which was lying on the paving stones under the wrought-iron table. 'Do you mind if I write some of this down? It is all getting a bit confusing. I am bound to forget the details.'

'You can always come over and check, dear,' Juliette said comfortably. 'And Mike knows it all. I don't know why he hasn't told you the whole grisly story.'

'He's quite reserved about Evie,' Lucy said thoughtfully. 'But perhaps it's my fault. I was so focused on finding out about her painting, which after all is the centre of my research; he may have thought I wasn't interested in the personal stuff.'

'Typical man!' Juliette grinned. 'I would have thought you would want to know all the shocking bits. I certainly would.'

There was a pause. Lucy smiled. 'Did Johnny talk about his uncle Ralph at all?' she asked. 'He would never have known him but –'

'He was haunted by his memory,' Juliette said. 'Ralph's whole story hung over the family.'

Lucy felt herself go pale. 'Haunted? It's a strong word.'

Juliette nodded. 'And I meant it. Literally.' She reached for her glass again.

'I don't understand,' Lucy said carefully. Her heart had started hammering under her ribs.

'Johnny used to have nightmares about him. They started when he was small, apparently. I blame his grandmother. Rachel was obsessed with Ralph's death. You know about that? He was shot down in the Battle of Britain. Right at the end. The whole family was devastated. Johnny started dreaming about him, then he said he used to see him. It can't have been healthy living in that house with his grandparents when they were so obsessed with Ralph's death. He was sure Ralph wanted to tell him something. It went on all his life, right up to the end. A few days before Johnny died – he was in the hospice in Chichester – he said to me that at last he would be able to speak to Ralph properly, face to face, and find out what it was he wanted to say to him.' She gave a tired smile. 'Presumably he knows by now.' She sighed. 'Right. Back to George: now there's a character. He loathed his father in spite of the fact that Edward left him so much money. He's hung on to it, though. Never even offered Johnny a loan when we were in pretty dire straits and I don't think he's given any to Christopher either, not that he's ever needed any.' She poured them both another drink from the jug and waved away an inquisitive wasp. 'George has been a widower for years and years now. His wife, Marjory, died of cancer. He runs an antique shop in Kensington. Very posh and very upmarket, selling goodies to rich people with pots of money and no taste of their own.' She snorted with laughter. 'Don't I sound a jealous cow. Scrub that last remark.'

Lucy laughed. 'Would he be prepared to speak to me, do you suppose?'

'I've no idea. He doesn't speak to us. Which is maybe what

this quarrel is about? I can't believe Johnny upset him in any way, he just wasn't like that, but they didn't get on, there is no getting away from that fact.' She sighed and took a sip from her glass. After a moment's silence she leaned back again and, pushing her sunglasses up onto her forehead she fixed Lucy with an intense gaze. 'What is it?' she asked gently.

Lucy was startled. She didn't realise her momentary abstraction was that obvious. She was trying to decide whether to tell Julliette about her own experience of Ralph. And if she did, was she going to admit that she had one of Evie's pictures and that she hadn't told Mike about it.

October 16th 1940

'I've brought a present for you.' Eddie held out a small parcel to Evie with a strangely bashful smile. 'I know I've been driving you hard, sweetheart, and I'm sorry. It is because I care about you. I so want you to be a success. You deserve to be a success.'

She took the parcel from him with a sigh. 'Thank you.'

They were standing in the kitchen at Box Wood Farm drinking tea. Evie had been out walking the fields with her parents and the man from the War Agricultural Committee. It was his job to suggest which extra fields they could plough for crops now that the last of their beef cattle had gone.

'Aren't you going to open it?' Eddie picked up his cup and took a deep gulp of tea.

Evie sighed. 'Of course.' She unknotted the string and carefully unfolded the paper. Inside was a lace-trimmed silk petticoat. Evie held it up, feeling the soft coldness of the material slide through her work-roughened fingers with delight in spite of herself.

'I thought you deserved a treat.' He smiled. 'I think it will fit you. Shall we go upstairs and try it on?'

Her eyes met his. She dropped the petticoat onto the table.

'Eddie, it's kind of you. But I can't accept it. Where did you get it?'

'What do you mean?' He looked affronted.

'It's black market, isn't it?'

'It is a present for the girl I love!' He pushed it towards her again. 'Them as asks no questions!' He tapped the side of his nose. 'Be a good girl, Evie. Just enjoy it.' Suddenly he was impatient again. 'Who's going to see it under your dress? It's our secret. Petticoats aren't rationed, for goodness' sake. Not yet anyway!' He glanced heavenward. 'Wear it for the next dance in the village hall. Then maybe someone will see a flash of lace as I swing you on my arm.' He smiled. 'But they won't know where it came from, will they! Now, what about another cup of tea before I go?'

When he left she took the petticoat upstairs to her bedroom and, just for a moment, held it up against her dungarees in front of her mirror, then with an exclamation of anger she bundled it up and pushed it into the bottom drawer of her chest of drawers. She had not allowed him to come upstairs with her; she had vowed never to let him touch her again. She pulled out her diary and sat down on the bed with it. Inside the front cover she had tucked a small photo of Tony, Tony who didn't want to see her any more. She sighed, staring at him for several seconds, and almost unwillingly brought it up and pressed it against her lips, then slowly she tore the photo in two.

That night Tony was sitting on his bed in the small bedroom he shared with another flying officer in Woodcote Farmhouse, the old building they were using as the Officers' Mess at Westhampnett. He was filling in his log book.

Patrol. Shot Enemy aircraft into water. Sitting target. Couldn't miss. Plane sank as we flew back to base. Action 30 miles out to sea.

'Coming up to The Unicorn for a pint?' Bill West stuck his head round the door. Downstairs someone had put on a record of Glenn Miller and a blast of music followed him into the room.

Tony looked up. He nodded and screwing the cap on his fountain pen he put it down and tossed the log book onto the locker beside his bed. He doubted if Evie would be there, but after all, that was where he had first met her properly and there was always a chance she might go for a drink with Ralph. He bit his lip. He was missing her terribly, but the message had come through loud and clear. Evie did not want to see him any more. Ralph had told him so and Evie's father had sent him a short curt note to that effect. Even without that, Evie's silence would have told him more clearly than anything anyone could have said that their affair was over.

He had had a letter from his mother that morning full of excitement about the girl he had met and fallen for and now he was going to have to write back to her and tell her it was all off. He shook his head unhappily. He might as well go out for a pint.

Wednesday 7th August

'Good to see you, Chris.' Mike led the way into the sitting room at Rosebank and gestured his cousin towards a chair. 'Long time no see.'

'Did she tell you she came round?' Christopher ignored the chair and strode towards the window. He turned and stood with his back to it. He was a short good-looking man with square features and neatly cut dark brown hair. His phone call an hour before had been curt, to put it mildly. 'Did she tell you she talked her way into the house, terrified Frances and took unauthorised photographs of the paintings?'

Mike sat down on the sofa and leaned back, crossing his legs, trying for a relaxed look. 'Lucy told me she went over to your house and that you were out,' he said calmly.

'Nothing else?'

'She said she spoke to Frances. She didn't mention taking any photographs.' Mike stirred uneasily. 'Did Frances say she was terrified? That seems odd. Lucy doesn't seem to me the type to terrify anyone.'

'Presumably because you have agreed to her demands and told her everything she wants to know. As Frances did in the end. I had to force it out of her. She wasn't going to tell me about the photos, that was going to be a secret, apparently! I can always tell when she's keeping something from me.' He glared at his cousin.

Mike inclined his head thoughtfully. Poor Frances. He didn't say it out loud. 'I have told Lucy as much as I feel is relevant to her book. But then I don't know of anything about Evie which should be a huge secret. If there is something there, Chris, I think you had better tell me what it is. So far I can see there's nothing wrong with Lucy writing a biography. I would have thought it could do nothing but good to raise Evie's profile. She was a great painter and she hasn't had the recognition she deserves.'

Glancing at Christopher he was shocked to see he had gone very white. His lips narrowed, he was radiating fury. 'Do you want people knocking on the door day and night demanding to see the house where she lived? Do you want people shouting that they have the right to rifle through your cupboards, looking for her belongings?' Christopher asked angrily.

'There is little chance of them finding anything here,' Mike reproved gently, 'you appear to have taken everything there was.'

'She left it all to me!' A patch of red appeared on the back Christopher's neck. 'I took nothing that her will didn't entitle me to. And I don't want people knocking on my door, especially spurious academics, trying to make a fast buck out of the family.' His voice was rising.

Mike smiled. 'Lucy is not a spurious academic,' he said. 'Her credentials are first class, as was one of her degrees.' He was managing to keep his voice level with difficulty. 'You still haven't told me any good reason to veto a biography, Chris. Your inconvenience, because you happen to hold the lion's share of her paintings, is just not good enough.' He levered himself off the sofa, unable to sit still a moment longer. 'What is it you're trying to hide?' He narrowed his eyes, studying Christopher's face.

'I am trying to protect the family.'

'From what?' Mike kept his voice even with extreme difficulty. 'Prowling academics! That just doesn't convince me. I'm sorry. If there is something there which warrants this attitude, Chris, you need to tell me what it is because as things stand you are not making any sense!'

'What do you know about the Box Wood portrait?' Christopher asked abruptly. He sat down suddenly, leaning forward, his elbows on his knees, hands cupped under his chin. He held Mike's gaze with ferocious intensity.

Mike eyed him cautiously 'I'm not sure I know which one that is.'

'It's the one Laurence Standish bought at an auction in Brighton in February.'

'Laurence Standish?' Mike echoed, puzzled. Then he frowned. 'You mean –'

'I mean, Lucy Standish's husband.'

There was a long silence. 'She hasn't mentioned it, has she?' Christopher said at last.

Mike shook his head.

'I understand it was destroyed in the car crash which killed him,' Christopher added after a moment.

'Lucy told you this?' Mike asked, bewildered.

'I haven't spoken to Mrs Standish.'

'So she told Frances?'

Christopher shook his head adamantly. 'I heard it from someone in London who had spoken to the expert Standish

220

was going to consult about the picture. He was going to make an offer for it once it had been authenticated.' He gave an icy smile. 'So, your oh-so-honest and above board academic hasn't been altogether open with you, Mike. How strange. I thought she had told you everything.'

Taken aback, Mike was silent for a long moment, then at last he sat down again opposite his cousin. 'If the picture was destroyed in her husband's car crash it is perhaps hardly surprising that she hasn't mentioned it. It must be part of an agonising memory.'

'Certainly in the cash department. If it was authentic, and I think there can have been little doubt about that because I have Evie's description of it, it was probably worth tens if not hundreds of thousands. I wonder if it was insured.'

Mike let out a disgusted groan. 'Is money all you can think about?'

'In this context, yes. I don't know these people but they were on the make. She still is. Believe me, Michael, before you make a complete fool of yourself!'

'No!' Mike gathered his wits at last. 'No, Lucy wouldn't lie to me. I don't believe you. I trust her.'

'More fool you.' Christopher stood up, shaking his head. 'Well, I've warned you. And you had better tell her, if you are determined to go on associating with her after what I've told you, that I shall be speaking to my solicitor about her actions on my property. She will be hearing from him.'

14

October 17th 1940

'He'll be all right.' Rachel looked at Evie, sitting opposite her at the kitchen table. Her words were as much to reassure herself as her daughter.

Evie gave a wan smile. 'I prayed today. I asked God to look after them.' Her eyes filled with tears. 'I can't even go down to the airfield.'

'You're thinking about Tony?'

Evie stared at her. 'Of course I'm thinking about Tony! About Rafie too, of course, but Tony is so alone . . .' Her tears brimmed again.

Rachel studied her face sadly. 'I'm so sorry it didn't work out, my darling.'

Evie clenched her fists. She compressed her lips into a miserable scowl to hold in the sobs. 'He didn't love me. I thought he did. I believed him.'

Rachel shook her head slowly. 'He loved you, Evie. Anyone could see that. But those boys are under intolerable strain. Perhaps he just couldn't cope with it all. Later, when it's all over,' she paused for a moment, trying to master her own voice, 'maybe then he will come back.' She heaved a deep sigh. 'We have other things to worry about, Evie. If the Germans come –'

'They won't! The Air Force won't let them!' Evie let out a wail.

Rachel shrugged her shoulders. 'There are so many of them, Evie, and so few of our boys.' She reached over and put her hands over her daughter's. 'Pray. That is all we can do. And you can paint and I can do what I can on the farm and everyone out there is doing the same. Your father, Eddie, all of them, willing our boys on.'

Sunday 11th August

Mike walked into the Standish Gallery just after midday and stood staring round at the exhibits. After a few minutes Robin pushed back the chair on which he had been sitting at the desk at the back of the room and wandered towards him. 'Can I help you, or would you rather look round uninterrupted?'

Mike jumped. He had been staring at a painting of the cathedral, lost in thought. He glanced over his shoulder, taking in the short, amiably smiling figure who had approached him.

'I actually came in on the off chance that Lucy was here,' he said after a moment.

'She'll be back later this afternoon.' Robin studied the newcomer for a moment.

'I heard she had a painting by Evelyn Lucas here,' Mike said after another pause. 'Or at least I believe she did some time ago. I was told it had been destroyed in a car crash. Is that right?'

Robin tensed. His hazel eyes narrowed behind his glasses. 'Lucy's husband died in the car crash,' he said cautiously. 'As to whether there was a painting in the car, I wouldn't know. Are you a friend of Lucy's?' His voice had an edge to it now.

Mike nodded. 'I'm Michael Marston. She has been working

with me over at Evelyn's studio. Perhaps she has mentioned it?'

'Of course she has mentioned it.' Robin continued to stare at him thoughtfully. 'I don't understand your enquiry. Why haven't you asked Lucy about this?'

Mike shook his head wearily. 'I have only just heard about the painting. I don't know why she hasn't told me that it existed.'

'Then perhaps it doesn't. Perhaps it never did.' Robin's voice was sharp. 'May I suggest you come back this afternoon if you want to speak to her?'

Mike hesitated for a fraction of a second then he nodded. 'I'll do that. I'm sure there has been a misunderstanding some-where down the line.' He turned towards the door.

Robin stood at the window and watched him walk slowly down the street. Only when he was out of sight did he go back to the desk and pick up the phone. 'Lucy, ducky, I think we may have a problem.'

Lucy dived into the gallery door ten minutes later and ran upstairs. 'Robin?' She was panting. 'Did he say who had told him?'

Robin was waiting for her in the kitchen. He shook his head. 'You didn't tell me you still hadn't told him about the picture,' he said reproachfully. 'I might have put my big foot in it.'

She gave a quick anxious smile. 'I have been feeling guilty about that but it just never seemed to be the right moment. With all these accusations flying around that I am in this just to make money it seemed wrong to waltz up to him and say by the way I have a large oil painting which is probably worth a bomb if it's verified.' She paused. 'But who has told him the picture was in the car with Larry? I don't understand that. Who else knows about it except for you and me?'

Robin drew in a deep breath. 'I don't like the sound of any of this, Luce.' He glanced at the studio door. 'I think you ought to be keeping that picture under lock and key.'

'The gallery is alarmed, Robin. No one can get in here.'

'Except by walking through the front door, coming upstairs

and going into the studio. If this guy is a friend of yours what more natural than that you invite him up to the flat?'

Lucy was silent. 'It's his cousin, Christopher. Somehow he's found out the picture exists.'

'Or existed. Michael seems to think it was destroyed in the crash.'

'So he must have known it was being taken to London for examination by David Solomon.' Lucy went on thoughtfully.

Robin nodded. 'Friends in the art world?'

'But not such close friends that they knew Solomon was ill and had postponed the meeting,' she mused. She walked over to the fridge, took out a bottle of wine and poured two glasses. She held one out to Robin. 'Of course there is an awful lot of gossip in the art world, but even so, I thought this would stay under wraps until Solomon had seen it. He hasn't rung me and I assumed he was being tactful Originally you told him we would get in touch when we were ready, didn't you?'

Robin nodded. He sipped his wine. 'What are you going to say to Michael when he comes back?'

'I'm not inviting him upstairs.' She glanced at the studio door. 'There isn't a lock.'

'That can be sorted fairly swiftly, but not quick enough for today.'

'Shall I deny it?'

'You don't want to show him the picture?'

She hesitated. 'No, I don't think I do. Not yet.'

'The longer you leave it the harder it will be to tell him in the end.' Robin eyed her shrewdly.

Lucy exhaled loudly. 'I don't know what to do for the best. He will find out in the end but I don't want him to see it yet. I just don't. There is a mystery there, Robin. I think Christopher knows what it is and I think he wants to make sure I don't find out.'

Robin grinned. 'What a mistake! He is obviously not an expert on the female mind otherwise he would realise that mysteries have to be solved.'

She gave him a gentle punch on the arm. 'As if you would know.'

He chuckled to himself as he leaned against the wall, arms folded. 'Shall I nip out and pick up a padlock?'

She shook her head. 'A padlock will immediately draw attention to the fact that there is something there we don't want people to see. Let's put a proper lock on the door – that will be less obvious. For now, I won't let Mike come upstairs. Simple as that. Besides, he's hardly likely to barge upstairs uninvited. He doesn't know that is, was, Larry's studio.'

'You think he will feel the same as his brother about the painting?'

'It's not his brother. Christopher is his cousin. I don't know what Mike will think, Robin. I just want time to think about it myself. I didn't mean to keep it from him. I've nearly told him on several occasions, but the time wasn't quite right, and now I've messed up. I know I have. I would have told him in the end, obviously, but the fact that Christopher is so against me makes me suspicious. Larry always used to say I had a suspicious mind.' She smiled wistfully. 'But there was usually a good reason.'

Robin pushed himself away from the wall and headed for the staircase. 'QED,' he said cheerfully. 'I'll let you know when he arrives.'

Lucy walked across to the sink and putting her hands on the cool rim leaned forward to look out of the window. She had blown it. One way or another she had completely blown it. If she confessed to owning the painting Mike would never trust her again. If she kept quiet about it she would never be able to mention it at all. But obviously someone knew Larry had bought it. Who? How did they know? It had been described in the catalogue as 'artist unknown'. The only person who could have told Christopher was Professor Solomon. It had to be him, and thinking about it, there was no reason why he should not have mentioned it. Larry was unlikely to have sworn him to secrecy. But then Larry was going to see him in order to confirm the identity of the painting. Surely the professor wouldn't have said anything without seeing it first?

Turning away from the window she sat down with a sigh at the kitchen table and put her head in her hands, her mind a turmoil. Solomon was one of the world authorities on British war artists, specialising in the Second World War. Perhaps this painting had been listed somewhere. Perhaps it had been stolen at some point. Had Larry sent him a photo of it? Perhaps Larry's description had been enough to alert the art world to its existence. And had he told the professor of his suspicions about the overpainting? Overpainting she should never have touched. Tampering with a painting as a total amateur as she had done was the worst possible crime. She might have done irreparable damage.

She heard what sounded like the creak of a floorboard from the studio and she looked up. 'Who's there?' Surely Mike could not have got in there? She pushed back her chair and stood up, feeling a sudden chill in the hot still air of the kitchen. She swallowed hard. If not Mike, then who? She tiptoed towards the door and stood, her ear pressed against it, listening. 'Ralph?' she whispered. 'Is that you?' She put her hand on the door knob and realised that she was shivering. Moving her hand away silently, without opening the door she took two steps back then she turned away. She couldn't face opening it. Not now, not with Mike even now perhaps heading up the stairs.

October 20th 1940

Scrabbling on the table in her studio for a penknife Evie paused for a moment, gazing across the room at the painting she had done of herself sitting on the gate with Tony behind her. Propped against the wall, it was usually hidden behind a pile of other canvasses but somehow it had been exposed the night before as she rummaged through some of her older works. She frowned. She should hide it again before Eddie saw it. Walking over to

227

it she pulled it free, holding it at arm's length and studying it. Originally she had planned to send it to Tony's mother but now she wasn't even sure if she was going to keep it. She could overpaint it and reuse the canvas. She touched Tony's face gently with a fingertip. The thought of him made her ache with longing. It was a good likeness. She had captured his carefree, joyous spirit. Her eye travelled down to her own face and she scowled. Why had she painted herself looking so cross? Perhaps even then she had known their relationship was doomed. With a sigh she turned the painting over and stacked it face to the wall, pulling some cardboard portfolios in front of it.

She had come upstairs to sharpen some pencils and collect her sketching things. More pictures were wanted apparently of gentle idyllic pre-war farm life, sentimental dreams for people sickened by war and pain. Grabbing the basket that contained her chalks and sketchbooks she ran down to the yard.

The old horse, Bella, was staring out over the stable door. Evie's father must have brought her in from the field to harness her. Evie walked over and rubbed the animal's nose fondly. She let herself into the loose box and groped on one of the beams behind the door to find a stiff body brush she usually left there. Giving the horse a brush before she started drawing would give Bella pleasure and be an outlet for some of her own frustration.

As she stooped to work on the animal's legs, brushing the thick white feathering until it was immaculate she heard the sound of a plane overhead. She straightened her back, listening. There had been a dogfight that morning over the farm, and later she had seen in the distance a mass formation of aircraft heading west. The sound of explosions had reached them from far away but whatever was going on it was somewhere out over the sea. This plane was low and very close. She pushed open the loose box door and stepped out into the yard, shading her eyes as she looked up. It was a Spitfire, making straight for them. It flew directly over the farmhouse and as it passed it waggled its wings once, then it was gone, soaring up over the hills and veering round back towards the south. She smiled. Was it Ralph, telling her he was all right, reassuring her he had survived yet another skirmish? Or was it Tony? It was the sort of thing he might do, but then why would he if he no longer loved her?

She was distracted by a nudge in the small of her back. The horse had pushed her way through the open door of her box and wandered out into the yard, wondering what had happened to her grooming. Evie turned and fondled her. 'That was Rafie, telling us he was OK,' she whispered in the horse's ear. 'I'm sure it was Rafie.'

Sunday 11th August

It was one forty-five. Lost in thought Lucy almost failed to register the soft slithering sound from behind the studio door. The noise came again and this time she turned to look round. Easing herself out of the chair she held her breath, listening. As she stood there, the silence was broken by a further sliding noise and then a sharp bang as though something had fallen to the floor. For a moment she couldn't move, paralysed with terror. For several seconds she stared at the door, hardly daring to breathe until at last she forced herself to move. Not giving herself any more time to think she walked over to the door and this time, she pulled it open.

The painting had fallen from the easel and was lying at its foot. A deep scratch had been scored across the corner of the sky.

Lucy gasped. She stared round apprehensively. The room was still and empty, the skylights tightly closed. There was no draught to catch the canvas and blow it from its place on the easel. It was a large picture. It had been clamped in place. It could not have slipped. 'Robin?' she whispered. 'Are you in here? Mike?'

There was no reply.

'Ralph?' Her voice wavered slightly. 'Ralph, did you do that?'

Stooping she lifted the picture off the floor and propped it upright, leaning it against the legs of the easel. She could feel him she realised suddenly. There was someone there, in the room with her, someone waiting and watching. She stared round, searching every corner, every shadow. There was no one there. Cold sweat broke out between her shoulder blades. There is nothing to be afraid of, she whispered to herself. This was Ralph, Evie's brother. He was trying to tell her something. She had no need to be afraid of him, no need at all. 'Ralph?' she whispered again. Her voice was dry and husky and her hands had started to shake. 'Ralph, is that you? Please. Speak to me.'

Nothing.

The room was very still, unnaturally so. She forced herself to stand her ground though every instinct was telling her to run. 'Ralph!' she murmured. 'Please.' She stepped away from the painting. 'Ralph!'

It was only when she slammed the studio door behind her and found herself leaning, hands on the edge of the table in the kitchen, panting, that she realised she had completely panicked. With a sob she ran towards the stairs and sped down to the gallery. 'Robin!' she called. She skidded to a halt. Mike was standing near the foot of the stairs.

'Lucy?' Mike reached out in concern. 'What is it? What's the matter?' Robin was standing next to him and the two men had been engaged in conversation.

Lucy subsided onto the bottom step, wrapping her arms round her knees. 'I'm sorry,' she whispered.

The two men glanced at each other. Robin stepped forward and put his hand gently on her shoulder. 'It's OK, Lucy,' he said softly. 'I was just explaining to Mike that you hadn't been feeling well. Come over here and sit down and I'll fetch you a glass of water.' He took her elbow and lifted her to her feet, guiding her towards the office area where he firmly pushed her into the armchair.

Her teeth were chattering and for a moment she found it impossible to focus. She heard the sound of Robin's feet on the stairs as he ran up to the kitchen. There was a pause as he found the glass and filled it then she heard him returning. It was only as he pressed it into her hand and folded her fingers round it that she raised her eyes and saw Mike sitting in the office chair opposite her. His eyes were fixed on her face.

'Are you all right, Luce?' Robin was standing over her.

She nodded imperceptibly.

'Perhaps, it would be better if you and Lucy discussed your queries at another time.' Robin turned to Mike. 'As you can see she is not herself today.'

Lucy saw the hesitation on Mike's face and managed a feeble smile. 'I'm sorry.'

'That's OK.' He stood up. 'I am so sorry you're not well. We'll talk next time you come over. I'm back in London tonight, but I will see you soon. Take care, OK?' He stepped away from the desk and for a moment she thought he was going to bend down and kiss her cheek. If he was, he thought better of it. He nodded towards Robin and headed across the gallery towards the door.

As it closed behind him Robin took his place on the chair by the desk and leaned forward. 'What happened?'

She looked at him wearily. 'The painting fell off the easel.'

He narrowed his eyes. 'Fell off?'

'I was in the kitchen. I heard it fall.'

'I see.' For a moment he fell silent. 'Was it damaged?'

She nodded. 'A scratch. A deep one.' She took a sip from the glass. 'At first I thought you or Mike must have done it.' She raised her hand as he opened his mouth to protest. 'I knew it wasn't you, of course I did. Then I wondered if Ralph had done it. I could sense someone there.'

'And that frightened you?'

'Of course it did. It terrified me!' She nodded again. 'Then suddenly I found myself thinking, this isn't like Ralph. It's someone else, and it was then I completely panicked.' There was a long pause, then she went on, 'I didn't realise Mike had arrived.'

'He seems to be a nice man.'

'He is.'

231

'But you still don't want to tell him about the picture?'

'No. Not yet.' She shook her head violently. For several seconds she said nothing. He waited patiently until she looked up again. 'There is something going on in the family, Robin. Perhaps when I have read all the diaries I'll understand better. They're hiding something, I'm sure they are. And if I am going to be a good biographer, an investigative biographer, I need to try and find out what it is.' She gave a tired smile.

Robin nodded slowly. 'Are you sure, Lucy? You're not getting just the tiniest bit obsessed? Do you really need to know all this?'

'Yes, I do. Of course I do. It's about Evie. I need to know everything about Evie. About her family, about the men in her life, about the motivation for her painting. And I need to know why Ralph wants to tell me something.'

'But you just said you didn't think this was Ralph.'

Her shoulders slumped and she sighed. 'No.'

'So what are you going to do?'

She gave an almost imperceptible shrug of the shoulders. 'I don't know, Robin. I just don't know. Are there two of them? Two ghosts in the picture? Am I imagining it? Am I going mad? I don't know what to do. I just want to get on quietly with my research. I want to write. I want to go to museums and galleries and record offices. I don't want to be too frightened to walk into my own kitchen!'

There was a long silence. Trying desperately to steady herself she picked up the glass and took a sip of water. 'I might ring Huw Redwood.'

Robin gave an exclamation of disgust. 'He doesn't seem to have done much good so far.'

'No.' She raised her eyes to his. 'I know you're not keen on the Church, Robin, any more than I am, but this is their job. They know about things like this. Huw is a nice man. And he is at least someone I can talk to.'

'And you can't talk to me? I suppose you still think I did it!'

She hesitated. Could he have done it? Could he be trying to drive her insane?

She smiled. The idea was ridiculous. 'Of course I can talk to you. I am talking to you at this moment. But ghosts are not your job, Robin. You don't believe in them.'

'From what you told me they are not his job either,' he retorted. 'Didn't you say he's supposed to go and ask his bishop?'

'I think he is, but this is something he has studied. He knows what to do. We are not talking about some fearsome possession by an evil spirit. We are talking about an unhappy young man who died when he was twenty-one years old, for God's sake. Or at least . . .' Her voice trailed away.

'Or at least you were before, but now you think there is someone else there?' Robin prompted.

'Put it this way, now I'm not so sure.'

'And he, it, whoever, frightened you,' Robin said.

'Yes. This was different. It was threatening.' She looked up at him again helplessly. 'Ralph's presence is uneasy and anxious. Rachel's was full of the most terrible grief but this –' Unable to finish the sentence she gestured helplessly with her hands. 'I have never felt such fear. One minute I was fine. I was chatting to Ralph as Huw said I should, about to examine the easel to see if any paint had scraped off on it to show where the picture had fallen, to understand how it got damaged, then I was over-whelmed by this complete stifling terror. I knew without a shadow of doubt that someone, he, it, was out to get me! I moved without knowing I was doing it. I was out of the studio before I could think. It was –' again the gesture – 'completely overwhelming.'

Robin was silent for a moment. 'Do you want to go up again now?' he asked at last. 'With me. We'll look at the painting and see how badly it's damaged.'

'I don't know.' She replied so quickly it surprised them both.

'Shall I go on my own? The door to the studio was shut

233

when I went up to get the water. Did you shut it when you ran out of the room?'

'I can't remember. I must have.'

'OK. I'll go on my own.' She saw a moment of brief hesitation then his usual cheery grin was back.

'Robin –' she said and paused. 'Be careful.'

'I will be so careful, ducky, you will wonder how I manage to get up there at all,' he replied. 'After all, I don't believe in all this supernatural stuff, remember.' He blew her a kiss. 'I may be some time, as they say.'

She sat frozen to the spot as he climbed once more to the kitchen, listening to the sound of his footsteps overhead. Slowly they died away. Five minutes passed. Her stomach was churning with apprehension when at last she stood up and went to the foot of the stairs. 'Robin?' she called up. 'Are you OK?'

There was no reply.

She put her hand on the knob of the newel post and clung there for a moment, her mouth dry with fear. 'Robin!' she called again, more loudly this time.

Still no reply.

She took a deep breath and put a foot on the bottom step. 'Robin!' Her voice was shrill this time.

Somehow she managed to drag herself up the stairs into the kitchen. The studio door was open. 'Robin,' she called again. Her voice was a whisper this time. She could hear nothing from within the studio. And then suddenly he was there in the doorway.

'Come and see this.' He beckoned her towards him. 'It's OK. There is no one here.'

For a moment she couldn't move, then at last she forced herself to go towards him. She stopped on the threshold and looked in. The picture was back on the easel. Beyond it, the studio looked much as it always did. 'What do you want me to look at?' she asked at last.

'The painting. Come and see.' He didn't seem frightened,

just perplexed. He went back to it and stood peering at it closely.

She had to force herself to walk towards him. Robin had pushed open one of the skylights and the room was full of fresh cool air. She could hear the sound of cars from the street below. 'What is it?' She looked at the picture and gasped. The figure behind Evie's shoulder had been obliterated by daubs of blue paint. She could see the oil glistening, smell it, see the marks of the brush, coarse and crude on the dry surface. 'Did you do this?' She spun to face him, eyes accusing.

'I shan't dignify that with an answer,' Robin replied shortly. 'I was looking at the brushes, look, he didn't use any of these. They are all clean and dry.' He gestured at Larry's work table.

'Someone must have come up here,' Lucy said, her voice husky.

Robin shook his head. 'How? We were never out of sight of the staircase. Not for one second.' He shivered suddenly. 'That paint is real, Lucy. Look.' He held up a finger and she saw a dab of blue paint on the end of it. 'Whoever did this is angry that Evie's young man has been revealed and whoever did this is real. It is not ghostly paint. It was not a ghostly brush! That is why I looked out of the window. I wondered if someone had crept along the roof from next door.' He shook his head with an exasperated sigh. 'Not possible. Even Spiderman couldn't have done it. I've checked all the rooms up here but there is nowhere someone could hide.'

'It was the ghost,' Lucy said softly.

'No! I'm sorry, Lucy, but it was a real person. It had to be. And it was a real person who is determined to ruin this picture. You were right in what you were saying downstairs, just now. There is something funny going on here to do with the Lucas family and this pilot chap, and I am going to help you get to the bottom of it.'

Lucy was still studying the painting. 'Thank you, Robin. You make me feel much better. I was so afraid. Somehow it reassures me to think this was done by a real person.' She still sounded doubtful though. 'If you're right.'

'Do you think Mike came here to distract us? He could have done, you know. We were so intent on you, we might not have noticed someone creeping in and climbing the stairs.'

'The bell on the door would have jangled.' She found her brain was beginning to function again.

'It might have been muffled.'

'That is easily checked.'

As if on cue the bell rang below them in the gallery. They glanced at each other then Robin turned and hurried across the floor to the stairs. Lucy stood where she was for a moment then slowly she followed him.

'Two postcards.' Robin was back in the kitchen a few minutes later. 'And it's begun to rain. I'd better close the skylight.' He went back into the studio. A few minutes later he reappeared turning out the lights after him. 'Two things occur to me. One, would you like to come and stay with me and Phil? I wouldn't blame you if you felt nervous being here on your own after this. And second, should we move the painting? If someone is determined to destroy it, it isn't safe here and besides, as you don't want Mike to see it we could take it to our place, or put it in the bank – do people still do that? Or find somewhere to store it safely.'

Lucy pulled out a chair and sat down at the kitchen table. 'I don't know what to do about the picture. But this is my home, Robin. I will not be driven out.' Even as she said it she felt a prickle of unease.

He sat down opposite her. 'Another idea. Why not let me and Phil move in here for a bit and you can go to ours? That would work.'

'And Phil wouldn't mind?'

'No, I don't think he would.'

October 20th 1940

Dudley Lucas was standing in the shadow of the barn watching his daughter as she sketched the old horse standing patiently between the shafts of the wagon. He smiled fondly, enjoying a few more minutes of peace before moving out into the sunlight.

'I've got to take Bella up to the field I'm afraid, Evie. We need the wagon up there,' he said gruffly. Why was it that even the sight of his daughter made him feel tearful, silly old fool that he was. She was so vulnerable, his girl, with her slim figure and her delicate hands roughened by the farm work but still so dextrous on the pencil she was using to sketch with. 'You going to paint that?'

She looked up at him and nodded. 'A picture of old England as she was in happy times. David Fuller seems to sell them as fast as I can paint them. I would have thought people would stop buying paintings with the war on, but it appears not.'

'I expect he tells people they will be a good investment,' Dudley said a little grimly. Ralph had told him that Evie knew about the loan. 'I had to tell her, Daddy,' he said. 'Not about Tony, of course not. God forbid she ever find out about Eddie's threats to him, but she had to know why we all have to be nice to Eddie.'

Nice! Dudley scowled at the memory of his son's tight-lipped admission. He began to untie the horse from the ring in the barn wall. It nosed his pocket hopefully. 'No more sugar lumps, sweetheart. I'm afraid they've gone for good,' he said with a fond ruffle of the animal's mane. He leaned over the fence and pulled a tuft of grass. The horse nibbled it without enthusiasm. 'I haven't seen Eddie recently,' he went on cautiously. Like Evie's mother he was careful how he spoke about Eddie to his daughter.

'He's busy,' Evie said bitterly. 'I never know when he will have time to come up here. When he's run out of paintings no doubt.' She had said nothing about the loan. Perhaps it was better not mentioned by anyone. She closed her sketchbook and put her pencils into the basket of sketching materials which stood at her feet. She glanced up at the sky. 'Do you reckon they have packed up and gone home for the day?' Save for that one single Spitfire, the sky had been empty for several hours. 'Perhaps they will let Rafie come out for the evening.'

Dudley gave a wry smile. 'I hope so, girlie.' He followed her gaze heavenwards. The sky was hot and almost white with glare. On the southern horizon storm clouds were gathering out to sea. 'No doubt Nazis dislike flying in a storm as much as our boys do.' He gripped the horse's bridle and began to turn her towards the field gate. 'Now you go in to your mother and see if she needs help with anything. I'll be in for supper later.'

Evie watched him as he clicked his tongue at the horse and headed away from the yard, walking easily beside the animal, whispering encouragement into the great flicking ears.

'There's a letter for you, Evie,' Rachel called from the pantry as Evie walked in. 'On the table.' Evie put down her basket and the sketchbook and walked over to the kitchen table. She picked up the envelope and stared at it curiously, not recognising the writing. Tearing it open she stood, the light from the sun shining onto the page through the back door.

Dear Evelyn, I felt I had to write to you after receiving the most heart-breaking note from Tony. My dear, why have you broken off your engagement? He was so excited when he wrote to his father and me about you –' Evie turned the letter over and looked at the signature. *Betty Anderson.* For a moment she was tempted to tear up the letter, but she couldn't. Her hands shaking, she went on reading. *He loves you so much, my dear, and because of that, his father and I love you too. He has told us so much about you in his letters, how could we not? Please don't break his heart. We know you too through the lovely portrait of him you sent to us – every brushstroke betrays your love for him. I know how difficult it must be for you with him in danger every single day, and we realise that living in Sussex as you do, you and your family are in constant danger yourselves, as is your brother, but please, please dear child, don't abandon Tony. There will be a future for you both when the war is over and I hope and pray every day for your safety and future happiness.*

Evie let out a little whimper of pain. She bit down hard on her lip, crunching the letter in her fist.

'Evie! What is it?' Rachel had been watching her from the pantry doorway.

Evie shook her head, unable to speak. Tears were flooding down her cheeks. Rachel stepped forward and took the crumpled letter out of her hand. Spreading it out on the table she bent over it and read it slowly. When at last she stood up there were tears in her own eyes. 'Poor woman. I didn't realise Tony had told anyone you were engaged.'

'We weren't. Not properly. It was a dream.'

'Oh, Evie.' Rachel pulled out a chair and sat down heavily.

'Why, Mummy, why did he have to break it off?' Evie wailed suddenly. 'His mother thinks it was me. It wasn't. It was Tony. He finished it.'

Rachel stared at her helplessly. 'I don't know, Evie.' She looked beyond Evie suddenly towards the door as a shadow filled the doorway and her expression hardened. 'Eddie! We weren't expecting you.'

Evie turned away from the doorway rapidly, rubbing the back of her hand across her face to remove her tears.

Eddie walked into the kitchen and put down a battered briefcase on the table. 'I'm glad I caught you both. I am sorry I haven't been over for a while. I've been up in London. We've had a lot to do at the Ministry. How are you Evie, darling?' He went over to her and leaned across to kiss her cheek. Evie stiffened, but she didn't move away. 'Hey,' he touched her face with his forefinger. 'You've been crying. What's happened?' His voice sharpened.

'Nothing that need concern you, Eddie.' Rachel stood up and, picking up the crumpled letter, tucked it into her apron pocket. 'I'll put on the kettle. I'm sure we could all do with a cup of tea.'

With a sniff Evie turned round and gave Eddie a watery smile. 'So, how are the picture sales going?'

'Well.' He gave her a long thoughtful look, then went on, 'Have you heard anything from the WAAC? I thought they were going to commission another painting from you. They were very pleased with your picture of the women in the Spitfire factory.'

'Which was bombed only days after I was there,' Evie said sadly. 'Those poor women. I'm sure they were all in the shelter, but even so. This bloody war!' She stamped her foot suddenly. Then she took a deep breath and calmed herself. 'I know the WAAC were pleased. I had a letter.'

Eddie nodded. He opened his briefcase and pulled out some newspaper clippings and a box. He passed her the papers almost shyly. 'I thought you'd like to see. I've been writing for one or two of the local papers. About art. And I've been reviewing one or two local exhibitions.'

She read his byline, Edward Marston and the dates at the top of the articles. He must have been doing this for some time and he had never mentioned it.

Evie glanced at them. 'That is brilliant, Eddie.'

He smiled. 'I will review your exhibitions when you have them, Evie. You can be sure of that.' He hesitated, then he handed her the box. 'I've never seen you use a camera, Evie,' he said, changing the subject. 'I don't know if you ever do, but I wondered if it would help when you are out and about. Not without permission of course, but a lot of artists use them to help with their work.' He pushed it over towards her. 'See what you think.'

Evie frowned. Carefully she began to open the box and extricated a Leica camera. She gave a little gasp of excitement. 'Eddie! This is amazing. We used them in college, but I've never had my own camera.'

He smiled. 'I thought I hadn't seen you with one. It's yours.' He hesitated. 'Do you know how to use it? Would you like me to show you? If you've used them in college you probably know.'

Her face had crumpled. The last time she had seen a camera

it had been in Tony's hands. He had taken several photos of her in front of the farmhouse, saying he would send them to his mother. Betty Anderson hadn't mentioned them in the letter. Perhaps he hadn't bothered. He had probably torn them up as she had torn up the photo he had given her of himself.

'Evie?' Eddie's voice was unexpectedly gentle. 'What's wrong?'

'There is nothing wrong,' Rachel interrupted. She put the teapot down on the table with a bang. 'Fetch the teacups, Eddie, if you would. You know where they are. Over there on the dresser.' She was glaring at Evie.

Evie straightened her shoulders. 'Thank you, Eddie. I would love you to show me. I've taken pictures, but I've never loaded the film or emptied the camera, and this one looks very complicated,' she said meekly. She felt her mother's intense gaze on her and she looked away. 'I was doing some sketches of the farm and the horse this afternoon. You said the WAAC would like to see some paintings of the land girls. Daddy was there, but I could easily substitute Patsy for him. I'll take a photo of her, then I needn't waste her time by asking her to pose for me. '

'Good idea.' Eddie put the cups on the table. He reached into his pocket for a pack of cigarettes. 'Can I offer you one, Mrs Lucas?'

Rachel shook her head. 'Leave it till you've had a scone, Eddie,' she said sharply. 'If we eat a bit of something now, then we can leave supper until late when Dudley comes in from the fields. I'm feeding the girls tonight too.' They had three land girls now, two sleeping upstairs in the spare room of the farmhouse and the third billeted in the village. Outside, the generator roared into life suddenly and for a moment the house seemed to shake, but the skies remained empty.

Evie walked with Eddie to his car after they had finished their tea. 'That was kind of you to give me the camera,' she said as they stood in the yard. She didn't look at him, watching the hens scratching round in the dried mud by the gate instead. He caught her hand.

'It's a pleasure, Evie,' he said gruffly. 'You know I like to make you happy.'

She gave him a quick glance. 'I know,' she said. She gently removed her hand from his.

'As I said, you'll be hearing from the War Artists any day,' he said.

She laughed rather grimly. 'I am so pleased. But they're still not giving me an official listing –'

'Give it time, sweetheart. They will.' He pulled open the door of the car and set one foot on the running board. 'They like what you've done. The picture of the women in the factory is going to be exhibited.'

'You didn't tell me that!' she cried.

'I only heard yesterday.'

'Where?'

'I'm not sure. Maybe London.'

She stared at him speechlessly.

He smiled and reached to touch her cheek. 'That would please you, eh? Fame at last. I'll let you know as soon as I hear any more.' He reached forward and gave her a quick kiss on the lips then he climbed into the car and pulled the door shut. 'TTFN!' he called.

She watched the car disappear down the lane in a cloud of dust and turned dreamily towards the house. Her mother was standing watching her. Evie skipped towards her. 'Eddie had some good news. The War Artists Advisory Commission is going to exhibit one of my paintings. Possibly in London!' She executed a small pirouette.

Rachel smiled. 'Congratulations, Evie. That is good news.' She studied her daughter's face for a moment. 'You're not fond of Eddie, are you, Evie?' She couldn't hide the sudden anxiety in her voice.

Evie stood stock-still. 'No!' she said sharply. 'No, I'm not. Not since Tony.' A shadow crossed her face. 'But Tony didn't want me, and it appears that Eddie does.'

'It doesn't have to be either, Evie,' Rachel said. 'Dozens of young men will fall in love with you, my darling. You will have the choice of all of them. Don't settle for Eddie just because he gives you expensive presents.'

Evie frowned crossly. 'I would never settle for Eddie. He and I have a business arrangement.'

'Oh, is that what it is?'

'You know it is. He sells my pictures and he knows all the important people in the art world.' For a moment Evie's face was very sober and her mother saw an expression there she didn't remember ever seeing before. Mature. Hard. Determined. 'Don't worry about Eddie, Mummy. I know exactly how to handle him.' Evie stepped past her into the kitchen. 'I'll go and change and help the girls until it gets dark.'

In her bedroom Evie sat on her bed, the camera in her hands. It was heavy, obviously expensive, with complicated shutter mechanisms. Quietly she put it down on the pillow and she walked over to the window and stood resting her elbows on the sill, looking out across the yard towards the fields. The clouds had drawn closer now and were full of portent. There was still no sign of aircraft anywhere. The enemy wasn't coming tonight.

For a long time she stood there staring out, then suddenly she turned towards her desk and rummaged in the drawer for some paper.

Darling Tony, she wrote. *I can't bear this. Please, please can we talk?*

At Westhampnett the CO called Tony into his office. 'A bit of a change for you, old boy. We've a bod from the Air Ministry coming down to do some portraits of you chaps. I've put you on the list.'

Tony flinched as though he had been hit. 'I don't think so.'

'Station Commander's orders, I'm afraid. We can't argue. I'm being done as well.' He glanced at Tony. 'I know this is not particularly tactful and all that, but we have to do what we are told. Evie is not official.'

'Evie and I are over. She hasn't been down here for days.'

'No. So, we have to submit to orders. I am told this chap won't take more than a couple of hours on each picture.'

Turps Orde was a man in his early fifties. He settled Tony down on a stool in the front room of the old house they used as a Mess and reached for his sketchbook and charcoal. 'So, you're one of the chosen few.' He had a friendly manner and put Tony at his ease. 'I'm told your girlfriend is a painter too.'

Tony nodded Glumly. 'She's had paintings commissioned by the WAAC.' No point in telling him she was no longer his girlfriend.

'Good for her. I shall keep a lookout for her work.' Turps reached for a piece of white chalk and began stroking highlights into his drawing. 'I'm having trouble doing portraits of you chaps. By the time the thing is finished you've probably been awarded a new medal.' He peered over his glasses.

Tony shook his head, embarrassed. 'Not me.'

'Ah.' Turps grinned. He tapped the side of his nose. 'Perhaps we should leave a space. I only sketch the best, you know, and a little bird told me there might be something in the pipeline for you, young man.'

15

Sunday 11th August, evening

Lucy was standing by her desk in the window. It was ten minutes since she had put down the phone and she was still staring out towards the floodlit spire of the cathedral which she could just see beyond the rooftops of the houses on the far side of the road. Huw was out. Before Robin had gone she had left a message begging Huw to come. Now there was nothing to do until she heard from him.

She glanced over her shoulder at the living room door. She had closed it behind her, leaving the kitchen across the landing with every light switched on and the radio playing quietly.

She paced up and down restlessly for a few minutes, then sitting down at last she reached for the pile of files on her desk. She still wasn't sure about what she was going to tell Mike and she was filled with foreboding. She didn't want to destroy their relationship. She paused, frowning. They didn't have a relationship; they were more like colleagues in a project. But whatever it was she didn't want to spoil it. The whole thing depended on her and Mike having complete trust in each other and now the mysterious Christopher was threatening to blow the whole thing out of the water. She couldn't afford to let that happen. With a sigh she pushed aside the files of documents and pulled Tony Anderson's log book towards her. Tony, whose face had been obliterated from Evie's portrait. Was she even sure it was Tony in the picture? No. Of course not. She wasn't sure of anything. She riffled through the book gently to see if there were any photos stuck in between the pages. There were a few pieces of paper, she had noticed before. Folded notes, one or two receipts at the end of the book which he had obviously tucked there for safekeeping and one letter on thin blue paper. Lucy unfolded it and caught her breath.

Darling Tony,

I can't bear this. Please, please can we talk? I don't know what I've done to upset you. I had a letter from your mother this morning. She sounded so kind. She said you had told her all about me and that then you had written to her and told her that our engagement was off. She thought it was my fault. She said you were unhappy.

I'm unhappy.

Please can I see you? I am going to ride down to the airfield gates this evening and bribe one of the guards to give you this. If you can, come up tonight.

I'll be waiting. E xxxxxxxx

Lucy stared down at the flimsy sheet of paper. It had been folded and unfolded so often that it was falling apart at the creases. Had he gone? Had Tony gone up to the farm? Had they made up their quarrel?

The sound of the front doorbell from the gallery below made her jump. She glanced at her wristwatch. It was nearly nine o'clock.

Huw looked exhausted when she pulled open the door and

let him in. 'I'm sorry I'm so late. Duty called. I had to go to the hospital,' he said as he followed her upstairs, 'but you sounded so distraught I felt I should come as soon as I could.'

Lucy felt a pang of guilt as she ushered him into the kitchen. 'I am really sorry. I didn't think. It wasn't late when I rang,' she defended herself.

He put his hand on her arm. 'It doesn't matter. I wasn't complaining.' He smiled. 'I was just worried that you had had to wait so long on your own. It sounded as though there had been developments.'

'There have.' Lucy glanced at the studio door. 'Let me show you.'

On the threshold of the studio she paused and took a deep breath before reaching in to flick on the lights. She led the way over to the painting on the easel and stopped dead.

'What is it?' Huw asked. He scanned her face and following her gaze turned to look at the picture. 'Is something wrong?'

She shook her head slowly. 'No, nothing is wrong.' Her voice was flat. There was no damage, no fresh paint. The young man's face, as cheery as ever peered over Evie's shoulder, unblemished. 'The whole corner of the painting was damaged,' she whispered. 'His face had been painted out.' She lifted a shaking finger and pointed. 'The picture was scratched. I found it on the floor.' For several seconds more she studied the portrait then she turned round to face him. 'Robin was here. He will tell you. He saw it. He helped me pick it up. He touched the wet paint and got some on his finger.' Again she faced the picture. She stepped up to it and examined it even more closely. 'It was so violently done I was afraid. We both were, and we decided it must have been an intruder, a real person, Huw, who had come in along the roof, perhaps, or slipped up from the gallery. Someone determined to destroy the picture, or at least the image of the young man. But now –'

'Now?' he responded gently.

'It wasn't, was it? Not a real person. A real person couldn't

247

have made all that go away. But,' she gazed at him helplessly, 'it wasn't Ralph.'

'What makes you think it wasn't Ralph?'

'I could sense it. I could feel it. It was a different –' She paused. 'A different sense,' she repeated lamely. 'As though . . .' Once again her voice petered out. 'That was why Robin and Phil stayed with me last night. I was suddenly so afraid.'

Huw waited several seconds. 'As though what?' he prompted again.

'It was someone quite different, that's all I know. Ralph is anxious, helpless, frustrated. This man was angry and strong and threatening.'

'You are sure it was a man?'

She nodded. Her back to him she approached the easel again. She bit her lip. 'Oh, yes. It's a man. No woman would have done this.'

Huw looked sceptical for a second, but he kept his thoughts to himself. 'And you were afraid,' he said gently. 'Both of you? How did Robin react to all this?'

'I told you. He thought it was a real person. So did Phil.'

'And they were prepared to leave you here alone?'

'No. They wouldn't go until I rang you.' She turned at last and smiled a little sheepishly. 'I told them you were on your way or they wouldn't have gone.'

'I'm sorry it took me so long.'

'It didn't matter. I was safe in the living room.'

'You didn't sense him in there?'

'No.'

For a long moment they were both silent, then Huw let out a drawn-out sigh. 'I will pray for the repose of the soul of whoever is haunting this place. That is all I can do, Lucy. Would you like to stay in here while I do it?'

Lucy shook her head. 'I'll go and put the kettle on.'

Huw smiled. 'Fair enough. I will join you shortly.'

In the doorway Lucy hesitated for a moment. Why not join

him? Why not support him with a murmured prayer even if she didn't think it would do any good? But what was the point of that? It might dilute whatever it was that he believed.

But, if she didn't believe in him why had she rung him?

Why had she rung him if, with part of her brain, she believed Robin; that whoever had done this was a real person, someone who had set her up? Someone who was determined she should abandon her research and leave Evie to her anonymity. Someone who was trying to scare her to death. Mike, or more likely, his cousin, Christopher Marston.

With a small perplexed grimace of confusion she made her way into the kitchen, gently pulling the studio door closed behind her. Reaching for the kettle she turned up the volume on the radio so that she couldn't hear anything that was happening behind the door.

Moments later she heard a shout followed by a crash. Footsteps pelted across the floor and someone was scrabbling frantically with the door handle. Frozen with terror for a second she couldn't move, then she ran towards the door just as it flew open and Huw almost fell into the kitchen. His face was ashen. Turning, he dragged the door shut then he staggered to the table and sat down. She could see the gleam of perspiration on his face. His hands were shaking as he brought them together on the table top and clasped them. She wasn't sure if he was praying or trying to steady himself.

'What happened?' she whispered.

He shook his head. 'He didn't wait to see what I was going to do. He picked up the canvas and threw it at me. I felt a rush of icy cold! I couldn't breathe! I felt hands round my throat!'

Lucy felt herself grow pale.

'You are right,' Huw went on. 'It is a man. A strong man. My dear,' he looked at her suddenly with such compassion she wanted to cry. 'I am sorry. This is beyond my experience and my capability. I must contact the bishop's office. This needs someone who is properly trained in the art of deliverance. I am not strong enough.'

Wearily he pushed back the chair and stood up. 'I want you to pack a case now, and come away with me. My wife will make you up a bed and in the morning we will discuss this with people who understand these things better than I. I was wrong and conceited and overconfident to think I could do this. A prayer for a lost soul is one thing. A confrontation with an angry and vengeful spirit is quite another.'

Lucy's immediate response was one of denial. 'I can't leave the gallery,' she gasped.

'Of course you can. Lock up, leave the lights on, set your alarm. It will be quite safe.'

'But not safe from him,' she said shakily. 'I will ring Robin and see if he and Phil will come back. Please, don't say anything to the bishop's office. This is my problem. I thought you could help me, but I don't want anyone else involved.'

'I have to tell them, Lucy.'

'No!' To her own surprise she shouted the word at him. 'No, I absolutely forbid it!' She paused in the sudden shocked silence that ensued. 'I don't think it's a ghost, Huw. I shouldn't have called you in. I think someone is trying to scare me off. I am not getting the Church involved. If it was a ghost, you would have been able to get rid of it. You would have sent it away. But if you can't do it, then it's not a ghost. I would rather you left. Please.' She was aware that she was sounding irrational, perhaps even a little mad. She tightened her lips. 'I am sorry but I would like you to go now. Whatever it is, however they did it, you've stirred things up. You've made it worse,'

'Lucy, my dear!' Huw looked anguished. 'I can't leave you here. I just can't! If you come with me we can discuss all this with my wife. Would you do that, at least? She is deeply intuitive, much more so than I am. She is nothing to do with the Church, I promise. In fact she probably feels as strongly about it as you do.'

Lucy shook her head. 'No. Thank you, Huw, but no. Please go.'

'But I can't leave you like this. At least let me stay with you till morning.'

She almost stamped her foot. 'Daylight makes no difference. It only seems more frightening in the dark, but he was here in broad daylight, in the sunshine. Please, just go.'

'Then let me wait until your friends arrive,' he pleaded. 'You mustn't be alone. If you now feel there is a real person behind this, then all the more reason you shouldn't be alone.'

'No need. Robin and Phil will come at once. I would rather you left.' She was suddenly desperate to have him out of the house. If he stayed, perhaps it would lead to a confrontation. Ghost or man, she was too frightened to contemplate it.

Huw rose to his feet. With a glance over his shoulder towards the studio door he moved away from the table and slowly pushed the chair back into place. 'I am so sorry to let you down. Remember, Lucy, it is my competence that has failed here, not God's.'

Lucy pursed her lips. 'I know you did your best. I don't blame you. Thank you for coming.'

He waited for another few seconds as though hoping she would change her mind then with a sigh he turned towards the door. She stood without moving as he walked slowly down-stairs, listening for his footsteps as he headed towards the gallery door, opened it with the faint jangling of the bell and then closed it again behind him. Then there was silence.

She put her face in her hands. She wasn't thinking rationally. She wasn't thinking at all. Why had she sent him away? At least he was company. At least he was there. With another glance over her shoulder she went through into the living room where she couldn't see the accusing blank which was the closed door of the studio. Reaching for the phone she punched in Robin's number. It went straight to voicemail. 'Oh, no!' She tried his mobile, then Phil's. All switched off. Desperately she glanced at her watch.

It was barely midnight and she was only just holding herself together.

Rosebank Cottage was in darkness. There had been no sign of Mike's car in its accustomed place and he had not answered the cottage phone. He must have gone back to London. The cottage was a refuge and she had the keys in her pocket. Cautiously she opened the front door and peered in. The place was very silent, the accustomed smell of polish and flowers and old wood surrounded her as she stepped inside and quietly pushed the front door closed behind her. She reached for the light switch and sighed with relief. It was as if she had been holding her breath for a very long time. If there were a ghost here it would be Evie, and Evie would keep her safe.

It didn't seem right to sleep upstairs. She pulled an old tartan rug off the settle in the bedroom, wondering how it had escaped Charlotte's modernising frenzy and huddled beneath it on the sofa in front of the empty fireplace. Exhausted by the events of the night she fell asleep at once.

October 22nd 1940

Evie woke suddenly, staring up into the darkness of her bedroom. It came again, a sharp crack against the window. She slid out of bed and tiptoed across the floor, pushing aside the blackout curtains and peering out into the night. There was a figure standing out in the yard looking up towards the window. 'Tony!' She turned and ran for the door, pattering down the stairs in bare feet and across the hall to the kitchen. She pulled open the back door and went out. 'Tony?' she whispered.

He appeared round the corner, pausing as he saw her in her white cotton nightdress and bare feet. 'Evie!'

In seconds he had wrapped her in his arms.

'Why didn't you come in?' she whispered when at last she could speak. 'You know the back door is never locked.'

'I was afraid I might run into one of your parents.'

'They are asleep, you silly. They are both so tired each night they would sleep through an air raid!'

Silently she took his hand and led him back towards the door. Her finger to her lips she guided him through the darkness of the kitchen to the staircase and up towards her bedroom. Once in there, the door closed, the key turned in the lock, they stood for a long time, their arms around one another, not speaking, not moving. She was the first to stir. Pushing him away slightly she groped for his belt and then his jacket and began to pull it off his shoulders. Quickly she unbuttoned his shirt and then reached for the waistband of his trousers.

'Evie,' he murmured. 'Are you sure?' She put her fingers on his lips to quiet him and determinedly went on divesting him of his clothes. Then she pulled him towards her bed.

It was a long time before they surfaced from beneath the eiderdown, tousled and giggling. 'I can't stay much longer, Evie. We might have a pre-dawn call,' he whispered. 'Sometimes Jerry sends spy planes over early ahead of the daytime attacks.' He ran his hand over her stomach and up to her breasts. 'Oh my darling, how I've missed you.'

'Then why did you break it off?' She rolled away and sat on the edge of the bed, the sheet round her shoulders as she groped for the matches so she could light the bedside candle, less risky than the overhead light. Suddenly she was shivering.

'I didn't. Evie, believe me it wasn't my idea.' He put his hand on her arm. 'Darling girl. I would never have broken up with you.' He climbed out of bed, reaching for his clothes. 'It wasn't my idea, sweetheart. Ralph had a word. He said there were reasons we couldn't be together.' He fastened his belt then he sat down next to her and put his arm round her shoulders. 'I don't understand.'

'Ralph told you?' Evie said after a short pause.

Tony nodded. 'And your Dad sent me a note.'

Oh God! Ralph. Eddie. Her father's loan. Evie's shoulders slumped as she remembered. Turning to him she put her arms round him and clung to him. That explained everything and she couldn't tell him however much she wanted to. Not yet. It was not her secret to tell.

'I love you, Tony. I have never loved anyone like this before,' she whispered.

He laughed gently. 'And there speaks the voice of how many years' experience?'

She giggled. 'Enough to know you are the one.'

'I'm glad to hear it.'

'But Ralph's right, we have to keep it a secret. Just for now. Just as I have to stay away from Westhampnett for a bit.'

He opened his mouth as if to argue, then closed it again. He nodded. Gently he pulled away the sheet, burying his face in her breasts. They sat still for a few moments then at last Tony stood up. 'I have to go, Evie.'

She nodded, biting her lip. It was bad enough for him without her making a fuss. 'How did you get here?' she whispered. 'I didn't hear Esmeralda.'

'I didn't dare make a noise. I cycled up. Don't worry. It won't take me long. Bill is covering for me and the lads at the gate will look the other way when I sneak back in.' He bent and kissed her.

They tiptoed down the stairs, holding their breath as one of the steps creaked under their feet. Evie followed him outside and across the yard. By the gate she stopped and watched as he vaulted over it and retrieved an old bicycle from the hedge.

'See you soon, my love,' he whispered. Pulling the bike round he scooted it down the lane a few paces and threw his leg over the saddle and began pedalling for all he was worth. Then he was gone.

Upstairs in the farmhouse Rachel heard the click of the back door closing softly and the patter of feet across the hall and up the stairs and she smiled to herself. So, the romance was back on. She hoped Evie had been careful. Beside her Dudley groaned and turned over. 'What's that,' he murmured. 'Is someone there?'

'No one,' she whispered. 'Just the wind. Go back to sleep. Morning will come soon enough.'

Monday 12th August

'Lucy!'

The voice penetrated her restless dreams and dragged her slowly awake.

'What are you doing here?' Dolly was standing beside the sofa staring down at her in astonishment. Lucy sat up slowly, stiff and uncomfortable and for a moment she couldn't remember where she was. Then it came back to her, the gallery, the picture, Huw's failure, and Mike. With a groan she sat up and glanced at her wristwatch. It was just after nine. The action gave her time to think of an excuse for her uninvited presence.

'I don't know how it happened. I was doing some extra work and I was suddenly so tired I thought I would lie down for a few minutes. Oh, Dolly. I'm sorry. How awful.' She swung her legs sideways off the sofa, and managed to stand up, running her fingers through her hair, which hung loose on her shoulders.

Dolly looked at her quizzically but all she said was, 'Go and wash your face, and I will put on some coffee. I've come in today to make up for the day I missed at the dentist.' She picked up her bags and made her way towards the kitchen where Lucy joined her ten minutes later.

'It was rather a hectic weekend,' Lucy said by way of explanation. 'I saw Michael – he came to the gallery – then I came over here a bit later hoping to see him again before he went back to London, but he had gone so I went over to the studio to catch up on a few things. I thought I would come in and

255

make some coffee to give me the energy to drive home and I suppose it all overwhelmed me.' She gave Dolly a hopeful smile.

Dolly merely nodded. 'Would you like some toast?'

'I would. Yes, please.'

'Did Mr Michael come over to talk to you about Christopher and what he had told him?' Dolly said. She had her back to Lucy, taking a loaf from the bread bin and reaching for the knife.

Lucy felt herself grow cold. So, he had told Dolly. 'He did, yes.' There was no point in lying any more.

'And have you got one of Evie's paintings?'

For a moment Lucy was about to deny it, then slowly she nodded. What was the point? It was all going to come out now. 'I don't know,' she said. 'We hoped so. My husband thought it might be. Then there was the car crash.'

'And the picture was destroyed.' Dolly seemed to take it as a fact. 'So that was why you became interested in Evie's work?'

Lucy hesitated. 'Not entirely. I was interested in the women war artists before, but seeing the picture focused me on Evie, yes.'

Now was the moment to say that the picture had survived, that it was in the gallery in Chichester and that it appeared to be haunted by a ghost who had chased her out of her own home last night, but somehow she didn't have the strength to say any more. She reached for the cafetière and poured herself a second mug of strong black coffee. 'Mike was angry I hadn't told him about it,' she said at last. 'But the moment never seemed right. The picture has never been authenticated. It is very different from the others of hers that I have seen.' All that was true.

If Dolly noticed the change of tense from was to is she didn't say anything and Lucy found herself suddenly wondering if the picture did still exist. She had not gone into the studio again last night. The ghost, if that was what it was, had thrown the canvas at Huw, that was what he had said. It had thrown it at him and he had run away. If it hadn't been a ghost and was some person, Christopher Marston, or even Mike playing some weird game with her, determined to get rid of the painting for some reason, it was in a way even more terrifying. Perhaps the picture was destroyed. She shivered. Dolly noticed that, at least.

'Are you all right, my dear? I hope you didn't take a chill last night. I saw you had the presence of mind to fetch down Evie's old rug.'

Lucy blushed. 'I must have woken up enough to realise that I was cold. I am feeling a bit shivery.'

'Well, you'd best go home and go to bed properly,' Dolly said firmly. 'We don't want you getting pneumonia, do we?'

The gallery was open when Lucy made her way from the car and pushed open the door. Robin was sitting at the desk writing something in the sales ledger. He peered at her over his reading glasses, then took them off and threw them down. 'OK, ducky. What's the story?'

She dropped her bag on the floor beside the desk and threw herself into the armchair beside him. 'I was chased out by the ghost. Huw couldn't cope.'

Robin leaned back in his chair and stared at her.

'Have you been upstairs?' she asked before he had a chance to speak.

'Of course I have. I went to look for you.'

'And is everything all right?'

'Apart from the fact that you left all the lights on, yes.'

'Have you been in the studio?' She could hear the tension in her voice.

He eyed her carefully. 'I have, yes.'

'And was the picture damaged?'

'No.'

'No?'

'No overpainting, no splodges of new paint, no scratches.'

'And it was on the easel?'

'Where else would it be?'

If it was Christopher he would have taken the painting. Wouldn't he? Or Mike? Always that nasty little caveat at the

257

back of her brain, could it be Mike? But Mike wouldn't do this to her, surely?

But Mike or Christopher, neither would risk damaging a valuable painting. The terrifying sinister entity which had been here last night wouldn't care, didn't care. It wanted to stop her, it wanted to frighten her. What did it want?

'He . . . someone . . . something . . . threw the picture at Huw. It sounded as though it had smashed. That was why I ran away.'

'Huw left you here alone?'

'No, he wanted me to go and stay with him and his wife. He . . . I . . . I was being unfair just now. He just said it was more than he could deal with and he would have to call in his God squad of ghostbusters and I said no. I was horrible to him. I tried to ring you too,' she added. She glanced at him apologetically. 'I didn't know what to do. I wondered,' she paused, 'I wondered if Mike or Christopher were behind this. If you are right and ghosts don't exist, maybe someone is pretending to be a ghost, but either way, I couldn't face staying here, so I went to Rosebank Cottage.'

'You WHAT?' Robin looked at her incredulously.

'I knew Mike wouldn't be there,' she said after a moment. 'He told us he was going back to London, remember? And I checked by calling first. I just didn't want to be here!'

'And if it was Mike behind all this?' Robin said gravely. 'It would mean he is a dangerous man. And yet you believed him when he said he was going back to London?'

Lucy pushed her hair back from her face with a sigh. Her head was splitting. 'I wasn't thinking straight.'

'No.' Robin exhaled loudly. He sat forward in the chair, tapping a pencil on the desk. 'So now what?'

'I don't know.' She felt like crying suddenly.

'It seems to me,' Robin said at last, 'that you have stirred up one hell of a wasps' nest here! And,' he added grudgingly, 'maybe not just in the present day, but perhaps in the past as well! I'm not sure the Marstons are capable of doing any of this, Luce. Didn't it start before they knew about the painting? If it is all a hoax it is an incredibly clever one. I searched that studio. No one could have got in there.'

'So, now you are telling me that you think it is a ghost?' She looked up at him miserably.

'I'm saying that all this is getting out of hand. You, we, can't cope with this on our own.'

'If it is a ghost, I don't want the Church involved.'

'Not even Huw?'

She slumped back in the chair. 'Huw is not like the other vicars I've met, like the one who did Larry's funeral. I like Huw. I trusted him.' Her shoulders hunched dejectedly. 'He did his best. He is a kind man. It was beyond him, that's all. When I realised he couldn't do it, I panicked and sent him away.' She groped in her pocket for a tissue. 'That was when I decided that maybe it wasn't a ghost after all, that maybe the Marstons were behind all this. I wanted to believe they were behind it.' She looked at him pleadingly.

'If the Marstons are behind this, Luce, we need the police,' Robin said quietly. 'But they aren't, are they? They may be angry with you, they may be furious with you and want to stop you researching Evie for some reason, but they are not capable of entering a locked room on the first floor and conjuring with disappearing paint and flying pictures!'

He reached across and took her hands. 'So, on the one hand, you seem to have wound up this Christopher person big time, and you've alienated Michael Marston into the bargain. On the other, you are being besieged by something weird. Whatever and whoever it is, you can't stay here with canvasses flying round your ears and doors slamming and oil paint being splodged over our portrait. Come on, Lucy. Get real! You are out of your depth. You have to move out and you have to call in the professionals.'

October 27th 1940

Waiting to taxi into position and take off into the pre-dawn light Tony smiled to himself. He had hardly slept at all after leaving Evie and crawling back into his bed at the Mess in the early hours, but this morning a mug of strong black tea and a cigarette had woken him sufficiently for him to feel on top of the world. As A flight roared over the grass and up into the air, heading over the spire of Chichester cathedral where it emerged from the early morning mist, and then climbed round towards the east he let out a whoop of joy.

'Squadron heading vector one twenty, climb to angels one five.' The sector controller's instructions crackled over his headphones. He glanced to the side and saw Bill do a thumbs up as he held position next to him as the first rays of the rising sun caught their wings and glittered on the Perspex hood over his head.

'One hundred and fifty plus bandits approaching Worthing at angels one eight. The buggers are early this morning, chaps. Let's give them what for!' The voice crackled again.

Tony smiled. He glanced across at Bill and returned the thumbs up sign, then the planes were wheeling south again, gaining height across the still-dark sea away from the chalk cliffs of Sussex.

Later that morning Ralph was grabbing a mug of tea, sitting in a shabby old deckchair outside the dispersal hut at Tangmere with a newspaper as his plane was refuelled when Al approached him. 'That was quite a spat this morning! Three of theirs shot down but two of ours damaged.' He grabbed a chair next to Ralph. 'One of them was Tony Anderson.'

Ralph looked up. 'Was he hurt?'

'Not much.' Al pursed his lips. 'Nothing a bit of sticking plaster and a good mechanic won't fix.' He rubbed his face with his hands wearily. 'Is Tony still keen on your sister?'

Ralph shook his head. 'No. I think that's over. Why?'

Al frowned. 'This is between us, yes?' He leaned forward, dropping his voice, his elbows resting on his knees. 'I've heard a rumour about Tony. It seems that he has enemies and I am not talking about Jerry.'

'What?'

Al reached into the breast pocket of his battledress and pulled out a pack of cigarettes. He passed one to Ralph and brought out his lighter.

'Someone told me in confidence that he thought we had a case of friendly fire. It was not officially reported but it looked to the observer as though it was intentional.'

Ralph stared at him, the cigarette burning untouched between his fingers. 'You're not serious?' He felt sick suddenly.

Al nodded. 'Serious enough to tip you the wink. I'm not sure who Tony's muckers are over at Westhampnett and I don't want to speak to the wrong person by mistake, but you might have a cautious word with him. Don't put the wind up the lad too much, but it wouldn't do any harm if he were to watch his back for a bit.'

'That is appalling!'

Al nodded. 'Not something we need just now. He's landed safely back at Westhampnett. I had a word with his CO on the phone after we got back. No accusations or anything, just a friendly enquiry. Don doesn't seem to have noticed anything suspicious, but then he might be being as cautious as me. I was told there weren't any bandits within range at the time.'

Ralph finally remembered the cigarette and raising it to his lips took a deep draw on it. 'I can't think of anyone who doesn't like Tony. But it's difficult to know what's going on, being based at different airfields.'

Al stood up. 'Just keep your eyes open, old boy.' He raised his hand to his rigger as the bowser finished refuelling his plane and pulled away. Al was ready to fly again. He headed for the dispersal hut.

Ralph stayed where he was, lost in thought. Of course Tony

had an enemy. But surely to God Eddie would not contemplate trying to kill him and even if it had crossed his mind, his clammy reach would not, could not, extend to someone in one of the squadrons. And anyway, Tony and Evie had broken it off. Or Tony had. Hadn't he?

From the flight hut behind him the sound of a telephone rang out. Time to go to work again. Eddie and Evie forgotten, he threw down the cigarette and reached for his helmet and goggles.

16

Monday 12th August

'The thing is, the picture hasn't actually been damaged.' Lucy and Robin had closed the gallery, stuck a 'Back at 2 p.m.' sign in the window and were having lunch in a bistro in South Street. 'It is all smoke and mirrors,' she went on. She had had a shower and a walk to clear her head and felt more rational now. 'We think damage has been done, we hear the crashes, we see and touch the wet paint, but it isn't real. It's some sort of hallucination.'

'You don't think there is a risk of this becoming real? Of it actually happening? Of the picture being destroyed?' Robin topped up her glass of wine and dug once more into his plate of linguini.

It was only when she had realised that she was starving that Lucy had remembered that she hadn't eaten for nearly twenty-four hours. With the door locked on the gallery and its problems, in the cheerful atmosphere of the crowded little restaurant, she felt marginally more relaxed. Safely away from the malign influence in the studio she felt a little more able to confront what had happened and to try and decide what to do next.

'I don't know. That might be a real possibility.' She tore a piece off her bread and dabbled it in the oil and vinegar dressing in the little dish between them. 'If this is a ghost of some sort and not a human, then I need to talk to Mike and tell him everything. I can't go on misleading him. I have to have him on side otherwise his evil cousin will manage to convince him I am all the bad things he suspects and more.'

Robin grinned. 'But that's my Luce. Evil to her core. A schemer in the grand manner.'

She smiled in spite of herself. 'It's not funny! The whole enterprise could go belly up. It's bad enough not having Christopher Marston's support, but if I have lost Mike's co-oper-ation then that would be the end of the biography. I couldn't do it without his help. And yet now, I have this constant fear in the back of my mind. What if Mike is part of it?'

'One way to sort it out, if only in the interim,' Robin sat forward earnestly, 'and I don't know why we didn't think of this before, is to get rid of the painting. It's obvious, isn't it. So, the first thing you have to do, Luce, is find somewhere safe to store it. The painting is the centre of all this. It obviously can't stay in that studio right next to your kitchen.'

'No.' She sounded doubtful.

'So, where do we store a haunted oil painting?'

'I don't know.'

'But I do. Or at least I have an idea,' he said. 'Leave it with me. I am going to call Phil.'

By five o'clock that afternoon the picture had been crated and removed from the premises.

'Don't tell me where you're taking it,' Lucy said firmly.

Robin stared at her. They had lifted it into the back of his car and slammed the hatch door on it. 'Why on earth not?'

'Then I can't tell anyone.'

'You think Christopher Marston is going to torture it out of you?'

She smiled uncomfortably. 'No, but he might try and persuade me, as might Mike. And so might Ralph, to say nothing of the other one.'

Robin grimaced. 'I would have thought Ralph would have his own methods of finding it. After all, he found it here.'

'Yes but he has been here before. He knows the gallery. He won't know the place where you are taking it. Will he?' she added anxiously

Robin shook his head. 'That, I can guarantee.'

'That's enough. I don't want to know any more. I am going upstairs and I am going to throw open the door and the skylights in the studio ·and I am going to blow all the evil influences away. Whatever has happened here, whoever has caused it, once the picture is gone, it will all stop.'

'Good girl. And I will see you tomorrow having dusted every trace of where I have been off my feet. Just don't worry about it, Luce, OK? It will be safe, I promise.'

She nodded. 'I trust you, Robin.'

'Good girl.' He went round to the front of the car and climbed in.

She waved him out of sight before going back inside the gallery. Flipping the sign on the door over to read *Closed* she switched on the downstairs alarms, then went up to the kitchen.

The place felt peaceful and somehow clean. She walked through into the studio and looked round before going to push open the skylights. The gentle murmur of distant traffic filled the room as she moved round tidying away the bottles and brushes which had been scattered over the table, pushing the easel back against the wall, restacking the portfolios in the corner. One day she would have to decide what to do with this room . If indeed she decided to stay at all. It could be her study, of course. That would be a sensible choice, somewhere to store her books and papers and put a proper desk at which she could do her research. Or it could become a second bedroom, some-where for visitors to stay. Or perhaps both. She sighed. In spite of what had happened over the last few days it still felt like

Larry's room. Larry's domain. It was going to be a long time before it would properly be hers Perhaps one day she should go and get rid of the responsibility of the gallery. For now, though, she had no choice. She had to write this book. For Larry, but also now for Evie. She had to know what happened to Evie, she had to know who the enigmatic young man with the joyous smile was. And who the *éminence grise*.

Leaving the door open behind her she went back into the kitchen and then through into the living room. On the table lay the books she had been studying. Sitting down she pulled the log book towards her once more and opened it. It was as she was leafing through the entries that she felt a cold draught blow through the flat. Behind her the studio door banged shut.

Wednesday 14th August

'She lied to you!' Charlotte was sitting in the small back garden of Mike's Bloomsbury flat sipping from a glass of prosecco as the shadows deepened. Soon it would start to get colder and it would be time to go in, but she had spent a long time worming out of him whatever it was that had been bugging him all week and at last he had come clean. Lucy Standish had failed to tell him the one important thing about her life. She owned, or at least had owned an Evelyn Lucas oil painting. 'The conniving bitch!'

Mike flinched. 'She didn't lie. She just didn't mention it. And I can see why. If it was destroyed in the fire which killed her husband it is hardly the sort of thing she would want to remember.'

'No. Of course not. She lost her man. But she also lost a fortune!' She was silent for a moment. 'Unless it was insured, of course.' She took another sip from her glass. 'Which goes for him as well, I suppose. One way and another she's probably a rich woman now.'

'Don't be such a cow!' he snapped at her.

She gave him a haughty look. 'Touched a nerve, have I? Oh, come on, Mike. Can't you see beyond her wistful looks and her big eyes. She's not a damsel in distress who needs rescuing. She is on the make. Your cousin is damn right about her. She is probably cleaning out Evie's studio as we speak now she's been warned off by him. When you next go down to Rosebank you will find it completely bare.'

Mike sighed. Levering himself out of the garden chair he wandered across to the French doors and went inside. 'It's bare already, Charlotte,' he called over his shoulder. 'That's the point. It has already been cleaned out by Chris. He helped himself to everything, including things which had been specifically left to people like Dolly who are not in a position to argue about it.' He had wandered over to the counter, opened the fridge and helped himself to another bottle of lager.

'Are you letting her continue sorting through the stuff?' Charlotte followed him inside.

'I didn't tell her not to.'

'Well then, you're a fool.' She put down her glass, elbowed him out of the way and went to the fridge in her turn. 'I called in at the deli on the way back. There are some nice things in here for supper.'

He watched her as she bent over, her silky hair sliding over her shoulder to expose her slim neck and tanned back in the scoop-necked dress, the delicate knobs of her spine looking strangely erotic as she moved. He was a lucky man to have such a beautiful woman in his kitchen however much she irritated him from time to time. As she brought out paper bags and cartons and began to lay out the food on plates he put down his bottle and caught her arm. 'Why not do that later?'

She smiled. 'Because I'm hungry! And I know you; you just want to change the subject from the sainted Lucy.' She smiled at him winningly. 'Go on, deny it.'

He felt another wave of irritation. 'I do want to change the

267

subject, yes. It is boring me. I am here now. I don't want to spend the whole week agonising about Rosebank Cottage.' He moved away from her and crossed to the couch which ran along the opposite wall. Throwing himself down he reached for the remote and turned on the TV.

Charlotte watched him for a moment through narrowed eyes, then she went back to the food, laying it out neatly, opening drawers to find knives and forks and napkins, reaching for condiments and wine.

'Do you want to eat over there in front of the telly?' she asked when it was all ready.

'May as well.' He didn't look round.

She scowled. She pulled out the heavy lacquer tray his mother had given him as a house-warming present and transferring the food and plates to it brought it over to the coffee table. '*Voilà!* All ready.'

He glanced up. 'That's great. Thank you.'

'My pleasure.' She stood still for a moment studying his profile as he looked back towards the screen and suddenly she was afraid. She had never fallen in love before. She wasn't sure if she had fallen in love now, but she was certain that this man was the nearest thing to a real lover that she had ever experienced. She wanted to spend the rest of her life with him and very probably she wanted to be married to him and suddenly tonight she had sensed her certainty that he felt the same way about her slip away. It wasn't that she had annoyed him – she had done that before, God knows, it wouldn't be a proper relationship if they didn't irritate each other sometimes – but it was as if a cold draught had blown through the room. Not antagonism; it was something less obvious, something more subtle, something which had made the skin crawl on the back of her neck, something which she knew if she looked at it more closely might be panic.

Sitting down next to him she found herself for a moment unable to move, so intensely aware was she of this internal radar which was saying: shut up, don't mention Evie, don't mention Lucy. Back off. Dangerous ground. Don't go there.

As though sensing her turmoil Mike turned and stared at her. 'All right?'

Wordlessly she nodded. 'Food.' She pointed at the table. That subject at least was safe.

October 29th 1940

Rachel was sitting at the kitchen table, looking very serious. She glanced over her shoulder to make sure they were alone. 'Evie, I know you've been seeing Tony again. Why didn't you tell us?'

Evie was standing by the door about to go out into the yard. She spun round to face her mother. 'How do you know I've seen him?'

'I could hear you both, darling, going downstairs.' Rachel sighed. 'I know you're a grown woman, and I know you love him and he loves you, but you must, please, respect the fact that you are living under our roof.' She bit her lip in anguish. 'If it was just me, I wouldn't –' She stopped abruptly.

'You wouldn't?' Evie's voice was harsh.

'I wouldn't say anything about him going up to your bedroom,' Rachel said crossly. 'I probably wouldn't mind. He is an honourable young man, I am sure he is, but your father, Evie!' She was twisting her handkerchief between her fingers. 'He has strong values. He would not want his daughter doing anything to shame him. He does not want you to have anything to do with Tony.'

'Shame?' Evie stared at her furiously. 'And whose shame is it he's really worried about? I think we both know, don't we?'

'What do you mean?' Rachel stood up and faced her daughter. The two women were of similar height and colouring, and as they stood glaring at each other it was for a moment as though

269

they were twins. Then Rachel turned away, her face crumpling, their age difference at once obvious. 'First you were absolutely miserable and it was all off, then suddenly you are wandering around the farm in a happy daze. You've left jobs untouched. I haven't seen you with a sketchbook in your hand for ages. Are you even painting any more? Please understand, Evie. Your father is old-fashioned in many ways. And he has noticed the change in you. He has told me he doesn't want you to see Tony any more.'

Evie stared at her mother incredulously. Then it dawned on her. Her mother didn't know. Of course. No one had told her about the loan. Her father had kept it from her and now Ralph too had kept his secret.

'I'm not painting because I'm tired, that's all. We are all tired!' she said wearily. She gave a deep sigh. 'And yes, I'm thinking about Tony. And Ralph, and all their friends. Of course I am. So are you. I see you standing there lost in thought sometimes, and I know you're thinking about Ralph.' She paused. 'You are always worrying about Ralph! You always have! I thought you would be on my side over Tony, but you've never loved me like you love him,' she went on sadly. 'If I love Tony and I want to marry him you should both be pleased instead of trying to come between us. Then I would get out of your hair and no longer be under your roof!' Unable to bear the confrontation any longer she groped for the door handle, pushed the kitchen door open and stumbled out into the yard.

Eddie was standing just outside. 'Evie!' His face was white.

'No, Eddie, I haven't time to talk about painting now!' Evie pushed past him and ran across the cobbles. For a moment he stood still, looking after her, then taking a deep breath he stepped into the kitchen. 'Hello, Rachel.'

Rachel had dropped into her chair again. She looked up at him, her eyes full of tears. One glance told her he had heard at least some of the conversation.

'Eddie, she didn't mean it!' she said, instinctively trying to appease him.

'Didn't mean what? That she wants to leave home? That she wants to marry Tony Anderson? That she is too tired to paint?' His voice was strangely flat. 'I think she meant every word of it, Rachel.' He dropped the parcel he was carrying tucked under his arm onto the table. 'No doubt she won't want this now. Perhaps you would like to pass it on to someone who would!' he said, his tone icy. He turned and walked out. Two minutes later she heard the bang of his car door followed moments later by the roar of the engine.

For a long time she sat staring at the table top then at last she pulled the parcel towards her and began to untie the string. Inside was a box of coloured pastels and a new sketchbook. Pushing them away from her with an angry shove, Rachel stood up wearily and walked across to the open door. The hens were placidly scratching in the yard outside, their gentle clucking undisturbed by the car that had raced past them.

Wednesday 14th August

Huw's face lit up when he saw Lucy standing at the door of his vicarage, then it clouded as he noted her agitation. 'Come in.' He ushered her into his study, a room littered with papers and books. She noted a small crucifix hanging on the wall near the desk but that was the only sign of his trade.

'Maggie, my wife, is out at the moment. At a meeting of the young wives,' he said. 'Sit down, Lucy. Tell me what has been happening.'

Lucy was silent for a moment. 'I wanted to apologise. I chased you out.' She sat down on the chair he indicated after he had removed a pile of books and sat there upright, tense, fiddling with the buttons on her jacket. 'I knew it wasn't Ralph,' she said at last. 'In the studio, it was someone else.'

'Yes.'

'You could tell?'

'Yes.' He sat down at his desk looking concerned. 'Do you know who it was?' he asked.

'No,' she whispered. 'We have moved the painting. Robin and Phil have stored it somewhere. They haven't told me where. We thought that best. I thought it would all be all right now.' She bit her lip, appalled to find she was near to tears.

'And it's not all right?' he prompted gently.

'No,' she whispered. 'It's not.' She jumped as the front door in the hall banged and they heard someone came into the house.

Huw stood up looking visibly relieved. He went to the door and looked out. 'Maggie, dear, I wonder if you can spare us a minute or two.' He turned to Lucy. 'You don't mind, do you, if we tell Maggie what's been happening? I promise you she is discreet and she could help us.'

He ducked back into the room followed by an attractive woman who looked as though she might be in her early sixties, her wavy ash-blond hair damp and curly from the rain, her face glowing from her walk. She held out her hand to Lucy. 'Hi, I'm Maggie, Huw's wife. I have been to a meeting of the young wives in the village and I am knackered! I need a drink. Would you like one?'

She left the room returning with two small glasses of whisky. 'Here.' She handed one to Lucy. 'Drink it or I will have to have them both.' She tipped some papers off the second spare chair and sat down. 'Before you ask, I am a young wife on account of being the vicar's wife, but also in this village young means anyone under eighty so all the wives qualify. In fact all females. In fact we have two men as well.' She took a sip from her glass and closed her eyes with a sigh, leaning back in the chair.

Huw ran his fingers through his hair, apparently silenced by this force of nature that was his wife. He glanced at her, satisfied himself that she had stopped talking and turned to Lucy. 'I'm not sure if I mentioned to you that my wife is the psychic one in this house. We met five years ago when I was training for the priesthood. I was a widower and we met because of our interest in trying to resolve the pain of lost souls.'

Maggie smiled. 'I am afraid I bollixed his chances of getting on the bishop's deliverance team. Huw knew I wouldn't be acceptable to them as a camp follower. I am not a God botherer. He told me about you, Lucy, I hope you don't mind. He said you and I would get on.'

Lucy was silent for a moment and Maggie frowned. She set down her glass and leaned forward in her chair. 'Would you like me to shut up and go away?'

Lucy shook her head. 'No. No, I would rather you stayed. I'm sorry. I was a bit taken aback. I didn't realise Huw had talked to anyone about me.'

'I did ask you, Lucy,' Huw interrupted.

'Yes, you did. I remember now.' Lucy rubbed her face ruefully. 'So much has happened. I can't cope with it all, somehow.' She took a sip from the whisky and felt the warmth run through her veins. 'I would like to talk to you, please. Both of you.'

Behind them the door creaked open a crack. Lucy felt herself tense, but already Maggie was laughing. 'Don't panic. It's Roger. As in Roger the Dodger, our cat. Do you mind cats? I'll chase him away if you do.'

Lucy managed a shaky smile. 'I love cats. We could never have one, living in the middle of the town as we do, otherwise I expect Larry and I would have had cats and dogs galore.'

She held out her hand to the magnificent ginger cat who walked into the room purring loudly as he went to Maggie and rubbed against her legs. He ignored Lucy.

'Roger is deeply jealous of the young wives,' Huw said, 'as am I.' He gave a tolerant chuckle. 'Roger is a one-woman cat I'm afraid, but if you are very good he may condescend to speak to you when he is used to your presence.' He turned to his desk. 'Now, Lucy. You were saying that the picture has been removed to a place of safety?'

Lucy nodded. 'I thought the problems would stop, but they haven't.'

'Tell us what happened.'

'The studio is still being haunted. There are noises; the door bangs; I can sense him there.'

'Ralph?' Huw asked

'No, the other one. The angry one, and I wondered, that is, it occurred to me, do you think it is Rachel? Do you think I brought her with me from Box Wood Farm?' Lucy looked from one to the other desperately.

Maggie was studying her thoughtfully. 'I can see the negative energy round you now, Lucy. It is a distinctly male energy. No,' she leaned forward with a restraining hand as Lucy leaped from her chair in a panic, 'don't be afraid. We can deal with it. You are very open and vulnerable at the moment. We have to teach you to protect yourself, to make sure you have a strong shield in place.' She glanced at her husband. 'Huw does this by way of prayer, but if you feel prayer doesn't do it for you, I can teach you some techniques which work just as well.' She gave a gurgle of laughter and then glanced back at Lucy. 'You can see why I am *persona non grata* with Huw's boss.'

'She is in spite of everything, a very good vicar's wife,' Huw put in loyally. 'I doubt if any of the young wives would ever guess what she gets up to in her spare time.'

Lucy found herself laughing with them as Maggie bent and lifted the cat onto her lap, stroking its head. It started to knead her knees with its paws.

'And are you able to tell me what or who this energy is?' Refusing to be distracted, Lucy brought the subject back to the negativity around her. She was feeling apprehensive and vulnerable.

Maggie put her head to one side. 'I can't at the moment, no. I can't see beyond a swirl of angry colours.'

'So does that mean it is definitely a ghost?' Lucy said after a moment's pause. She couldn't hide her discomfort. 'It definitely isn't a real man who has been doing this? Setting me up.'

They both looked at her solemnly. 'Someone may be threatening you, Lucy,' Maggie said after a moment, 'but this energy around you, I would say is so diffused, so strange, my guess is that it is what you call a ghost, yes. The anger of a live person you have encountered would contain a different pattern of colours, it would be structured differently.'

'So, is this what they call an aura?' Lucy couldn't quite keep the scepticism out of her voice.

'I am trying to avoid the word.' Maggie smiled. There were deep laugh lines at the outer corners of her eyes and Lucy found herself liking the woman more and more. 'It usually turns people off although it is a perfectly good word for describing what is in essence indescribable.'

Huw cleared his throat. 'I should at this point be saying that I don't believe in all this and that only the power of prayer can intervene, but I believe that God has given some people the ability to see beyond the norm, and that he gives some of those people the power to heal this sort of situation just as he gives some people the vocation to be doctors.'

'So, what I need is healing,' Lucy said thoughtfully, 'but not before I have discovered who is haunting me and what he can reveal about Evie's story?'

Maggie burst out laughing. 'Oh, my dear, you are only asking for miracles! But I like your attitude. You are prepared to suffer for your art, even if it puts,' she hesitated for a fraction of a second, 'if it puts your peace of mind at risk.'

'As long as it is just my peace of mind,' Lucy murmured. She looked up in time to see husband and wife exchange a quick glance. 'Which is not what you were going to say, was it?'

'No.' Maggie's face lost all trace of humour. 'No, I was going to say, your sanity, or even your life.' She grimaced. 'But I thought better of it because it would never come to that. Whatever is going on here, it is not the stuff of life and death,

I am sure. It is sadness and anger – normal human emotions – which have for whatever reason become trapped in our space and time. We can work with this, and sort it, I promise.'

She smiled again and Lucy tried to return the smile. Why when Maggie sounded so reassuring did she not feel the least bit reassured?

November 4th 1940

Eddie stared at the young man who had brought the note. 'Who gave you this?' he said sharply.

'One of the airmen. He said it was urgent.' The messenger was no more than a boy, Eddie saw now. Too young to enlist.

'You did right to bring it straight away,' he said, suppressing a smile. He reached into his pocket and brought out a sixpence. The boy had bony shoulders, angular wrists sticking out from rolled-up sleeves, scraggy knees protruding from threadbare shorts. 'Keep your eyes open. There might be more messages for me.'

'Yes, sir!' The boy had bright intelligent eyes. No, not intelligent. Knowing. Eddie smiled again. 'Good lad. Off you go.'

He slid his thumb under the flap of the envelope and pulled out the single sheet of paper. *Near miss. Better luck next time.* It was unsigned.

Eddie scowled. Tearing up the note he held his lighter to the pieces and dropped them on the ground, grinding the ashes into the mud with his heel.

Thursday 15th August

Mike's mother stepped out of her small bright blue Volkswagen Lupo and surveyed her nephew's abode with an expression of quizzical distaste. In coming to see Christopher, she was about to interfere and she knew Mike would be furious with her, but interfering was what she did best! With a sigh she slammed the car door and turned towards the house. The front door opened as she mounted the steps.

'Juliette!' Frances Marston smiled at her. 'How lovely to see you after such a long time.'

The two women air kissed and Frances led the way inside.

'It seemed foolish to come to Midhurst and not look in if you were at home,' Juliette said cheerfully. She proffered a small box of handmade chocolates as a peace offering. Today she was wearing a vivid green tunic over black harem pants with open-toed red sandals. As she handed over the chocolates her bangles rattled noisily.

Taking the sweets, Frances turned and gave her a bleak smile. She had, Juliette noticed suddenly, a black eye, fading, and well covered with make-up, but nevertheless obvious as she moved into the beam of sunlight which fell through the French windows. Frances sat down on the sofa and Juliette followed suit, positioning herself opposite her, on the far side of the coffee table with her back to the window.

'Is Christopher home?' Juliette enquired after an awkward pause. She tried to keep her voice nonchalant.

Frances shook her head. 'Just me, I'm afraid.'

'That's good,' Juliette said firmly. 'If I remember rightly Christopher has a tendency to take over every conversation and I wanted to see you.'

'What you really mean is, that you want to talk about this woman who is writing Evie's biography,' Frances said with a grimace.

No need for oblique approaches to the subject, then, Juliette thought dryly. 'The topic was bound to come up,' she said. 'I gather Christopher is not happy about it.'

'No. He's not.'

Juliette clasped her hands in her lap. 'Why?'

The directness of the question appeared to take Frances aback for a moment. 'Isn't it obvious?' she said after a moment.

'Not to me.'

This time the silence stretched out for what seemed to Juliette like minutes. 'Is there some kind of a problem here I don't know about?' she said at last, her voice gentle. 'If I don't know what it is, how can I help?'

'It just needs for everyone to mind their own business!' Frances cried. She rammed the heels of her hands into her eye sockets for a moment as though trying to stem her tears.

'But Evelyn Lucas is everyone's business, Frances,' Juliette remonstrated softly. 'She is a national treasure. You can't pretend she is of no interest to the world. If Lucy Standish hadn't decided to write her biography, someone else would, and someone a lot less sensitive than Lucy. If you tell me why there is this huge problem, then perhaps I can mediate in some way between you all. Mike doesn't seem to know what the problem is. He is happy for the book to go ahead. I haven't spoken to George, but I am sure –'

'Don't!' Frances looked up furiously. 'Don't speak to Chris's father. You mustn't. Chris would be livid.'

'OK. But why not?'

'I don't know.' Suddenly Frances's fury had dissipated. Her words came out as a wail. 'I don't know about any of this. Chris won't tell me. When I asked him he was livid with me. He said it was none of my business. He was so angry when I said Lucy had been here I thought –' Again she stopped. 'I thought he was going to kill me,' she finished in a whisper. 'The children were due back today. They're in Scotland with my parents. He rang them up last night and said they couldn't come home. He said we had to go away and they should stay there till the end of the holidays.'

'And your parents were happy with this?" Juliette asked tentatively.

'Oh, yes. They love the kids, and Hannah and Ollie will be very happy there. And safe.' Frances wrapped her arms around herself with a shiver.

'And are you going away?' Juliette had long ago stopped feeling impatient with this poor fragile woman. Her sympathy was mounting with every second.

'I don't know.' Frances stood up suddenly. 'I think you'd better go, Juliette. It was nice of you to drop in, but I never know when he, when Chris, might come back suddenly. I would hate him to find you here.'

'Why? I am his aunt!'

Frances smiled. 'I don't think he is a great one for family loyalties.'

'Although he loves family inheritances.' Juliette was tight-lipped as she levered herself off the sofa.

Frances gave a small nod. She led the way out of the room into the hall. 'I liked Lucy,' she whispered as she pulled open the door. 'She seemed a nice person.'

'She is.' Juliette stepped outside then she turned. 'You do know where I live, don't you, Frances? I want you to remember you can come to me any time, my dear. Any time at all.' She reached over and kissed Frances's cheek then she turned away, but not before she saw the other woman's eyes flood with tears again as she stepped back inside and shut the door.

At the gallery in Westgate Huw and Maggie followed Lucy up the stairs. They had turned the Closed sign over on the door, and Lucy had bolted it. The flat was hot and airless and very quiet. Lucy found she was clenching her fists as she stopped on the landing.

'Let me go first,' Huw said quietly. He stepped past her, opened the kitchen door and went inside. The studio beyond was empty, tidy. They saw him standing still and looking round.

Maggie turned to Lucy and smiled. 'Me next,' she whispered. 'You don't have to come in if you don't want to.'

Lucy remained where she was. Her heart was thudding in her chest as she strained her ears. She could see Huw and Maggie standing in the middle of the floor in silence. Both appeared to be listening intently. Huw put his hand in his pocket and drew out a small book. A Bible? She saw Maggie reach out and touch his shoulder. She pointed to something and Huw turned to look. He nodded and moved towards whatever it was. Lucy took a step forward. The board creaked under her foot and she caught her breath in fear. Neither Huw nor Maggie seemed to have heard.

She could see Huw's face now. He was murmuring something, the book held in front of him in both hands. Maggie was watching him intently. Slowly Huw moved forward, towards the studio door. He put out his hand towards something she couldn't see. Lucy bit her lip. The tension was becoming intolerable.

Suddenly, sunshine flooded in through the skylight and Lucy heard Huw's exclamation of surprise.

He was looking shaken. 'He was here,' he said. 'The other one. The stronger one. The angry one.'

Lucy cringed away. 'What did he look like?'

'I couldn't see, not clearly. Red. He was a swirl of red. He was angry.'

Maggie had moved beside her husband. Her face was white.

'Has he gone?' Lucy whispered.

Huw nodded. 'He's gone. For now.'

Downstairs in the gallery the doorbell rang suddenly.

'Ignore it,' Huw commanded.

'Lucy!' A woman's voice rang through the shop downstairs, presumably calling through the letterbox. 'It's Juliette. Mike's mother. Can I come in?'

'It's up to you, Lucy,' Maggie said sternly. 'The moment has passed here for now. Our visitor has gone.'

'Are you sure?' Lucy was shaking visibly.

'I'm sure.' Maggie smiled. 'Maybe someone else here would be a good thing. It will clear the air.'

Lucy ran downstairs and pulled open the door. Juliette was standing on the doorstep. For a moment they stared at each

280

other in silence. Lucy found she was incapable of speech, then abruptly her eyes filled with tears.

'Oh, no!' Juliette was horrified. 'You are the second person I've made cry in as many hours. Oh, Lucy, my dear. I am so sorry. Shall I go away?'

Wordlessly Lucy shook her head. She caught Juliette's hand and pulled her inside.

Maggie appeared on the staircase behind her. 'Lucy, dear, are you all right?'

'It's a friend of mine,' Lucy stammered. 'From Brighton.'

'Which sounds a bit like Coleridge's person from Porlock!' Juliette said cautiously. 'I'll disappear.'

'No. I would like you to stay. I want you to know what has been happening. Please.'

'Juliette?' Maggie Redwood recognised the newcomer first. 'What on earth are you doing here?' She ran down the last few steps, holding out her arms.

'Maggie?' Juliette let out a gurgle of delight. 'My God, what a small world!' She turned to Lucy. 'Maggie's husband, Huw, married Rick and me. Maggie offered to organise the flowers in the church and we realised we had known each other years ago in London when we were carefree and young.'

'Which we aren't any more!' Maggie said with a grimace. 'Lucy, my dear. Whatever serendipity this might appear to be, it is up to you whether Juliette stays.'

'I would like her to,' Lucy said again. 'She is Mike's mother! I want her to know about the picture. I am so tired of all the secrets and misunderstandings, and there is something so awful going on here.' She turned to the stairs and led the way up.

As they sat down in the sitting room Lucy launched into an explanation.

'I didn't tell Mike I had an oil painting by Evie Lucas and now he thinks I have been lying to him because I kept it from him. Christopher found out first and is furious and he told Mike.' She looked down at her hands, linked together on her lap.

'So, this picture is why Christopher is so angry and wants to stop you writing about Evie?' Juliette asked slowly. 'I've just been to see Frances. Poor love, she is terrorised by that man.' She pushed her bangles up her wrists in a businesslike way. 'But I'm not sure how you two fit in?' She glanced at Maggie. 'Am I being obtuse?'

'It appears that the painting is at the centre of some kind of psychic attack. Huw and Maggie have come over to help me deal with it.' Lucy gave a helpless smile at Juliette who was staring at her open-mouthed.

'For the first time in my life I am speechless,' Juliette said at last. 'I take it you are all being perfectly serious?'

Maggie leaned across and put her hand over Juliette's. 'Lucy has been in great distress. She needs your support.'

'And she will have it.' Juliette said firmly.

'I didn't mean to lie to Mike,' Lucy said in anguish. 'It has all got so complicated. I so nearly told you. I wanted to tell you. I didn't know which way to turn.'

'Can I see the painting?' Juliette asked. She glanced at Huw, who was sitting next to his wife in silence. The Bible was still clutched between his fingers.

'I was too frightened to let it stay here,' Lucy replied. 'Awful things were happening. Robin, my assistant in the gallery, has taken it away and hidden it somewhere safe. The picture was being attacked by someone. Something. That's why Huw and Maggie have come over.'

'My God!' Juliette looked taken aback for a moment, then she smiled. 'I remember Maggie in the old days. She was always doing the Tarot cards and crystals. But Huw?'

'Huw has come to pray for Ralph's soul. You remember you told me Mike's father was haunted by him?'

Juliette paled. 'It never occurred to me that this had affected other people. I thought it was just Johnny.'

'Would you rather go, now you know the situation?' Lucy smiled sadly.

'No way.' Juliette said. 'I am part of this. Or I think I am.

282

And, Lucy,' she paused, looking Lucy in the eyes, 'I think it's up to you to tell Mike about this painting. I think you should do it soon, but I won't say anything until you're ready, OK? And I would like to stay, as long as you don't think I will be in the way. I'd like to think that I might be able to help in some way. I am not psychic, but I firmly believe in these things. I couldn't have lived with Johnny all those years and not have felt that it was all terribly real, at least for him. I never saw anything, but he did. I know he did.'

'Perhaps Maggie and I should go back into the studio, Lucy,' Huw put in at last. 'To say a final prayer.'

They stood up. Maggie reached over and touched Lucy's hand gently. 'It will be all right,' she whispered.

When they were alone Lucy looked at Juliette. 'I'm not afraid, not when there are other people here. But when I'm on my own –'

'I don't blame you.' Juliette pushed her bangles up her wrists with a sigh. 'And you must come and stay with me. You can't stay here.' She raised her hand as Lucy started to protest, then she interrupted herself. 'But Ralph would never harm anyone, I'm sure he wouldn't.'

Lucy sighed. 'I don't think it's Ralph,' she whispered.

They both looked at the studio door. Huw had left it ajar and they could hear voices talking softly.

'He's praying,' Lucy murmured.

Juliette nodded.

'It's kind of you to ask me to stay,' Lucy went on. 'But I want to stay here. I have to stay here. I don't know if you can understand, but this is my home. I am not going to let them chase me away.'

Behind them the phone rang.

Lucy turned towards it. She hesitated then picked it up.

'Lucy!' It was Robin. 'Something terrible has happened. The storehouse where we left the painting. It's caught fire.'

17

November 12th 1940

'You did know Tony took one of the WAAFs to a dance last night?' Eddie dropped the remark casually into the conversation.

'What?' Evie dropped the potato knife into the sink and stared at him, her hands dripping with muddy water. He was seated at the kitchen table, his briefcase beside him on the floor.

'I was surprised, I must say.' He leaned back in his chair and folded his arms, his face carefully neutral. 'He seems to have got over his relationship with you very quickly.' He narrowed his eyes. 'I assume he has stopped creeping around you in the middle of the night, or is he still pretending you are the only woman in his life?'

'I don't believe you!' Her face was white.

He hesitated before replying. 'Maybe I got it wrong. I probably misheard –'

'No! You told me deliberately to upset me!' She reached across to the roller towel on the back of the door.

'I didn't mean to.'

'You did.' She put her hands on her hips. 'Why have you come? Haven't you got work to do?'

'I have, Evie, yes.' He adopted an infuriatingly conciliatory tone. 'I needn't have come but I felt I had to. I wanted to make sure you are all right. I care about you.' He looked away. When she made no response he stood up and bent to retrieve his briefcase. 'I brought you some money from the gallery. They've done well with some of your sketches. If you have any more I could take them –'

'I haven't. I've had too much on my mind to do any drawing. Or painting. What's the point? It's hardly helping the war effort!'

'Evie.' He looked seriously concerned now. 'But haven't you had a new commission?'

'I'm not in the mood.' She almost stamped her foot.

'Ah, now that is childish. If you don't behave like a responsible adult you won't get any more,' he said furiously. 'I worked very hard to get you that contract, Evie. If you mess it up I will look a complete fool.'

'You will look a fool?' She headed for the door. 'And how will I look if Tony has been taking other girls to dances?'

She had gone before he could answer, slamming the door behind her.

'What did you say to her?' Rachel must have been standing in the hall. She came in, her arms full of dirty overalls and threw them down into the basket on the floor near the sink. 'Eddie, you never seem to learn!'

He was standing staring after Evie. 'No.' He looked crestfallen. 'I'm a fool. She will come round, though, won't she?' They both looked up at the ceiling as the sound of aircraft approached from the south. Rachel opened the back door and went out into the yard.

'They're heading for Portsmouth.' Eddie had followed her, squinting up into the sun. 'My God, there are hundreds of them.'

'There are our boys now.' Rachel bit her lip. Was Ralph up there? They stood watching as the tight-packed formation of German bombers with their fighter escort thundered high along the coast. Then the fighter squadrons were there, Spitfires and

Hurricanes on their tail, breaking the formation, harrying the enemy, smashing their lines, the vapour trails all that could be seen now as they climbed out of sight, lacing the sky with deceptively delicate patterns.

Eddie glanced at Rachel. 'He'll be all right,' he said with surprising gentleness. 'Ralph is a damn good pilot.'

She nodded wordlessly. Behind them Dudley and one of the land girls had appeared, the dogs at their heels, walking across the paddock. Both stopped to look up, then they walked on. The sight had become commonplace. There was work to do.

Dudley waited until he could hear Rachel breathing evenly in bed beside him, then he eased himself carefully from their bed. He had left his clothes in a pile on the chair. Catching them up he tiptoed to the door and holding his breath he inched it open. The landing was draughty and the night cold as he dressed in the dark and crept in his socks down the stairs. His boots were by the kitchen door, his jacket on the hook. He glanced down at the two dogs which, tails wagging, had materialised out of the dark as he entered the kitchen and with a stern snap of the fingers sent them back to their blanket in the corner. There was no place for them where he was going.

He had been approached several weeks before as the threat of invasion became ever greater, by two neighbouring farmers. There were five of them now in the Auxiliary Unit; five local men in reserved occupations who were, as far as the locals knew, now members of the Local Defence Volunteers. What even their wives didn't know was that these particular men, meeting secretly at night at a hidden base, had been taught how to handle weapons, and had been given instruction in the art of sabotage and demolition. Like Dudley, the others had been born and bred in the area. They knew it like the backs of their hands. In the event of an invasion they would be ready, not just to defend their homes against the enemy but to take the battle to them. They were part of a secret army, with hidden dumps of weapons and supplies. They had been trained to kill and if necessary to die rather than divulge their secrets. And their discretion was guaranteed by the signing of the Official Secrets Act. They were to tell no one what they were doing, not even their immediate families.

Dudley glanced at his watch as he walked silently across the yard. He was late for their rendezvous. Rachel had been up until past midnight, and then as so often, too tired to sleep when at last she did go to bed. He gave a grim smile. Never mind. If he missed the start of the cross-country exercise they were planning for tonight it would be up to him to track the others down. Good practice.

He stopped suddenly as he heard a sound in the lane. Someone was out there in the dark. He shrank back into the shadows, edging along the side of the house and round the front, straining his eyes into the deeper black of the hedgerow as he heard the quiet squeak of the gate hinges.

Bending almost double he ran quickly across the yard and was on the man as he turned to close the gate after him. His hand groped for the mouth to silence him and he dragged him backwards towards the dairy, hearing the frantic scrabble of heels as his captive tried to regain his balance and fight back. Pulling him into the dairy he slammed his opponent against the wall and pinioning him with his elbow he groped in his pocket for his torch.

The wavering beam was trained for a moment on the intruder's face. It was Tony, eyes wide and frightened as he leaned against the wall, panting.

'My God, boy, what are you doing here?' Dudley let him go. 'Do you know how near I came to breaking your neck?'

Tony nodded, still gasping. 'I know. I'm sorry.'

'Sorry!' Dudley reached forward and grabbed the front of Tony's battledress, pulling him away from the wall. 'You will be a great deal sorrier if you can't give me a good reason for being here. I hope you were not expecting to meet my daughter!'

Tony put his hands up and as firmly as he could disengaged

Dudley's fists. 'I'm sorry,' he repeated, trying to catch his breath. 'We are so busy it isn't possible to get here in the daytime to see her.' He paused, suddenly realising what he had said. 'She didn't know I was coming. You mustn't blame her.'

'And how did you expect to see her?' Dudley's face was growing more angry by the second. 'She is asleep.'

Tony shook his head. 'I was going to throw stones at her window. We wouldn't have done anything wrong. Just a quick talk.' He looked at Dudley hopefully.

'Forget it!' Dudley switched off the torch. 'Go now. Before I get really angry. Go, and never come back here again, do you hear me? Leave Evie alone. I hear nothing but bad reports of you and her. She is not for you, boy, understood?' He sensed rather than saw the disbelief in Tony's eyes as the young man began to protest. 'Out!' he ordered. 'Out now and don't come back.' He reached again for Tony's arm and propelled him out of the dairy into the yard. 'Go! Before I set the dogs on you!'

Tony let himself out of the gate and stumbled back down the lane to where he had left the bike lying in the hedge. He glanced back once, but the yard behind him was silent and the house still in total darkness. He gave a grim smile. He could have got Dudley for flashing a torch around in the blackout if he had thought of it. Thank God Evie's dad hadn't caught him inside the house. Then there really would have been hell to pay. He took a deep breath. Poor Evie. He hoped her dad wouldn't make trouble for her tomorrow. He had said she didn't know anything about him coming, but that wasn't quite true. She expected him every night. Expected and hoped. He had only managed to come up to the farm two or three times, but when he had it had been worth it! He gave a quick secret smile at the memory of creeping up the stairs in the dark, letting himself into her bedroom, listening for a few seconds to the soft murmuring sounds she sometimes made in her sleep before undressing and sliding quietly into the bed beside her to wake her with his kisses.

Gripping the handlebars he was about to vault onto the saddle when he paused thoughtfully. What had Dudley been doing out in the yard at this time of night, anyway? It had been incredible bad luck, but he had not been expecting him, clearly, so who had he been waiting for? A chance movement of the torch beam had shown that Evie's father had been fully dressed in some sort of camouflage and his reactions to intercepting an unexpected intruder had been efficient and professional. Tony shivered. He had never thought much about Evie's father, beyond a tendency to avoid him if he could. He was to all outward appearances a quiet, hard-working farmer, with stern old-fashioned views, especially about his daughter, which Rachel and Evie both seemed to respect even if they honoured them in the breach rather than the observance. But he was so often out on the farm when Tony was there he had not registered that much. Pushing the bike, Tony headed down the lane, deep in thought. Surely Dudley Lucas could not be a spy?

Thursday 15th August

The fire was out when they got there. The fire engine was still parked in the road outside the small warehouse as Huw drew up behind it. Lucy threw herself out of the car before it had come to a halt.

'Robin? What happened? Has the painting gone?'

Robin and Phil were standing on the pavement with two fire officers and a policeman.

'It's OK.' Robin put his arms round her. 'Calm down. The painting is safe.'

Maggie and Juliette had climbed out of the car and followed Huw, stopping to look at the warehouse in horror. From the outside there was no sign of damage save some smoke stains above a window at the side. A hose disappeared into the wide open doors at the front of the building but the firemen were standing, arms folded, chatting with the policeman. All three appeared calm.

'It looks as though it was an electrical short circuit of some sort,' Phil said. 'Luckily someone saw the smoke before anything too awful happened. There was nothing much stored in there and the picture's completely safe. It's in Robin's car.'

Two hours later they were all gathered in the sitting room of St Margaret's Rectory at Chilverly. The picture, still in its wooden crate, was leaning against the wall in the hall.

'Are you sure it will be OK to leave it here?' Lucy asked for the fourth time.

Maggie nodded. 'I'm sure.' She glanced at Huw. 'We agree. Whatever is going on Huw and I will deal with it.'

'Aren't you the least bit scared?'

Huw sighed. 'Maggie is my rock in these matters. Diocesan deliverance team or Maggie Redwood, give me Maggie any time. But I have a feeling nothing will happen while it is here. I don't believe the fire was anything to do with it. The investigation guys from the fire brigade know what they are doing. They catch on very quickly if it is arson.'

'Do ghosts count as arson?' Lucy asked.

'They don't believe in spontaneous spiritual combustion, put it that way.' Robin smiled.

'But you didn't tell them –'

'No, of course I didn't tell them.' He shook his head.

'So,' Maggie had seated them all in the sitting room at the vicarage. 'What we have is a conundrum. Ralph it is generally accepted was a nice guy, agreed?' She looked round the room. 'But now,' she focused on Lucy, 'we have this other presence making itself felt in the gallery and this one appears to be far from nice. Either Ralph has undergone an extreme character change, or it is someone completely different and he was sufficiently strong for something of his energy to remain with Lucy when she came here. He appears to have been determined to smash the picture, and maybe, although this is doubtful, he was behind the fire today. We already knew someone was determined to interfere with the painting. In what, for the sake of argument, I shall call real life, person or persons unknown have in the past tried to paint out the unknown figure standing behind Evelyn Lucas in the picture.'

The door behind her was nudged open a crack. Roger the Dodger walked in and stood surveying the scene.

'He's not unknown,' Lucy interrupted, her voice husky. 'His name was Tony Anderson. He was another pilot, like Ralph.'

The cat walked slowly through the room towards Maggie and majestically jumped onto her knee. She put her hand on its head as it settled down, paws folded neatly beneath its chest. It fixed its unwinking gaze on Lucy.

'I can't be sure, of course,' Lucy added, 'I am guessing. I think he and Evie fell in love with each other after they met In the summer of 1940.'

'So, what happened to him?' Juliette asked.

'I don't know. I am, as you know, going through what letters and notebooks I can find of Evie's. Sadly most of them, if they exist at all, must have been collected up by Christopher, but from one or two diaries I have been able to read Tony and Evie were very much in love.'

'But, for whatever reason, they split up?' Juliette went on. 'Do you think he was killed?'

Lucy nodded slowly. 'I suppose that is a strong possibility.'

'And so maybe it was Evie herself who painted out his figure in the picture. She couldn't bear to look at him after he died.' Juliette looked at them all in turn.

Lucy nodded. 'I had wondered that too.'

'It's strange,' Juliette said thoughtfully. 'I don't think I ever remember Johnny mentioning anyone called Tony. You would think if he was such an important part of his mother's life she would have said something, even if only much later when time had healed the hurt a little. After all, she married and had children, so she wasn't inconsolable forever.'

'She may have kept it to herself just because it was such a painful memory,' Phil put in slowly. He was sitting next to Robin on the sofa near the empty fireplace. With six of them in the room it seemed very crowded.

Maggie nodded. 'My instinct tells me that could be the most likely reason for not mentioning him. For now we will have to put that down as an unknown.'

'You don't think it is the ghost of Tony who is doing this?' Robin put in suddenly. 'He might be thoroughly pissed off at being painted out.'

There was a moment's silence. One by one they fastened their eyes on Maggie.

She smiled. 'Don't know. Huw?'

He shook his head. 'I don't know either. I have had no sense as to the identity of anyone in this story. I have assumed Ralph because we know what happened to him, and because Lucy recognised him from a photo, but he is the only personality in this story we have tried to contact.'

'Do you think the painting is going to be safe here?' Robin put in at last. 'Do you think you are going to be safe with the painting?' he added. He sounded subdued and Lucy found herself shivering.

Huw nodded. He glanced across at his wife. 'If Maggie says so, then I am content with that. I feel that surrounded by prayers, and safely in its box, it will at least remain quiescent for the time being.'

Phil looked from husband to wife and his face broke into a quizzical smile. 'Would it be very indiscreet to ask how you two manage to combine your different belief systems without coming to blows?'

They both laughed. 'Easily,' Maggie said. 'Our beliefs are actually very similar though we differ slightly as to how things work. As long as we come to the same conclusions, we are able to back each other up admirably.' She glanced at her husband with a fond smile. 'And if we cannot agree, then Roger has the casting vote.' She rested her hand on the cat's head again. 'For instance, if there was the slightest danger from that painting now, Roger would not be sitting here on my knee. He would be in the next county. Cats know about these things.'

Huw stood up. 'My friends, I feel we need to move on. May I suggest that Maggie and I return with Lucy to her flat and just check that all is well there, and that Phil and Robin return to check out your warehouse. Knowing about these things as I do, I fear the police and fire officers may still be there. Juliette, I am sure Maggie will be in touch soon.' He reached across to kiss her on the cheek.

'We have been dismissed, guys.' Juliette stood up, her bangles jangling.

'Only temporarily.' Huw beamed at her.

As they all moved into the hall Roger stalked past the picture, pausing to give it a cursory examination. Lucy found herself holding her breath as she watched, but he gave no sign of being upset, trotting happily past them all into the garden.

November 13th 1940

Tony telephoned Box Wood Farm twice the next morning and both times the phone was answered by Rachel. On each occasion she said that Evie was out in the fields. Her tone was clipped and unfriendly. He walked away wondering what had transpired when Dudley had told them about their meeting the night before. With A flight on standby he had no further chance to get near the telephone in the Mess that day, flying three sorties one after the other without a chance to get his breath back, never mind leave the dispersal area.

When at last the pilots returned to the Mess that night his friend Bill West was not there. Nothing was said but when at last Tony turned in, the other bed in their room was still empty. Heavy-hearted he threw himself down and tried to force himself to relax. His flight was on early duty the next day so their batman would call him at six with a cup of tea; he would be ready to go over to the dispersal hut with the others at six thirty. Even if Bill was still missing there was always the chance that he had landed somewhere safely. Best to hope. And pray.

When he woke there was a note with his tea. 'Young lady delivered it, I gather, late last night,' his batman said with a wink. Neither of them looked towards the empty bed. 'Your hot water for shaving is ready, sir.' And he had gone.

Tony sat down on the bed and ripped open the envelope.

Tony, I gather Daddy has found out that you've been coming up here. Please don't come again till I tell you it's safe. Love, E xxx

That was all. So, Dudley hadn't told Evie any details of their meeting. He frowned. So far he had not had time to think about Dudley's night-time sortie, and what if anything he should do about it. Tony drank his tea and tucked the envelope into the back of his log book. There was only just time to shave before grabbing a piece of toast and going out into the cold, dew-sodden dawn.

Friday 16th August

Lucy read the note twice and pushed it back gently into its envelope. Reading these personal letters still made her feel intrusive and a little guilty. She must be the first person to see them since Tony. Obviously it had reached him, so presumably he had read it. But of course she couldn't even be sure of that. Once more at home she was sitting at the table in the front room, nibbling a piece of toast. Behind her the kitchen door was closed. In the background the *Today* programme was on the radio. She glanced at her watch. In thirty-five minutes she would have to open up shop. That gave her time to read some more of the log book, trying to put together a sequence from the entries she found in it. Some entries were no more than the single word 'sortie' or 'patrol', some were far more detailed, but each made up a certain portion of Tony Anderson's day and, day by day, took him through the last weeks of the Battle of Britain. Twice he noted almost sheepishly that he had shot down an enemy plane, his earlier excited reports now toned down and world-weary. She found another note, confirming that his friend Bill West had been shot down over the English Channel and the plane had not been recovered. His belongings had been quietly cleared away and Tony's room in the Mess was now being shared by a chap called Peter Warrender, who seemed to be a good egg. Lucy smiled at the description. Was this the page from a letter Tony had been going to send to someone, and had forgotten to post? He often seemed to slot things into his log book. She wondered what his CO, Don Irving, had thought when every month the log book had been submitted for inspection. She examined the stamp, signed and dated. Perhaps it had been hard to get time alone to write letters. She could imagine Tony sitting on his bed in the small bedroom in the Mess when the call had come to hurry off and go back on duty; or perhaps he had just caved in to total exhaustion, pushing whatever letter he was writing inside the nearest safe place before collapsing back onto the pillow.

The trouble with the log book was that it contained nothing at all of his personal life except for these few scraps tucked so tightly in that they had become almost bound in with the other pages.

She turned to Evie's diary for the corresponding month. Two more commissions had been received from the WAAC. Far from being overjoyed Evie seemed almost bitter in her scribbled entry. *No doubt Eddie has prevailed on them to give me this. Let them wait!* Lucy grimaced. Something was obviously wrong.

On the next page she had written:. *More bribes. Sketchbook. Paints. At least he hasn't brought me any silk knickers this time.*

295

Lucy laughed out loud. Presumably she was talking about Eddie and his heavy-handed efforts to encourage her to paint.

Then came another entry.

I was asked to go to Southampton last week to visit a factory and make sketches. While I was there the air raid warning sounded. I was in a shelter with dozens of women and children. It was hot and dusty and claustrophobic but we could feel the ground shaking round us as the bombs fell. It was horrible. When we came out the damage in the roads only two streets away was total. Houses flat. I could hear a woman screaming and screaming and screaming. It was awful. It made my stomach go all cold. I didn't want to draw anything, it didn't seem fair when so many people were suffering, too intrusive, too insensitive, but something made me do it. This is all I can do to help, after all. It's silly to refuse to paint because it's Eddie who wants me to. There are an awful lot of people at the WAAC who know more than him. If painting can help bring this war to an end in any way at all, I must do it. It is all I am fit for. I started on a big canvas today. It will be called, The End of the Street.

Lucy sat back thoughtfully. That was one of the paintings listed in the Imperial War Museum's catalogue so presumably it still existed. She turned to her pile of books and references then shook her head. She could check it on line and probably download a copy of the picture later when she went to the gallery.

She reached for the log book again and then paused, looking up. Was that a sound from the kitchen? She turned in her chair and stared towards the door, holding her breath. All was silent.

'Ralph?' Her voice sounded husky as she called his name. 'Is that you?'

Silence.

Outside a car drove down the street, its engine noisy, echoing between the walls of the houses. It emphasised the silence of the room. Lucy stood up. She took a deep breath, then she walked steadily into the kitchen. Crossing it she went to the studio door and pulled it open. The room was empty, tidy. Still.

November 16th 1940

'Your father is not well, Evie.' Rachel was skimming the top off the cream in the dairy. The milk was thin these days; she didn't know how long it would be worth carrying on with the remaining cows. 'I know you don't mean to, but you worry him, darling. You must try and be a bit more considerate.'

Evie had been stacking bowls on a shelf. She turned, astonished. 'What have I done now?' She walked across to check the bags of curd dripping into pans on the table. 'I am painting again. It takes some of my time. It has to!'

'It's not that, Evie. He is proud of your painting. But I told you before, it is the fact you are still spending time with Tony.'

Evie stared at her. 'I haven't seen Tony for ages!'

'Oh!' Rachel looked genuinely surprised. 'I thought –'

'You thought wrong! He hasn't even phoned me.' Evie turned away but not before Rachel saw the hurt on her face. 'Eddie thinks he's taking some other woman to dances. That should please you and Daddy!'

'I see.' Rachel's cheeks coloured slightly. Her interception of Tony's calls had left her feeling guilty, but anything was better than Dudley's rage at the mention of the boy's name. 'I'm sorry, Evie. I know it's hard, but your father seemed so angry about him I thought he must have been up here again.' She picked up the cream jug. In the doorway she turned. 'I don't know what's wrong with him. He won't go and see the doctor,' she said sadly. 'He is exhausted and angry and short-tempered with everyone. He gets these pains –' She put her hand on her heart.

Evie stared after her as her mother walked back across the yard and disappeared into the kitchen.

That was as near as her mother had ever come to admitting how stressful life was now at the farm.

'The CO wants to see you, old son.' Peter Warrender, his new room mate, put his head in to their bedroom where Tony was lying on his bed, dozing. They had spent an exhausting few days on almost constant alert, with patrol after patrol in the face of increasingly heavy enemy attacks on Portsmouth.

Tony opened his eyes. 'Can't a chap have forty winks in peace?'

'Nope. At the double, there.'

Tony groaned. He levered himself off the bed. 'Will you get a beer lined up for me at the bar? If I am to be skinned alive I will need it and if I fail to survive you can drink it for me. Where is he, in the office?'

Peter nodded and disappeared from view.

Don Irving was seated at a desk covered in papers and forms, a heap of log books to one side, an overflowing ashtray by the telephone. The room was full of cigarette smoke.

He looked up as Tony entered and waved him to a chair. He looked very serious. 'How are things, Tony?'

Tony moved uneasily in the seat. 'All right?' It was a question rather than an answer.

'In all aspects of your life?'

Tony frowned. 'What have I done?'

Don grinned. 'I'm not sure, to be honest.' He leaned forward on his elbows, his chin cupped on the back of his hands, studying Tony's face. 'Is there anything worrying you? More girlfriend trouble? I've noticed Evie Lucas hasn't been coming down to the base. I'm glad she's stayed away. As you know, she's been getting some unwanted attention from the powers that be.' He paused, then seeing Tony colour slightly went on, 'This is not normally any of my business, old boy, but if it impacts on the safety of one of my pilots then it is. I've been tipped the wink that maybe someone out there is out to hurt you.'

Tony's mouth dropped open. 'I don't understand!'

'No, neither do I exactly, but I've been told to warn you that there may be someone, somewhere, who does not wish you well. It would be good if you were to have eyes in the back of your head, which I would expect anyway if you value your scraggy neck!' He grinned again. 'If this is something to do with

298

Evie ,' he added, 'it's a rotten shame, but better just leave it for a bit, eh?'

'Are you saying her father –'

'I'm not saying anything.'

Tony chewed his lip for a moment. 'Maybe there is something I should tell you. I've been wondering, to be honest, if I should tell someone.' He rubbed the back of his neck uncomfortably as though already feeling a presence behind him. 'Dudley Lucas caught me going up to the farm a few days back. It was after midnight.' He looked down as he saw his CO's expression. 'It was before A flight was put on early standby. My flying wouldn't have suffered. The thing is, he was outside, fully dressed, with a scarf pulled up over his face and, well, I think he was up to something.' Tony scowled. 'I kept telling myself that after all he is a farmer. He was probably out delivering a calf or some-thing, but it just didn't feel right. He was being,' he hesitated, 'furtive. You don't think,' again he stopped uncomfortably, 'you don't think he's a spy, do you?'

'And trying to kill you to cover up the fact that you saw him?' Don ran his fingers through his hair.

'Kill me?' Tony stood up. 'You've been trying to tell me someone is trying to kill me?'

'Well, you already know the entire Luftwaffe is, but yes, I suppose I am saying that.' Don came round his desk and perched on the corner of it. 'This is a bit beyond me, Tony. Normally I would say this is all imagination, but as someone else has alerted us to this, I can't ignore it. An argument over a girl is one thing, but now after what you've told me.' He sighed. 'I think I will have to go to someone else about this. It is potentially very serious.'

'I'm glad you think so.' Tony was growing ever more agitated. 'If someone is trying to kill me –'

'If someone is spying for the enemy,' Don corrected gently. He whistled through his teeth. 'All right.' He was suddenly resolute. 'I will talk to the powers that be, and in the meantime, be careful. There is no suggestion that anyone on our squadron is involved in this, but when you are taking part in a general mêlée, with planes from other bases, watch your tail even before you get near the bandits.'

Tony headed for the door. He stopped and turned. 'You will tell me if you find out anything?'

Don nodded. He waited for Tony to close the door behind him, then he reached for his telephone.

18

Sunday 18th August, early

To Lucy's relief there was no sign of anyone in the cottage. The garden was deserted, the only sound the excited gossip of the family of swallows sitting in a line on the telephone wire. She still hadn't seen Mike since their meeting in the gallery and she had arrived full of trepidation.

The envelope full of old letters had been slotted into the back of a tattered volume on Renaissance art. Lucy wasn't sure what had made her pull the book out, but a cascade of cuttings had dropped around her feet as she did so, and with them this torn, crumpled envelope.

Her heart beating with excitement she carried the whole lot to the table and pulled up her stool. She had arrived at Rosebank Cottage as the morning sun disappeared behind a bank of cloud and the studio was shadowy as she let herself in.

One by one she pulled the letters from their hiding place and carefully unfolding them, laid them out before her.

The first, dated October 1940, was from the War Artists Advisory Committee, signed by E. M. O'Rourke Dickey, who if

Lucy recalled correctly was the secretary, offering the sum of twenty guineas for three of Evie's paintings: *The Market Never Closes*; *Southampton Defies Danger*; and *Girls Pull Together*. There was no clue as to what the paintings depicted, though Lucy felt the titles were probably self-explanatory. She didn't recognise any of them.

The next letter on flimsy airmail paper was from someone who signed themselves P. Dated March 1941 it was obviously one of her friends from the Royal College, now evacuated to Cumbria. *Evie darling, you would love it here. The hills are so dramatic and the light is almost perverse in its intensity, but oh the boredom! We have nothing to do but paint!!! I think some of the chaps are planning a party though. Things could improve.*

This was like striking gold. These letters were part of a commentary on Evie's painting life. Lucy drew the next one closer and caught her breath excitedly. She recognised the writing from his log book.

My darling I hardly dare write to you. Everyone and everything seems to be against us. Please tell me you don't feel the same. I miss you so much. I have spoken to your mother twice on the phone and she said you weren't there, but you never rang back.

I wonder if your dad ever told you I had a run-in with him one night and he sent me away. I think I put my foot in it seeing him outside at that hour but I could hardly pretend I was there for a casual walk. I am going to post this before we take off this morning and hope you get to it before anyone else in your house. You can always write to me c/o the Mess at WH. Don't mention to anyone that I've been in touch. I love you so –

Lucy turned the page but that was all. Nothing else. The second page was missing.

She read it again, a lump in her throat, then, putting it gently aside she looked at the other documents. There were two receipts. She stared at them. *The Fuller Gallery, Westgate, Chichester*. Her address, though the name of the gallery was different. She found her hands were shaking. David Fuller had paid Evie two guineas each for two watercolour paintings of the cathedral, one at sunset, one with two Spitfires flying past the spire and another of ducks flying at sunset. Where, she wondered, were those pictures now?

She was reaching for the next piece of paper when the door opened behind her. She turned on the stool and found herself face to face with Charlotte Ponsonby.

For a moment they stared at each other in silence before Charlotte stepped inside and shut the door behind her and leaned against it. 'I thought it must be you when I saw the lights on in here,' she said.

Lucy glanced past her at the door. 'Is Mike here with you?'

'I'm not in the habit of coming down here alone.' Charlotte was wearing a short pink linen coat over a dress of the same colour and purple high-heeled sandals. She did not look, Lucy thought to herself idly, as though she was dressed for a weekend in the country.

'He is coming down in the other car but I seem to have arrived first,' Charlotte went on, 'which gives us a chance to have a little chat.'

Lucy swept all the papers on the table into a careful pile and tucked them back into the book, then she folded her arms. 'What sort of chat?'

'A chat about you and Mike.' Charlotte moved to the other side of the table and pulling up a second stool perched on it, her eyes fixed on Lucy's.

Lucy stood up. She picked up the book and held it to her chest defensively. 'There is no "me and Mike", as you put it. What on earth makes you think there is? I am working here, that is all.'

'He is obsessed with you.' Charlotte's eyes were hard.

Lucy stared at her. 'What nonsense! Last time I saw him he was angry with me, but that was the result of a misunderstanding.' Suddenly she was furious. She was damned if she was going to make excuses to this woman. 'If you have a

303

problem with Mike I suggest you take it up with him. He and I barely know each other. We've had lunch twice and on every occasion we have met it has been to talk about his grandmother. If you are feeling insecure in your relationship, I suggest you look closer to home! I doubt if he likes the clingy type.'

She stopped abruptly, shocked at her own bitchiness. Bending over, she picked up her briefcase and laptop bag. 'I'll leave you to it. I would hate to be intrusive.'

She turned to the door.

'Stop!' Charlotte had risen from her stool. 'What is that book?'

Lucy still had it clutched in her arms. She held it tighter. 'It is a textbook on Renaissance art. Probably from Evie's days at college.'

'Did Mike say you could take it away?' Lucy could feel the hostility coming off the woman in waves.

'Mike said I could take anything I wanted,' she said with exaggerated patience. It is all going to be returned, I assure you. And I assure you equally that, if it is the monetary value of this book that worries you, it is probably not even worth a fiver. If I tried to sell it, it would fetch nothing; it would be pulped.'

'Then why are you taking it?'

'Because I am interested in art; I am interested in Evie. I am writing a book about Evie and anything that interested her, interests me.' Lucy slotted the book into her bag. 'Any further questions?' She held Charlotte's gaze for a full three seconds and was pleased to see the woman quail slightly.

She opened the door. 'Have a nice weekend,' she called over her shoulder as she closed it with care behind her. She hoped she hadn't sounded too sarcastic.

Mike was standing by her car in the lane. 'Don't worry, I'm going.' She fumbled in her pocket for the keys.

'You don't have to.'

'Oh, I think I do. I have enough to cope with trying to sort out your family, Mike, without being accused of trying to seduce you by your girlfriend!' Her anger had sparked up again at the sight of him. 'I'll keep out of your way for a bit. Perhaps that is best anyway, given your suspicions about my motives!' Pulling open the car door she threw in her laptop and bag and climbed in after them.

'Wait, wait, wait!' Mike grabbed the door handle as she made to pull it shut. 'What is all this about. What has she said?'

'Ask her.' Giving up on the door, Lucy inserted the key into the ignition and turned it.

'No.' Mike was still holding onto the handle. 'I need to talk to you. Now, please. This is crazy, Lucy. What did Charlotte say?'

Lucy sat back and closed her eyes, her head pressed against the head rest. 'The exact word she chose was obsession. Yours, not mine. She thinks you are obsessed with me.'

There was a long silence and when she opened her eyes at last to look at him he was staring at her, an unreadable expression on his face.

'Exactly!' she said tartly. 'I told her to sort it out with you. Please take your hand off my car.'

He stepped back without a word.

'And when you see her you might explain that any books I remove from the studio are part of my research and I will return them.' She was astonished at the hostility she felt towards him suddenly.

He stood back out of the way as she pulled into the lane and drove up the hill. She glanced in the mirror and saw him still standing looking after her as she turned the corner into the village.

November 19th 1940

Tony was flying at twenty thousand feet. It didn't make any difference knowing someone might be trying to sabotage him, not when there were hundreds of ME 109s out there all bent on the same thing. He wasn't hearing the RT any more, just the voice in his own head dictating the moves one by one.

Lock onto the enemy; follow him, finger on the tit, fire. Another burst. I've hit him. He's on fire; he's going down. Watch out behind. No time to check, dive away out of line. Constantly dodge and weave. Never stay on one course for a second. There is another one. Finger on the tit, fire. The gun button is hot. No, it's my hands in the gloves; the whole cockpit is hot. Please let me not be on fire too. No, I'm flying too close to the sun. Joke. Dodge. Watch out, someone behind me, but it's someone with a black cross on his tail. Swoop away, watch for tracer bullets, come up under another chap and fire. Got him. Check fuel. Nearly out. Look down. The sea as far as I can see. Better break away and go down lower. Head for home. Sweat, it's sweat dripping into my eyes. Sweat shouldn't be red. Am I hit? I can see the coast now. Make a course west. Can I reach our airfield? I'm much lower now. Turn off the oxygen. Wrench back the canopy. The blast of fresh air clears my head. It's just a scratch. It can't be any more. The Spit doesn't seem to be damaged, so how can there be blood? Feeling woozy. Maybe I shouldn't have turned off the oxygen. There it is, Chichester spire. I can make it. Turn into wind. Lower and lower still till the wheels hit the deck and we bump across the grass towards the dispersal huts. The boys are waiting for the plane. Am I late? The others are back. Slowly we drift to a halt and I just sit there, waiting for something to happen. More sweeps I expect. More patrols. More encounters out to sea.

It was just a scratch. A splinter deflected from a hole in the Perspex of the hood. How could he not have known that the plane had been hit? A cup of sweet tea and a dressing over the cut and he was back on readiness.

'How are you, Tony?' Don was waiting for him in the Mess. 'Two shot down confirmed, and two probables, I hear. If you go on like this we'll have to give you a gong, old boy.' Tony was conscious of the man's steel-grey eyes steadily scrutinising his face and he knew what he was thinking. Don't go mad; just because you think you are going to die, don't take unnecessary risks. It doesn't work that way. Keep calm. Keep thinking. Don't go looking for trouble because the next time it will find you and we can't spare you. Not yet.

There was a letter waiting for him on the locker by his bed. His batman must have put it there earlier.

I'm missing you too, but Daddy is not well. Please don't come up for a bit. I'll let you know when. Be careful, my darling. With all my love, E xxx

He kissed the sheet of paper and tucked it under his pillow, then he lay back and closed his eyes. He dreaded this interlude before blessed sleep took him because suddenly he could again feel the vibration of the plane through his whole body, feel the joystick in his hands, feel the angle of the wings as he soared up towards the sky.

Sunday 18th August

'Just drive in to the Goodwood Motor Circuit,' Robin's friend Ted Bairstow had said. 'Drive through the tunnel and pass all the parking areas. The hangar where we are working is on your right. If I'm not there one of the boys will let you in and you can walk through to the airfield beyond. It is much the same as it was in 1940. Still grass. The farmhouse they used as a Mess is still there. It's a private house now.'

She had been planning this visit for ages; background information; seeing the real place, the scene of so many of Evie's paintings. Finally getting round to a visit to Westhampnett seemed to be a good idea by way of taking her mind off her encounter at Rosebank. Lucy parked her car and climbed out staring round. Behind her, empty parking bays stretched back towards the gate in the distance; in front she could see the control tower and the airfield. Now, as she had seen from the map, it was called Chichester or, more often, Goodwood Aerodrome. When Tony had flown from here it had been called RAF Westhampnett after the nearest village.

Ted was there; a stout, cheerful man in his late fifties, dressed in blue overalls, he showed her round the hangar where, with a group of friends, he was restoring the carcass of a Mark IX Spitfire. She stared at it. She had seen these planes before in photographs and paintings, not least Evie's, but nothing had prepared her for how small they were in real life. This little aircraft with its pretty rounded wings and cramped single-seater cockpit covered by a Perspex hood hardly seemed robust enough to have flown into battle, never mind helped to win a war. He showed her the ports for cannon in the wings. 'There would normally have been eight machine guns in 1940,' he explained, 'in the Mark I and II, otherwise scarcely any difference in appearance.' He grinned at her. 'If you want to go up in one, there are one or two two-seater Mark IXs about nowadays. You could put your name down, though it might take a few years to get to the top of the list.'

She glanced at him to see if he was joking; he wasn't. She took photographs, and unable to stop herself, rested her hand on the nose of the aircraft near the propeller. She could almost feel how keen it was to fly again.

Ted opened the full-height hangar doors which fronted the airfield just a crack and waved her through. She walked out, clutching her camera. In the far distance she could see the spire of Chichester cathedral rising above some trees. There were a few private modern planes drawn up round the perimeter, and a windsock flying in the distance, but otherwise there was no one there. The airfield was quiet. She shivered. As she stepped out of the shelter of the hangar she had heard Ted pulling the doors closed behind her, anxious to keep the cold wind and the dust out of the hangar. She stood staring out across the field to where the sun was beginning to set in a bank of cloud, turning the edges of the slate-coloured haze every shade of flame.

The Spitfire was standing facing into wind in the distance, a silhouette against the sunset. As she watched it began to move, racing across the grass towards the west and rising up to fly low and steady towards the spire. Her eyes narrowed, she put her hand up, trying to see against the glare as the plane swung round in the far distance and turned back towards the airfield. She could hear the throaty roar of the engine now as it approached, low and fast, heading straight for the row of hangars where she stood. She watched spellbound as it flew closer and almost ducked as it thundered over her head with a quick waggle of its wings and was lost almost at once in the distant haze.

She waited to see if it would return, then she retraced her footsteps to the hangar doors. Someone slid them back a couple of feet so she could slip inside and they closed behind her. The lights were on now, two figures bending over a piece of engine on the work-bench in the corner. She walked up to Ted.

'Did you hear it? I didn't realise there were any Spitfires flying from here. It was wonderful! I am so pleased I saw it.' Her eyes were shining, her earlier tangle with Charlotte and Mike forgotten.

Ted looked at her puzzled. 'There are no Spitfires here at the moment, or at least only this old lady.' He jerked his thumb towards the plane behind him.

'But I saw it take off. Just now.' She felt foolish suddenly. 'Perhaps it wasn't a Spitfire. It flew right over the hangar. It waggled its wings like they do sometimes at an airshow when they've finished and they are going away and then it flew off up towards Tangmere.'

She stopped abruptly. Towards Tangmere. Why had she said that? How had she known where it was going? Ted was watching her speculatively and she found herself shaking her head.

'I must have imagined it,' she said with an embarrassed smile. 'It is all too emotive, seeing your plane here after I've been doing so much research into 1940.' Her voice trailed away.

Ralph had been based at Tangmere. He must have come here from time to time, surely.

'There are vintage planes here aplenty,' Ted said thoughtfully, 'and Spitfires fly displays quite often in the summer, but I am pretty sure there aren't any here now. Besides, no one is allowed to fly this late. Did you see the letters?' She realised that Ted was still talking to her.

'The letters?'

'On the fuselage. They all have letters to denote the squadron they came from and then a number.' He pointed at his plane.

She shook her head. 'It was going too fast to see. I didn't think.'

'Maybe an echo from the past?' Ted said comfortably. He reached for a rag and began to wipe the oil from his hands. 'I sometimes think it's still all very close, you know.' He was silent for a moment, lost in thoughts of his own. Then he grinned at her and went on, 'Look, we're packing up now, Lucy, so I had better chase you out. Come again any time, OK?' He looked at her closely. 'Are you all right?'

She nodded.

It had been Ralph flying that plane, she knew it had.

Sunday 18th August, late

Charlotte was sitting in Rosebank Cottage in the dark. She had made a cup of tea for herself, but it had grown cold and the milk in it had skimmed over. She had rung Mike again and again, frantic with worry when he didn't show up at the cottage. She rang the London number and Dolly and in the end she had rung Mike's mother as well. Juliette was short with her, but sounded worried herself when Charlotte explained they had planned to meet at lunchtime, driving down in separate cars.

'Please, you will ring me back if you hear from him?' Charlotte knew it sounded feeble, but she was near to tears.

'Of course I will.' Juliette hung up.

Charlotte sat staring at the window, watching the reflections in the glass and finally she stood up and pulled the curtains across, not comfortable with the thought of the empty garden and the isolated studio beyond. She shivered before miserably confronting the thought which had been haunting her all afternoon. Had Lucy rung Mike and told him everything Charlotte had said to her?

The first thing Juliette did was ring Mike's number. He answered at once. 'So, if you are not at Rosebank, where are you?' she asked crisply.

He was at her house within twenty minutes.

'I know she was worried. She rang about every five damn minutes.' He threw himself down on the floor in front of the empty fireplace, leaning back against the sofa seat, his ankles crossed on the rug. He reached up for the bottle of lager his mother passed him.

'So what happened?' Juliette perched on the edge of a chair opposite him. Her son was looking miserable and exhausted.

'I got to the cottage and I met Lucy Standish coming away. She was in a rare old strop. She and Charlotte had had words and Charlotte had told her –' He paused suddenly and Juliette saw a touch of colour flush his pale face. She waited several seconds before prompting him. 'Charlotte told her . . .?'

'Charlotte is under the impression that I like Lucy. I gather she told Lucy I am obsessed with her and she told Lucy to go.'

'Ah, I see.' Juliette nodded wisely. 'And are you obsessed with her?'

'No of course I'm not!'

'So, why did you not go straight in and tell Charlotte as much?'

Mike took a long draught from his bottle. 'I don't know.' His shoulders slumped back against the sofa and he closed his eyes.

'Do you love Charlotte?' Juliette asked after a long silence.

311

'I don't know that either.'

'Not enough, obviously, to go in and reassure her.'

'Perhaps not. She's possessive.' He stopped as though considering what he had just said for the first time. 'She is the one who is obsessed by Lucy.'

'I like Lucy.' Juliette leaned forward, elbows on knees. 'I've seen a bit of her since you brought her here.'

'No doubt she is keen to find out as much as she can from you about Evie.' He sounded bitter. 'She is the one who is obsessed round here. With Evie.'

Juliette frowned. 'I'm happy to tell her all I know. I thought that was the point of you bringing her here in the first place.' She fixed him with a fierce look. 'So, why did you go round to her gallery and make all kinds of accusations about her? Do you really believe she is trying to cheat you, or did you get all that from Christopher? What the hell is going on with Christopher, Mike?'

Mike hesitated, then he shook his head. 'I have no idea.' He sighed.

'Did you know he hits Frances?'

Mike opened his eyes. He leaned forward and stared at her. 'No, of course I didn't know that. How did you find out?' Suddenly he was suspicious. 'Have you been to see her as well? This is all to do with Lucy, isn't it? It's her fault Chris was angry with Frances. He came to see me about it. Lucy is bloody persistent and she is causing a lot of friction in this family! I wish I hadn't brought her to meet you, now.'

'Well, I'm glad you did. As I said, I like her.'

'Did Lucy tell you she and her husband had a painting of Evie's?'

'Yes, she did.' She decided not to mention the fact that she had seen it – or at least seen its crate. What had happened between her and Lucy and the Redwoods was probably best kept to herself for now.

Mike frowned. 'So, it's only me she doesn't trust.'

'It looks like it.' Juliette leaned back against the cushions and contemplated her son in silence.

He was staring down morosely at his empty bottle. 'Somehow I've messed all this up,' he said at last.

'Indeed.'

He looked up at his mother and gave a wry grin. 'So, tell me what to do.'

'You don't mean that.'

'Don't I?'

'No. You have always gone your own way. Just think before you act.' She stood up and went to find a second bottle for him. 'Do you think your uncle George would know what's going on?' she called over her shoulder.

Mike thought for a moment then he shook his head. 'I've no idea. I haven't seen him for years. He and Dad didn't exactly get on, did they?' He scrambled to his feet and followed her. 'Is this all to do with the inheritance, d'you think?'

She nodded slowly. 'That's my guess. There is a lot of money at stake here, and if Evie becomes famous, properly famous, suddenly, anyone who has one of her paintings will benefit.'

'You mean Lucy?'

'I mean Christopher. He appears to have cornered the market.'

'So, wouldn't you think he would be pleased about the publicity?' Mike perched on the arm of a chair. 'Would you go and see George?'

'No.'

He looked at her in astonishment. 'No?'

'No, Mike. I told you, he and Johnny didn't really get on and we saw very little of him, considering they were brothers. I found him very standoffish and difficult. He's never so much as sent me a Christmas card since Johnny died. If you want to go and see him, that's up to you, but leave me out of it.'

The sound of the phone ringing broke the silence that

followed her outburst. They both looked at it, then Juliette picked it up.

'It's Charlotte,' she said, passing it to him.

November 20th 1940

Ralph had driven Tony out to the Old Ship Inn at Bosham. It was his favourite pub. He carried the two pints back to the table in the window and set them down.

'Still no sign of the Hun this morning!'

Tony shook his head. 'They are focusing on poor old London. I wouldn't be there for the world.' He reached for his drink. 'How is Evie?'

Ralph took a long swig from his pint and put it down with a firm bang on the table. 'She's all right.' He studied the contents of his tankard with unnecessary concentration then after a few moments he looked up.

Tony was watching him warily. 'So, you're going to tell me to give up on her,' he said at last. 'Everyone else has.'

Ralph sighed. 'You know who is behind all this effort to split you both up, don't you?'

'I've guessed. It's your dad.'

Ralph was silent for a moment. 'Partly, yes. Daddy is against all the sneaking around at night. I heard about that.' He gave Tony a searching look. 'But if your intentions are honourable and you mean to marry Evie then I don't think he would have any problem from that point of view. Look, Tony, I've been thinking about this a lot and there is something you need to know. A family secret. I've told Evie and I made her promise not to tell you, but this is all getting out of hand and it's not fair on either of you if you don't know what is going on.' He took another gulp of beer. He glanced round the bar, which was smoky still from the previous night's drinkers but which at this hour was empty save for the barmaid who, her back to them, was drying glasses and returning them to their places on the shelf.

He lowered his voice still further. 'I've been talking to Mummy. She dislikes Eddie intensely but she pretends to welcome him for Evie's sake. He takes advantage of the fact that he is the gateway to the War Artists Advisory Committee and she thinks Eddie is in love with Evie. Really in love.' He glanced up at Tony. 'He is a strange man. Very clever. Very manipulative.' He paused again, reaching into his pocket for a packet of cigarettes. He passed one to Tony and brought out his lighter. 'I think he could be quite unscrupulous.' Flipping the lid on the lighter open he stroked his thumb across the wheel and held out the light. 'She only knows half the story. Eddie lent Daddy some money,' he went on gravely. 'To get him out of debt. And now he is threatening to tell the whole world and shame him, if Daddy doesn't throw you out. He is blackmailing him, trying to make him force Evie to forget you.'

'He wants to marry her himself?' Tony's voice hardened.

Ralph nodded. 'I assume so. To keep his interest in the money with her share of the farm. I don't know how much it was he lent, but I suspect it was more than my dad has admitted. It must be. He wouldn't sell his daughter unless –'

'Unless he was desperate.'

Ralph gave a grim nod. 'I don't think Eddie is interested in getting the money back, even if we had it. He's a wealthy man. But this gives him one hell of a hold over my father. Eddie doesn't like being thwarted, I know that much about him. And he will not put up with any competition.'

Tony leaned forward and drew on the cigarette. 'So you are telling me he could be dangerous?'

'I'm telling you to be careful.'

'The CO told me the same thing,' Tony said carefully. 'But with no names.'

Both men smoked quietly for a while. 'Should I go and confront him?' Tony asked at last.

'No!' Ralph spoke out loudly and raised his hand to the barmaid as she looked round, startled. He pushed back his chair and stood up. 'I'll get us another one. When are you rostered on?'

'Tomorrow. More sweeps, I suspect. I wonder what the Hun are up to.'

Ralph nodded. 'Don't say anything at the moment, especially not to Evie. She has a very complicated relationship with Eddie. He told her you were dating another girl, but she didn't believe him. She didn't say anything though. She knows her career rests with him, or she thinks it does. I suspect that is what he has told her. She's painting again.' He went over to the bar to pick up the fresh drinks. 'I wasn't sure if you knew she had stopped, but the committee asked her to do some more of the street scenes in Southampton after the bombing. She was there during a raid and it affected her very deeply. You can imagine, it is very hard to stand by and make sketches when people have been so terribly injured and their homes destroyed.'

'And that is our fault. We let the bastards through.' Tony clamped his jaw shut.

'We do our best.' Ralph sat down again. He rubbed his face wearily. 'In fact we do more than our best. When you think how many of them there are. Those great formations of bombers coming in over the coast, heading for London.' He shuddered. 'I shall dream about them to my dying day.'

'So, if you don't think I should go and confront Eddie, what do you think I should do? I have already been warned to watch my tail.' Tony sounded bitter. 'I can't just sit there in my plane and wait for some low life in Eddie's pay to take a pot shot at me when they should be trying to take down a Junkers 88!'

'No.'

'Does Evie still love me?' Tony leaned forward towards Ralph suddenly. 'Does she ever talk about me?'

Ralph looked evasive. 'I've never encouraged her to, to be

honest. Besides, I've hardly been home, and when I am there are other people there.'

'I tried to ring her. Your mother answers every time. She didn't pass on my messages. Does she know about all this?'

Ralph shook his head. 'I don't think so. Daddy told me not to tell her. But she is very loyal to my dad. If she thinks he is against you –'

'You said he wasn't, not if I plan to marry Evie.'

'That was before Eddie started tightening the screws.'

Tony sighed. He reached for another cigarette.

'And what did Evie say last time you discussed it with her?' Ralph asked curiously.

'She loves me, Ralph.' Tony shook his head, clearly bewildered. 'She wants to get married, but there is always something in the way. She doesn't want me to go up there or phone any more. Now I know why. She must be completely torn in two.'

'She is, poor kid.' Ralph downed the rest of his pint and stood up. 'Come on, we'd best be getting back. I'll drop you off on the way past the Mess. There is a young lady near here I need to see before I go back to Tangmere.' He gave a coy wink. 'I don't know what you should do, Tony. Just be bloody careful.'

'Would you speak to her for me? Tell her I know and I understand it's difficult. Tell her I love her.'

Ralph held the door for him as they walked out into the village street. He nodded reluctantly. 'Of course I will. But I may not get the chance to get up there for a few days and if I do I may not get the chance to speak to her alone. I'll do my best.'

It was bitterly cold with a sharp wind blowing. Both men pulled up their collars.

They climbed into the Morgan. 'If she asks I will tell her you would make a great brother-in-law,' Ralph said with a laugh. 'God forbid that Eddie should step up to that position!'

Monday 19th August

Lucy was on duty in the gallery the next day; Robin was looking after Phil's bookshop in North Street and Phil had gone to Brighton to visit a friend in hospital. The gallery was quiet and Lucy was taking the chance to catch up on checking the books and ordering some more greetings cards. When the door opened she looked up and, not recognising the man who walked in, bent once more to the computer screen. The sound of card hitting glass, however, made her look up again. He had flipped the open/closed sign over and he was bolting the door.

'What are you doing?' She was shocked by his sudden action and not a little apprehensive.

'I take it you are Lucy Standish?'

He was fairly short, about forty, good-looking, with neat dark hair and a smart expensive suit. His eyes were hard as flint.

'Christopher Marston?' It was an easy guess. The man radiated hostility.

'Are you surprised I'm here?' He walked towards her and came to a standstill some four feet away, folding his arms as he looked at her.

She stood up and felt better, nearer his height. 'I was expecting you to come in person in the end.' Adrenaline was coursing through her body but she managed to keep her voice steady. 'I'm glad. We need to talk. Please, sit down.' She indicated the armchair.

He ignored her invitation. 'I want you to stop interfering in my family's business. I give you two days to return to me any papers or articles which belong to my grandmother's estate and if you do not comply with my wishes I will take out an injunction against you. Is that clear?'

Lucy looked at him, stunned. 'I have taken nothing without the permission of the current owner, your cousin Mike. I don't believe anything I have belongs to you.'

'As a senior member of the family I have the right of veto. There will be no biography.'

'I believe your father, George Marston, is the senior surviving member of the family,' Lucy said, thinking fast. 'Are you acting with his authority?'

Christopher narrowed his eyes. 'My father knows nothing of this whole débâcle! He is not well. He is not to be bothered by any of this.'

'I see.' Lucy paused. 'I am sorry to hear he is not well.' Her brain was racing. 'I will consult my solicitor about your request and your desire to veto the biography. You do understand that I have academic backing for it, and considerable interest has been shown by a great many people. The biography doesn't need authorisation by anyone.' She was pretty certain that was true.

She saw two red patches appear just below his cheekbones and realised too late just how angry he was becoming. He leaned forward and seized her arm, twisting it up behind her. She heard herself gasp as the pain knifed through her shoulder. 'I suggest you do as I say,' he hissed in her ear. 'Don't underestimate me, Mrs Standish; I am accustomed to being obeyed. Is that clear?'

She was incapable of replying.

'Do I make myself clear?' he repeated. He jerked her arm up a little further.

Her scream seemed to come from some distant place far inside herself, and it was sufficiently loud for him to drop her wrist. 'This is what you do to your wife, is it?' she gasped. 'You're a vicious bully but you have made a big mistake taking me on.' She wasn't sure where the words were coming from. 'Don't you dare threaten me! Go!' She pointed to the door. 'Go now. I have activated the security alarm. The police will be here in less than two minutes and it won't look good if you are arrested for attacking me.'

To her astonishment he seemed to believe her. He gave her one more furiously angry glance, then turning on his heel he strode towards the door and drawing back the bolt he pulled

319

it open and walked out, leaving it swinging to and fro behind him.

For several moments Lucy just stood there incapable of moving. The pain in her arm and shoulder was excruciating but worse than that was the shock at what had just happened. She couldn't think what to do. She wanted to ring Robin but that wasn't fair. He was busy. She should shut the door and lock it in case Christopher returned. The voice from the doorway made her jump painfully.

'Lucy, are you all right?' It was Maggie Redwood. 'I was in Chichester today so I thought I would call in passing and make sure you were OK. My dear, what on earth has happened?' As she walked in Lucy burst into tears.

They relocked the door and they went upstairs.

'We should call the police.' Maggie was immediately practical. 'He can't get away with this.'

'No.' Lucy shook her head. 'I did something stupid. I let him know that I knew he beat his wife.'

'Then it's even more important we report him.'

'She will never admit it and there is no proof.'

'You are proof, my dear.' Maggie took Lucy's arm and gently pushed back the sleeve. 'Look at the marks on your wrist. I know someone in the police who will handle this sensitively –'

'No! Please.' Lucy walked over to the sink and ran some cool water over her wrist. As she was patting it dry on a towel they heard a loud crash coming from the studio. Both women looked towards the door, startled.

'Oh, no.' Lucy paled.

'Stay out here.' Maggie went over to the door and pushed it open. She glanced in and then disappeared into the room.

The door banged behind her.

Lucy watched in anguish for a moment then taking a deep breath she went over and reached out to the handle. It refused to budge. 'Maggie!' she called. 'Are you all right?'

There was another crash from inside the room. And then she heard the sound of splintering wood. 'Maggie!' she screamed. She dragged at the handle and this time the door opened.

Maggie was just the other side of it. Her hair was wild as though she had been out in the wind and her clothes dishevelled. 'Stay away!' she cried. 'Ring Huw.'

Lucy ran towards the living room and grabbed her phone. Behind her she could hear the sound of crashing again and then Maggie's voice. It sounded as though she was swearing.

As soon as it had started it was over. Maggie appeared in the living room. She looked exhausted but she was smiling. 'We have a real evil so-and-so here. Something has stirred him up and I reckon it was Christopher. Did he come upstairs at all? Did you reach Huw?'

Lucy nodded. She was shaking. 'He's on his way.'

'Good. I am sorry, Lucy. This is awful for you and not that good for me, to be honest.' Maggie blew her hair out of her eyes with a great sigh. 'I have never come across anything like this before. Testing times.' She gave Lucy a determined smile. 'I want you to come and stay with us for a few days. I suggest you pack a bag, my dear. Bring your research material – anything to do with Evie and her story – and we'll put a notice on the door downstairs saying that the gallery will be closed for a bit. I know it's not good for business, but better we sort this out completely. I want you to be able to be happy and safe here.'

This time Lucy didn't argue. By the time Huw arrived she had collected up all her research, her letters and notes and books and thrown some clothes into a suitcase.

He ran upstairs two at a time after Maggie went down to let him in.

Lucy was happy to leave it to them. She sat looking out of the window, her eyes fixed on the rooftops opposite where a crow was sitting on the TV aerial surveying the street below. Straining her ears in the direction of the studio Lucy clenched her fists. She could hear nothing. Minutes passed. She ought to get up and go and see if they were all right, but she was too afraid.

'It's all right, Lucy. It's over for now.' She realised that Huw was standing beside her and she hadn't heard anything he had said. 'There is nothing there now. All is quiet and Maggie and I have surrounded the room with prayer, each in our own way.' He smiled at her reassuringly. 'Leave it now. Have you rung Robin to tell him what is happening?'

'No.' It was a whisper.

'Would you like me to?'

She couldn't believe she nodded. She felt like a frightened child.

Obediently she followed them down the staircase and climbed into Huw's car. Maggie leaned in after her and kissed the top of her head. 'Huw will drive you back home. I'll go and pick up my car from the car park and follow you.'

Her bedroom at the vicarage was small and pretty and cosy. To her relief there had been no sign of the crated picture in the hall. They must have moved it somewhere and for the time being she didn't even want to ask where it was. It seemed ironic that she had followed it here and that once more she was under the same roof as the cause of all her troubles. She dragged in her belongings and sat down on the bed with a sigh. No one knew where she was. Here she was safe. From Christopher, from Mike and Charlotte, and hopefully from her unwanted ghostly intruder as well. As though to confirm her situation the door opened and Roger strolled in. He gave her bags a cursory sniff and then jumped on the bed, circling three times before curling up on the pillow. Lucy smiled. Maggie, she was sure, would take this as a benison, three times a circle, a magic blessing and a sign that all was well.

19

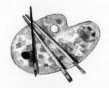

November 22nd 1940

Tony drove up the lane and parked in the farmyard right by the back door. He climbed out of his little Morris and walked straight into the kitchen. Rachel's sewing basket lay on the table. There was no one about. He went through into the hall and stood at the bottom of the stairs, holding the newel post, looking up. 'Rachel? Evie? Is there anyone there?' For a moment he thought the place was empty, then he heard a door opening and the rattle of footsteps on the stairs.

'Tony?' It was Evie.

She hung over the banister on the landing above his head. 'What are you doing here?' she whispered.

'I need to talk to you.' He took the stairs two at a time and swept her into his arms. For a long moment she clung to him, her whole body melting against his, then she pushed him away. 'You can't stay. It's not safe.'

'What do you mean, it's not safe?'

'My parents might see you.'

'I don't care. I want to marry you, Evie. I've been thinking and I can't let all this misunderstanding and delay go on. Let's do it now. As soon as we can. We can get a special licence. My parents are wealthy people, Evie. If there is a need for money for the farm, they will help. They could pay Eddie off. Surely your father won't forbid us if this is what you want? We'll ask him to give you away. Ralph can be my best man.' He put his hands on her shoulders and held her for a moment, looking into her eyes. 'I love you, Evie. I want you to be my wife. Nothing has changed. I've wanted to marry you since the first time I set eyes on you.'

She was about to answer when a loud voice floated down from the landing above. 'But she doesn't want to marry you.'

Eddie walked slowly and deliberately down the stairs, coming to a stop only when he had reached them.

'What were you doing up there?' Tony stared at him in shock, his hands falling away from Evie's shoulders. He looked at her. 'Well, what were you both doing?'

Eddie smiled slowly. 'What do you think we were doing?'

'We were in my studio, looking at pictures,' Evie said hotly. 'What else?' She thrust Tony away from her. 'Stop it, both of you. I can't cope with this!'

'You heard her,' Eddie said. 'She wants you to go.'

Evie turned on him. 'It is not for you to tell anyone to go, Eddie. I want you out of here as well. I want some peace to paint!'

'And I want you to make some decisions,' Eddie snapped back. 'You need to get your priorities in place, Evelyn. Either you want a career as an artist or you don't. It is time you made some choices. If you want to play with boys,' he threw a sneering glance at Tony, 'so be it, but don't expect me to waste any more time on you or your work.'

Both men were silent for a moment. Eddie stepped forward. 'After you.' Grim-faced he gestured at Tony to go down.

Tony was clenching his fists. 'I don't think so. Not till I've finished my conversation with Evie.'

Eddie stepped forward, his jaw clenched, his eyes narrowed with hatred, reaching out as if he intended to punch Tony in the chest. Evie stepped between them but she was halted in her tracks by a shout from Rachel, who had appeared in the hall at the foot of the stairs.

'What do you think you are doing?' She was staring up in horror. 'What is all the noise about? Your father's in there, Evie,' she pointed towards the kitchen, 'and he is ill. He's collapsed!'

Evie pushed between the two men and ran down towards her. Not waiting she elbowed her way past her mother and ran into the kitchen where Dudley was sitting at the table, his hand pressed to his chest. He was sweating profusely. Evie hardly noticed him. She ran past, on out into the yard.

Tony tore downstairs after her, not seeing Dudley at all, and only stopped when he reached his car. There was no sign of her. He gazed round. 'Evie!' he called. 'Evie, darling, where are you?'

Eddie had not followed them; there was no sign of him.

Tony made his way towards the dairy and peered in. It was empty, as was the barn next to it. He stood in the yard and stared around in confusion. 'Evie,' he called again. 'My darling, please. Where are you?'

There was no reply.

He waited for several minutes by the gate then dejectedly he went to the car and climbed in, sitting staring unmoving through the windscreen before climbing out again and bending forlornly to the starting handle.

Evie heard the engine fire up from the stable. Tears were pouring down her cheeks. Distraught, she put her arms round the neck of the old horse, who was stoically munching her hay, and sobbed into the animal's sturdy neck as though her heart would break.

In the house Dudley took a deep breath and reached for his handkerchief, trying to stop his hands from shaking. It was

Eddie who stood over him with soothing words and went to fetch a glass of water.

Tuesday 20th August

The painting, still in its crate, had been put in Huw's little private chapel. 'This is one of the spare rooms really,' Maggie said with an indulgent smile, 'the smallest, but he's fixed it up beautifully. I come and sit in here sometimes, to think and pray.' She pushed the door open and ushered Lucy in. Lucy and the portrait might be back under the same roof, but here, with Maggie and Huw to protect her, it didn't seem to matter.

The altar was a small table in the corner with a cross standing on it and a sturdy candle much decorated with drops and whorls of melted wax. On the wall behind it there was a reproduction of Duccio's *Madonna and Child with Angels*. There were two low chairs facing it, and leaning against the wall behind them, the crate. Lucy's eyes went straight to it. She shivered.

'It's strange that such a personal thing, such a lovely thing in so many ways, can suddenly become so threatening.'

'It's not threatening in itself, Lucy. All we have to do is detach whatever – whoever – it is who is clinging to it.' Maggie went and sat down on one of the chairs and after a moment's hesitation Lucy sat beside her. Bright sunshine was pouring through the window and she could see the branches of the apple tree on the lawn moving gently in the breeze outside. The little room felt very peaceful and safe.

Lucy glanced sideways at Maggie. 'I thought you didn't believe in God.'

'No, my dear. I believe in God, otherwise, as I told your friend Phil, I doubt if Huw and I could get on. It's just the Church I find hard to stomach. Too much structure, too much concentration on good works. Too many meetings and rules. Don't get me wrong, good works and meetings and rules are all good in their place but I think they can sometimes get in the way of the spiritual stuff. People forget that is what it is all about. So I worship out in the wind and rain and sunshine. My cathedral is under the trees.' She grinned. 'Sorry, does that shock you? It sounds very pagan, but Huw understands. I think sometimes he secretly agrees. And my way of worship allows me to believe in all things in heaven and earth like it says in the Creed. If I see a ghost it is part of the way things work. I don't have to call for the deliverance men or wait for a psychiatrist, I trust my instincts. Ghosts are a natural part of the way things work. Roger the cat finds them natural just as robins and rabbits are natural.' She smiled. 'But things go wrong in nature. All is not peaceful all the time. I am not naïve. I can see that. Ralph Lucas has been trapped by some problem which is or was worrying him so much he has to try and resolve it on this earth and it is hard for us to communicate with him as he is working now from a different –' she paused trying to choose the right word – 'a different format, if you like.'

'I saw him in his Spitfire,' Lucy said after a moment. 'After I met Charlotte at Rosebank Cottage I went to the airfield where Tony was stationed and I saw a Spitfire fly over very low. They said it couldn't have been a Spitfire. There were none flying that day.'

'But you feel it was Ralph?'

Lucy nodded. 'Somehow I knew it wasn't Tony.' She shook her head. 'I'm becoming obsessed with the family, aren't I!'

'Isn't that part of the job of a biographer? Through Evie, you've formed a link with them.'

'And the other entity?' Lucy asked softly.

'I don't know. Maybe him too. He too has a problem. His is different, but only from our perspective. From his, it must be as urgent as Ralph's.' She sighed. 'I'm not pretending this is all serendipity, Lucy. I know there is something potentially dangerous going on here and I'm not so conceited that I can be sure I can cope with it alone. I need Huw and his prayers.

327

He is a powerful man with a strong connection – a hotline, if you like – to God. Prayer is good. It is powerful. I pray. And so should you.' She looked at Lucy shrewdly. 'God didn't answer your prayers and bring back your husband, Lucy. That doesn't mean God doesn't exist, my dear. It means, almost certainly that your Larry has moved on. Not everyone is trapped here by sudden death. Sometimes, yes, but some souls have a clear vision –'

'I loved him much more than he loved me,' Lucy interrupted suddenly. 'I am beginning to be more realistic and honest with myself now. He wasn't sentimental. He would have thought "Lucy can cope".'

Maggie was silent.

'He would have looked forward, not back. You're right.' There were tears in Lucy's eyes. Her mind was a turmoil of grief for Larry, fear for herself and a growing determination that she was not going to be beaten by all the problems which were being thrown at her.

Maggie squeezed her arm gently. 'Your husband bequeathed you quite a challenge with the painting, my dear, and I think he is now confident that you can cope with it, so, what are you going to do next?'

They both turned to look at the crate.

Lucy took a deep breath. 'I have to be able to go back to Westgate,' she said after a moment. 'I can't let this bastard, whoever he is, ghost, or Christopher Marston, get the better of me.' She gave a small grimace. 'What with that and being chased out of Evie's studio as well by Mike's girlfriend I'm not doing very well at the moment. My confidence has taken a bit of a knock, to put it mildly. But this is something I have to face. I can't leave it all to you and Huw. For my own peace of mind I have to get out and fight.'

'That's very brave.' Maggie grinned at her. 'Have you spoken to Mike about his girlfriend yet?'

She nodded. 'But I was angry.'

Maggie smiled. 'Oh dear.'

'And he hasn't rung me back. I wasn't sure I would still be welcome before. Now I might have blown it completely. Perhaps he won't let me go there again. He might be like Christopher and ban me from the whole project.' She grimaced unhappily. 'But I am not going to give up. I have to know what happened. I have to! I live and sleep Evie now. I can't get her out of my head. I need to know what happened to them all. Not just for the book but because I need to know what happened and how it all ended. I have to know. It might be more sensible to sell the painting, give up the grant and forget the whole project but I can't. I won't.' She gave Maggie an apologetic smile. 'I owe it to Evie.' She paused again. 'I do have another line of enquiry. George Marston. Evie's younger son is still alive. I am going to go and see him if he'll let me. Perhaps he can explain the mystery behind all this.'

November 23rd 1940

'Listen to me, Evie!' Ralph caught her arm as he used to when they were children. 'Shut up and listen for once in your life!'

They were walking up on the Downs behind the farm, far away from listening ears. The sky above them was quiet, clouds massing in the distance, a tension in the air which came not from the imminent threat of yet more planes but from the knowledge that there hadn't been any sign of the enemy for several days.

'I want to know what has been going on. Is Dad ill? He looks as though he's at death's door. Has Tony been up here? And Eddie?'

Evie nodded. 'They were both here. Mummy says Daddy's heart is giving him trouble. She seems to think it would kill him if Tony came up here again.'

329

Ralph stared at her incredulously. 'I had no idea there was anything wrong with him.'

'No.' She groped in the pocket of her dungarees for a hanky. 'Oh God, Evie, what a mess.'

'Tony came up here, Ralph, when Eddie was here to talk about the paintings. They had a terrible row. Eddie was unspeakably awful.' She raised her eyes to his and he saw how pale and thin she had become. 'I don't know what to do.'

Ralph shoved his hands into his pockets. He let out a soundless whistle and slowly shook his head. 'The trouble is this is not just about you and Tony any more, is it, Sis, there are others involved. Besides Daddy, I mean. My CO, for a start. And Tony's. I was asked to have a chat with Tony about all this.' He glanced at her sideways. The sight of the misery on her face decided him. What was the point of making things worse by telling her that someone might be trying to hurt Tony, someone who was supposed to be their ally? He wandered on, a few paces in front of her. Was Eddie the culprit? Everything pointed to him. He was jealous and angry and had resented Tony from the start, but would he really be in a position to get someone to try and kill his rival? Almost as the thought crossed his mind he realised it was perfectly possible. Eddie had contacts everywhere. He was a fixer and he was not someone who would allow himself to be crossed. Ralph stopped, staring down across the stubble fields below them. All their fields would be under cultivation next spring. There would be no more grazing sheep, only a cow for milk and the old horse in the orchard and the pigs. His poor father, no longer the master of the farm, not only in hock to Eddie, but obeying orders from the government, ploughing up ancient meadows to feed the nation. No wonder he was ill.

Evie caught up with him. 'What shall I do, Ralph?'

'Nothing for now. Let Tony do his job and,' he turned to face her and gripped her upper arms, forcing her to face him, 'watch out for Eddie, Sis. Don't antagonise him but don't let him get too close either. Concentrate on your painting. That is your bit for the war effort, and important, and it is your life.' He paused, holding her gaze.

She nodded slowly.

'Plenty of time after the war to think about Tony. It will be over soon and anyway you needn't worry about him. He'll make it. He's a survivor.' He wished he felt as certain as he sounded. 'You mustn't distract him, Evie. None of us can afford to be distracted. One lapse of concentration for even a second could be the difference between life and death.'

She looked appalled. 'You are saying I am putting his life at risk?'

He nodded. 'Let him go. Just for now. Just for a while.'

When he had gone she climbed wearily to her studio and stood looking round the room. She loved it up here with the low sun slanting through the skylight. It was peaceful in here and safe. She must never let Eddie come up here again. He spoiled the atmosphere with his eagle eyes darting round the place, cataloguing the paintings and sketches in his mind, checking what she was doing against some list he carried in his head. She walked over to her easel. The canvas depicted a scene of desolation and destruction, the predominant colours greys and browns and black. In the foreground she had painted a mother carrying a baby in her arms. They were both swathed in a blue shawl, the colour standing out, drawing in the eye, the baby reaching out towards his mother's face in total trust, the shawl a safe warm place, apart from the rest of the scene. In the background she had sketched in the faces of three ARP wardens watching her anxiously as they dispensed blankets and tea to the shadowy figures around them. Evie shook her head slowly. She hadn't realised she had drawn a Madonna and Child. Without conscious thought she picked up her palette knife and reached for a tube of paint. In minutes she was immersed in the painting, oblivious to everything around her, filling in a sea of faces, depicting their horror and their fear, showing that fear lessening as they focused on the wonder of the little group at the centre of the picture, showing the terror and stress dissolving in the faces close to the central scene to be replaced by a look of wonder and joy.

She painted on until it was too dark to see properly and at last she put down her palette with a sigh. She stood back staring at the picture, unaware that she was resting her hand gently on her stomach in the age-old gesture of a woman protecting her unborn child.

Tuesday 20th August

Charlotte's brief phone conversation with Mike earlier that evening had been very unsatisfactory. He had mentioned that he was with his mother, which she supposed was some sort of a relief as she had been terribly afraid he was with Lucy. She rather rashly retorted that in that case she might as well not have come down to Rosebank, and that in fact she might as well stay in London for the rest of the summer, and to her dismay he had agreed. 'I know you've got a busy schedule, Charlotte,' he said. 'It might be easier than racing up and down to Sussex. Just for a few weeks, anyway.' She hadn't been sure if that was an effort at reconciliation. Somehow it didn't feel like it.

What about their meetings, at the cottage, and the romantic meals to follow? What had happened to them? Why had he gone to see his mother again? She wondered if bloody Lucy had rung Juliette and told her everything. Of course she had!

Wednesday 21st August

Rosebank Cottage was in darkness when Lucy arrived. There were no lights on in the front room or upstairs, as far as she could see. Almost certainly Mike had gone back to London. She had driven past the place where he usually left his car and it was empty, as was the verge at the top of the lane where Charlotte parked. She parked there herself, tucking her car in close to the hedge, then retraced her steps down the lane. She opened the gate and climbed the steps to the front door, and then, her nerve failing as she reached into her pocket for the key, she ducked around the side, over the steep front garden with its rockery and flowers and onto the back lawn. A glance at the cottage showed no lights there either.

She had been too restless to sleep after supper at the vicarage; instead of going to bed she had gone out and climbed into the car, heading almost automatically back towards Rosebank. It was nearly midnight when she got here and the whole village was in darkness as she drove across the small green, past the church and turned down the lane. The pull of this place was too strong to resist. Evie's very soul was here, waiting for her. Whatever terrors the research held, the draw of Evie was greater. She refused to think about Mike. Charlotte seemed to think she liked him, which was ridiculous. As if she would be so disloyal to Larry. The woman also seemed to think Mike liked her. Not very likely now, although once or twice – for a moment she relived the occasions they had touched hands. Had there been a spark there? No. Nothing more than the shock of two people accidentally brushing against one another in a crowded space.

She followed the path across the grass to the studio and unlocked it, pushing open the door and peering in. She was reluctant to turn on the lights but there was no alternative. She clicked on the central lamp which hung low over the table and glanced round. Nothing had changed, as far as she could see. The piles of books and papers were as she had left them, the boxes and suitcases stacked against the far wall. With a sigh of relief she closed the door behind her and walked over to the table. There were various things she had meant to take away, a box of receipts and bills from the battered desk, an old leather satchel which she had discovered in one of the suitcases, some envelope files which she had found stacked on a high shelf over the window. If she could take those with her she could work on them without coming back to the studio for a while, and avoid the risk of another meeting with Mike or Charlotte. It was as she began to collect things together she noticed another box on the floor in the corner. In it were some more notebooks – maybe diaries – written in Evie's hand. Where had they come from? Dolly must have found them somewhere and put them in the studio for her. She picked the box up and began to glance through its contents, her heart hammering with excitement as she saw more and more items in Evie's distinctive untidy handwriting. Underneath them was a wad of newspaper cuttings held together by a rusty paperclip. She held them up to the light and saw they were articles and reviews of exhibitions all written by Edward Marston. Not surprising, come to think of it, considering his interest in art and all his contacts in the art world.

A noise behind her as she stacked the books and papers on the table made her freeze. For several seconds she didn't move then slowly she turned towards the door. Nothing had moved in the studio. The door was still closed. She glanced at the nearest window. It was so black outside all she could see was the reflection of the room behind her. Hastily she shoved everything she needed into the large canvas shopping bag she had brought with her and put it by the door. Again she looked round. Was there anything else she would need? She could feel herself getting more and more nervous as she seized another couple of cases at random. She doubted if she could carry any more. Tidying the chair back into place and checking that nothing had obviously been moved she made her way back to the door and, turning out the light, silently pulled it open.

Light was streaming out across the grass from the kitchen window. Lucy caught her breath. Mike must have come back.

Or both of them. Silently lugging the bag and cases outside, she closed the door as quietly as she could and turned the key. The patch of light from the window reached almost to her feet as she crept down the side of the lawn, aware that her footsteps would be clearly visible in the heavy dew. She reached the pergola and peered round to the front of the cottage. The windows there were lit now as well and she could see a car pulled up close to the gate. She thought she recognised the outline of Mike's Discovery, but she couldn't be sure in the play of shadows beyond the hedge. Why didn't they pull the curtains? It was impossible to get out of the garden without using the front path. She piled the bag and cases near the apple tree in the deepest shadow and waited. She was not prepared to have him catch her creeping about like a thief, and if Charlotte was with him that would be worse. She froze suddenly. She was parked in Charlotte's usual place at the top of the lane. They could not have failed to see her car and surely they must have seen the light in the studio.

She shivered, her wet feet growing colder as she waited, pondering the wisdom of trying to climb down the rockery and over the fence to drop into the lane. Almost as she decided she would have to do it someone in the house drew the curtains across the front window and a minute or so later the bedroom light went on, to be muted almost at once in its turn by the curtains. She gave a sigh of relief. Reclaiming her bags she tiptoed over the wet grass to the path and ran down it, letting herself out of the gate and turning up the lane as fast as she could. As far as she could see there was no sign of Charlotte's car, but she only relaxed when she had reached her own, thrown the bags in the boot and climbed into the front. In seconds she had started the engine and pulled away from the hedge.

It was nearly two in the morning when at last she drew in behind Huw's car at the vicarage and let herself into the hall. They had left the light on for her and Roger the cat was sitting on the bottom step of the stairs studying her with a look of faint disapproval. She lugged the bags in and as quietly as she could made her way up to her bedroom.

It was only when she was sitting on the edge of her bed that she took out her mobile and saw that it was switched off. When she turned it on she saw there was a message from Mike: *Stop skulking and come in for a coffee.* He had sent it at twelve forty-five when she was standing under his apple tree.

November 25th 1940

Tony had heard nothing from Evie since their meeting up at the farm, nothing about her since his CO had called him into his office. Now he had summoned him again. 'That incident we discussed. Evie's father.' Don looked at him closely. 'Dudley Lucas has been checked out. No problem there. All right? He was merely looking out for his daughter. And please, old boy, no more midnight trysts!'

An orderly put his head round the door. 'Sorry to interrupt. A Flight at readiness in five minutes!'

So, what had Dudley been up to? Tony put it out of his mind as much as he could. Talking about Evie had brought his unhappiness back. Pretending that Dudley had been looking out for Evie only made the whole episode worse.

The patrol went up to more than thirty thousand feet. At that height the planes were bitterly cold and the windscreens froze. The pilots were on the lookout for unidentified planes but they saw nothing and returned to base with hands and feet so cold they could barely walk when they climbed from the cockpits.

Tony returned to the Mess to find an envelope lying on his bed. His batman, by now used to his role in the clandestine affair, must have put it there earlier. Sitting down he tore it open.

Darling Tony,

I am missing you so much. Daddy is ill and he is so cross about you coming up here we can't risk you doing it again, but please don't give up on me. I love you so. I will see if Ralph can arrange for us to meet somewhere else soon.

With all my love,
Evie. xxxxxxxxxx

Tony sat staring at the letter then he lifted it and pressed it against his lips. He was sure he could smell Evie's distinctive scent of flowers and oil paint. He smiled fondly. Tomorrow he would see if he could raise Ralph on the telephone, or even drive over to Tangmere to see him. There had to be some way he and Evie could get together, some way he could persuade Ralph to help him in spite of everything.

In the event, though, he didn't get the chance. They flew almost constant patrols over the next few days and Tony and his room-mate Peter found themselves too tired to do more than throw themselves on their beds in the evenings, drifting to sleep to the sound of Benny Goodman and Ella Fitzgerald wafting up the stairs from the almost deserted front room, which served them as bar and sitting room, where only one or two hardy souls stayed up late, winding and rewinding the gramophone.

20

Friday 23rd August

Lucy walked slowly down Kensington Church Street on the opposite side to the shop. George Marston's gallery was very smart, Gothic windows in place of a full-size display window, the wooden frames painted black with gold lettering and scrolled decoration. Now that she was so close her nerve was failing her but George was the key to so much of Evie's story. It had been a deliberate decision not to ring first. On current form the Marston family were far too touchy for her to give him a chance to fend her off before she even put a foot over the threshold. Better to arrive unannounced and hope he would let her in.

Taking a deep breath she crossed the road, dodging between taxis and bicycles, and approached the door. It was locked. There was nothing unusual in that. She glanced through the window but could see nothing beyond the rather funereal arrangement of dried flowers on a pedestal in the centre of the staging. It was then she saw the note affixed inside the window glass. *By appointment only.* There followed a phone number.

She grabbed her mobile and entered the number, waiting for it to ring before she had time to change her mind.

The voice that answered was male, alert and perfectly civil. For a split second Lucy wondered if she should lie to him and pretend to be interested in buying something from his shop. No. Being devious had brought her nothing but trouble with Mike. This time she would be upfront about why she was there.

'This is Lucy Standish,' she said. 'I wondered if it would be possible to talk to you? I am sorry at the short notice, but I am in London, standing outside your shop. I would really appreciate the chance to chat about Evelyn Lucas.'

There was a short silence. 'Evelyn?' he repeated at last. 'You mean my mother?'

'Yes, your mother.' Strangely it did not sound as though he knew what she was talking about. She wondered briefly if he was ill, as Christopher had said; perhaps not quite in possession of his wits. Or perhaps after all Christopher hadn't warned his father against her.

'Come in.'

Before she had a chance to think further the door in front of her buzzed open and, taking a deep breath, she stepped inside the shop. Juliette had been right. It was very up-market, very expensive and in very good taste. For several seconds she stood staring round, taking in the quality of the furniture and paintings. Nothing here would cost less than five thousand pounds, she reckoned. A bit different from the dear old Standish Gallery.

A door opened at the rear of the shop and George Marston appeared. She would have recognised him even if she had not been speaking to him. He had the same build and colouring as his son. His hair was nearly white and his eyes very different, softer behind their glasses, a paler shade of grey, but apart from that the way he held himself, his build, his mouth were alike. Even the voice was similar in timbre. 'Please come through to the back,' he said courteously after he had shaken hands with her.

She followed him through a curtained doorway into a bright, comfortable office which opened onto a small courtyard, and he gestured her towards a chair. 'So, tell me,' he said as he settled himself opposite her. 'What is it you want to know about my mother?'

Lucy hesitated. 'I assumed that Christopher would have mentioned me to you,' she said at last.

'My son, Christopher?' There was a hint of bewilderment in his eyes now.

She nodded.

'I'm afraid Christopher and I do not talk very often these days,' he said after a moment and there was a distinct note of regret in his voice. 'We inhabit such contrasting worlds. He is a City man and they have very different values to those I appreciate. I'm a bit old-fashioned.' He smiled.

Lucy found she was warming to him. 'Then I will start at the beginning,' she said.

He allowed her to talk without interruption until her story was told. She did not mention the ghosts or her painting or her visit to Frances, or the extent of Christopher's opposition to her involvement with his family, but otherwise she left nothing out.

When she stopped there was a long silence during which she watched George anxiously, feeling her nervousness increasing by the moment. He seemed lost in some distant world of his own and it was several minutes before he levered himself out of his chair.

'A small sherry is called for, I think,' he said. He walked across to a rosewood side table where a beautiful cut-glass decanter stood on a lacquer tray with several small glasses. He poured them each a thimbleful and passed one to her. 'I do actually have several of my mother's paintings,' he said when he had taken a sip and savoured it for a moment. 'I would be delighted to show them to you. I think it is quite definitely time that Mama was given her due recognition. She has always had a following amongst the cognoscenti, of course, but she did not enjoy the idea of fame. She was an intensely private person, Christopher is right about that.'

'But you don't object – you don't think she would object – to a book about her?'

'I think she would be very pleased.' He smiled at her over the rim of the glass. 'So, you have won the approval of Dolly, have you?'

Lucy nodded. 'It took time.'

'I can imagine. I was very fond of Dolly. She looked after my mother for a long time and was the most intensely loyal person I think I have ever met.'

'But you haven't kept in touch with her?'

Just for a second she saw the shutters come down behind his eyes. He shook his head. 'After Mama died –' There was a long pause. 'I didn't care to go to Rosebank Cottage again. It wasn't the same without her.'

'Were you sad that Mike inherited it?' she asked cautiously. She didn't want to jeopardise her relationship with this man.

He was staring into the distance now. 'I never knew Mike. Not really. I expect someone has told you that his father and I did not get on. That was not my choice, but sadly it meant our families did not see much of each other.'

'Would it be prying to ask why you didn't like each other?' Lucy took another sip of the sherry.

'I think it went back to when I was born. I have given it much thought over the years.' He was silent again and she thought for a moment he was going to expand on some theory, but he didn't, contenting himself with: 'Sibling rivalry, I suppose. Johnny had no time for a new little brother. I came along four years after he was born and instead of getting over it, he seemed to became more and more entrenched in his dislike of me as the years went on.' He pursed his lips. 'Sad.

341

Very sad. But too late to do anything about it now. I have nothing against Michael, nothing at all, but I would not like to presume that he would welcome me into his life. I prefer to keep my distance. I am too old to cope with more rejection.'

Lucy felt a wave of sympathy as he allowed this glimpse of loneliness to show for a moment. She changed the subject. 'Do you remember watching your mother paint?'

He smiled. 'Oh, yes. She never minded us going into the studio. We would sit there spellbound. Sometimes she told us stories about the subjects she was painting and once in a while Johnny or I would be allowed to hold a brush and put in one or two strokes. She used to joke that when she was famous it would fool the experts when they realised someone else had helped her with the painting. The old masters used to do that, she told us. They allowed the apprentices to fill in the boring bits of their masterpieces.'

'It sounds like a happy childhood.'

'It was in some ways. But not when my father was there. They didn't get on. Mama was very unhappy a lot of the time. She locked herself away in her studio when he was there.'

'That's sad. And what about your grandparents? Do you remember them?'

'I liked Dad's parents. They farmed properly. A big farm with lots of cows.' He smiled nostalgically. 'Evie's parents got rid of most of the animals during the war. There was an old horse, I remember, and various dogs and cats, and some ducks on the pond behind the byre. But the farm was down to arable then and when her dad died they leased out the land. We were living in London by then in a huge old house in Hampstead. It had a garden, which I loved. We lived with her parents before that but we were a bit much for poor old Dudley. He was quite ill at the end and we were noisy so Dad took us away to London. Mama was distraught though she tried to hide it, and Johnny and I were incredibly upset. Johnny loved his new school, though, and I suppose I got to like mine in the end.' He gave her a grin.

'So you and Johnny did get on then, when you were young?'

He hesitated and gave her a sad shake of the head. 'You know, when I was about four or five I remember Johnny in an especially horrible mood getting me in a corner and telling me that Mama only pretended to love me more than him – that was it, of course, the jealousy, the lack of confidence – because I was adopted. I didn't know what it meant, but the word stayed with me and a long time later – years later – I asked her if it was true.' He stopped, staring into space. 'She said no, but I had a feeling she was lying.'

Lucy wasn't sure what to say. Nothing in this encounter had gone the way she expected but above all these were glimpses of a vulnerable and lonely man quite unlike the tyrant she had anticipated.

'But your birth certificate –'

'Was normal as far as I could tell. I managed to acquire a lifetime's worth of passports with it.' He laughed ruefully. 'Have I said too much? Probably. Please don't quote me on this.'

'Of course not.'

'An old man gabbles.'

It was her turn to laugh. 'Not so old! Good heavens, you can only be in your sixties.'

'And feel a hundred.'

Again she found herself anxious to change the subject. 'You said you would show me Evie's pictures.'

He nodded. 'And I will. But not today, I'm afraid.' He looked at his wristwatch. 'We have talked for too long, I fear. They are at home in my house and alas I am going out this evening to the opera, which would not give us enough time to go and see them now. I will give you my home address and phone number and mobile and all that and we shall meet again soon, I hope. You must let me take you out to lunch or something, and bring your tape recorder and I will fill you in on as many anecdotes about my mother as I can remember. And if it gets up my son's nose so much the better.' He chuckled.

As he showed her to the door he caught her hand and squeezed it gently. 'I am so glad you came to see me, Lucy. And please, if you think it is appropriate, will you tell Michael that I would like to be his friend? Whatever there was that didn't gel between me and his father, it doesn't have to be the same for us.'

Friday 23rd August, late

The opera had been wonderful. With a smile of contentment George fumbled for the key in his pocket and let himself into his house. Keats Grove was quiet; he loved this stroll back from the underground station during which he had the chance to unwind after a day in the shop followed by the theatre or the cinema, or like today a treat at Covent Garden with one of his colleagues from the antique world.

Over a light supper the two men had discussed his unexpected visit from Lucy.

'Do you know, I had never realised you were Evie Lucas's son.' Derek Hemingway leaned forward across the table, his eyes alight with interest. 'She had a formidable talent. I always wondered what became of her.'

The two men looked up as the waiter approached and they gave him their order. George reached for his glass and took a sip of the very passable rioja. 'I'm surprised you have even heard of her,' he said thoughtfully. 'I suppose there are too few of her paintings in the public domain for her to be a household name.'

'Did she not produce very much in the course of her career? I know there is one in the Tate.'

George stared down at the table thoughtfully. 'You are right.

Why only one? Where are her other paintings? She was always painting when I was a child, as I told Lucy. The farmhouse where we were brought up was full of her paintings and then when we moved to London I remember them being stacked along the passage on the top floor. But then –' He paused thoughtfully. 'My parents got divorced after Granny Rachel died and she and my brother and I moved to a small cottage in Sussex. I suspect a lot of the pictures got left behind with my father. I can still remember that time. I think it was all very acrimonious. He kept the house, of course, and pretty much everything. My brother and I adored the new cottage though. Johnny was much older than me and he didn't live at home any more, but I revelled in living in the country again.' He chuckled. 'It's strange I don't count myself a country boy. My whole life is antiques and paintings and London-centred but I suppose I was about fifteen then and into sport and stuff. She sent me to Lancing College and I loved it. Very churchy. That fabulous chapel. Smells and bells. I began to appreciate art there. At home, it was just Mum's paintings. I suppose I was a bit blasé.' He sighed. 'The collection my mother left – most of them painted after we moved in 1960 – was bequeathed directly to my son. He always said it was because she was afraid I would sell them, but I wouldn't have.' There was a long silence.

Derek waited for him to continue. He noticed George's glass was empty and reached for the bottle. 'Did you and your mother not get along then?' he asked at last.

George sighed. 'We got along fine. Really well. Perhaps she and my dad had some sort of an agreement. My brother, Johnny, inherited all her stuff and I inherited from my father. His house, his money, a few paintings.' He paused again. 'But not all.'

George went to the keypad and unset the alarm, closed the door behind him and stood for a moment looking down at the hall stand. His cleaning lady had picked up the post and laid it out there for him. One cursory glance told him there was nothing there he wanted to see. He turned into the living room and switched on the lights. It was a gracious room, subtle, he always liked to think, with perfect handpicked furniture. Every now and then he would change the pieces round, bring some things back from the shop, change the mood, but for now it was a restful place, gentle on the eye and perfect as a setting for the five Lucas paintings which hung on the walls. They were all examples of her later work, three that she had given him herself, as were the two sketch portraits he kept in his bedroom. Those he had bought from an auction in Brighton. Over the fireplace was a painting which had been given to him by an old friend of his mother's who no longer had any room for it. It was large, more strident than her usual palette, in some ways uncomfortable in its depiction of a stormy scene on the Downs, the great trees of Chanctonbury Ring in the background, trees which had later been felled by the great storm of 1987. He loved that painting. It was elemental; violent. It contained rage and frustration and sorrow, somehow predicting the violent end the trees would suffer, and yet, there in the distance was a break in the clouds with a promise of gentle warmth and summer skies to come.

He went over to the front window and drew the curtains. The tree outside was moving slowly in the slight breeze from the heath which had teased his hair as he approached the house. He would enjoy showing Lucy the paintings and if she wanted he would allow her to photograph them for her book. His mother would be pleased, he was sure. He smiled again, aware that supporting Lucy would undoubtedly piss off Christopher.

The noise behind him made him turn round with mild curiosity. He still attributed any untoward noises in the house to dear old Marcus, his wonderful, much missed, tabby cat, alas now departed to the great cat hotel in the sky, although, sometimes, he had to admit he did wonder if his beloved wife,

Marjory, though she had been dead for over twenty years, still kept an eye on him. There was no one there, of course. There never was. The house, so full of furniture and paintings and beauty, was, sometimes achingly, empty. He took a step towards the door and another, suddenly aware that there was a shadow there, a shadow which looked strangely like that of a man.

'Hello?' he called. He felt nervous now, suspicious. 'Is someone there?'

To his astonishment the hazy figure that appeared looked exactly like his father.

November 30th 1940

Evie had made Ralph drive her out towards the coast. They parked at last in a lonely lane near Pagham. Ralph pulled on the handbrake and turned towards her. 'Not another mile till you tell me what this is all about.' It was raining hard and a cold wind had scoured the last leaves from the hedgerows.

'It's Tony. I have to see him.'

Ralph let out a groan. 'For goodness' sake. We have been over this so many times. Can you please leave me out of it! Ring him. Meet him in Chi or somewhere. Daddy will never see you there, but look out for Eddie. You and Tony are both miserable. You are making everyone else miserable. You are both being annoying.' It was the closest she had seen him to being angry with her for a long time.

'I did ring him. I left two messages at the Mess and I had no reply. If he cared he would have come to see me. He could have done it. He could have found out when Daddy was away from the farm and come up to see me. He did before.'

Ralph let out a groan. 'Evie, the poor guy is fighting a war! He does have to do other things. He can't just chase after you all the time.'

He took her hands in his. They were very cold and he could

see the stains from the oil paints in her fingernails. A wave of compassion swept over him. His baby sister always brought out the soft side in him and he cursed himself for it.

'All right. Just one more time. I will tell him, but if you two can't arrange something this time then that is it. The end. Right? If he can't or won't meet you then you must give up. It means he just can't do it now. You are putting so much pressure on the chap, Evie, and he is being harangued on every side, being told to leave you alone.'

'I hate Eddie.' She said it so quietly he had to bend towards her to hear. 'It is Eddie, isn't it?'

'Eddie is very protective of you, I do know that. And he's very jealous. So, for God's sake don't blurt out that you still love Tony. Eddie is too important to your career.'

Two more of her paintings had been bought by the Commission and were even now on display in London. She had had a personal message from Sir Kenneth Clark praising her work and asking her to produce more sketches of the women of Southampton rallying round to bring some semblance of normality to their lives after the endless repeated bombing of their city. Even now there was a painting on the easel in her studio showing two young women with a group of small children. Their hair tied up in colourful scarves, their coats flapping open over dull brown dresses, the women, barely more than girls themselves were playing with the children in an underground shelter. The small faces were thin and grey with fatigue but they were laughing, as were the adults round them as they all looked down at a game of spillikins, the pins lying on the ground in a small patch of sunshine. The picture had moved Ralph to tears.

'You heard they have given Tony the DFC?' he said suddenly. He looked up at her.

She was staring out of the windscreen. A dead leaf had plastered itself on the glass. She shivered. 'No one told me. That's good. He's a brave man.' She gave a sad little smile.

Ralph frowned incredulously. 'Aren't you pleased?'

'Of course I am. He's a hero. He's in danger every day.' Her voice trembled.

'Yes, he is,' Ralph replied. 'So why can't you see that you have to give him a bit of space, Evie?' He didn't point out that all this applied to him as well. That he too was in danger every day, that he too was exhausted and under interminable pressure. She had never even asked if he had a girlfriend, someone somewhere who worried about him and maybe cried when he was late back from a sortie. As far as she was concerned Ralph was her property, there for her and her alone. He reached for the starter button. One of these days he would tell her about Sylvie. 'I must take you back. There is someone else I have to see before I get back to Tangmere.'

She didn't even ask who it was.

21

Saturday 24th August

Christopher and Frances were seated in silence at the kitchen table when the doorbell rang. It was nine o'clock in the morning. The table was bare save for a coffee pot and two mugs. Christopher swore as the bell rang again. 'Well,' he said, 'you might as well go and see.'

Frances pushed back her chair and walked out into the hall. She was dressed and made up, and her hair was neatly brushed in a half-fringe so that it more or less covered the fading black eye. She unlocked the door and pulled it open. There were two uniformed police officers on the doorstep.

'Mrs Marston?' The elder of the two looked at her with such a solemn face she felt her stomach turn over. 'The children?' she gasped. 'Has something happened to the children?'

'No, Mrs Marston. We are not here about your children.' The older man had his cap tucked under his arm. 'I am Sergeant David Hawkins and this is Constable Simon Jones. I wonder, is your husband in, Mrs Marston?'

She turned to call Christopher but he had followed her out of the kitchen and was standing in the hall. 'What is it?' he called. 'What's happened?'

'If we might come in please, sir.'

The two policemen followed them into the sitting room. 'Does your father live in Keats Grove, Hampstead, sir?'

'Oh God!' Christopher said. His face had drained of colour. 'What has happened?'

'I am afraid your father has been found dead, sir.'

Christopher opened his mouth to say something, found himself incapable of speech and sat down heavily on one of the armchairs.

'What happened?' Frances echoed in a whisper. 'Did he have a heart attack?'

'At present we don't know the cause of death. I'm sorry.'

'You must know something! Who found him? That useless cleaning lady of his, I suppose.' Christopher looked wildly from one man to the other.

'At present we know very little, sir. I gather he was found downstairs in his living room. He was alone and there were no signs of a forced entry, but a painting which I gather had been hanging over the fireplace was lying near him. It had been badly damaged. His neighbour found him. I gather he had a key to your father's house and when he couldn't get an answer this morning and saw the curtains still shut he let himself in. They had an arrangement to go out together, I understand, and he thought it strange that your father hadn't rung to tell him if there was a change of plan.'

Christopher seemed incapable of speech. It was Frances who told the police that they had been estranged from Christopher's father and had not seen him for several years, that he had been ill on and off with a bad heart, that they knew nothing about his friends or business colleagues and who might have seen him last, and it was Frances who calmly locked up and ushered her husband into the back of the police car before climbing in beside him for the drive to London.

The body had been removed when they got there; the painting of Chanctonbury Ring was lying where the police had found it on the carpet in front of the fireplace. There was an ugly hole ripped in the centre. With an exclamation of horror Christopher moved forward to pick it up. The sergeant stepped forward to stop him. 'I am sorry, sir, but just for now we mustn't touch anything. Detective Inspector Swire will be here in a moment to speak to you.'

Christopher moved back. He was still staring at the picture. 'That's Evie's,' he whispered to Frances. 'One of Evie's from the seventies. How the hell did he get hold of it?'

'She was his mother,' Frances retorted, rather more sharply than she had intended. They both glanced at the sergeant, who pretended not to have heard the exchange. 'I am sure he had a great many of his mother's pictures. Surely you didn't think you had the total monopoly.'

'Why did he smash it like that?' Christopher appeared far more concerned about the damage to the picture than his father's death. He swung round as another man walked into the room.

'Detective Inspector Swire, sir.' Medium height, compact build and thinning fair hair gave the inspector a deceptively meek appearance as he held out his hand. 'Could you tell us, just for the record, where you were last night between midnight and the early hours of this morning?'

'You can't possibly think –' Christopher exploded.

'No, sir, I don't.' Inspector Swire's voice was cold and surprisingly powerful. 'Nevertheless I would like to confirm your whereabouts.'

'We were at home in bed.'

'And do you know a Mr Derek Hemingway?'

Christopher looked blank. 'No.'

'Or,' the inspector consulted a piece of paper, 'a Mrs Lucy Standish?'

December 5th 1940

'I want to marry your sister.' Tony was sitting opposite Ralph in The Unicorn bar. The continuing run of bad weather meant they were grounded for the time being, as was, presumably, the enemy. 'I don't know where I am with her any more. And I miss her so much. To keep everything above board, I want your permission to ask her. I can't ask your father, he will only say no. I know why he has taken against me, and I understand that Eddie is threatening everybody, but I need to be with her and I need to know that she wants to be with me! I love her so much. We can be married by special licence and if you are there it will make it respectable.'

Ralph shook his head. 'I'm not sure that's right, Tony.' He picked up his glass. 'I'm not sure she wants to rush into this, however much she loves you.' If she loves you, he almost added. He wasn't sure now. 'She adores Daddy and she won't want to risk him getting angry. You do know how ill he is, don't you? Can't you just put it all off for a bit?'

Tony's shoulders slumped. 'Supposing I give her a ring? Then she will know I mean it.' He sat back on his seat, his face a picture of anguish. 'I have one. I asked my mother to send Grandmother's ring down to me. It was always going to be for the girl I marry. It is very pretty. I think Evie would like it. I'll tell her not to show it to anyone. Eddie mustn't see it, or your father, but we would be secretly engaged.'

Ralph pursed his lips. 'It's an idea, certainly.'

'But how am I going to ask her if she won't see me?'

'Write to her and I will see she gets the letter. That way there can be no mistake. I will guarantee to give it to her personally and I will bring her reply. How about that?'

It had to be up to them to sort this out but he could help, he could let them have one more chance to see each other. Didn't he owe them both that much? Ralph sighed as from the rain-swept night outside the air raid siren began its eerie wail.

'I don't believe it,' he said. 'Not in this weather. It will be a false alarm.'

Tony smiled for the first time. 'There hasn't been a raid for days. I reckon they have forgotten about us.' He sat forward. 'Ralph, there is a rumour my squadron is going to be posted. I have to know before I go. Supposing they send us back to Scotland?'

'Write the letter. If you go to Scotland perhaps that would be a good thing. If Evie wants to marry you she can jump on a train and meet you up there. You could go to Gretna.'

For a moment the two young men held each other's gaze.

'Write it now so I can take it with me,' Ralph said at last. 'Ask for a bit of paper at the bar.'

A sheet of notepaper and an envelope were produced and Tony retired with it to the corner. Barely half the people drinking had left to seek the air raid shelters. The others downed their beers steadfastly, half an eye on the blacked-out windows and door. There was no noise of overhead planes and only ten minutes later the all clear sounded.

'Here.' Tony folded the letter into the envelope and wrote Evie's name on it. 'Shall I give you the ring?'

'You have it here?' Ralph stared at him

'I've carried it since my mother sent it. Just in case.' Tony rummaged in his battledress and felt in an inner pocket. The pretty sapphire ring sparkled in the dim light of the bar. 'Tell her I will put it on her finger myself when she says yes.' He grinned weakly. 'Remind her about the milkwort flower. I've told her this is the last chance, Ralph. If she says no, that will be it. If she chooses her dad and Eddie over me, I won't push her any more; I can't fight them unless she wants me to. I won't ask again.' He pushed back the chair. 'I don't want the ring back. There will never be anyone else. Let's go. You can drop me off.'

As he climbed out of the Morgan at the gate to Westhampnett Tony stooped to Ralph's window. 'If I don't hear from her I will know it is all off this time. That will be it. I will go back to Scotland and she will never see or hear from me again. You will persuade her, won't you?'

Ralph nodded. He raised his thumb. 'I might not get up there for a few days, but don't worry, I'll see she gets the letter.' He couldn't promise any more than that.

Monday 26th August

Huw walked up the stairs ahead of Lucy. Behind them, Robin followed them into the kitchen and straight through into the studio. The skylights were open and sunshine poured into the room.

'It's clear.' Huw turned to Lucy. 'He has gone.'

'How do you know?' Her mouth was dry.

'I can feel it. But Robin and I agree, the painting should not return here, and maybe you would be more comfortable staying with us a little bit longer.'

'I want you to take another week or so off, Luce.' Robin folded his arms. 'This has all been an awful strain on you.'

The police had arrived at ten a.m. and Robin had hesitantly told them where Lucy was staying. Maggie had sat with Lucy when they told her of George's death. Her alibi for Friday night was cast iron – she had been on the train by six, still had a receipt for coffee from Victoria Station, and another for the train ticket. She had spent the evening with Huw and Maggie and one of the churchwardens and his wife who had come to supper and stayed till almost midnight. She had been able to tell them nothing about George other than that he had been going to the opera that evening. Her sadness for the loss of someone who to her had been kind and friendly was compounded by the irreplaceable loss of information about Evie's life.

Juliette rang them later at the vicarage. 'Frances told me.

355

The police took them up to town to see if anything had been stolen, which of course they didn't know, and then they had to go and identify him. It is just so awful.'

'So they think it was a robbery?' Maggie had passed the phone to Lucy.

'They don't know, but one of Evie's paintings was badly damaged. It was lying on the floor when they went into the house. Obviously George wouldn't have done it. There was no sign he was trying to move it or anything. He would have had to stand on something and there was nothing near him. They think maybe he disturbed someone who was trying to steal it. They will know more after the post mortem.'

After she had hung up the phone Lucy looked at Maggie and grimaced. 'You don't think . . .?' She hesitated for a moment. 'The entity who tried to destroy Evie's painting in my studio. You don't think he had turned his attention to George? You don't think he followed me to London?' The colour had drained from her face. 'Huw was so sure it had left the studio. Did I take it with me? Did I cause George's death?'

'Don't even think about it, Lucy.' Maggie shook her head. 'It was probably some low-life scum who followed him home.' She gave a sad smile. 'Don't tell Huw I said that. I know I should forgive and understand but I get angry! This sort of thing is so needless!'

'And now he will never make friends with Mike,' Lucy said wistfully.

'No, but you can tell Mike that was his wish. That will help them both.'

Lucy sighed. 'I suppose I have to speak to Mike.'

'Of course you do. Ring him today. At once.'

'And that will help George how?'

'It will ease his way. He died suddenly and unprepared. He will have left unfinished business amongst which is his relationship with you and Mike.'

'Oh great! So now he is going to haunt me as well!'

'No. Sorry.' Maggie ran her fingers through her hair. 'I shouldn't have said that. Ring Mike, Lucy.'

Mike picked up her call at once. 'Lucy? Where are you?'

'Staying in Chilverly.'

'Mum rang and told me about George. It's terrible. Listen, I am at Rosebank Cottage. I have taken a few days off from the office. I can work from here if necessary. Can you come over? We need to talk.'

Lucy felt a lightening of her spirits. 'Is Charlotte there?' she asked cautiously.

'No.'

They met two hours later. As they sat in the living room of the cottage Lucy could hear the quiet roar of an ancient Hoover upstairs, thudding over the carpets on the uneven boards. 'Dolly's day?' She smiled.

'Not usually. She has to go to the dentist again tomorrow. She will be glad to see you. She said she would make us some coffee as soon as you arrived.' He sat down on the sofa and in the light from the window she saw the strain on his face. 'I didn't realise you had gone to see George. I didn't realise he was well enough to see anyone.'

'Perhaps he wasn't,' she responded sadly. 'I would hate to think I could have been responsible in any way for his death. He had a bad heart, I gather.'

'But you didn't upset him, did you?'

'Of course not.' She was indignant. 'We were going to meet again and he was going to tell me lots of stories about Evie. He was looking forward to going to the opera that evening. He was fine. Cheerful. The only thing that had made him sad was the estrangement from the family, and, Mike, he was so keen to meet you and be friends with you. He seemed so upset about his difficult relationship with your father. He implied it was Johnny's choice, not his.' She shook her head. 'He was going to show me his pictures. He had several that Evie had given him over the years and now I suppose they will go to

Christopher.' She scowled. 'Sorry. That sounded awful. It must confirm your worst suspicions of me.'

'About that,' Mike put in. 'I'm sorry. We got off on the wrong foot about Christopher and his accusations about your painting –' He broke off as Dolly came in with a tray. Lucy hadn't noticed that the sound of vacuuming had stopped. Mike changed the subject swiftly. 'Dolly, do you remember George living here?' He pounced on one of Dolly's homemade biscuits and then as a second thought passed one to Lucy.

'Of course I do.' Dolly nodded emphatically. 'He was a bit younger than your father who had gone off to university when they first moved here. He was a nice boy, George. There was a terrible row over him living here, of course. Evie's husband wanted him to stay with him in London. George ran away from his father's house and came down on the train by himself. I suppose he was about fifteen, and he hitchhiked here from Chichester. I can still remember Evie hugging him and telling him he didn't have to go back. His father used to beat him. Mr Edward came after him, of course, but there was nothing he could do.'

Mike and Lucy looked shocked. 'He never mentioned that,' Lucy said.

'Well, he wouldn't. He was terrified of his father, though. I remember one day when they thought Mr Edward was coming down to take George back to London by force. Evie sent George to stay with some school friends and she nerved herself to have a fight about it, but Mr Edward never came. I'm not sure if he actually threatened to go to court but I think if he did he gave up for some reason. I don't think it was ever mentioned again. George was a gentle boy, quite sensitive. Artistic like his mother.' She bit her lip. 'How very sad that he could have come down here. He loved this house, but when Mr Johnny inherited it, that was that.'

'But he told me that his father left him all his money?' Lucy queried.

'Oh, yes, Mr Edward was very rich, according to Evie.' Dolly seemed to have lost her usual reserve. 'He never gave her any money to support the two boys. He was a penny-pinching sort of a man.' She pursed her lips. 'But he left it all to George. Never a penny piece to Johnny.'

After Dolly went back to work Mike suggested they go to the pub for a sandwich. 'Peace offering. Please. Can we start again?' he said. As they sat in the courtyard at the back of the pub he made his suggestion. 'There is a spare room at the cottage, you know. You could stay if you wanted to be closer to the studio. It would save you having to drive back and forth. How much do you reckon is still there to look through?'

She still hadn't told him about the ghost. All she had said was that Robin had suggested she take a few days off to concentrate on the book. Mike hadn't asked why she was staying with Huw and Maggie and she wondered suddenly whether his mother had told him what had been going on. She glanced up. He was cutting a wedge of cheese and didn't notice. He looked tired and there were deep dark circles under his eyes.

'There is a lot more than I first thought,' she said carefully. 'I suppose it would save time if I could stay over here occasionally. But what would Charlotte think?'

She saw his face tighten. 'There is no reason why she should find out.'

'Obviously I wouldn't be here next time she came.'

'No.'

He pushed his chair back abruptly. 'Would you like another glass of wine?'

She nodded. Subject changed and off limits. Interesting.

Tuesday 27th August

Lucy had found another batch of letters. Evie had obviously had no system whatsoever for filing things at any point in her

359

life. This time they were in an old torn brown foolscap envelope which was labelled *Galleries*. Excitedly Lucy carried it over to the table and pulled out a wedge, not of gallery details but a stack of personal letters held together with a rusty metal paperclip.

Hitching the stool closer she sat down and carefully removed the clip.

December 13th 1940, morning

Ralph had gulped down his early morning tea as he shaved and dressed. It was as he was leaving the room that he remembered Tony's letter and the ring. He still hadn't had a chance to get up to Box Wood Farm. His only day off he had gone into Chichester to meet Sylvie. One of these days he would introduce her to the rest of the family, but not yet. Life at Box Wood was too complicated. He didn't want to risk upsetting his father, though why a sweet girl like Sylvie would do that he wasn't sure. Evie was causing enough trouble for now. He hesitated then took the letter and the ring out of his pocket and stuffed them into the drawer of the cabinet beside his bed. His silver St Christopher had become entangled with the ring. For a moment he hesitated, about to put the medal back in his pocket but a voice called him from the corridor and leaving it where it was he hurried out and followed the others down the stairs.

It was a foggy, windy morning after all the rain and they were instructed to fly out over the Channel to intercept some stray 109s which had been seen approaching under cover of the cloud. It was going to be cold up there. The pilots gathered at flight dispersal and almost at once were sent to their planes.

'Chilly old morning!' Ralph's rigger greeted him. 'Don't worry. She's warmed up and ready to go!'

He climbed into his Spitfire and settled into the seat, closing the cockpit hood and drawing on his gloves as almost at once the flight leader's voice crackled over the radio.

They flew in formation out over the coast above a sea which was suddenly unimaginably blue in a patch of winter sunshine and began to climb.

'Bandits ahead. God! Bloody hundreds of them!' The voice came again. 'Go for it, boys, and good luck!'

Tony pushed the last of his belongings into his bag and set it outside the door to be collected with everyone else's to be loaded onto the transports, destined for Prestwick. After the days of rumour the squadron had been posted at last and they were setting off that morning. They were due some respite after being in the front line for several months and normally he would have been over the moon with relief and joy to be going home, near enough to his parents to visit them as often as he got the chance. As he glanced at his watch he noticed his log book had fallen down behind the locker. He bent to retrieve it and put it to one side. An important document, not something to leave behind.

His thoughts went back to Evie. Ralph would by now have had plenty of time to deliver his letter and the ring to Evie but he had heard nothing from her.

'Ready old boy?' A pilot from B flight ran up the stairs two at a time. 'They 've copped some more action over at Tangmere this morning. One of the squadrons has lost a couple of planes. Damn bad luck that. Come on. The CO is about to call time on this place! We're well out of it all.'

Tony smiled. 'One more thing I've got to do.' He ran into the office. It was empty. He grabbed the phone and dialled Box Wood Farm. He couldn't just leave it. Suppose Ralph hadn't had the chance to speak to Evie? Supposing she was going to ring him but hadn't had time? She didn't know he was flying out. He had to give her one more chance. He listened to the ring tone, picturing the phone echoing in the hall at Box Wood. If Evie didn't answer please let it be Rachel.

It was Dudley. His message was clear. 'My daughter never wants to see you again.' The man sounded as though he was about to explode with fury. 'How many times does she have to tell you, boy!'

The phone was slammed down and Tony was left staring at the empty desk in an empty room. Only seconds later someone put their head round the door. 'We're off!'

Standing up slowly Tony turned away from the desk. He could hardly see for sudden unmanly tears. His log book was forgotten.

Tuesday 27th August

Dear Rachel, the letter said. It was dated 14th December 1940.

We were so desperately sorry to hear about Ralph. No words can express the appallingness of your loss at this time. All I can say is that he died for his country and his country will be eternally in his and your debt.

Lucy read the letter twice. Her eyes were brimming with tears. So this was it. Ralph had died on 13th December and someone had written this letter to his mother. She bit her lip and turned to the next in the pile.

They were all there. The letter from Ralph's commanding officer, two from his fellow pilots, several from neighbours, one from a woman called Sylvie who Lucy guessed might have been a girlfriend. She frowned. Had there been a mention of Sylvie in any of the stuff she had found so far? She scrutinised the anguished letter again. 'My darling Rafie,' the woman had called him. Rafie. That was Evie's name for him. Did Evie know her? There had been no mention of her in Evie's diaries. If Sylvie was Ralph's girlfriend, how awful to have lost the man she loved before she was even officially a part of the family. Did that explain Evie and Tony's desperate need to marry so quickly after they had met? Poor Sylvie, whoever she was, seemed to have mourned and wept alone.

Most of the letters were addressed to Rachel or Rachel and Dudley. There was nothing to convey the desolation of the recipients of the condolences, nothing to echo the faint desperate cry which Lucy had heard echoing through Box Wood Farm on the evening she had spent with Elizabeth. She clipped the letters together and sadly put them back in the envelope, feeling in some strange way that these tragic missives were none of her business, however much in her heart she was inextricably linked to the family in their agony.

Wednesday 28th August

Charlotte put down her phone and switched it off. She was frozen with shock. Mike had been telling her about some replanting he was planning to do in the garden in the autumn. They were chatting comfortably, laughing, not making plans exactly, but the implication was there that they would see one another soon, and she could hear him pottering round in the kitchen at Rosebank as he talked, clattering pans, running the tap and she pictured him with his mobile tucked between his shoulder and his ear as he prepared himself some supper; late supper. She had glanced at her watch as they talked. It was after eleven. It was then she had heard a voice in the background, clear, fluting, full of laughter.

'Mike, you're not really going to make us some supper at this hour? Honestly, a sandwich will be enough –' And then the voice had stopped abruptly and Charlotte could picture Mike gesturing frantically that he was on the phone. Lucy was there with him. That was why he had decided to stay down in Sussex; that was why he had so easily and casually told her to stay in London. Lucy was there at eleven o'clock at night.

Charlotte walked over to the fridge and bent to open it, taking out a bottle of wine. She felt numb. Lucy was there, with him, at the cottage. She slopped some wine into a glass and gulped it down. The bitch, the utter bitch. She had set her cap at him from the very first time she had set eyes on him and he was such a fool he hadn't seen it. He wouldn't even realise what was happening until it was too late and Lucy had her claws well and truly stuck in. She poured some more wine into the glass, this time filling it to the brim. What to do, that was the question. How to get rid of Lucy bloody Standish? Engage brain. Think.

She walked towards the window, slopping some wine over her bare feet and stared out into the light-spangled darkness of the London night. This could not be allowed to happen. Mike was the man for her. She had chosen him, decided, planned their future in that house, planned how to get rid of Evie's stuff, visualised new furniture, even looked up the local schools for their children when they came. Evie. It was all Evie's fault, always had been. Without her, Lucy would never have come, never had the excuse to inveigle herself into Mike's life.

She drained the glass and put it down, unsteadily balancing it on the edge of the bookcase, brushing the tears out of her eyes. Easily sorted. It would all be easily sorted. As soon as it was light she would drive down to Sussex and sort things out. She would make sure that Mike was gone. A phone call would do that, make sure that he was somewhere else and then she would sort things out. She gave a feral smile as she walked back across the room and picked up her phone. She glanced at it. Three missed calls. All from Mike. So he was scared, trying to make it all right, trying to explain. Too late. It was up to her now to sort things out.

Trailing her fingers along the back of the sofa, she made

her way along to her bedroom door and pushed it open. So many of her things were missing now, left at Mike's London place or left at Rosebank. She had hinted so often that they should move in together properly but always he had resisted, making excuses. And now she knew why. Even before Lucy had barged her way onto the scene he had been keeping his options open. She hadn't been enough for him. Tears began to trickle down her cheeks again. She threw herself down on her bed and closed her eyes and quietly began to sob.

Half an hour later she had given up on sleep. She got dressed and put on a jacket. She drank two cups of black coffee and then made her way down to the garage under the building. Climbing into her car she backed out of her parking space and turned into the road. She negotiated the narrow streets with the tightly parked cars on either side without incident, and then set off towards the south. Aware that the cool night air had made her feel slightly dizzy she slid down the window and took deep breaths of the breeze in her face, leaning forward towards the dash to find some music and letting the blast of sound echo behind the car as it steered down the echoing sleeping streets.

Thursday 29th August, the early hours

In Brighton Mike lay staring up at the ceiling of the spare room in his mother's house. He wasn't sure why he had decided to bail out of Rosebank for the night. It was one in the morning by the time he reached Brighton but it seemed suddenly important that Lucy did not feel in any way pressured. She had been doubtful about staying at the cottage even when he had shown her to the small spare room. Perhaps sharing a bathroom was too intimate, or even the thought of breakfast together. She had been too tired to drive back to the vicarage, though, that he was sure of. Better to let her find her feet alone. He would be back, he had told her, mid-morning tomorrow. He wasn't sure if the slightly taken aback expression he had caught on her face after they had finished their coffee at midnight contained an element of disappointment or relief. Whatever her feelings, he couldn't deal with them now. Not with his guilt and confusion about Charlotte weighing so heavily on his mind. With a sigh he turned over and pulled the sheet up over his head. Within minutes he was asleep and dreaming about one of his mother's Cordon Bleu breakfasts.

December 23rd 1940

The old place had not changed one bit since he had last seen it in July. Tony stared at the front of his parents' farmhouse with a feeling of indescribable confusion. He had hitched a lift over from Prestwick and was looking forward to his first few days of leave for a long time with relief and longing and misery. He had to tell them that it was all over with Evie. Heaving his kitbag up onto his shoulder he trudged up the drive, noting the bare branches of the trees in their familiar arabesques over the stone slabs on the roof, the ancient lichen whorls showing yellow against the patches of snow and the outline of the distant hills against a sky as white as the ground beneath. The first thing he would have to do was find a car to drive. The sale of his little Morris Cowley back at Westhampnett had been entrusted to his batman, who was fairly sure he could get six pounds for dear old Esmeralda. The buying and selling of cars as pilots failed to return or as their squadrons came and went was something of a local industry at all the airfields. At Prestwick he was already nego-tiating to buy an old motorbike. That would save him having to cadge lifts, as he had this morning.

The door opened when he was only halfway up the drive and the two shelties streaked out to greet him, leaping around him with sharp barks of excitement. Dropping his bag he squatted down to hug them, ruffling their ears and dropping kisses on warm russet heads. He glanced up and raised a hand as he saw his parents standing side by side in the doorway. 'Come on, lads,' he muttered. 'Let's go and say hello.'

'Brucy and Bob are pleased to see you, darling.' His mother held out her arms and suddenly she was crying. 'Oh, Tony. We wondered if we would ever see you again!'

And his father was hugging him too, too overwhelmed to speak, and the dogs were nosing between them all, not wanting to be left out, and all Tony could think was,

Evie.

22

Thursday 29th August, early

Lucy's car was parked where she usually left her own. Charlotte drew up behind it and pulled on the handbrake with a vicious wrench before pushing open the door and climbing out of the car. She took a deep breath of the cool air and glanced at her watch. It was nearly four a.m.

Grabbing her bag she hurled the car door shut and headed towards the cottage. The long drive had not improved her temper but, after a pause for a black coffee at an all-night service station, she felt far more sober now. She pushed the gate open and walked up the path, groping in her bag for her key. The cottage lay in darkness, bathed in the scent of roses and new-mown grass. Above, in the dark velvet of the sky, a waning moon hung low over the silhouette of the apple tree. She slotted the key into the lock and turned it. Nothing happened. The door was bolted from the inside. Furiously she made her way round to the back door, stumbling in the darkness on the mossy path. The door opened. As usual he had forgotten to bolt this one. With a smile she slid into the kitchen.

She groped on the wall for the switches and snapped on the lights, suddenly not caring if they heard her, and for several seconds she stood still, listening. She could still smell the after-echo of tomato and herbs from whatever they had eaten for supper and the stronger pungent odour of Mike's favourite brand of coffee. She could see, stacked in the sink, two plates, two saucepans, two forks and an empty oily salad bowl. She swallowed a moan of unhappiness and turned towards the living room. The room was tidy, save for the two empty cups on the low table. Slowly she made her way to the staircase.

Throwing open the door of the bedroom she grabbed for the light switches and flooded the room in light. The bed was empty, still made, cold, the curtains not even drawn.

She spun round as the door to the tiny spare room opened behind her and she was confronted by the sight of Lucy, tousled with sleep, confused, wrapped in one of Evie's Indian shawls. 'What's happened?' Lucy mumbled.

Charlotte didn't bother to reply. She pushed Lucy aside and went into the room. 'Where's Mike? Don't bother to pretend he isn't here!'

'But he's not,' Lucy protested. She was waking up fast. 'He went to stay with his mother in Brighton. What is it? What's happened?' Under the shawl she was naked but for her underwear. She shivered suddenly. 'Charlotte, I wish you would get it into your head that Mike and I are not having an affair!' Suddenly she was furiously cross. 'What is the matter with you? We had supper because I was still working late and he suggested I stay because the cottage would be empty. Go and see. Go to Brighton. Check on him!' She was fully awake now, pushing her hair back from her eyes. 'This is all in your head. I am no threat to you!'

Charlotte stared at her, her mind whirling with anger and hatred. Without this woman's intrusion into their lives Mike would be here now, in bed with her, not trailing after some stranger with an art degree!

The box of matches was next to the candlestick on the book-case by the bedroom door. Grabbing the matches Charlotte gave an ugly laugh. 'This will sort the problem out,' she shouted almost incoherent with the jumble of emotions in her head. 'This will sort out everything!' She whirled away to the top of the stairs and ran down, leaving Lucy on the landing staring after her. Pulling the back door open she ran out onto the grass. It was wet with dew but she didn't notice as she ran towards the studio. The door was locked and she rattled it frantically, unaware of the string of expletives pouring from her mouth. Not to be thwarted she pulled her arm back and thrust her elbow through the nearest window, swearing even harder as a streak of blood ran down her wrist.

In the house Lucy had dialled Mike's mobile. 'I'm so sorry to wake you, but Charlotte is here. She seems to have gone mad. I think it might be best if you come back. She's got some matches. I am so sorry –'

She glanced out of the window and it was then she saw the streak of flame from the studio. 'Oh dear God, no!' she gasped. 'Please, no!'

Pulling on her jeans and a sweater she ran down the stairs and out into the garden, not pausing to find her shoes. There was no sign of Charlotte. She ran across the grass, groping in the pocket of her jeans for the key which she had slipped in there the night before.

The studio lay in darkness. From here she could see no signs of the fire. She paused on the steps and listened, her mouth dry with fear, terrified she was going to hear the roar and crackle of burning wood. Nothing. Slipping the key into the lock she turned it and carefully pushed the door open a crack. The place was completely dark. She pushed the door open a bit further and saw the flare of a match.

Charlotte was standing inside by the broken window. She struck one match after another, her hands shaking. 'Bloody thing! It won't stay alight!'

Lucy walked over to her, aware of a strong smell of charring paper.

'Give me those matches,' she said as calmly as she could. 'Please, Charlotte. Let me have them.'

Charlotte gave a small bitter laugh. 'I don't think so.' She took another match out of the box with a shaking hand. It fell to the floor and she gave an exclamation of annoyance. 'Go away, Lucy, unless you want to get hurt!' she snarled. Another match fell on the ground. Lucy took a step towards her. Charlotte didn't notice. Her hands were shaking more violently now and suddenly the whole box flew out of her fingers. Matches fell in all directions and she let out a small shriek of anger. She fell to her knees, frantically trying to gather up the matches and then she was crying.

Stamping on the matchbox and kicking away the matches with her bare foot, Lucy reached for the light switches. The side window, with the broken pane, had been opened so Charlotte must have climbed in that way. She had picked up some sketchbooks and papers and piled them together, lighting them on the floor where they had briefly flared and gone out.

Almost subconsciously Lucy noticed with relief that there was nothing of value there as far as she could see and at the same moment became aware that she could hear a fire engine in the distance. She looked down at Charlotte. 'The fire brigade is on its way. Mike must have called them from Brighton after I rang him,' she said bleakly.

Charlotte scowled. 'The fire went out. Even now she's won.' Her voice had gone flat. All the fight had drained out of her.

'Who?' Lucy didn't understand for a moment.

'Evie.' Charlotte's voice was full of venom. 'She will always win.'

Outside the strobing blue light of the fire engine shone through the broken window for a moment as it drew up in the lane. It was turned off and Lucy heard the gate squeak as the first fireman ran up the path. 'I'll go and tell them it's out,' she said.

The senior officer insisted on accompanying her back to the studio to check for himself. 'I've told them that it was a mistake,' she said to Charlotte, who was standing up now, leaning against the wall. 'You lit some rubbish in the bin without thinking.'

'Why not tell him I was drunk.' Charlotte didn't try to mask her bitterness.

Lucy glanced at the fire officer. 'I'm sorry. There was a bit of a family row. I rang her partner who is in Brighton and he misunderstood. He thought it was worse than it was and called you. I am really sorry.'

She could see the man didn't believe her. The floor was covered in scraps of burned paper; there was no bin. He walked round the studio, turning over piles of papers, checking every corner, then he turned back to Lucy.

'I'll have to make a report, but I can see it was a genuine call. Conflagration extinguished before we arrived.'

Lucy managed a smile. 'Thank you. Some of the stuff in here is quite valuable. The former owner was a famous artist so it could have been very serious.' She hoped he didn't hear Charlotte's snort of disgust.

'And you are happy for me to leave you to sort out the mess?' he asked. He glanced meaningfully at Charlotte. 'Are you two on your own here? You wouldn't like the police to attend?'

'Oh good Lord, no,' Lucy was genuinely horrified. 'Thank you,' she added hurriedly. 'We can sort this out, can't we, Charlotte? Mike will be on his way back. He'll be here very soon.'

The man looked round and nodded. She could see he was no fool. He probably attended scenes like this all the time – two women obviously quarrelling, a spiteful act of revenge, a dodgy box of matches and some paper which had grown damp and thwarted whatever intention there was to burn the place down. She realised she was clenching her fists and relaxed them deliberately at her side.

'Can we offer you some tea, officer, to say thank you for

372

coming so promptly?' she said meekly. 'I really appreciate it. It could have been catastrophic.'

'Thank you, no.' He gave her what appeared to be a genuinely friendly smile. 'We have to get back to base.' Already the men with him were retreating across the lawn and climbing back on to the appliance. 'You take care now. Both of you.' He gave one more cursory kick at the scorched paper on the floor and withdrew, leaving them alone.

Lucy bent to pick up the pieces of paper. 'No harm done, as it happens,' she said shortly.

Charlotte gave a sneer. 'This time.'

Lucy straightened and looked at her. 'Do you want Mike to dump you?'

Charlotte made no response for several seconds, then, 'He already has,' she said. 'Hasn't he?'

'I have no idea.' Lucy sighed impatiently. 'I don't know or care what is going on between you two. For the thousandth time, I have told you it has nothing to do with me.' She began to stack the pieces of paper on the table. 'Do you know the name of a local handyman who will come and mend the window?' She noticed that Charlotte had taken her hand out of her pocket. It was dripping blood on the floor. 'We had better go in and see to that cut. It looks pretty bad. Thank goodness the fireman didn't see it or he would have called an ambulance as well. Have you any idea how lucky you are he believed me?'

'He didn't believe you. He knew exactly what had happened. He just didn't want to get involved.' Charlotte turned towards the door and headed out across the lawn. With a quick glance round to make sure everything was all right Lucy followed her, leaving the lights on and the door wide open.

When Mike and Juliette arrived forty minutes later Charlotte's hand had been bound up and the two women were sitting in silence with cups of tea between them on the table. It was growing light and the only sound in the sitting room was from a robin singing in the rose bush near the front door. As Mike led the way in Charlotte burst into tears.

He stared at her for a moment. 'What happened?' His face was grey with fatigue.

'I tried to burn the studio down.' Charlotte's voice was flat. 'I'll go and pack my things up in a minute. I know it's all over. Evie won.'

Juliette sat down beside Charlotte. 'What have you done to your hand?' Blood was seeping through the bandage.

'I broke the window.'

Lucy got up and made her way out to the kitchen. Neither Juliette nor Mike had looked at her. Wearily she put the kettle on again, wondering if anyone would notice if she crept away back to bed upstairs.

'It looks as though you saved the day.' Mike was suddenly behind her. 'I knew I should have stayed here.'

She turned. 'I am so sorry. It's my fault.'

'How do you work that out?'

'She still thinks you and I are having an affair.'

He gave an irritated sigh. 'I told her it wasn't true but she wouldn't believe me. She's as jealous as hell of you. But there is more to it than that, isn't there? Ever since I first met her she has resented Evie, who in her eyes is standing between her and ownership of this cottage.'

'But that's absurd.'

'No. Actually she's right. Except that she is not the one I would choose to redesign this place should it ever need doing.' He didn't linger over the words, holding her eye as he said it, he merely turned away and pulled the lid off the biscuit tin. There was nothing to read in what he had said beyond the words themselves. She was astonished at the pang of regret she felt. Was Charlotte right after all? Did she, deep down inside, secretly, fancy Mike? If she did then it was obvious he did not reciprocate the feeling. Horrified at herself and her disloyalty to Larry she turned away from him.

374

'You'll need the spare room for your mother. I'll go back to the vicarage. It's morning now anyway.' She forced herself to meet his eye. 'Better I'm not here while you sort out what to do about Charlotte. Let me know when it's safe to come back.' She managed a smile. 'I'll get my stuff and leave you to it.'

When she walked down the path and out into the lane ten minutes later no one looked out of the window to watch her go.

December 23rd 1940

The memorial service was at St Margaret's Church. There was no interment, no coffin. Ralph had been shot down miles out over the Channel, and there had been no sign of him or his plane after he plunged into the sea.

The church was full. Families came from miles around. The Lucases were well known and liked, and Ralph had been popular locally. He was not the first son to be torn from a Downland family and would not be the last, but every bereavement brought a fresh wave of despair to the old men, the women, the children who had been left at home.

Rachel sat between Dudley and Evie, clutching a handkerchief, her eyes on the arrangement of winter flowers below the pulpit, the wreaths lying on the worn blue carpet of the chancel step where the coffin would have stood. She wrung her handkerchief between her hands, dabbing at her streaming eyes, unable to look to left or right, staggering to her feet with a barely suppressed sob when the vicar came in. Beside her, Dudley was stony-faced, his black tie tied too tightly round his collar, his eyes, too, fixed on the wreaths.

Behind them someone was sobbing as though their heart would break. Evie turned and glanced back. A WAAF, supported by two friends, was standing at the back of the church. She was pretty, just the sort of girl Ralph would have liked. For a second Evie wondered if she had been someone special, someone

Ralph had cared about, but then her own grief swept over her again and she turned away. Whoever she was she would have to cope with her grief in her own way. Her own heart seemed to have turned to stone. She had lost Ralph and she had lost Tony, who had left without a word. What was left?

Dudley had given Evie the news that Tony's squadron had been posted back to Scotland. He did not mention Tony's phone call. Her grief that Tony had gone without a word was somehow subsumed in her grief for her brother's death. Perhaps she could not bring herself to contemplate it. She would never forget the terrible scream her mother had given when the news had been brought to Box Wood Farm. Later Ralph's CO would bring his belongings back to the farm and Rachel would put them away somewhere without looking at them. She had barely spoken since. It was Eddie who rallied round, who ordered the memorial tablet for the church, who had visited each day for long enough to make sure they were all managing to keep going.

Sitting on her bed, staring out of the window, Evie shivered. The house was cold. Snow had swept in over the Downs and her father had kept to his little office behind the dining room. Rachel had sat endlessly day after day in the kitchen, receiving her friends as one by one they called to express their condolences and bring little gifts of comfort to a family who could not imagine ever finding comfort or happiness again.

Evie's last picture, of the mother and baby amongst the ruins, still sat on her easel. Her sketchbook lay on the floor beside her bed, filled with its drawings of the women of Southampton queuing in the evenings at the station with their bedding and their children, determined to get out of the city before the night's bombing began. She had not lifted a paintbrush since the terrible 13th of December.

'I'm pregnant.' The thought drifted into her mind like a wisp of thistledown. 'It's two months now. I'm pregnant and it's Tony's.'

She sat without moving until long after it was dark then

went downstairs to the kitchen. Rachel was listlessly stirring something in the pan on the stove. The land girls had gone down to the pub. The farmhouse was no longer the cheerful place it had been in the evenings and they sought company and solace elsewhere. The imminent arrival of Christmas seemed to have been forgotten.

Sitting down at the scrubbed table Evie watched her mother for a long time without speaking, then at last she came out with it. 'I'm going to have a baby.'

Rachel dropped the spoon in the pan. She turned to face her daughter. 'I hope I didn't hear you say that.' Her face was animated for the first time in days.

Evie looked away. 'I'm sorry. I don't know what to do.'

'What to do? You'll marry him, of course!'

Evie stared at her. 'How can I? He's gone. He didn't want me.' Her voice was heavy with despair.

'What do you mean, he's gone?' Rachel sat down beside her. She seized Evie's hands. 'He's been here every day!'

Evie stared at her. 'Mummy, it's Tony's baby.'

'No.' Rachel shook her head. 'No, it isn't. It's Eddie's. You've always loved Eddie. You'll have to marry him before your father finds out. It would kill him, Evie, if he thought you were going to have a baby out of wedlock. You know it would!' Her mother's voice was bordering on the hysterical.

Evie stared at her. 'But it's Tony's. Eddie and I haven't been together for months.'

'Then you had better put that right.' Rachel stood up. She was almost spitting now. 'Your father must not find out about this, do you hear me? It would kill him. You cannot do this to him, Evie. Not after Rafie –' As always after the mention of Ralph's name she dissolved into tears. She took a deep breath. 'You cannot inflict a bastard child on this family, Evie. You can't. Tony has gone. He abandoned you. He didn't care what happened to you, did he? He couldn't even pick up the phone to say goodbye.' She was sobbing loudly. 'You must marry Eddie.

Then everything will be all right. I will not have you bring this family's name into disrepute.'

'But I could still marry Tony. I could contact him somehow, I'm sure I could.' Even as she protested Evie knew it was no use. He had flown back to Scotland without a word. She had been nothing but a passing amusement just as Eddie had said.

Christmas came and went almost unnoticed.

Friday 30th August

'Don't you see, she sent someone to steal the painting.' Christopher was standing in Mike's London flat. Mike had only returned from Rosebank a few hours before. 'It all fits. Someone was there by invitation. My father let them in, then at some point there was a struggle. The police believe the painting was damaged in a fight. Dad had opened the door normally when he came back from the opera and switched off the alarm. The records show that, and exactly when he did it. It was very late, but still he let whoever it was in. He must have been expecting them. The police think someone brought the painting down on Dad's head. Perhaps he tried to snatch it back from them.'

'That is completely illogical,' Mike said. 'Why destroy the thing you have come to steal?'

'Because he fought back, because he changed his mind. Who knows? Lucy Standish had been to see my father that afternoon. She knew he had more paintings. She knew they were worth a fortune.'

'Have the police confirmed the cause of death?' Mike was leaning with one shoulder against the wall of the hallway. He had not asked Christopher to come into the sitting room. He shoved his hands into his pockets. He was exhausted and fed up, sick at the mess he had found at Rosebank, furious that he had to return to London for a meeting which could not be missed, and above all cross that he had opened the door to Christopher.

378

'They think it was a heart attack.'

'But what about head injuries if someone smashed a painting over his head?'

'There appear to be no signs of a head injury. But he was hit by the canvas. That would not necessarily have left a mark.'

'If the impact was hard enough to tear the canvas surely the stretchers would have injured him? What about fingerprints?'

'He wore gloves.'

'You mean there were no prints?'

'No.' Christopher glared at him. 'I'm not suggesting this woman did it herself. She must have employed someone professional and it all went wrong.'

'Obviously.' Mike let his scepticism show.

'Have you seen her since this happened?'

'Lucy? Yes.'

'And?'

'And what? She didn't say, "Oh, Mike, I tried to steal some of your uncle's paintings and it all went wrong and I killed him," if that is what you are waiting to hear. Far from it. She was gutted when she heard George was dead. He had promised her stories, anecdotes about his mother, family information about growing up with a great artist.' Mike scowled. 'Information that was vital and wonderful and unique to your father and she has lost that opportunity now. There is no way it can ever be recovered. She would have been mad to put all that in jeopardy. And he had promised her photos of all his paintings. He was proud of Evie and he wanted to share her with the world, unlike his son who appears to want to squirrel everything away forever like some Dickensian miser.'

'You just don't get it, do you!'

'No, frankly I don't.'

Christopher heaved a deep sigh and, realising he was not going to be asked in any further, moved back towards the front door. 'There is no more to be said then. I have told the police that they should treat Lucy as a suspect. No doubt they will be calling on her.'

'They called on her the day after your father died,' Mike said calmly. 'You had already fingered her, I gather. Luckily she had an alibi.'

Christopher sneered sarcastically. 'For herself, maybe. For every contact she has in the shadier side of the art world? I doubt it.' He pulled open the door. 'I leave that to the police. Take care, Mike. Don't be any more fooled by her than you have already. She is after everything she can get her hands on by whatever means.'

Mike gave a cold smile. 'Then I am in no danger, Chris, as you took everything of any value in the cottage. Maybe you are the one who should be careful.'

It was only after he had watched Christopher walk away and cross the street that he wished he hadn't made that last remark. It would make things, if anything, even more tricky for Lucy.

23

December 27th 1940

It was easy to manoeuvre Eddie into taking her out to dinner.
The house was a sea of misery, her mother barely able to drag
herself to the kitchen to put on a kettle for the girls' breakfasts.
Eddie came and collected her and drove her to eat at The
Spread Eagle in Midhurst. There was a roaring fire and they
finished with plum pudding, which Evie found herself
consuming ravenously. Eddie went out of his way to be
charming and she relaxed in the warmth and the gentle background noise of conversation. For once he didn't push her on
the subject of her paintings and she found herself eyeing him
thoughtfully. Would it be so bad to marry this man? After all,
she had fancied him once. She sat back in her chair and sighed.
But that had been before Tony. She frowned, unaware that
he was studying her face. Tony had gone. He hadn't cared.
He hadn't meant it when he had asked her to marry him. His
gestures of everlasting love had meant nothing. She had loved
him to distraction and she would, she knew, love him forever,
but she had to forget him.

'Evie?' She realised Eddie was talking to her. 'Are you all right?'

She nodded. 'Just thinking.'

He smiled sympathetically. 'I know. It's hard.'

She bit her lip, suddenly afraid she would cry.

When they returned to the farm the place was in darkness. From the direction of the tentative bark from Jez she guessed her father had locked the dogs in the stables. Evie pushed open the kitchen door and looked in.

'Mummy and Daddy must have gone to bed.' She pulled Eddie in and closed the door before switching on the light. Outside the generator rumbled into life. 'Shall I make us some tea?' She smiled at him.

'I'll get some more tea for your mother,' he said as he sat down at the table. 'I know it won't help but running out would be the last straw.'

Evie set the kettle on the stove. It was still hot. She reached for the coal bucket and filled it as the kettle began to hiss on the hotplate. 'Will you stay tonight, Eddie,' she said without looking at him. 'It is so lonely here.' The sob in her throat was genuine.

He pushed back his chair and came to put his arm round her. 'You know I will.'

Monday 2nd September

There was more damage in the studio at Rosebank than Lucy had suspected. When she returned she looked around in horror. In places the wall was blackened and scorched, a portfolio, luckily empty, had been badly burned and one of the chairs had been broken. 'I couldn't believe she would do such a thing,' she said over her shoulder to Dolly.

'It looks as if she made several attempts to light it,' Dolly said through pursed lips. 'The woman is an evil witch.'

382

Lucy glanced at her in surprise. 'That's strong language,' she said with a gentle smile.

'Oh, yes. And warranted.' Dolly stooped to pick up a cushion which had fallen from one of the chairs. 'The firemen came back to check everything was safe. They asked Mr Mike again if he wanted to prosecute but he said no. I think he told them she was a little bit unstable and maybe a bit drunk, which I gather was true.' She gave a grim smile. 'He had a call about some meeting in London and he had to go but he said I wasn't to touch anything until you had had a look just in case, then I will clean it up once you say what you want to keep.'

'But didn't he want to check himself?'

Dolly shook her head. 'When he rang to ask me to come in today he said to leave it to you. He was very angry about what happened. I pity that Charlotte Thingy when he gets his hands on her.'

Lucy hid a smile. 'So do I,' she murmured.

She spent a long time in the studio after Dolly had opened the windows to try and get rid of the sour smell of burned wood and paper. The fire had somehow concentrated her mind. She had been working slowly, imagining she had as long as she liked to go through the archive but now, she realised, time might be short. There were too many people intent on stopping her telling Evie's story and the story itself was becoming more and more convoluted and urgent. Over the last two days she had sat at the vicarage kitchen table and written down every single thing she could remember of her visit to George's gallery. It was sad that so much of the precious time she had spent there had been taken up with telling him what she knew rather than her asking him for his story. But then neither of them had known that time had run out. Of course she didn't know then either that Dolly had such a strong recollection of George as a boy. As they sat over some soup at lunchtime in the cottage kitchen she wrote down all Dolly's memories of the young

George and cross-checked them with the few snippets George had told her himself.

One thing had stuck in her mind. 'George told me that when he was little his brother John had told him he was adopted,' she said cautiously. 'The thought had always haunted him. Do you think that was true?'

Dolly looked shocked. 'No. No, Evie would have told me. He was born at Box Wood, like Johnny.'

'And when she moved here you said she left George with his father.'

'I doubt she had any choice. Her husband was a complete so-and-so.'

'And George ran away from him?'

Dolly nodded. 'I do remember that. He arrived by himself one night, poor lamb. He had come on the train to Chichester and then made his way five miles across country with nothing but a haversack. Mr Edward came after him, of course, and he and Evie had a terrible quarrel.'

Lucy waited a few seconds. 'Which you overheard?' she prompted.

Dolly coloured slightly. 'One could not have failed to.'

'Can you tell me what they said?'

Dolly shook her head vehemently. 'There is nothing that you need to know. Just nastiness. On his part. He was a mean-spirited man and a bully. He left in the end and though I think he threatened to come back and to go to the courts and to drag George away by force, he never did. I believe he came back a few times to try and force her to give him some paintings but I'm sure she wouldn't have done it. I don't think she was frightened of him any more. George stayed here until he left school, and he still came back during the holidays when he was at college in Italy. He lived abroad a lot when he was younger. He met his wife in Rome. She was a sculptress, a lovely lady. They moved back to London quite near his father, in Hampstead, and Christopher was

born in 1972. She died when Christopher was fifteen. Cancer.'
Dolly shuddered.

Lucy was making notes. 'And George stayed in London?'

Dolly nodded. 'He went to Italy a lot, with Christopher, then
Christopher decided to study economics. I think that confused
George. It wasn't something he understood, but he supported
him and encouraged him and then slowly they became
estranged, I never quite understood why.'

'He said it was because they inhabited different worlds,' Lucy
said thoughtfully, 'which I suppose would be true, though it is
sad if it came between them.'

'I think Johnny had something to do with that,' Dolly said
after a long silence. She stood up and removed their plates,
switching on the electric kettle before she sat down again.
'Johnny resented his mother being so close to George. He
didn't like it that he had already left home when she bought
this place. He was very angry when he heard George had
run away from London and come here and Evie was going
to let him live with her.' She stood up again and began to
make the coffee. 'There was something very sad about
Johnny. He loved his grandfather – both his grandfathers
– and I think he would have loved to have been a farmer.
He didn't enjoy London. In some ways he was a lost soul.'
She sighed. 'I liked Johnny very much. I liked them both.
It broke Evie's heart that they didn't get on. And then there
was Ralph.'

'Ralph?' Lucy echoed sharply.

Dolly nodded. 'Johnny was obsessed by him, the heroic uncle
who had died before he was born. He used to say Ralph haunted
him. He appeared to the boy in his dreams and talked to him.'
She shivered. 'That used to give me the heebie-jeebies. And it
terrified Evie. She couldn't bear it when Johnny told her about
it. She got so angry. She forbade him to mention it.' She was
pouring Lucy's coffee and stopped suddenly. 'What is it? What
have I said?'

January 6th 1941

Evie wore a cream suit to her wedding, altered from a dress of her mother's, and she carried a posy of snowdrops and winter aconite interspersed with small spikes of sweet box from the farm. There were some two dozen guests at the service in St Margaret's, where such a short time before they had attended the memorial service for her brother. Her father took her up the aisle on his arm and handed her over to Eddie before walking back to stand beside his wife, his face like carved stone. On the other side of the church sat Eddie's parents and his two sisters.

As she repeated the age-old words of the marriage service Evie felt as if she were in a dream, but it wasn't the dream of a blissful bride, it was a nightmare from which she would never wake up. This was all wrong. She should be standing beside Tony. Ralph should be the best man, not this stranger, smirking at her round Eddie's shoulder, and her husband, standing at her side and placing the gold band on her finger, should be a laughing, blue-eyed pilot, not Eddie . . .

She managed the responses somehow, her voice husky, her excuse of a heavy cold by now a reality as she clutched her handkerchief and dabbed at streaming eyes and reddened nose. She saw Eddie look at her and for a moment thought she saw disgust in his glance, but then he grinned and gave her hand a squeeze. She did her best to smile back.

As they signed the register an air raid warning sounded in the far distance and the congregation exchanged uneasy glances as they listened to the wheezy notes of the organ, played, in the absence of the regular organist in the Navy, by the grand-mother of Sally who ran the shop; Sally who had at the last moment rushed round some gardens in the village to collect several vases of honeysuckle and witch hazel, winter jasmine and hazel catkins to cheer the gloom of the grey stone church. No one could have expected Rachel to do it, not after losing her son, and Evie hadn't been well, the whole village knew that. Sorry for the Lucases, and guessing something of their despair, Sally had determined that the church at least would look pretty. She succeeded. The sun had disappeared behind banks of cloud and raindrops were beginning to fall on the churchyard as Evie and Eddie made their way back down the aisle as husband and wife, and stood in the porch for photos, the scent of daphne from the rector's garden filling the air around them. There were no rose petals for confetti, so two little girls from the village showered them with dried dead leaves.

Afterwards the two families and their guests went back to Box Wood Farm and ate the wedding cake, which Rachel, managing to shake off her apathy, had conjured from a recipe in one of her magazines. She smiled at her daughter as Evie and Eddie cut into it and everyone cheered. Evie, meeting her eye at last, managed to smile back. Dudley, for whom this ultimate sacrifice had been concocted, scowled once again at his new son-in-law and took himself outside to check on the cows.

January 29th 1941

The call came three weeks after the wedding. Rachel answered the phone and spoke to someone who announced themselves as 'Tony Anderson's friend, Jim, up in Prestwick'.

'Eddie Marston's mother gave me your number. I'm one of his ground crew, but Tony was a mate as well, and I know he would have wanted Eddie to know if anything happened.'

Rachel froze. 'If anything happened?' she echoed

'I'm sorry. He flew out yesterday testing a Mark Two. He didn't return.'

Rachel's hand tightened round the receiver. She couldn't speak.

387

'Will you tell Eddie?' the voice went on.

'I'll tell him,' she whispered.

She was still sitting in the hall when Dudley came in, stamping snow off his boots in the kitchen. 'Rachel?' He could see her through the door and stopped in his tracks, struck by her stillness. He went to her, his face tight with anxiety. 'What's happened?'

'Tony.' She said. 'He's missing.'

'Tony?' Dudley stood, his hands in his pockets. 'And why did they feel they had to tell us?' He was furious suddenly. They had no business upsetting Evie again, bringing it all back, reminding her of Ralph so soon.

'I expect they thought it was a kindness,' she stammered. 'Evie loved him so much.'

Dudley frowned. 'Not enough, obviously. Anyway, Tony is in the past. Don't even mention it to her.'

'I have to, Dudley. How could I not?' Rachel climbed wearily to her feet.

'Where is she?'

'Upstairs in the studio.'

'And Eddie?'

'He went out this morning early.' She was visibly trying to pull herself together. 'The man who rang asked me to tell Eddie, not Evie. That seems odd.'

'Probably thought he could break it to her.' Dudley turned and went back into the kitchen and held his chilled hands over the stove for warmth. 'He was a nice boy,' he conceded roughly, 'just not for her.'

'Why not?' Rachel followed him in. 'Why was everyone so against him?'

That was a question Dudley would never answer. Since the wedding Eddie had made it clear there would be no question now of ever paying back the loan. 'Obviously she really loved Eddie, or she wouldn't have married him,' he said firmly.

Rachel sighed but she said nothing.

'Don't tell them, Rachel. The boy has gone. It will only upset Evie and that will make Eddie angry.' Dudley moved over to the window and looked out thoughtfully. 'He is a very possessive man. Better for Evie if she puts Tony completely out of her head. It was a passing infatuation, no more.'

Rachel moved over to the sink and picked up the teapot. 'I think it was a little more than that,' she murmured to herself. Dudley didn't hear her and she didn't repeat what she had said.

She had walked up to the village shop, her basket on her arm, her head and shoulders swathed in a thick scarf, and returned just as Eddie came in. He had moved into Box Wood Farm on his marriage and they had taken over the larger of the two spare rooms, swapping it with the land girls, who had moved another bed into Evie's old bedroom. Dudley saw him as he headed for the staircase and beckoned him into his office.

'We had a call from Scotland,' he said. He eyed his son-in-law with distaste mixed with gratitude. It was an unpleasant combination of emotions to deal with. Secretly he couldn't understand why Evie had suddenly changed her mind and accepted Eddie's proposal of marriage. Presumably her hurt and anger at Tony leaving her without a word had rebounded and she had thrown herself at Eddie as a sop to her own wounded pride. Well, thank God she had! The marriage had taken place by special licence – another of Eddie's fiddles, no doubt, but it was done now and all was at peace within the farm. Without Ralph, Evie would inherit everything one day and a farm needed a strong man to run it. He was under no illusion that Eddie would turn his hand to farming himself, but he had money. He could employ a manager. Dudley moved over and closed the door behind Eddie. The pair were man and wife and that was that. He waved his son-in-law to a chair. 'Tony Anderson has been killed,' he said. 'They wanted me to tell you, I suspect so you can break it to Evie. It would be dreadful if she heard somewhere else.'

He was watching Eddie's expression. The man showed not a flicker of emotion. 'Do you know what happened?'

'Missing out at sea. Like Ralph.' Dudley's voice cracked. 'This bloody war!'

'Odd. On the west coast of Scotland,' Eddie said thoughtfully. 'Not exactly the front line.'

'The Germans would be attacking Clydeside,' Dudley retorted shortly. 'Hardly a respite from the war. But as it happens, I gather he was testing a plane that had been repaired.'

Eddie took a deep breath and Dudley realised that he was trying to hide the gleam of triumph in his eyes. His distaste intensified. 'Do you want to tell her, or shall I?'

'I will,' Eddie said quietly. 'Don't worry. I'll pick the right moment. You're right. She has to know.'

As he climbed the stairs to Evie's studio Eddie allowed himself a small smile. He pushed the door and went in. She was standing in front of the easel, a brush in her hand, wearing her usual dungarees, her hair, for once free of its scarf, tangled around her shoulders. His eyes dropped to her stomach. She had put on a little weight. He walked over to stand behind her. She was working on another study of the women of Southampton and for a moment he was caught by the intensity of the expressions on their faces, their terror half-eclipsed by their grim determination. Almost automatically he scanned the table near her hand to see how the paints were holding out. This constant palette of brown and grey was using up her supplies of burned umber and ivory black, the darker blues, the tubes squeezed and almost empty. She didn't look at him as she squinted closer to the canvas. 'The light is going. I'll have to stop soon.'

'That is a very powerful scene,' he said. He waited as she put down her brush and reached for a rag. 'Evie, I have some sad news.'

She turned and looked at him at last. Her expression echoed that of the women in the picture. It was almost as though she had drawn a self-portrait. 'What?' she asked.

'Tony,' he said.

She went white. For a moment he thought she was going to collapse and he held out his hand, resting it lightly on her arm. 'Do you want to sit down?'

She shook her head. 'What's happened?'

'I gather he was flying out over the sea. He didn't come back.'

'Like Ralph,' she echoed her father's words.

He shook his head. 'Ralph was killed in action. I gather Tony was just test flying a plane that had been repaired.'

'Just test flying,' she repeated.

He nodded. She had grown very frail, he realised. She staggered a few steps away from him, turning her back, her shoulders rigid. 'Just test flying.' She said the words again as though unable to believe them.

She turned back and he saw the tears in her eyes. She looked stricken. 'Can you leave me alone for a bit, Eddie?' she said, her hand on her stomach. 'I'll be all right in a minute.'

His gaze dropped again to her midriff and suddenly he knew.

The ice-cold shaft of hatred and jealousy that sliced through him took even him by surprise. 'You're pregnant!' he said softly. 'You're carrying his baby!' The flash of fear which crossed her face confirmed it. 'So, that was why you were so keen to marry me. It was nothing to do with loving me. You needed a father for his bastard!'

'Eddie –' She moved towards him but he stepped back.

'You cheating, lying, little trollop!'

'Eddie, please!'

He looked her up and down again and then turned on his heel. He walked out of the studio, slamming the door behind him and she heard his footsteps as he ran down the stairs.

He went into their bedroom and sat down on the bed. He was shaking all over, his fists clenched, his eyes blazing. When she appeared some fifteen minutes later he was still sitting there. Outside it had begun to grow dark. She walked in and closed

391

the door. The blackout wasn't drawn and she made no attempt to turn on the light. 'I am sorry, Eddie.'

'So am I.' His voice was harsh.

'What are you going to do?'

'What can I do?' He clenched his hands even tighter. 'We are married. Everything that is yours is mine and that presumably includes Tony Anderson's bastard. I presume you didn't want your father to find out. He would have thrown you out, old-fashioned puritan that he is, and he still might, but we don't want to risk you being disinherited, do we? After all, you will now inherit your brother's share of this farm, which will be worth a bit when the war is over. So why don't I just add a child to the list of assets. Your paintings, your farm and your child. I will acknowledge it as mine, but don't expect me ever to forget that it was fathered by someone else!'

The slam of the door could be heard all over the farmhouse. Dudley glanced up from his desk and frowned but he made no move to see what had happened.

Thursday 5th September

Dolly had found the extra boxes of papers and books in one of the outhouses. Sitting at the low coffee table in the cottage Lucy had piled them in the corner, ready to take them back to the vicarage. She had enjoyed her few days staying at the cottage but at the same time, she didn't feel safe. It was too exposed. Every time she heard a car in the lane she looked up and waited, afraid it might stop, afraid it might be Charlotte. Mike had assured her that Charlotte wouldn't be coming back, ever, that he had taken her key, that he and she were no longer an item, no longer even speaking, but still Lucy didn't trust the long quiet evenings. She had rung Maggie that afternoon and Maggie had begged her to come back to the vicarage, at least for a night or two. She considered the offer. It was tempting but she had sworn she would not be chased away from the gallery. In the end she compromised. She said she would drive back the next day, via the gallery in Chichester, where she would look in on Robin and make sure everything was all right. Having made the decision she was surprised at just how much of a relief it was. Her very real fear was still there, close beneath the surface, she had to acknowledge the fact.

The first thing she had taken out of the dustiest of the boxes was a fat notebook with a cardboard cover. Inside it was full of Evie's writing – great blocks of writing, very small, unlike her usual untidy scrawl. Lucy carried it over to the lamp, and squinting slightly, began to read.

It was a log of her paintings, each one described, dated, with a note of the place Evie had gone to make her original sketches. Biting her lip with excitement, Lucy turned the pages. There were dozens of them, page after page of detailed descriptions, the dates running from August 1940 to September 1945. Holding her breath she started at the beginning, working her way slowly in. Several had notes of how much she had sold them for, and to whom. Most of those were initialled, either WAAC, or FG, which Lucy took to mean the Fuller Gallery. Those pictures had passed through her own front door, though obviously they had sold on and presumably fairly fast. Evie must have had a steady fan base or David Fuller had had a very shrewd eye for what his customers wanted. Judging by the descriptions the pictures which went to him were more likely to be country and farm scenes and birds, whilst the War Artists were required to paint aspects of the war. Again and again there was a note about a painting of *Westhampnett, Dispersal*. Or *Westhampnett, The Officers' Mess at Woodcote Farm*, *Westhampnett, Dave and Luke, T's fitter and rigger*. Most of these were pencil sketches, or charcoal or pastel, but some were oils. And there were portraits, some named, some, frustratingly, anonymous.

Deeply engrossed, she turned another page and stared. The

entry had been crossed out with a vicious scribble but it was still legible. *Me and Tony at the Gate, August 1940, oil.* Was that their painting, the one Larry had bought? Almost certainly. Had it been crossed out at the same time as Tony had been painted out? And what had happened to the painting after that? Evie had not kept it, nor presumably had it gone to the gallery and sold on, as it had been languishing in a sale room. Lucy studied it, willing the entry to give up its secret. She turned on further. The entries went on fairly regularly with a long gap in 1941 and another in 1944.

When she had finished glancing through the list she sat back, numb with excitement. Here was a catalogue of Evie's paintings from the most iconic period of her life, and the list which filled in some of the gaps in her diaries. How many of these paintings and drawings still existed? She thought wistfully of George and his suggestion that she photograph his paintings. What would happen to them now she wondered? They would go to Christopher, of course, and disappear from the public domain with the rest of the items he had taken from Rosebank Cottage. She thought back over the pictures Frances had shown her. None of them dated from the war years, she was pretty sure of that, or none of the ones on display. What else he had squirrelled away? Who knew?

The discovery of this log of Evie's work explained why she so seldom mentioned her paintings in her diaries. Obviously the two notebooks ran concurrently. Did that mean there were other logs lying around, relating to her later work? Lucy felt a kick of adrenaline under her ribs. If one had turned up here, perhaps there would be others, and for a start she could look in the box sitting on the table beside her and after that in the sheds in the garden she had never even considered searching, assuming them to be full of gardening equipment. Sitting forward on the edge of the chair she reached into the box again and began systematically to unpack it, horrified to find the stuff at the bottom wet through and mildewed. Going in search of some paper kitchen towels she spread wads of them out and laid out the notebooks and papers, not daring to open them until they had dried.

January 29th 1941

Evie sat dry-eyed in her studio in the dark. Her head was reeling, her stomach sick, all her dreams and fantasies crumbling around her. She hadn't consciously realised she still had dreams that Tony would return or that he would phone from Scotland and beg her to come north to be with him; she hadn't recognised that even after her wedding she had prayed that somehow he would change his mind and rescue her, but it would never happen now. She would never see him again. She was married to Eddie, who had suddenly revealed himself to be far more cruel and unkind than she had ever suspected, and she had nowhere to escape to. She put her hand on her stomach, for the first time aware that she was doing it, aware that this precious little scrap of life, hidden inside her, was all there was left of Tony Anderson.

Tears were coursing down her cheeks now as she sat hugging herself in the dark. There was no sound from outside the room. At least Eddie hadn't followed her upstairs.

Evie!

The whisper was softer than the hiss of snow which had begun to fall outside, barely touching the glass of the windows as it drifted down into the farmyard below.

Evie!

She straightened and looked round. 'Ralph?' Her eyes widened in the darkness.

Evie, I'm sorry—

She stood up, suddenly afraid. 'Ralph?' Her voice trembled.

I'm so sorry. I let you down.

She backed across the room, her eyes scanning the shadows.

I'm so sorry . . .

Scrabbling for the door handle she let herself out onto the landing and ran towards the stairs. She couldn't run down, Eddie was downstairs. Instead she headed up towards her studio.

In the distance she heard the phone ringing in the hall. With a sob she let herself into the dark room and scrabbled for the light switch. The blackouts were drawn across the skylights, the room filled suddenly with cold white light. She slammed the door and stood with her back to it, her heart thudding with fear. She had imagined it. Of course she had. And even if it was Ralph's – she balked at the word ghost – why should she be afraid? Her beloved brother would never hurt her.

'Ralph?' she whispered his name out loud.

There was no reply.

She was alone the next day when the pilot came. He was riding a motorbike and swept into the farmyard in a cloud of blue smoke. Evie went to the kitchen door and looked out. For the first time in ages her fingers itched for a pencil. He was a good-looking lad, red-haired, freckle-nosed, with piercing blue-green eyes surveying her from under bushy eyebrows.

'Evie Lucas?' he guessed, his voice hesitant.

She nodded.

He turned and reached into one of the panniers on the back of the bike and pulled out a parcel wrapped in brown paper. He faced her again. 'I'm based at Westhampnett. We took over when 911 squadron was posted back to Scotland.'

Evie swallowed hard. She had a suspicion this must have something to do with Tony.

He met her eye as if reading her thoughts. 'I took over Tony Anderson's room,' he said awkwardly. 'The squadron left in a bit of a hurry, by all accounts, and he left his log book behind. I found it on the floor behind his locker. I was going to forward it on to him. As you know, he'd be in trouble for losing it, but then –' He stopped.

'Then he was killed,' Evie prompted in a murmur.

'One of the WAAFs knew you and he were –' Again he

stopped. 'Close,' he went on unhappily, 'and she thought you might like to keep it. I'm sure no one will miss it.' He was still clutching the parcel to his chest as though afraid to offer it to her.

For a moment Evie didn't trust herself to speak. Silently she held out her hands. He put the packet into them. 'I'm so sorry,' he said awkwardly.

'Thank you.' She managed a smile.

'I'd better go.' He gestured over his shoulder towards the bike. 'The enemy are still demanding our attention.'

'You haven't told me your name,' Evie called out as he turned away.

'Josh Andrews.' He gave her a warm smile.

She held out her hand to him. He took it and shook it hard. 'Thank you, Josh. I will treasure it,' she said with an effort. Somehow she held back her tears. She stood watching as he drove out of the yard then she turned back inside. She needed to hide this somewhere no one would ever find it.

24

Friday 6th September

Lucy had allowed herself one more night at Rosebank Cottage, alone with Evie's memory. She made herself an omelette and then retreated to the small bedroom with the box of notebooks. One of the damp, mouldy items she lifted from the bottom of the box turned out to be an address book. Cautiously she prised the wet pages open. It was laden with addresses, all in an unknown hand. She frowned, staring at it intently, looking for names she recognised. There were no Lucases, no Andersons but there were three Marstons so perhaps this had belonged to Eddie. She looked up David Fuller and sure enough, there he was, his address the same as hers, the telephone number Chichester plus just three digits. She smiled. It was as though she had met a friend in this damp box of long forgotten papers. She tried to turn the page and it stuck to its neighbour, beginning to tear. Better to set it aside and wait for it to dry rather than inadvertently destroy some priceless piece of information.

Next she picked up a tooled leather folder, the pale dust of mildew hiding a faded green colouring which must have once been rich and elegant. Inside were several sheets of paper, old letter drafts, bills – Lucy gave a wry smile – always bills. She picked out a crumpled sheet of paper which had obviously been screwed up and thrown away and then presumably retrieved and flattened and restored to its place in the folder.

Dear Alistair and Betty,
    I was so sorry to hear of Tony's death. One of the boys from Westhampnett brought me his log book. He has the bed Tony used to sleep in. He didn't want to get Tony into trouble and he had been going to send it on to him but after Tony died one of the girls in the WAAF told him Tony and I had been in love. I have it here and I wondered if you would like it—

The fragment of easily recognisable writing ended with a scrawl of the pen. Evie hadn't been able to go on. Nor had she sent the log book. Presumably she had been unable to part with it after all.

Lucy wondered who Alistair and Betty were – his parents, perhaps. She glanced at the letter again. It was undated. Poor Evie. So, that was how his log book had come to be with her diaries. The love of her life had been killed and that was all she was left with.

Gently she tucked the piece of paper away. Did this explain why Tony had been painted out? In her grief Evie had not been able to bear looking at him? But surely the reverse would have been true. She would have treasured this painting and kept it close.

She leafed back through her notebooks and glanced at the photo of the painting which she kept there to remind her of any detail she might have forgotten, unlikely as it was. Every brushstroke was burned into her brain. The reflection from the desk lamp fell on the glossy surface of the print and she caught her breath. Just for a second had she seen a resemblance to Mike there in the young man's face? She reached for her notes and scanned the dates. Could it be that Tony was Johnny's father,

Mike's grandfather? Surely not. She sat for a while pondering on this enigma and only slowly did she become aware that she could feel the hairs on the back of her neck stirring as though a cold draught had found its way into the room.

January 30th 1941

Refreshed after a second spot of overdue leave Tony walked into the Mess at Prestwick and looked round. His CO was sitting at the bar nursing a glass of beer. Tony slid onto a stool beside him. 'Where is everybody?'

'Heaven knows.' Don gestured towards the steward to pour another. 'Have this one on me. Good to see you alive and well.'

Tony reached for the glass. 'Thanks. Why, weren't you expecting to?'

Don glanced across at him. 'You haven't heard then? We lost OL5.'

Tony felt himself go cold. That was the Spit he usually flew. 'Who was flying?'

'Bob Fine.'

Tony exhaled sharply. 'Poor blighter. Shot down?'

'No. There was no enemy around. They were too busy beating up the poor old Forth Bridge that day.'

'Then what?' Tony could feel the blood beating in his ears. 'You think someone is still after me?'

'Not necessarily.' Don downed his drink and pushed the empty glass towards the steward for another half. 'You mustn't blame yourself. We've had some suspicions that there have been possible attempts at sabotage on the planes.' He signed for the drinks.

Tony frowned. 'No, you don't mean it!'

'Reds. Communist infiltrators. They are quite strong on Clydeside.' He paused for a moment, a grim look on his face. 'We found a stick of gelignite strapped to an exhaust

400

manifold. We are dealing with that, and I don't have to tell you that that is to be kept absolutely under wraps. However, in this case, I have to consider too that you do have enemies, Tony.'

Tony nodded gloomily. 'If it was something personal, to do with Evie, I thought it would stop after I disappeared from Sussex,' he said bitterly.

The two men stared at their drinks in silence for several minutes then Don looked up. 'As it happens, old boy, you are moving on again anyway. You've been posted away from the squadron.' He gave a rueful grin. 'We are going to miss you, but you've had a long stressful time with a good many kills under your belt and it appears the powers that be have decided it's time you had a bit of a break and that you would be a good person to teach some youngsters to fly at an operational training unit.'

In the village of Prestwick a shadowy figure let himself into the phone box and allowed the heavy door to swing shut behind him. He took a deep draw on the cigarette hanging from the corner of his mouth before feeding some change into the slot and dialling a number. When a voice answered the other end he pressed button A and waited for the change to drop. 'Hello?' he glanced over his shoulder to check the street was deserted in the winter's darkness. 'Just to let you know, Anderson wasn't flying yesterday after all. He was on leave. It was another pilot who was killed so your target is still with us. Do you want us to try again?'

There was a moment's silence then a quiet laugh echoed down the line. 'No, I don't think we need to bother you further. One wasted plane is enough. Tony Anderson is dead to us. That is all that matters.'

Saturday 7th September

Christopher Marston had hired a van to bring the most valuable items away from his father's house as soon as the police had moved out.

'Are you sure you can do that?' Frances had asked as he climbed out and went round to open the doors. Ollie, newly returned with his sister from their stay with the grandparents, had gone with him and the boy glanced at his mother with something like scorn.

'Why not?' he said.

'What about things like probate?' Frances asked.

Christopher glanced over his shoulder with a look of utter disdain. 'Those bloody fools know nothing about art. They wouldn't be interested. Besides, these were all rightfully mine anyway. The lawyers can quibble over the house and the furniture if they want to but not Evie's pictures. I want them out of sight. The only one they know about is Chanctonbury Ring, and that is badly damaged so I doubt if it's worth anything. Anyway they have taken it away in case it's a murder weapon. 'Here, Ollie, help me with this.' He handed a box to the boy. 'Put it in the hall. Frances, go and make yourself useful by putting the kettle on and stop wittering!' He was tired and more stressed by the expedition to his father's house than he would like to admit. Poking round in his father's bedroom and study had been an unnerving experience. As he walked round the house, he had had the feeling his father's eyes were following him everywhere he went.

He reached into the van for another box of framed sketches and followed Ollie indoors. The boy was just about old enough to be useful now. God knew where Hannah was.

Put them upstairs, out of sight.

The voice in his ear was quiet but insistent.

Don't leave them lying around where anyone can see them.

Christopher looked round. 'Ollie?'

The boy had put the box down and gone back out to the van for another.

Christopher put down his own load and retraced his steps to the door. He was imagining things.

Don't be a fool. Anyone can see them there.

Christopher turned round indignantly. 'Frances!' he bellowed. There was no sign of her. The hall was empty. Outside he could see Ollie's back as he bent to pick up something out of the van. The boy was straining to pull it towards him. He was out of earshot; Frances was presumably in the kitchen. Christopher turned away from the door and walked to the foot of the stairs. 'Hello?' He called. 'Who's there?'

There was no reply.

Was it his father's voice he had heard? He shivered as he looked round again, perplexed, then with a shake of the head he walked out to the van and reached for one of the larger frames he had stacked in the back. 'Give me a hand with this big one, Ollie.' It had been hanging in his father's bedroom over the fireplace, one of the war paintings of a Spitfire with the letters OL5 painted on the fuselage. The blanket he had so hastily wrapped round it had fallen off. He stared at it. The pilot was standing by the plane, helmet and goggles in his hand. He was looking out of the picture smiling towards the viewer – or the painter. Evie.

He was blond, cheerful, his hair blowing into his eyes and Christopher too was struck suddenly by how much the young man looked like his cousin Mike. He stared at it for several seconds and then he gave a quiet chuckle.

'What is it?' Ollie looked at him, Ollie who was squarely built, dark of hair and slightly swarthy of skin like all the rest of Christopher's family.

'Who does that remind you of?' Christopher asked, pointing.

Ollie stared at the painting. 'No one. Should it?'

Christopher shook his head. 'No, of course not.' He pulled the blanket over the picture again. 'Come on, give me a hand

403

with this. We'll stow it in the attic for now until I decide where to hang it.'

It was later when Ollie was ensconced in front of his laptop in his bedroom that Christopher took Frances upstairs to the attic. 'Look at this.' He had leaned the picture against the wall with three others of the larger ones from George's collection.

Frances studied the painting for several seconds in the harsh light of the naked bulb.

'Well?' he said.

She glanced at him. 'You think he was Johnny's father?' she said at last.

'So, you can see the likeness?'

She nodded. She glanced at him nervously, unsure what else he wanted her to say.

'It looks as though my grandfather reared another man's child as his own. Do you think he knew?'

Frances hesitated. 'Johnny was very fair, certainly, and George was dark-haired like you,' she said cautiously.

Christopher let out a cynical laugh. 'No wonder George didn't get on with his brother. They had different fathers. That explains a lot.'

'It's only guesswork but if you're right it would certainly explain the difference in colouring. He did look like that young man. Do you know who he was? Do you think George knew?' Frances stepped closer, peering at the face of the pilot.

'I don't know. He had the picture in his bedroom in pride of place. Would he have done that if this was the family cuckoo in the nest? So, Granny was a bit of a goer in her time!'

Frances smiled. 'She was a very attractive woman.'

'I suppose so. When she was young, anyway.' He turned away from the picture. 'What that Standish woman would give to know that little piece of gossip, if it's true, eh?' He paused and turned back towards her. 'Don't even think about it,' he said softly, 'because if I found out that you had told her, Frances, your life would not be worth living. Do I make

404

myself clear?' He didn't wait to see her frightened nod. He was already descending the steep attic stairs.

'Mum.' Ollie came into the kitchen as Frances was preparing supper. 'You know what you said about probate and Grandfather's will?' He sat on the edge of the table and picked an apple out of the fruit bowl. 'I think Dad burned the will.'

'What?' Frances turned to face him, shocked.

'I didn't think about it till you said that, but when we went into the house Dad went straight into the study and began to go through the desk. I had never been there before but he seemed to know his way round. He was really hurrying and impatient and cross. Then he found this envelope and opened it. He skimmed through whatever it was and swore. Then he laughed. He saw me watching and he told me to go and get everything off the walls upstairs and stack them in the hall but I kind of hung around.' He took a bite of his apple.

'And?' Frances had laid the vegetable knife on the kitchen island.

'And, he burned it. In the fireplace. He was very pleased with himself then he stirred up the ashes and he chortled.'

'Chortled?'

He nodded.

'So, if it was George's will he hadn't left the stuff to your father, had he?' she said.

Ollie shook his head ruefully. 'No, I think he might have left the paintings to the nation. He muttered something about "if the country wants them the country can bloody well buy them".' He shook his head in confusion. 'Should I have tried to stop him?'

'No, darling.' Frances sighed. 'Nothing will change your father's mind once he has made it up. Don't mention this again. Forget it. What will be will be.'

'Why do you stay with him, Mum?' Ollie hurled the apple core towards the bin. It hit the lid and bounced off. He didn't move.

'Yes, Frances, why do you stay with me?' The cold voice

405

from the doorway made them both jump. Ollie slid off the table and backed away towards his mother.

'Dad! I didn't hear you come in.'

'Clearly.' Christopher walked into the room. Frances took a step backwards.

'Leave us!' he shouted at Ollie.

The boy jumped again but he straightened his shoulders. 'No, Dad. I'm not leaving Mum. I am not going to let you hit her again.' He clenched his fists.

'And what are you going to do about it?' Christopher advanced on the boy threateningly.

'I am going to stand up to you.'

Christopher smiled. 'Are you indeed?'

He looked from his wife to his son and back, then he shook his head. 'Plenty of time to sort you two out,' he said calmly. 'Thank goodness Hannah has more sense than to defy me.' Turning on his heel he walked out, leaving them staring after him in silence.

'You can't stay, Mum,' Ollie whispered at last after the door closed. 'Surely you can see that?'

She picked up a dishcloth and nervously wiped her hands. 'I've no choice, Ollie.'

'Everyone has a choice. He's a bully and a bastard!' He walked across and retrieved the apple core, tossing it into the compost bin by the sink. 'Can't you see? If you stay, one day he might really hurt you badly.'

February 10th 1941

Eddie was out the whole time now, returning late at night, often after Evie was in bed. She turned her back to him as he climbed in beside her, clenching her fists in misery, lying tense and angry until he began to breathe evenly. Only then would she turn on her back and lie staring at the ceiling in the dark, listening for the roar of night-time bombers heading west towards Portsmouth and Southampton.

She hadn't been spying deliberately when she found the photo. He had left a jacket on the back of a chair and, going to hang it up, she had almost stepped on his wallet as it tumbled out of the pocket. She picked it up and was about to put it on the chest of drawers when something made her open it. There were several five-pound notes folded inside, a couple of receipts and some stamps, and there, in an inner pocket, the photo of a young woman she did not recognise. She was glamorous, with tightly permed dark hair, full lips and large dark eyes. In her hand a long cigarette holder caressed her mouth suggestively. Evie turned the picture over and read the inscription, cold shock washing over her as she stared at the bold writing.

To my darling Eddie, from Vinnikins, Arundel, June 1940

He had an art scout in Arundel, she knew, a woman who looked for pictures for him. From time to time she rang the farm and he would listen and make notes and smile and promise he would go and collect whatever it was she had found. The way he had described her she was middle-aged, plump, widowed. Lavinia Gresham. That was her name. Evie had spoken to her several times, taken down details of some sketches she had found, passed the message on to Eddie. Vinnikins indeed.

She even knew the woman's address. She had seen it scribbled more than once on labels and in notebooks lying on Eddie's desk in what had once been the dining room of the farmhouse but which was now his den.

It was several days before she managed to get the loan of her father's car on the pretext of picking up some special pastels at a studio supplier in Arundel. Her father would never check up; he would never be sufficiently interested. Besides, he refused her nothing these days.

She found the cottage easily and parked outside, walking up the garden path without hesitation. She wasn't sure what she was going to say or do; part of her was hoping Lavinia would turn out to be the woman Eddie had described and not the vamp in the photograph. When she opened the door Evie's heart sank. She was every bit as glamorous as her picture, if not more so.

For a moment the two women looked at each other. 'Evelyn.' Lavinia obviously recognised her. It was almost as if she had been expecting Evie. She turned and led the way into the sitting room. 'I knew you would come one day,' she confirmed. 'Did Eddie tell you about me?'

Evie perched on the edge of the sofa, pulling her dress down over her knees as though trying to hide the evidence of the growing baby.

'No, he didn't. He doesn't know I've come.'

'How did you find out then?'

'He carries a snapshot of you in his wallet.'

Lavinia suppressed a smile. 'So, why are you here?'

Evie shook her head slowly. 'I'm not sure. It was a shock when I realised he had a girlfriend, then I asked myself if I really cared after all. Does he love you?'

Lavinia gave her a searching glance. 'I don't know, if I'm honest.'

'Do you love him?'

The other woman nodded at once. 'He's the only one for me.' She heaved a sigh, then she shot another quick look at Evie from under her eyebrows. 'He told me about your fella getting killed. I'm sorry.'

Evie put her hand on her stomach. 'I've known Eddie much longer than I did Tony. Eddie was sort of the boy next door.' She gave a wistful smile.

Lavinia nodded. 'It's the sort of thing he would do. Give another man's child his name. He's a good bloke.'

Evie stared at her. 'You know?'

She nodded. 'He told me everything.'

'And you don't mind him marrying me? Didn't you want to marry him yourself?'

Lavinia shook her head slowly. She stood up and walked across the room to stare out of the window towards the distant view of Arundel Castle beyond some old willow trees. 'I'm married already. My bloke is overseas somewhere. He and I don't keep in touch.' She turned and came back to resume her seat. 'For all I know he is dead.'

'And you would have married Eddie if you had the chance?'

Lavinia smiled. She had a warm smile, Evie realised, and a genuinely kind face. 'I suppose I would if he had asked me, but he wouldn't have. He is a high flyer, Eddie. I have nothing to bring him. You have a farm as well as all your talents. It would have been no contest. Better for me to imagine that he held back because I was already married.'

Evie was shocked into silence by this pragmatic approach. 'If I were you, I would hate me,' she said softly after a long pause.

Lavinia chuckled. 'Good thing you ain't me, then. Please don't think too bad of me. I don't see him often. I'm no danger.'

A moment later Lavinia rose to her feet. She touched Evie's shoulder lightly. 'Shall we keep your visit between ourselves? I don't suppose either of us wants to put him in a bad mood, do we?'

Evie groped for a handkerchief. 'No,' she whispered.

'And you take care of that little one,' Lavinia went on. 'That was my only sorrow, no kids. But it was not to be and it would have complicated matters, let's face it.'

Saturday 7th September

In the attic Christopher had pulled the painting under the lights so he could scrutinise it more closely. He had forgotten Frances and Ollie downstairs in the kitchen. This was one of Evie's war paintings and as such deserved a place in the Imperial War Museum at the very least. He felt a quick thrill of excitement. That was obviously why his father had wanted to give it to the nation. More fool him. He squatted down to examine the painting more closely. It didn't matter a hoot who the young airman was. What mattered was that this was a genuine Lucas and had been painted during the Battle of Britain. Had she signed it? He couldn't see any sign of a signature but maybe it was hidden by the frame. Anyway, the provenance was sound. No one could claim it wasn't genuine and he could always get it verified by David Solomon if necessary. He sat back on his heels with a quiet smile of satisfaction.

The light flickered and he glanced up at the bulb. The attic storey of the old house consisted of two long rooms under the roof beams. They smelled strongly of the ancient wood and, unfurnished and uncarpeted, had for the fifteen years the family had lived there, become the repository of all their unwanted possessions. Piles of unused furniture, boxes of old toys, empty frames stood around the edges of the long dark rooms. He had never bothered to decorate this top floor; there was more than enough room in the house downstairs. The light flickered again and he saw the bulb swinging on its length of flex in the draught, sending wild shadows whirling round the room. He straightened, frowning, wondering if someone had opened a door downstairs. 'Hello?' He rested the painting against the wall and turned to the doorway. The narrow upper flight of stairs led up between the two attic rooms and it was dark out there with no external light.

'Ollie, is that you?'

He squinted in the darkness. There was a figure standing there in the doorway. 'What do you want?'

He could see him now, a young man, with a thin face, mousy hair, dressed in the blue-grey uniform of the Royal Air Force. 'Who the hell are you?' He stepped towards him aggressively. 'What the devil are you doing in my house?'

The figure disappeared.

Christopher went to the door and stared down the stairs. There was no sign of anyone there. He swung round and went back to the painting. He was imagining things. He thought he had seen the figure from the painting. He looked again hard at the figure of the young man with his helmet and goggles and shook his head. Not him. It was someone else. The figure in the painting was fair-haired, with a wild curly mop. The figure he had seen in the doorway was a taller, thinner figure with darker straighter hair and sad, shadowed eyes. Above all he realised he had noticed the eyes.

For the first time he felt a shiver of unease. He stood unmoving, unaccountably uncertain what to do. The air was cold, draughts swirling round the attics and he was aware now of the sound of rain beating down on the roof tiles above his head. He shivered.

Downstairs his wife and his son were waiting, full of antagonism and dislike, if not actual hatred, for him. He didn't want to confront them and he didn't want to move, he realised suddenly, in case that figure was still there, round the corner.

With an angry exclamation he shook himself and turned to switch off the light. He headed for the stairs and began to run down. At the bottom he strode along the landing to Hannah's room. He knocked on the door. 'Hannah?'

'Hi, Daddy.' Her voice was bored.

He opened her door and looked in. 'Are you busy?'

She was lying on her stomach on the bed, propped on her elbows, her mobile phone in her hand. The open suitcases on the floor under the window were half packed, ready for school the following week. He walked in and sat down on the end of her bed.

'Do you believe in ghosts?' he asked. She dropped the phone and sat up.

'Oh my God! Have you seen one?' Her long hair was hanging round her face and he couldn't see her expression.

He hadn't meant to say it. He hadn't even realised that was what he was thinking. Had he seen a ghost?

'Cool.' Hannah seemed anything but phased by the question. 'What did it look like?'

He hesitated. 'He was wearing wartime uniform. RAF uniform.'

She nodded. 'Do you think it was Granny's brother?'

'Granny?' he frowned, confused.

'Your granny, Evie. You were always telling us how famous she was and how her brother was killed in the Battle of Britain. Don't you remember? Ollie loved those stories. It was so sad. He was incredibly young. He had a funny name.'

'Ralph,' Christopher murmured. He shivered again. He rose to his feet and went over to the window, lifting the curtain a little so he could peer out into the dark.

'What was he doing? Why would he come here? He never came to this house so why would he haunt it? Is he haunting us?' Hannah climbed to her feet and came to stand beside him.

He studied his daughter. She was wearing hideous floral leggings and a striped dress of equal ugliness. He sighed. How had he sired a child with such poor taste? Her feet were bare and rather grubby, as was her hair, but her face was alight with excitement.

'Where did you see him? Do you think I can see him too?'

Christopher shook his head. 'I was imagining it, darling. I just thought I saw something moving in the shadows up in the attic. I was looking at the pictures I brought back from your grandfather's house. There is one there of a young pilot –'

'– and it's Great-uncle Ralph?'

'No.' He shook his head. 'No, it's not him.' He paused for a moment, deep in thought. 'This chap I thought I saw, his face was so clear.'

'Then you weren't imagining him.'

He shook his head. 'I suppose not.'

'Have you any photos of him? Or portraits? Surely Great-granny painted her own brother?'

He moved over and sat down on the stool in front of her dressing table. 'I've never seen one, but you're right. There must be a portrait of him somewhere.'

'Perhaps it's in the National Gallery.'

He looked startled. 'What makes you think that?'

'Well, there is one of hers in Tate Britain, isn't there? She was very famous, Daddy. I've Googled it. It shows women in the war amidst all the bombed buildings. It's amazing.'

He gave a hesitant smile. 'I didn't know you were interested in art.'

'You don't know what I'm interested in. You've never bothered with anything either of us do.' She sounded resigned rather than angry. 'Have you any idea what makes Ollie tick?' She gave him a tenth of a second to answer. 'No. I didn't think so. Poor Mum has to do everything. She trails up to the parents' evenings, and dutifully comes to our plays and matches.' She sat down cross-legged on the bed. 'Don't look so crestfallen. You're a businessman. Lots of business fathers don't show up at school.' She leaned forward. 'Shall we go upstairs and see if he's still there?'

'No!'

The force of his answer surprised them both. She looked hurt. 'Why not?' She slid off the bed and came to stand in front of him again. 'Are you scared?'

'No.'

'Why, then?'

'I just don't want to.' He stood up too. 'Leave it, Hannah.'

She glared at him. 'I'm going. I want to see him.'

'No!' How could he explain to her the sudden wave of fear which had enveloped him as he ran down the attic stairs? The certainty that the apparition, whoever, whatever, it was, meant him no good. He tried to take a firm grip on himself. 'Come on downstairs. Your mother is making supper. Let's go and open a bottle of wine.'

Her face broke into a smile. 'Do you mean that?'

He realised what he had said. The pretence that his kids were too young to drink was a nonsense they all subscribed to.

Ollie was frightened of his father; she wasn't. She stood up to him. If her pathetic mother did the same the family would be a lot happier, Christopher thought yet again. Instinctively his daughter knew he respected her for not being afraid of him and equally instinctively she realised that something had happened up there in the attic which had frightened him and she had never seen him afraid before.

Lucy had been working hard, safe in the small spare room at the vicarage and with all the time she needed, secure in the knowledge that Robin was taking care of the gallery. She had decided to keep a low profile for a while as far as Mike was concerned, and anyway she had more than enough material to be going on with. She paused, thinking about Mike. She couldn't decide how she felt about him. Or how he felt about her. Did he trust her again now? He seemed to. He hadn't forbidden her to go back to Rosebank, as had seemed a real possibility at one point. He seemed happy for her to go on working there and happy for her to go on digging into Evie's life. She sat back staring at the screen. On the other hand she had a strong feeling that he had real reservations about her motivation, thanks to his cousin. She frowned at the thought of Christopher. His presence in the background was a definite threat. She put her hand on the mouse as the screensaver kicked in, bringing her manuscript back to life. The book was taking shape at last. The book. Yes, she was beginning to see it as a book, beginning to write paragraphs of linking prose, to make notes of which illustrations would best fit the narrative and draw out a plan of how to fit in the details of Evie's later life as they emerged. Evie was opening up to her, slowly, reluctantly, revealing her secrets one by one, emerging as a rounded fascinating, poignant figure, a real person in every sense, surrounded by a cast of characters who in their turn were fleshing out, stepping onto the stage.

Putting Mike and Christopher to the back of her mind, she sat in front of her laptop scrolling down through the list of dates she had filled in. The events she had unearthed regarding Evie's life, at first so sparse, were becoming more and more detailed. The small room was filling with books and papers, each one annotated, liberally bristling with coloured stickers, each fact now entered onto the computer, each supposed or guessed category of information a different colour and font.

The later years of the war seemed to have been a more stable time in Evie's life. After the birth of Johnny in 1941 she seemed to have settled into a routine of painting for the WAAC. From the infrequent diary entries and the more detailed painting notes a pattern emerged where her mother took over much of the daily care of her son while she visited Chichester and Southampton to record the daily life of the women in factories and in the services and in their homes. In her studio she worked long hours, noting from time to time that little Johnny had joined her at his small easel and was showing marked artistic talent. Lucy smiled indulgently at that, noting the 1944 date. The child was only three!

Then in September 1944 came a note about more personal issues and a rare mention of Eddie in a letter to Johnny's godmother, Sarah Besant. *You won't believe this, but I am expecting another baby! Eddie is so pleased. I am going to finish the large painting of the women queuing with their empty baskets and then cut back a little on work. I seem to get very tired all the time. Mummy and Daddy are brilliant with Johnny but Eddie is out so often. I wish I knew where he goes.*

Lucy cross-checked some dates in her timeline. This must have been the first announcement of George's imminent arrival. She glanced up sadly. The personal blow at his loss, apart from a natural sense of unfairness at the death of a nice, gentle man, was doubled by the loss of all the information he could have given her about his mother.

She noted down the date of the letter on her notepad and then went back to the letter. *I wish I knew where he goes.* Did that sound angry or poignant or just worried? She was getting a fairly clear picture of Eddie as she worked through the diaries. A bit of a bully, a man with fingers in a lot of pies; an entrepreneur, shrewd and with many contacts; she still couldn't make up her mind if he had known about Tony Anderson. Evie and Eddie had married soon after what must have been Evie's breakup with Tony. Had she preferred the older man all along – she glanced at her date chart. Eddie was twenty-nine when they married; Tony Anderson, from his portrait, looked much younger.

June 18th 1941

Eddie carried the painting into David Fuller's gallery and put it down, leaning it against the wall. 'I have something for you here.'

The gallery owner's eyes lit up. 'Something of Evie's? I've been missing her work. Now Sir Kenneth Clark has first dibs on everything it leaves very little for me, so it seems.'

Eddie gave a quiet smile. 'Then this will please you mightily.' He bent and pulled off the brown paper it was wrapped in.

David gasped. 'It's a self-portrait! You can't want me to sell this.' He reached for his spectacles and perched them on his nose. 'Who is this young man with her?' He glanced up over the spectacles, his blue eyes shrewd as he searched Eddie's face.

'He was a boyfriend. I am going to ask you a favour here, David.' Eddie sat down on the bottom step of the staircase, his hands linked loosely between his knees. 'Evie was keen on this chap. Very keen. Right at the beginning of the Battle of Britain. The guy was killed. It upsets her to see it now. I thought perhaps she would get over it but she found the picture the other day and cried all over it. She asked me to take it away and burn it. I took it away but I can't bring myself to burn it. I thought you could sell it for me and we'll keep it between ourselves. I don't want the WAAC to have it either. They would display it somewhere and cause even more grief for her. Before you sell it, I thought you could do something to make sure that even if it did emerge that we had sold it, it wouldn't hurt her any more. I want you to paint out the pilot.'

David stared at him. 'Me?'

'You. Don't tell me you don't know how. You've cleaned up enough pictures in your time, you old rogue.' Eddie gave a thin smile. 'Call it portrait of a girl, and sell it to a dealer as far away as you can. We'll go fifty-fifty on it.'

'But you know you could get far more if it is put on the market as a Lucas.' David was confused and not a little suspicious.

'I know. But I happen to love my wife. She is preoccupied with the new baby at the moment, so hopefully she will forget about it.' Eddie stood up and dusted his hands together. He had not looked at Evie's baby for two days after he was born, had not come home the first night. If her parents thought it strange they said nothing. They were at her bedside and fulsome with their adoration and that was all she wanted. When Eddie finally came upstairs to look at the boy who everyone thought was his son he grunted a few words of congratulation and left the room. He had not brought mother or child any gifts.

Now, he gazed down at the picture again. 'It should make a good price. I'll look forward to hearing from you when the deed is done.'

David Fuller began to paint out the figure of the airman behind Evie's shoulder that same evening. He did it carefully, with feather-light strokes of the brush, well aware that at any time the thin layer of paint could be removed by someone who knew what they were doing. The overpainting was not good. The quality of paint was inferior now; Evie had obviously used pre-war oils which were of a far better consistency,

417

but once it was dry it probably wouldn't show. He covered the blank section of the canvas with cloud in a fair imitation of Evie's sky and stood back to admire it, then he rang one of his best customers, a collector who lived in the Downs some sixteen miles away. 'I've got something for you,' he said with a huge smile. 'Quite an interesting story attached to it. Come in as soon as you can.'

It was agreed that the painting would stay under cover until the end of the war. The price paid was one hundred guineas. David pocketed fifty and split the remaining sum with Eddie. Evie did not notice that the picture had gone for another three months. She had no reason to disbelieve Eddie when he told her he had found it one day when collecting another painting from her studio, and that he had burned it. The tears she wept were private tears, snuffled miserably into Johnny's soft hair as he clung to her breast.

25

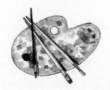

Saturday 7th September

Robin was seated at the desk at the back of the gallery when Lucy pushed open the door and went in.

'Luce! How are you?' He leaped to his feet and gave her a hug. 'It's so good to see you. Are you ready to come home?'

Lucy nodded. 'How is it upstairs?'

'It's OK.' He caught her hand. 'Come up while the shop is empty. We've been doing rather well, the last few days. I've sold another two paintings and there is someone interested in your little sculpture in the window there.'

She followed him up, unable to suppress the small tremor of nervousness as she climbed the stairs. The flat was spotless and the kitchen full of sunlight. She glanced at the door of the studio. 'Is it alright?'

'As far as I can tell. Your friend Maggie came in yesterday. She opened all the windows and did some magical mumbo jumbo.' He gave a broad smile. 'I can't see what it achieved but the whole place has felt marvellous ever since. I think your evil guy has gone elsewhere.'

'I need to know what it was he was trying to do, Robin. He came here for a purpose. To destroy the picture. I've found out much more about the family in the last few days.' Lucy walked towards the door and pushed it open. The studio was neat and tidy and, like the kitchen, full of sunlight. She walked over to the skylight and pushed it open further. 'Apparently Tony Anderson died. It was so sad. He was killed in Scotland. Evie seems to have married Eddie Marston on the rebound shortly afterwards. The picture shows her happy with Tony, so maybe someone wants that happy time forgotten.'

'Eddie?'

She nodded thoughtfully. 'I am beginning to wonder if it might be him.'

'When did he die?'

'That's easy. In 1989.'

'So he lived until relatively recently.'

She nodded. 'Could he be our bad guy? From my research he is beginning to come over as a bit of a bully. Quite unpleasant, in fact. I think he was born in about 1912. So he was seventy-seven when he died. I don't think there is an age limit on being a ghost, is there?' She grimaced. 'How strange that we have two ghosts. Ralph, who was only twenty-one and possibly Eddie, in his seventies.'

'So, what unfinished business did Eddie leave? Isn't that what your ghostbuster friends say is the reason for somebody haunting? He was obviously angry about something. Very angry. Angry enough to rage about it even though he's dead.'

'It's Tony. It must be. He's the catalyst. It all fits. We found the picture of him and I've begun to dig into the past. Either he just hated Tony so much he wants him forgotten forever, or there is something else he wants hidden.' In the cold light of day she had discounted her theory that the portrait of Tony resembled Mike. She had taken her photo out into the daylight and scrutinised it carefully. Whatever passing resemblance she had seen in the lamplight the night before had gone.

'And Ralph?'

'I think Ralph wants us to know about it.'

'A cosmic battle.' Robin shook his head sceptically. 'It sounds far-fetched.'

'The whole ghost thing sounds far-fetched,' Lucy said crossly. 'But listen. This has not just happened to us. Ralph haunted Johnny Marston. Juliette, his widow, told me. Literally, as a ghost and in nightmares.'

'So why can't your mates Maggie and Huw interview these two guys and find out what they are on about and tell them to shake hands. It is all in the past.'

Lucy nodded glumly. 'I suppose it is. Or is it that it is still going on?' She felt herself grow suddenly cold. 'My interference has summoned them back. I've stirred it up again.'

That evening she went back to the leather folder and found amongst a load of other stuff a letter folded very small and tucked into the back flap. Once again it was dated 1941, shortly after Johnny was born.

Ambleside, June 1941

Dear Evie,

I was so excited to hear you had had a little boy. What wonderful news. You and Eddie must be so thrilled. Thank you for the photos. What a darling! I suppose all small babies have fair hair? What a joy it must be for you and your parents. I was so pleased you have called him after Ralph. Your brother would have been so proud of his nephew. And I am so proud to have been asked to be his godmother. Thank you. Tell me as soon as you have a date for the christening and I will be there to hold John Ralph over the font. Don't forget to make lots of sketches of him and save one for me. Now you are so famous it will be very exciting to have a genuine Evelyn Lucas on the wall! (I'm not jealous – honestly!)

Make sure you give me time to get back to Sussex.

It's an awful long way and I will have to find a way round poor old London. I'm so looking forward to seeing you, and my godson.

With all my love,
Sarah

With a gasp of excitement Lucy read the letter again and reached for her list of Dramatis Personae. Sarah Besant was one of Evie's friends from the Royal College of Art, which had been evacuated from South Kensington to Cumbria in December 1940 to try and escape the London Blitz. And there was a date at the top of the letter. She glanced from her list of characters in Evie's life to her sketched timeline, and back at her photo of the portrait. So, Evie had had an eight-month baby. She chewed her lip thoughtfully. Why had Sarah Besant made the point about the baby having fair hair? Was that just a chance remark from an artist who presumably had an eye for such details, or was that a hint that she knew Johnny was Tony Anderson's child? Poor Tony Anderson, who appeared to have been killed soon after he was posted with his squadron back to Scotland in December 1940.

That might explain a lot.

The next account she read jumped the story forward by three years.

October 10th 1944

'Where have you been?' Evie greeted Eddie at the door of the kitchen. She was feeling sick and exhausted, and Johnny had been running round all day out of control. Her parents had gone into Chichester and she was well aware that her last painting was weeks overdue for an exhibition which was being planned for the autumn. 'Have you been out with that woman?'

Eddie stared at her blankly. 'What woman?' He took off his greatcoat and, pushing past Johnny, who was playing with a small wooden horse, hung it from the peg on the back of the kitchen door. 'Don't be so stupid, Evie. When have I time to see any women?'

Did he still not realise that she had gone to see Lavinia Gresham before Johnny was born? She had been so sure that Lavinia would tell him, but the expected explosion of fury had never come. There were plenty of other things which set him off, above all her protective adoration of her son, but on the whole he kept away from the farmhouse. The conception of the new baby was the result of an evening after the whole family had been sampling some homemade ale at a dance in the village hall. Evie had become quite giggly and flirtatious – not with him, it had to be said, but with a young soldier on leave with his parents in the next village – and Eddie's anger had exploded in the privacy of their bedroom later that night. What had occurred was undeniably rape; the next day Evie had told him that she never wanted to share a bed with him again, and although he had ignored that angry tearful plea he had slept resolutely with his back to her ever since.

'Lavinia!' She glared at him. 'Did you think I didn't know about her? I've known for years!'

Eddie looked astonished for a moment. Then his face darkened. 'So, you've been prying into my affairs?'

'Prying?' she said furiously. 'You carry her photo with you everywhere. It is hardly tactful!'

He laughed. 'Well, my married life at home is not exactly rewarding, Evie, darling,' he said. 'Of course I go elsewhere. I've known Lavinia since we were teenagers. She is warm and loving and doesn't argue every time she opens her mouth.' He walked past her and went out into the hall. She heard him run up the stairs and, suddenly too angry to care, she went up after him leaving Johnny crying bitterly behind her.

'So, you don't deny it?' she cried, following him into their bedroom.

'No, of course I don't deny it.'

'Why don't we get divorced then?' she screamed. 'That would suit me fine and leave you to marry her, if she's so warm and loving!'

'I will never divorce you, Evie.' He froze suddenly, looking at her. 'So don't mention such a thing again. Do you hear me?'

Behind them the door opened and Johnny peered in. 'Mummy?' The little voice sounded scared. Neither adult paid him any attention.

'Are you threatening me?' Evie asked coldly. Suddenly she was in total control of her temper.

'I do believe I am.' Eddie held her gaze, his expression full of contempt.

'Mummy?' The little boy was clinging to her skirt now.

'I think it might be a good thing if you left this house,' Evie said calmly. She stooped and swung Johnny off his feet.

'Put that child down.' Eddie stepped towards her.

'And if I don't?'

'Then I might hit him by mistake.'

She stared at him in horror. 'Get out!'

Eddie lunged at her, pulling Johnny from her arms and throwing him none too gently onto the bed. The child let out a piercing scream as Eddie raised his hand and slapped Evie across the face, hard. Off balance, she lost her footing and crashed against the corner of the chest of drawers. She let out a cry of agony as she collapsed onto the floor, clutching her stomach. With a look of total disgust Eddie turned and walked out of the room as Johnny climbed off the bed and ran to his mother, sobbing bitterly.

'Eddie!' Evie's voice rose in panic. 'Eddie, come back. I'm bleeding.'

All she heard was the thump of his footsteps as he ran down the stairs.

Monday 9th September

Mike put his key into the lock at Rosebank and pushed open the door. There was someone in the kitchen and he felt his spirits rise in anticipation. 'Lucy?'

'It's me, Mr Mike,' Dolly called back. Of course, Lucy's car would have been in the lane if it was her. He walked in and stared round. 'Good heavens, what is going on?' The kitchen table was stacked high with dusty boxes and cases.

Dolly sat down heavily on one of the kitchen stools and let out a sigh. 'I'm going through everything of Evie's, like you told me. There is much more than I thought. I got young Bob Parsons from the pub to come and go up into the attic for me and out in the mower shed.'

Mike sat down opposite her. 'Has Lucy seen all this?'

Dolly shook her head. 'I haven't seen her for several days.' She gave him a stern look. 'Did you and she have a quarrel?'

'No.' He gave her a fond smile. 'Far from it. It's just I've been busy, and so, I guess has she. Shall we ring her and tell her you've found all this?'

Dolly looked doubtful. 'I'm going through it first. I'll put the stuff I think she should have on one side. She doesn't want to be doing with Evie's old clothes and things.'

'Still no sketchbooks?'

'No,' she said. 'But Mr Christopher rang me last night at home. He wanted to know where Lucy was.'

'What did you say?' Mike felt an undercurrent of worry wash through him.

'I told him I hadn't seen her for a while and had no reason to think there was anything left here for her to interest herself in.'

'Good for you.' Mike gave her a conspiratorial grin. 'And is there?' He indicated the piles of things on the table.

'There is quite a lot of personal stuff there, Mr Mike. I'm just not sure how much she wants to know about the family.'

'Everything. I thought we had agreed on that.'

Dolly frowned. 'You might not want her to see everything here.'

'Really?' Mike reached forward and pulled a shoebox towards him. 'What sort of things?' He took the lid off and looked inside. The box was full of bits of lace and feathers.

Dolly laughed. 'Trimmings for hats. I reckon Evie must have made her own. After the war when she started having exhibitions in London she would have worn hats.'

Mike picked out a cockade of black feathers. 'These are lovely.'

'Funereal.' Dolly's mouth turned down.

She pushed back the stool and stood up with a groan. 'Last time I saw Lucy she gave me a copy of what she calls her time line, with the family tree. Did she give you one?'

Mike sighed, hiding another twinge of hurt that yet again she had shown how little she trusted him. 'She probably thought I knew it all.'

'Maybe. Well, take a look and see if you can improve on it. That's what she told me to do. She said I was to write on it and cross it out, anything I wanted, as we made our way towards the truth.' She held his gaze. 'That's what she wants. The truth.'

Mike frowned. 'And don't we want the same?'

'Perhaps.' She pushed a transparent folder towards him. He opened it and scrutinised the photocopy with its small neat writing, some appearing to have been inked, some pencilled. He recognised Dolly's carefully inscribed rounded hand in some of the amendments and Lucy's own scribbles where she had changed her mind.

'My goodness. She's made a list of Evie's exhibitions as well.'

Dolly nodded.

'It's really coming together, isn't it?' He gave Dolly another cautious glance. 'So what is bothering you?'

'She's getting too close.'

'To what?'

Dolly walked across to the window and stared out into the

garden. 'I don't know. That is what Mr Christopher said. She is getting too close and she has to be stopped.'

October 10th 1944

Evie awoke, lying in a haze of pain and fear. How long she had been like that she didn't know. As she drifted back to consciousness she realised that Johnny was lying with her, wrapped in her arms. The little boy was crying quietly.

'Johnny,' she whispered.

He snuggled closer.

'Johnny, darling, I want you to go downstairs and fetch Granny. Can you do that for me?'

She felt him shake his head.

'Please, Johnny.' She tried to keep her voice steady. 'I need to see Granny. Will you be a very big grown-up boy and see if she is in the kitchen?' She prayed quietly that her mother had come home. Moving slightly she became aware of a wet stickiness beneath her and realised she was lying in a pool of blood. She closed her eyes with a sob. She didn't need to be told she was losing the baby.

Carefully she pushed Johnny away from her. 'Stand up, darling. Be a good boy. Is Granny downstairs?'

He nodded.

'Did you hear her come in? Can you call her for me? Tell her Mummy isn't very well.' She was trying to speak calmly.

He still clung to her for a few more moments and then he seemed to understand finally what she wanted. He ran towards the door and pulled at the handle. For one terrible moment she thought Eddie had locked her in, but the door opened and Johnny disappeared. She heard him talking to himself as he went downstairs. 'Call Granny. Call Granny. Come see Mummy.'

For a long time she heard nothing then at last she heard her mother's anxious steps on the stairs. 'Evie? What's happened?'

After that there was a blur of activity. Somehow Rachel managed to help Evie onto the bed; Johnny was dispatched downstairs to Dudley's care, the doctor was called, then Eddie. Evie said nothing. She had fallen, she said, that was all.

Monday 9th September

Ollie did not like his sister coming into his bedroom but she had arrived before he could lock the door. She looked round with an expression of disgust.

'Don't you ever get this room cleaned?' She didn't wait for his reply. 'What is going on with Dad?'

He took off his headphones with reluctance and laid them on the desk. 'Him and Mum, you mean?'

She shook her head. 'That's nothing new. Mum has to learn to stick up for herself. She's a complete nerd when it comes to understanding men.'

Ollie snorted. 'And you're the expert, I suppose.'

She nodded without a trace of humour. 'I've got him here, like this.' She waggled her little finger.

Ollie sneered. 'So, what do you mean, then?'

'When you went to London with him to Grandfather's house. Something happened there.'

'Well, duh, yes.' He loaded the words with sarcasm. 'We brought all the loot back.'

'And stashed it in the attic?'

He nodded, getting bored.

'Well, it's gone.'

Ollie's eyes flew open. 'Gone?'

She nodded. 'I went up there just now. The place is as empty as it was before. Just junk. There are no pictures there now.'

Ollie gave a silent whistle. 'I wonder where he's put them. Dad saw something up there. He was freaked by it.' Ollie frowned. 'There is something really weird going on. Not just

Dad being a dickhead as usual, something sinister. Do you reckon Evie's pictures are worth millions?'

Hannah nodded. 'I think they must be. You know what he's like about money. I heard him talking to Mum about Mike at Rosebank Cottage. He thinks there is more stuff there which he missed when he went there to collect everything. You would think he's got enough, but he obviously wants to get his hands on it.' Hannah sat down on the floor and drew her legs up under her. 'I don't think our father is an awfully nice man,' she said thoughtfully.

Ollie was startled. 'I thought you worshipped him.'

Hannah gave an angelic smile. 'His wallet, maybe.'

Ollie laughed. 'I'm surprised you've even seen it.' He sat down and leaned towards her. 'Mum is really frightened of him. I think she ought to leave him.'

Hannah looked thoughtful, then she nodded. 'Where would she go?'

'Back to Granny and Grandpa in Scotland. She would be safe there. Grandpa wouldn't let anything happen to her. He adores her. Men always adore their daughters.' He looked resigned. 'That's why you can get away with being such a cow sometimes.'

Hannah giggled. 'He didn't let me see the pictures though. He wouldn't go back up there and by the time I got the chance they had gone. He came in to see me when he had just come down the stairs. He was white and kind of shaky. He asked me if I believe in ghosts.'

'What did you say?' Ollie was curious in spite of himself.

'I'm not sure I answered. I'm not sure if I do. He said it was a young man in RAF uniform and we thought it was Uncle Ralph. But why would he be frightened of Uncle Ralph?'

'I would have thought that was obvious. Because he was a ghost!'

'And why is he haunting us suddenly?' she said thoughtfully.

'Not us. We haven't seen him. He's haunting Father.'

'So, has Father stolen those pictures?' Hannah was picking her nails. She asked the question casually without looking up at him.

Slowly Ollie nodded. 'I think he has. I think Grandfather left them to the National Gallery or somewhere. Dad said if they wanted them then they could pay for them.'

'Money as always.' She sounded disgusted.

He nodded again. They both sat in silence for a while, gazing gloomily into space.

'Pity we have to go away to school,' Ollie said suddenly. 'I vote we insist we stay for Grandfather's funeral. After all, they must give compassionate leave or something after a family member has been murdered.'

'Murdered?' Hannah looked at him in horror.

'Maybe.'

'So, what do we do?' Hannah said after a while.

'Nothing.' he said after another silence. 'Just wait. Maybe have a word with Mum. Something will happen. It always does.'

26

October 20th 1944

Lavinia had been a scout for Eddie for years, working for him even before the war, and continuing after it started, looking for paintings and pieces of furniture which he acquired at discount prices from people desperate for cash in war-strapped England and stashed away in a warehouse where they could wait until the prices began to rise again. It was too early yet, but soon the war would end and he was quietly confident that not long after it happened the markets would begin to rise. When they did he would be sitting on a fortune.

Lavinia was standing at the window waiting for him when he drew up outside the Arundel house. She watched as he climbed out of the car, chewing her lips with nerves. He looked remarkably pleased with himself, his hat just that little bit to one side as he always wore it, his greatcoat hanging open just enough to give him a swagger. He glanced round as he opened the gate and walked up her drive and only then seemed to notice that she was standing in the window. He raised a hand.

She met him in the doorway and raised her face for a kiss.

'I haven't seen you for ages,' she said, forgetting her resolution not to nag him.

He gave her a quick peck on the cheek. 'Busy, busy,' he said airily. 'You know how it is. So, darling girl, what have you got for me?' He bounded ahead of her into her front room. On the ground floor, it looked out onto the rose garden at the back, blighted now by the stormy weather, and if one stood to one side of the chair carefully placed in a small bay to make the most of the view, one could see the castle, magnificent in the evening sunlight.

Lavinia looked at him, trying to judge the right moment to spring her surprise and for the first time noticed how tired he appeared. 'What's up, love?' She went over to the tray on the sideboard and reached for the gin bottle. 'Do you want one?'

He shook his head and sat down on the chair.

She put the bottle down nervously. Perching on another chair opposite him she waited, aware that something bad must have happened.

'It's Evie,' he said at last.

Lavinia scowled. She had no desire to hear about his wife. 'What's up with her?' she asked coldly.

'She was expecting a baby. Mine. She lost it.'

Lavinia went white. 'What happened?'

He shook his head. 'Some sort of woman's problem. Who knows? The doc thought she might die.' His bravado had suddenly gone. 'My son.' He leaned back in the chair and closed his eyes.

'Oh, Eddie I am so sorry.' Lavinia was struck dumb for a moment before she pulled herself together and asked, 'But she can have more, right?'

She fixed her eyes on his face.

He shook his head slowly. 'Unlikely. She's been very ill.'

'I'm so sorry, love. But at least you've got little Johnny.'

Eddie's face hardened. 'At least I've got little Johnny,' he repeated bitterly.

In the end she thought it better not to tell him her secret. It could wait.

Saturday 14th September, morning

'We wanted to talk about the ghosts,' Maggie announced as she and Huw sat down in the living room at Rosebank and, at Mike's invitation, took the role of mother, and poured coffee into Evie's old porcelain cups. They were freckled with hairline cracks and chips, but still extraordinarily pretty. Mike had only just managed to rescue them from Charlotte's desire to bin them.

'Ghosts?' Mike stared at his guests in astonishment.

'Ah.' Maggie glanced at her husband. 'Lucy hasn't mentioned them to you?'

She pictured herself and Huw as viewed through his eyes. Elderly couple, bit scatty, clergyman with wild hair. Not a good image!

Mike was waiting for them to go on.

'The ghost of your great-uncle, Ralph Lucas,' Huw put in.

'Ah. Yes. I do know about that. My dad always claimed Ralph was trying to contact him. When he was a little boy at Box Wood Farm where my grandparents lived when they were first married – with Evie's mother and father, and then I think all through his life. It was a bit spooky. I was scared by his stories and I think my mother told him to stop talking about it.'

'Lucy has seen him too, Mike.' Maggie leaned forward and put her hand on his arm. 'He has been seen several times at her gallery in Chichester.'

'I see.' Mike looked cautiously from one to the other. 'So, we believe in ghosts, do we? I know she is finding out lots of stuff from all the papers she has found here. She hasn't necessarily had time to keep me updated on everything.'

433

'I suspect she is finding the research rather overwhelming,' Maggie said gently. 'She has certainly been very busy writing.'

'You mentioned ghosts in the plural,' Mike said. 'Assuming there are such things, do we know who the other ghosts are?'

His guests looked at each other and he saw the look of concern which passed between them. 'What is it? Is it Evie?'

They both shook their heads. 'Not Evie, no,' Huw said carefully. 'It is the ghost of a man, a very forceful individual, who seems intent on hiding much of the evidence that Lucy is uncovering.'

Mike sat back and folded his arms. 'That would be Grandfather. If anyone is being a ghost round here, it would be him.'

'That's Edward Marston?'

Mike nodded. 'He and Evie were divorced in 1960. They didn't have a happy marriage as far as I know and after the divorce Evie came to live here with my father and my uncle George, and Grandfather Eddie did everything in his power to deprive her of her paintings. '

'Do you remember him?' Maggie asked.

'I was about thirteen when he died. I don't think we ever saw him, but I know my father used to be furious at the way he hounded Granny. Her paintings were potentially very valuable even then and he wanted them, even those she painted long after they were divorced. I think he claimed he was her agent and there was some kind of legal tie.'

'And his interest descended to his younger son, George, and now to Christopher?'

Mike looked at her with interest. 'You know my cousin?'

'I know Frances,' Maggie put in hurriedly.

Mike nodded thoughtfully. 'Of course.'

Mike took a sip from his cup and leaned back in his chair. 'So, you think Eddie is haunting Lucy? That wouldn't be good.'

'Are you prepared to believe in ghosts?' Huw asked bluntly.

Mike paused for a moment before he answered. 'I've never

seen one, but I have heard enough to have an open mind.' He sounded cautious.

'Good. So,' Huw went on, 'we can discuss the form this haunting is taking. It is of sufficient violence to frighten everyone who has witnessed it and we want to try and find out if there is some specific moment which has triggered this, or if it is just the overweening ego of a man who is not prepared to accept that he is no longer able to influence events he has left behind.'

'Wow.' Mike grinned. 'Violence, you say?' Suddenly he frowned. 'You mean this ghost has tried to hurt Lucy?'

'It has repeatedly tried to destroy the painting of your grand-mother with the young pilot who was, we suspect, her lover during the Battle of Britain.'

'What painting?' Mike looked puzzled.

'The painting in her studio –' Huw stopped abruptly as Maggie aimed a kick at his shin under the table.

'The painting she told me had been destroyed in her husband's car crash,' Mike went on. 'I see. So Christopher was right. It does still exist.'

There was a long silence. Huw rubbed his face with his hands. 'I'm sorry. I thought you knew.'

Mike gave a deep sigh. 'Lucy chose not to tell me. Perhaps it's my fault that she didn't trust me enough.'

'She trusts you, Mike,' Maggie put in. 'Perhaps there was a misunderstanding.'

He gave a bleak smile. 'Perhaps.' He folded his arms. 'You were saying, you thought the ghost was trying to destroy this painting?'

Huw nodded slowly. 'It has come very close once or twice. The painting has been damaged a couple of times; then the place where it was stored caught fire.'

'And where is it now?'

Huw looked at his wife. 'In our vicarage. Lucy was terrified alone in her gallery with the picture still there. Who or, whatever it was, was threatening her, smashing things up, causing doors to open and shut, hurling the canvas off the easel. We thought it best if it came to the chapel in our house where we can surround it with prayer.'

Mike gave a quiet laugh. 'Well, if it is Eddie, prayer won't have the slightest effect. From what I gather he was not a religious man.' He stood up restlessly. 'How could she not have realised that I didn't know? I don't understand. I thought I was her friend!'

'Christopher frightened her,' Maggie said. 'Don't blame her, Mike. We have all been confused and worried about this picture and the seeds of evil it seems to contain.'

Mike shook his head slowly. 'No, that's not good enough. I have helped her; I have given her everything I could find of Evie's. I have introduced her to my family. I have trusted her, but it seems she was not prepared to trust me.' He was becoming increasingly angry. 'Maybe Christopher was right. He could well be a better judge of character than I am, anyway. She stands to make a lot of money from this book of hers, no doubt, and boosting Evie's fame will make this painting far more valuable.'

'Mike, wait a minute.' Maggie could feel the colour flaring in her cheeks as her temper rose to match his. 'Are you really suggesting she would have gone to all this trouble and effort and hard work, planning to take months if not years out of her life, to boost the value of one picture?'

'If it's worth a million, yes.'

'A million?' Huw echoed. 'Are you serious?'

'I don't know. I don't own any of my grandmother's oil paintings.' Mike pushed his hands into his pockets. 'Look, I'm sorry. I'm not sure what you came here for, but if it was to make sure I knew about the painting, then thank you, you have succeeded. You have given me a lot to think about. And now, perhaps if you wouldn't mind leaving. I have a great deal to do.'

Huw and Maggie glanced at each other as they walked up the lane towards the village. 'What have I done?' Huw shook his head slowly. 'I am such an idiot! Couldn't keep my big mouth shut.'

'He had to find out, Huw. Someone was bound to tell him,' Maggie said.

'But it didn't have to be me!' He sighed bitterly. 'Poor Lucy, I have ruined everything for her.'

June 1944

Tony's latest posting had arrived out of the blue. He had been supervising gunnery training in Hawarden in North Wales for several months, then he had been posted up to Peterhead in Scotland where he was running 14 APS, armoured practice camp, training men in the use of air-to-air and air-to-ground machine guns and cannon. There had been rumours that the camp was closing – the war in Europe was winding down after the D-Day landings, but nothing firm had been said.

And now this. He stared down at the signal, trying to take in the implications. Squadron Leader Anderson had been posted. He was to report to Liverpool. He was to board the troop carrier, HMS *Britannic*, heading for who knew where. Oh God, this was it. He was destined for the Far East.

Over the last three years Tony had been posted to a succession of air training schools in England and Scotland, managing to visit his parents at infrequent intervals. As he walked up the drive to the farmhouse this time he was full of dread as to what his mother was going to say at his news. He stooped to greet the dogs as usual and found her in the garden where she was deadheading the roses. They embraced and almost at once he found her studying his face in that way she had which seemed to read his very soul.

'What is it, darling? What's happened?'

He gave her a cheeky grin. 'What will I do when I really want to hide something from you?'

'You can't.' She pushed her gloves into her pocket and waited.

'I've been posted again,' he said, giving up the idea of breaking it to her gently. 'Overseas.'

'What?' He saw her cheeks pale. 'Where?'

'That's the trouble, I don't know. I have been ordered to join the *Britannic* at Liverpool. We have sealed orders as to where she will be going. I'm going to be the security officer.' He grinned.

His mother glared at him. 'You are not in the Navy.'

'Not yet. Sounds as though I shall be quite close.'

He saw her sigh as she turned towards the house and led the way slowly inside. 'Is it a promotion?'

'Probably.'

He had wondered what had led to this posting himself and had a strong suspicion that his old CO, Don, had something to do with the transfer. Over the last couple of years or so he had found himself moved abruptly from station to station at short notice and although it happened to everyone now and again, he wondered if his former CO was still keeping a fatherly eye on him from the distance of whatever lofty rank he now possessed. If so, he was pleased. There had been no other unforeseen incidents threatening his life, beyond the small matter of the war!

As though reading his thoughts his mother turned to him as they walked into the sitting room. She had gone over to her desk, which stood in the window. From a pile of papers and books she retrieved a newspaper cutting. 'Do you ever hear from Evelyn Lucas?' If she saw the wince of pain on his face at Evie's name, she gave no sign.

He shook his head.

'I thought you might be interested to see what she is doing now,' she said. She handed him the cutting and he stared down at it. There was a small picture of Evie. She looked older and more serious than he ever remembered her looking in the past.

Well-known artist, Evelyn Lucas, features in new exhibition

in the National Gallery in London. Miss Lucas has contributed some two dozen paintings to the exhibition which centres on the bravery and endurance of the people of this country . . . Miss Lucas is married to art critic and collector, Edward Marston and the couple have one son. They live in Sussex.

Tony realised that his eyes were blurred. He handed it back to his mother. 'Good for her.'

She studied him carefully. 'No regrets?'

He shook his head.

'You'll find someone else, darling.' She reached over and touched his hand for a moment. Unspoken, the thought of oceans and submarines and distant theatres of war rose between them. 'Don't tell your father I've shown you this,' she whispered. 'He said I shouldn't, but I thought it better you know she is –' she stopped short, then ploughed on, 'she is getting on with her life, darling, and so must you.'

He nodded sadly and wondered, not for the first time, what had happened to the portrait of himself which used to hang above the fireplace. It had mysteriously disappeared after he had been posted back to Scotland. He had, half-ashamed, half-embarrassed, poked around the house, even searching the store-rooms in the attic, but he never found a trace of it and he never plucked up the courage to ask. He guessed his parents were being tactful, but nevertheless he would have hated to think they had destroyed it. It was a picture of him, after all, and had been painted by a famous artist for a purpose – to remember him by if he were killed.

His job was no sinecure. HMS *Britannic* was carrying some five thousand troops, Army and ATS, Navy and Wrens, and Air Force and WAAFS, and his duties mainly involved the mainte-nance of some kind of discipline on board. The ship was crowded, the troops sleeping on hammocks below decks and the scope for mischief was vast. One of his duties was to try to keep the men and women from becoming too friendly with one another, in a vain attempt at preventing too much immorality, for instance, checking that amorous couples had not climbed into the lifeboats at night, and he and his team were also charged with the censoring of the letters, which would be posted at their first port of call. Their destination was under seal until they had passed Gibraltar but it was easy to guess. The war in Europe was winding down and this was part of the redirection of much needed troops from the theatre in Europe towards the war still raging against the Japanese.

The upside of the posting, as the ship ploughed out into the Atlantic and headed south, was that he had his own cabin and the ship, whose last port of call before Liverpool had been in the US, was laden with food such as hadn't been seen in Britain for years. Besides, his duties were not so onerous he couldn't enjoy the feeling of being on a great ship out at sea with plenty of time for himself.

Standing at the rail staring out at the heaving grey water he prayed, like most of those on board, that Hitler's submarines would stay focused on the Channel and fail to spot them. The ship was fast and modern; this was one of the great White Star Line which had been called up just before the war and it tackled the waves with ease, to Tony's relief. As an airman he had not been too sure how he would take to the sailor's life! In the event he enjoyed it.

Having left the stormy waters of the Atlantic and headed in through the Straits of Gibraltar, the ship cruised through the Mediterranean, following the north coast of Africa. The air grew warm and balmy and from time to time as they sat on deck in the evenings they could see the shadow of the Dark Continent looming up out of the haze to the south.

As it turned out they were not destined for the Far East at all. They disembarked at Port Said, the troops heading for the transit railway to Cairo. Tony left the train at the transit camp at Heliopolis from where he was flown to El Ballah, where he was to run a gunnery school in the desert. It was there, sitting in his tent, one hot November morning, that he opened his mail to find yet another cutting forwarded by his mother describing Evelyn Lucas's latest exhibition and mentioning in the last few lines that Evie, married to the art critic Edward Marston, was expecting her second child. With a cry of misery he screwed up the paper and threw it down on the sand. Was he never going to escape her memory?

January 1945

The war was heading uneasily towards its close but for the time being life was no easier for the people of Britain. Evie was still painting the aftermath of the bombing and they had been hearing for months now about the attacks of Hitler's so-called secret weapon, the V2 rockets. However, the wireless was relentlessly optimistic and it was hard to be sad all the time, especially when the sun shone on the frost-covered fields. Evie's health was improving now and as it did she went more and more often to her studio where Johnny loved to sit near her at his own little table.

He was drawing while she was blocking in the background of a new painting. The studio was full of sunlight. Glancing down at her son, Evie smiled. The light was catching his curly blond hair as he leaned forward over his piece of paper, concentrating hard. Quietly she reached over to the table and took up her sketchbook. She caught his expression just as he became aware that he was being watched and looked up. He gave her one of his lovely broad smiles.

'Mummy, have you finished? Can we go and ride Bella?' He dropped his pencil and pushed back the little stool he had been sitting on. 'What's that?' He came over and leaned against her, staring down at the sketchbook.

'That's you.' She smiled at him. 'Can you see? There's your hair and your eyes and your jumper.'

'My jumper is blue.'

'And it will be blue here as well, when I paint it.'

She looked up at the sound of heavy steps on the stairs and eyed the door warily. To her relief, it opened to reveal her father. He was breathing heavily after the climb. 'So, this is where you both are.'

'We're drawing, Grandpa.' Johnny ran to him as Dudley walked across the studio and sat heavily on the chair next to the table, trying to get his breath back. 'Mummy is going to paint my jumper blue.'

He smiled indulgently. 'That seems like a wise decision.'

Evie put down her pencil. 'Are you all right, Daddy? You shouldn't climb up here. We could have come down. We have been wondering if Johnny can have a ride on Bella.'

'Of course he can.' He smiled fondly at the child. 'We should start to think about getting him a pony if he likes riding. A farm horse is hardly ideal.'

'She is perfect. She is steady and kind and it's like riding a sofa.' Evie laughed. 'I agree it won't teach him to have a good seat on a horse, but there's plenty of time to see if he really enjoys it.'

Dudley patted Johnny on the head. 'He's growing more and more like his father, isn't he?' he said.

Evie stared at him, startled. 'Eddie is so much darker –'

'He's not Eddie's boy.' Dudley shook his head. 'I'm not blind, Evie.'

'But –' She stared at him speechlessly. 'How long have you known?' she asked at last. She felt suddenly helpless.

'Since before you were married.'

'So I needn't have married Eddie!' Suddenly she was furious. 'You let me go ahead and tie myself to him for life, knowing Johnny wasn't his.'

'You had to have a husband, Evie,' Dudley said calmly. 'You know you did. Eddie's made a good father to Johnny.'

She stared at him in disbelief. 'And you think he's made a good husband to me?' she whispered piteously.

'You could have done a lot worse.' Dudley stood up with an effort. 'Enough, in front of the child. Now, you come down and we'll find out how Bella is feeling about trotting round the paddock with young Johnny here.' He gave a deep sigh. 'Your mother is not feeling up to much today. Maybe you and I can find something for lunch, eh? We can't have our little hero starving to death, can we?'

'Where is Eddie?' Evie called to him as he preceded her down the stairs.

'Gone to see David Fuller.'

'With some of my pictures?'

'I assume so.' Dudley stopped in his tracks and turned, looking up at her. 'He does you very well, Evie, looking after your interests,' he said firmly. 'You've got a good man there. You should be grateful for the way it turned out.'

Evie stared down at him speechless. But what could she say? He hits me, Daddy, where you and Mummy can't see. He hurts me. He threatens to hurt Johnny unless I do as he says. He tells me what to paint and takes the pictures before they're even dry. He gives me no money – he says I don't need it as I'm living at home. Why do you think I lost the baby? He hit me and I fell against the corner of the dresser . . .

Somehow she summoned a smile. 'Come on, Johnny. Let's go for a little ride before lunch. Then you can help me see if there are any eggs and maybe if there are we can have a lovely omelette.'

Her eyes met her father's briefly over Johnny's head and just for a second she saw something there which looked like guilt or perhaps remorse. Whatever it was it was gone in a second.

Saturday 14th September, morning

From behind the curtain Hannah had watched the rest of the family go out in the car, pleading her time-of-the-month excuse as a reason not to go shopping with them. To the children's amazement their parents had agreed that they should delay the return to school until after the funeral and as yet, as far as they knew, no date had been arranged.

As her father's car disappeared round the corner of the drive Hannah ran up to her bedroom and retrieved the books from beneath her mattress. Most of them had come from her friend Tab, who was a witch. Or she said she was. They shared a study bedroom at school and Tab, who at first had terrified her, had drawn her in with her spooky stories and confident pronouncements of arcane facts about the afterlife.

Now that the moment had come Hannah was terrified all over again, but she was determined to go on. She had been waiting for a chance like this for ages and to discover there was a ghost in her own house was a gift to her from the spiritual realms. Wait until she told Tab and the others at school about this!

She opened one of the books at the carefully marked page and ran her eyes down the close lines of print. For backup she needed holy water, a candle, matches obviously, salt. She had been stymied by the holy water bit, but elsewhere in the book it had said to put some salt in spring water and bless it. That sounded easy enough. She collected the scented candle she had bought specially, matches and her mother's pack of Maldon salt from the pantry; organic and from the sea, it should be perfect. The bottle of spring water came from Waitrose. If there was to be an exorcism she would be ready. Another of her books, carefully collected over the several months of her increasing interest in the subject, had suggested smudging if the atmosphere in your house was uncomfortable. Smudging consisted of wafting a bunch of smouldering herbs around and directing the sacred smoke into the darkest corners of a room by fanning it with a feather. She had found a pheasant's tail feather in the garden, and made the bundle of smudging herbs with sage from her mother's pots of herbs. Sage was what the Native Americans

444

used and they knew a lot about this sort of stuff. Her bundle looked green and moist and she wasn't sure how she would get it to light, but it was the authentic herb of choice. All this was in case of trouble, but her aim was to summon the spirit, have a chat. In one of the books it said it was possible to do this. Talk to the dead. Treat them as though they were alive. Explain to them what you wanted. Tab did it all the time.

Piling all her paraphernalia into one of her mother's baskets she stood at the bottom of the attic stairs and looked up. Her mouth had gone dry and behind her the house felt extraordinarily empty and quiet. She took a deep breath and put her foot on the bottom step.

Every step creaked. Her heart was thudding uncomfortably when she reached the top and stopped, looking round the landing. The doors to the two attic rooms were open now, the new pictures gone, only the ones that had been there before and the rest of the family junk left. She put down her basket and held her breath, listening. It was quite dark, the only light from the attic windows, one at the far end of each room, set into the roof gables. They allowed only a small amount of light even though outside the sun was shining. It did not occur to her to turn on the electric lights.

She glanced down at her basket, realising suddenly that she should have prepared things before she came upstairs. Her holy water was still just salt and water. She had collected a small ceramic bowl from the kitchen dresser for her basket of tools so she had better make that up quickly now. With shaking hands she unscrewed the spring water and poured a little into the bowl then she tipped a little salt in. How much? Did it matter? The book hadn't said. Should she stir it? She chewed her lip uncomfortably, trying to stem her overwhelming desire to turn round and run back downstairs, dive into her bedroom and hide under her duvet. But she might not get the chance to do this again for a while. It wasn't often the whole family went out together and her excuse wouldn't work a second time.

She set her chin determinedly as she put the salt packet away in the basket.

Somewhere in the room on the left she thought she heard something move. She stared in through the doorway.

'Hello?' Her voice sounded very timid. She glanced round again, forcing herself to stand her ground as she stirred the water with her finger. All she had to do now was bless it. She hadn't been to church since she was confirmed at school. No one had made her, no one had been much interested, certainly not her parents. She had loved the lessons, loved the glamour of the service, but her enthusiasm had died almost as quickly as it had come, subsumed beneath her interest in the paranormal and Tab's scorn for the Church in any form. But she remembered the Lord's Prayer. Everyone knew that. Quietly she put her hand over the water and began to recite it, realising suddenly that she was paying attention to the words with a sincerity she did not remember feeling before. The action comforted her.

Taking a deep breath she stepped into the room and looked round. 'Hello,' she whispered. 'Are you there?'

She waited for a reply, the bowl of water in her hand trembling. She looked nervously over her shoulder. Should she try smudging? Or light the candle at this point? But she didn't want to exorcise him by mistake.

'Hello? Are you there? I know you tried to speak to my father. Can you talk to me?'

She could sense someone there, she was sure she could. She swallowed hard, her eyes searching every corner of the room, without daring to move.

'Speak to me. I want to help you. Daddy said he saw you up here.'

Cautiously she began to walk backwards towards the door. All she wanted to do was run but somehow she managed to make herself move slowly.

And then she saw him; a figure was standing in the light from the window, shadowy, indistinct, by the wall, bending over a stack of her father's pictures. Slowly he appeared to straighten and he looked directly at her. For several seconds she stood rooted to the spot, aware that she had stopped breathing, then she turned and fled.

On the landing her basket was lying on its side, the sage shredded, the salt scattered all over the floor. She looked at it in total disbelief for several seconds before dropping the bowl of water which was miraculously still clutched in her hand and running back down the stairs as fast as she could.

Several steps from the bottom she slipped and missed her footing, half-tumbling down onto the rug. She scrambled to her feet and ran towards her bedroom in a complete panic.

As she reached the door it slammed in her face.

27

Saturday 14th September, early afternoon

'I am so sorry.' Huw looked at Lucy and then at Juliette. 'I am a complete klutz. I should know better. All my training and experience and instincts should have screamed at me to watch what I was saying and I jumped in, obliviously, and with both feet. Maggie kicked me, but it was too late.'

Lucy was sitting on Juliette's sofa in the Brighton house with her arms wrapped round her knees. She was completely numb. 'It's not your fault,' she said at last. 'Absolutely it is not your fault. I should have told him ages ago. I've had enough opportunities. I had even half convinced myself that he knew, or had guessed.'

'I thought he knew,' Juliette added. 'I mentioned it to him, I'm sure I did, but looking back I think he assumed I was talking about it before it was destroyed. It could have been me putting my foot in it as easily as you, Huw.'

'I should have been upfront with him the first time we met,' Lucy went on as if they hadn't spoken. 'I just thought he would get the wrong idea about my motives. And now he has the wrong idea anyway.' She looked for a moment as though she were near to tears.

Huw moved over and sat down beside her, putting his arm round her shoulders. 'It will be all right, Lucy. Somehow I will make it my business to put it right.'

Lucy buried her face in her knees, trying not to cry. Why did she care so much? It wasn't just that Mike might withdraw his co-operation and ask for all the papers back, which let's face it, he had already threatened to do. It was far, far more than that. It was personal. It mattered terribly that he thought well of her, that he trusted her, that he didn't think that Christopher had been right all along to assume she was a trickster and a cheat and a thief.

The door opened and Juliette looked up. Her face assumed an expression of utter astonishment. 'Mike?'

'Sorry, Ma, I let myself in. Something awful has happened –' He paused as he entered the room and looked round, shocked.

'I'll go.' Lucy scrambled to her feet.

'No, wait.' Huw stood too and tried to catch her arm.

She wrenched it away from him and grabbed her bag. Without looking at Mike she pushed past him and ran out through the hall and into the street. In seconds she had disappeared round the corner.

Mike stood still, his face a picture of horrified surprise. At last he turned to Huw. 'I had no idea you were going to come straight here. What business have you with my mother?'

'We wanted to try and put things right,' Maggie said softly.

'Right!' Mike echoed bitterly. 'What is there to put right? Someone finally told me the truth. I don't know why I should be angry with you. You were the only people to have been honest with me.' He threw himself down on the sofa where Lucy had been sitting.

'Shall I go after her?' Huw asked Maggie.

She shook her head. 'Let her go for now. You'll never find her anyway if she's wandering round Brighton.' She turned to

Mike. 'Lucy did not deceive you, Mike. She withheld part of the story until it was the right moment to tell you, that's all.'

Saturday 14th September, afternoon

Hannah had never run so fast in all her life. From the moment she had pushed the door open and peered into the attic room she had, she realised now, been filled with an overwhelming feeling of dread. The emotion had washed over her, followed by blind rage from somewhere outside herself which had hit her like a physical punch to the stomach. Had she really seen a figure there? She wasn't sure now but at the time she had been clearly aware of the craggy face, the stooped shoulders, the bright, vicious eyes, and the sight had completely freaked her out.

Backing out of the room she had taken the attic stairs in what had seemed like one jump, landing in a heap somehow without breaking her ankle. Confronted by her closed bedroom door she turned and hurtling on down the main staircase had raced out of the front door, which she left open behind her. She pelted down the drive and out into the lane without looking back, falling at last at the foot of the old oak tree at the corner where the lane joined the road back into Midhurst.

She was clutching her ribs, trying to get her breath back when a car had drawn up.

'Hannah? Is that you, dear?'

It was Minna Fairbrother, she saw, one of their neighbours from further up the lane. Somehow she scrambled to her feet, pushing her hair out of her eyes.

'Can you give me a lift? Please.' At some level she was aware of how odd she must look and she managed to smile, still trying desperately to get her breathing under control. 'I overslept and I'm supposed to be meeting a friend. If I miss her she will go and think I've missed her on purpose.'

She got into the car, realising at once that she had neither phone nor money on her, intensely aware that nothing on earth would persuade her to go back to the house.

'Where shall I drop you?' Minna turned to look at her as they slowed at a crossroads. She was well aware of the gossip surrounding the Marston household and the fact that from time to time Frances turned up in the village with heavy make-up and dark glasses in a vain attempt to hide a black eye. So, he had turned on the daughter now. She frowned. 'I can take you anywhere you want to go, my dear.'

Hannah was trying to gather her thoughts. 'I suppose,' she hesitated. 'I mean, where were you going?'

Minna smiled. 'To the station at Petersfield. I'm on my way to London.'

'Could you take me there, please?' Hannah was beginning to shiver.

'To London?'

Hannah managed a smile. 'No. To Petersfield.'

'But what about your friend?'

'She'll come and get me.'

Minna drew up at the side of the road and turned to look at her. 'There is something wrong, isn't there, Hannah? Please tell me. Maybe I can help.'

Hannah bit her lip. 'I've come out without any money. Could you lend me some?' She saw the other woman's face close. 'Just enough for a phone call. I've forgotten my phone as well.' And then the inspiration had stuck. 'I need to ring my father's aunt. She lives in Brighton and she will come and fetch me. Please.'

Ollie had told her about Juliette's visit to their mother when they were away. Frances had confided in him that she seemed a nice woman, as though anxious to let her son know that there were nice people in the family. The visit was a secret from their father, so he was to tell no one. He had of course told Hannah that same evening.

Minna sighed. She started the car again. 'My bag is on the

back seat. My phone is in there,' she instructed. 'Do you know her number?'

Hannah shook her head.

'Or her address?'

Again Hannah looked blank.

'So, how do you propose to find her?'

'I don't know.' And suddenly Hannah was crying huge tears which rolled down her cheeks and soaked into her T-shirt.

Minna glanced at her watch with a sigh. Her train was growing ever more distant as an achievable goal, but how could she leave this child in such a distressed state? 'Supposing we take you home and you find your mobile and some money and your aunt's phone number and address?' she proposed gently.

'No. I can't.' Hannah looked so terrified that she confirmed Minna's worst suspicions.

'Would you like me to take you to the police, Hannah?'

'No!' She sounded panic-stricken.

'Where is your mother?'

'She and Dad are out with Ollie.'

'And they left you at home alone?'

Hannah nodded. She was winding a strand of hair around her finger.

'Well, if you are too afraid to go home, there must be someone else you can go to. What about a friend in the village?'

'I haven't got any friends. I go away to school.'

Minna leaned back and closed her eyes in despair. It was too late for the train now. 'All right, supposing you tell me why you are afraid to go back to your house.'

'There's a ghost in there.'

The whisper was so faint Minna thought she had misheard. 'Did you say a ghost?'

'Yes.'

'What sort of ghost?'

'An old man. A hideous old man.' Hannah wiped her eyes with her knuckles.

This was getting beyond a joke. Minna sighed. 'So, who will know where your aunt lives?'

'It will be in the address book.' Hannah gave her a pleading look. 'I can't go back in.'

'Then I'll go in and look if you tell me where it is.'

And suddenly it was easy. She reversed the car into a gateway, turned round in the lane and drove up to Cornstone House, leaving Hannah shaking in the front seat. The front door was, as Hannah predicted, still open and in the hall was a table with an old-fashioned telephone on it; beside it was a bulging address book. Juliette Marston had been crossed out and re-entered as Juliette Bell. Her address and phone number were there. Minna copied them down, all the time glancing up to scan the depths of the hall and the staircase, feeling the intense cold in the house in spite of the warm sunlight outside. She didn't linger to make the call from the phone on the table in front of her. Turning, she ran back outside, pulling the door closed behind her and returned to her car where she dived back into the driving seat. 'Here. Ring her.' She tossed her piece of paper into Hannah's lap. 'If she is happy for you to turn up I will drive you to Brighton and then take the train from there.' She started the engine and was already heading for the gates.

Behind her the house settled back into silence.

March 1945

Lavinia told Eddie that she was pregnant on his next visit. As she stood, her eyes fixed anxiously on his, waiting for his reaction, she felt nothing but fear. She saw the different emotions crossing the harsh narrow planes of his face, anger, anxiety, indignation and then, curiously, triumph. She was standing by her small square dining table near the front window of the room, her fingers locked on the back of the chair in front of her, her knuckles white, half-expecting him to turn round and

453

walk out. Instead he strolled over to the chair which stood by the back window overlooking the garden and the view of the castle and only when he was comfortably seated, one knee crossed casually over the other, did he at last ask, 'When?'

She found she was barely able to speak. 'July.'

He nodded.

'What do I do?' she whispered.

'What do you mean?'

Had she really hoped he would tell her he would divorce Evie, demand she divorce her husband, Peter, wherever he was, marry her, create for her a warm loving home?

'I mean what are you going to do? It is your baby.'

He scratched his chin. 'I will give you some money. You've got a wedding ring.'

She glanced down at the narrow band on her hand. 'You mean I should go on living here?' She tried to hide the hurt in her voice.

'I don't see why not. Will your landlady object?' His voice was cold, unengaged. It was as if it was of absolutely no concern to him what her neighbours and friends would think, or the midwife, or the doctor.

'But they'll know it isn't Pete's.'

'Why should they care one way or the other? Just tell them he came home on a bit of leave.'

She held back her tears. This was Eddie. This was the way he was. She had always known it. 'Will you tell Evie?'

His face darkened. 'That would hardly be tactful after she has lost a baby herself.'

She gave a half-smile. Since when had he considered himself tactful? Slowly she sat down at the table and with a sigh forced herself to look at him.

'Have you any pictures for me? Or silver? I can dispose of silver.'

She couldn't believe he was talking about business again as if the interlude with the baby had never happened, but that was how their relationship was to continue over the next months.

Mary Brown, her landlady, turned out to be endlessly sympathetic when, realising she could no longer hide her condition, Lavinia had knocked on the door of the upper flat one evening and confessed everything. There was no question of putting Lavinia out on the street, far from it; she was supportive and even excited about the coming event. When the time of the birth arrived it was Mary who rang the midwife, Mary who boiled endless kettles of water and it was Mary who first held the tiny scrap which was Lavinia's son. Eddie did not appear for three days after being alerted that Lavinia had gone into labour. When he came, to give him his due, he brought flowers and a bottle of wine, most of which he drank himself, and showed every sign of being impressed at the small bundle of furious life which was his child. He gave her money for a pram and for a cot and came more and more frequently, watching in fascination as the little boy developed, ever aware that this was his baby, his child, his son, as Johnny never could be.

Saturday 14th September, afternoon

'What a nice woman,' Juliette said as Minna drove off down the street. She ushered Hannah inside and closed the door. Huw and Maggie and Mike had left barely an hour before and Lucy had not returned. 'Come outside into the garden and we'll have a glass of fruit juice, then I want you to tell me from the beginning what happened.'

The only lie Hannah had told was that she had left a note for her parents, so they wouldn't be worried.

When Juliette rang Huw there was no reply. She thought for a long time about what to do, then rang again and left a message asking him to ring her back. She needed him and Maggie to return as soon as they could.

Hannah appeared to be in a state of near collapse. Nervously she followed Juliette into the kitchen and back to the garden. She picked at the food she was offered, constantly staring round as though afraid that the ghost had followed her.

'Do you want to ring your mother?' Juliette said yet again.

Hannah shook her head. 'I told you. I left her a note.' She was beginning to believe it herself. She shivered, hugging her arms around herself. 'Can I stay here? Please.'

'Yes, of course you can stay. But only if your mother says so, Hannah. You must see we have to make sure it is all right.'

At last Hannah nodded. She went to Juliette's phone and dialled. Juliette listened to the call from the kitchen. 'Hi, Mum. Listen, I'm OK. I'm in Brighton with Aunt Juliette. Can I stay for a bit?' There was a pause during which Juliette imagined Frances frantically trying to find out what had happened. 'No, honest, I'm fine. She's going to take me shopping in the Lanes.' Hannah took a deep breath, listening again. 'OK. I'll ring you when I want a lift home. Thanks.' From where Juliette was standing the phone was shielded by Hannah's body and Juliette couldn't see the girl's finger firmly holding it disconnected.

Juliette ducked back out of sight. 'OK?' she said as Hannah appeared.

Hannah nodded. 'Sure. She doesn't mind if I stay a bit. I didn't tell her about the ghost. I knew Dad would freak. So, can I stay? Please?'

'Yes, you can' Juliette realised she had been manipulated masterfully. Still, late night shopping was perhaps a good way to defuse the situation until Huw and Maggie got there. 'Let me show you my spare room so you can have a wash and settle in, then we'll go out.'

The spare room was next to the bathroom on the first floor. Juliette led the way in. 'There are clean sheets on the bed and towels in here.' She opened a cupboard and passed a couple of pink fluffy towels to Hannah. 'Come down when you're ready.'

In the event Huw and Maggie were not to come back until the

next morning just after ten. 'Sorry not to have been able to come last night. We were tied up,' Huw said enigmatically. He and Maggie had followed Juliette into her living room. 'Then I had to take early communion as it's Sunday. Lucy has gone in to the gallery to pick up some stuff and then she's off to have lunch with her assistant, Robin, so we have time now to hear Hannah's story.'

Huw, at Juliette's suggestion, was wearing his dog collar and the sight of it certainly seemed to have had a calming effect on the girl.

'You mean you are an exorcist?' she asked him with wide eyes as he explained why he was there.

He nodded. This was not the time for prevarication.

'And you are a psychic?' she went on, looking at Maggie. 'A real one?' A real one as opposed to Tab, whose advice and competence she was seriously beginning to doubt. Maggie too nodded gravely. Hannah needed to have confidence in them.

Juliette glanced at Maggie.

Maggie in turn looked at Huw. 'So, what do we do next?'

Huw stood up. 'Will you excuse me if I go out for a while, ladies? Half an hour perhaps. I won't be any longer, I promise. Having heard Hannah's story I need to think about it. Why don't you girls get something to eat? I bet Hannah is hungry.' He smiled.

Juliette turned to Maggie when he had left. 'Was it something I said?'

Maggie smiled, shaking her head. 'He's gone out to pray. He often does that. He prays while he walks. I expect he'll go down on the beach. He needs to ask what to do for the best.' She saw the sceptical look on Hannah's face. 'God is his boss, Hannah. He's just contacting base. It's enormously helpful.'

Hannah scowled. 'My father says God doesn't exist.'

'Why am I not surprised?' Juliette put in. 'And does he allow you to think for yourself?'

'Of course he does.' Hannah looked defensive.

'I think that is obvious or you wouldn't have gone looking for the ghost,' said Maggie gently. 'That took a lot of courage.'

'But I did it all wrong. Tab said I could banish him but I needed to see him first.' Hannah bit her lip hard, obviously finding it hard to talk about it. 'I was so stupid. I thought it would be easy. I thought he would go away when I asked and Dad would be impressed, because he was frightened and I wasn't.' Her eyes filled with tears.

'You were courageous, Hannah,' Maggie repeated. 'If anyone is to blame it is your friend who does not understand fully what she is talking about, and the books you read which didn't warn you that what you were doing could be dangerous.'

Juliette stood up. 'Come on, let's find something to eat. I think brunch would be a good idea. Nice and grounding. Hannah, let me show you where the dining room is and perhaps you could lay the table for us.'

She led the way to the dining room door and opened it. 'OK? The cutlery is in the dresser drawer there.'

Hannah didn't move. There was a short pause. 'Hannah?' Juliette realised suddenly that Hannah was staring at a picture on the wall on the far side of the room, her eyes rounded in horror, her face white.

'That's him!' Hannah cried. 'Oh my God, that's him. The ghost. It's him!' Pushing between the two women she ran back into the drawing room and dropped onto the sofa sobbing.

Juliette was looking at the picture. She too had gone white. 'That's Johnny's father,' she whispered. 'That's Eddie Marston.'

Saturday 14th September, late afternoon

'Hannah? We're back. Are you feeling better, darling?' On returning home the day before, Frances had stopped on the landing and stared at the dropped basket and its scattered contents for several seconds before knocking on her daughter's bedroom door. There was no reply. 'Hannah?' Frances opened it and looked inside. The room was empty. She stared round with her usual feeling of helpless dismay at the mess in which Hannah lived. Automatically she stooped to pick up various garments and put them on the bed. She sighed. There was no sign of Hannah downstairs. Unlikely as it seemed, perhaps she had gone out for a walk. Closing the door behind her Frances went back down to the kitchen. Minutes later Ollie appeared. 'Any sign of her?' He looked worried.

Frances shook her head.

'Did you see the stuff on the landing?'

Frances nodded towards the kitchen island. The basket stood there with its strange contents, gathered from the carpet upstairs. 'I can't think what that was all about.'

Ollie bit his lip. Hannah didn't know he had sussed her interest in ghosts. For a while he had quite fancied Tabitha when she had come to stay last summer and he kept a quiet but constant watch on Tab's activities on Facebook. He knew enough to be suspicious of the contents of the basket he had stepped over on his way to his own room, and after his mother had gone downstairs he had rummaged under his sister's mattress and withdrawn the books she had hidden there. Her bookmarks were still in place.

He wasn't sure what to do about it.

Christopher walked in to the kitchen. 'Any sign of Hannah?'

Frances and Ollie both shook their heads.

He threw the newspaper he had been carrying under his arm onto the table. 'She must be feeling better.'

Frances gave a tight little smile. 'Good. She hasn't been looking very well for several days.'

'Did you look in the attic?' Ollie blurted out suddenly.

Both his parents looked at him in puzzlement. 'What on earth would she be doing there?'

'She, she, she . . .' He paused, stammering slightly.

'Well, boy, spit it out.' Christopher glared at him.

'She was talking about the ghost you saw.'

Christopher went white. 'What did you say?'

459

'She was intrigued. She said she had never seen one and –' Again Ollie fell silent. Hannah would kill him for this. 'I think she may have stayed at home to get the chance to be on her own.' His glance shifted towards the basket on the table. 'Those are things people use to get rid of ghosts.'

'I did not see a ghost!' Christopher said abruptly through gritted teeth. 'Do you hear me?' He glared at Frances. 'Who said I did?'

'I said nothing,' Frances said quickly.

Christopher shook his head in exasperation. 'Go upstairs, Ollie. Check if she's up there.'

Ollie turned towards the doorway and for a moment he hesitated. One glance at his father's face made up his mind for him and he headed out into the hall towards the staircase.

The attic landing was dark, the doors to the two rooms closed. Nervously he stood there for a moment at the top of the stairs plucking up the courage to let go of the banister. The two way switch at the foot of the stairs had failed to turn on the light. He took two paces forward and reached out for the switch up here. It had no effect. The light was broken. He swallowed hard. 'Hannah?' he whispered. 'Are you up here?'

There was no reply.

'Hannah?' He took a deep breath and headed for the door on his left. Grabbing the handle he pushed it, expecting it to be locked. It swung open with a slight squeak of the hinge. For a moment he stood without moving, then he managed to force himself to take a step forward. He groped inside the door for the light switch. This light did not work either. Clicking it up and down he cursed under his breath. There must have been a fuse. Stupid. He should have brought a torch. He stood irresolutely in the doorway. He could see there was no one in there. Enough light was percolating through the window to illuminate the shadowed corners and the areas behind the piled furniture and old suitcases. He scanned the room carefully and then backed out, pulling the door closed behind him.

Leave it. This is not your business, boy.

The voice in his ear was a harsh whisper. Ollie let out a yelp of fright. 'Hannah?' he gasped. 'Stop it. Where are you?' His eyes were like saucers as he stared down the narrow landing. It wasn't his sister's voice he had heard; it was a man's voice, deep and rasping. He focused on the other door. Cautiously taking a couple of steps forward he reached out towards the door knob. He turned it and pushed. The door was locked. He shook it. 'Hannah? Are you in there?'

'Well, is she up here?' His father's voice from the landing below made him jump. Christopher took the stairs two at a time. 'Why are you up here in the dark you stupid boy?' He put his hand out towards the light switch. The light came on at once.

Ollie stared indignantly. 'But it wouldn't work –'

'Of course it works. Is she in there?' Christopher stretched past Ollie and turned the door knob. Silently, almost obediently the door swung open. Ollie watched as his father stepped into the room and turned on this light as well. There was no sign of Hannah. Christopher looked round carefully scanning the piled boxes then turned out the light and closed the door. 'Where the hell is she? Wretched girl.' He turned and ran back downstairs leaving Ollie standing where he was. Ollie glanced back at the door.

'Hannah?' he called softly. 'Where are you?'

There was no answer.

May 8th 1945 VE Day

There was to be a service in the church and then in the evening a party in the village hall. People had been putting up red, white and blue bunting all over the village. Rachel and Dudley and Evie went to church with Johnny sitting proudly beside them in the pew, then they went back to the farmhouse. There was no sign of Eddie. Outside it was drizzling, the blossom on the trees hanging wet and disconsolate, some of it being torn down and scattered on the ground. The actual day was almost an anti-climax after it

461

had been predicted for so long, and it seemed wrong to celebrate when the war was still going on in the Far East, but Hitler's death had been announced on 1st May and that in itself was reason to celebrate. Evie helped with the refreshments in the village hall and danced once or twice with the old men from the village. The Civil Defence and the Home Guard had already been disbanded and there were some young men around, mostly those who had been invalided out of the Army or the Air Force, so there were plenty of partners for her to choose from, but everyone there was conscious of the heartbreaking gaps which would never be filled, boys like Ralph and the son of the village baker.

And, of course, there was still no sign of Eddie. Was he with Lavinia, she wondered. If he was she found she didn't care. Good luck to the poor woman.

That night she wrote it all down in her diary, complete with some sketches of the dance. The entry made cheerier reading than many she had written lately.

Saturday 14th September, evening

Mike had been back at the cottage for only a few minutes when a car drew up outside, parking in the narrow lane with two wheels on the bank by his front steps. Christopher climbed out and ran up to the front door. Mike answered the aggressive knock at once. One glance told him something was wrong as he stepped back to allow his cousin into the hall.

'Is Hannah here?' Christopher burst out.

Mike shook his head. 'I haven't seen Hannah for years. Why would you think she might be here?'

'Because of this Evie business.' Christopher pushed past him into the sitting room and stood there looking round. 'She's disappeared. We can't find her; wherever she is, she's not got her mobile with her, which is unheard of. There is no trace of her anywhere in the house at home. She has been missing for hours.'

Mike perched on the arm of the sofa. 'Have you told the police?'

Christopher shook his head. 'Not yet.'

'Why not?'

'Because she must be somewhere. We have been ringing people up and down the country. Frances's parents – Hannah loved being with them in the holidays. Her school friends –' He paused abruptly, thinking of the awkward conversation he had had at Ollie's instigation with the mother of Hannah's schoolfriend Tab before she had passed the phone to her daughter. The girl's superior laugh, her enigmatic pseudo, American spook-film-psychic speak. 'I sense she has gone beyond the veil; you must seek her in the land of the dead . . .' Christopher had frozen at her words, then dismissed them as he heard the manic laughter the other end. He wanted to wring her neck, to kill her, to demand her to give the phone back to her mother, but he hadn't. He had frozen her out with a caustic reply and hung up.

'Well done, Dad,' Ollie had said. He had been listening in the doorway. 'If she does know where Hanny is, you will never get her to talk now.'

Ollie had told him about her fascination with the ghost and the fact that Hannah had collected some books on the subject, that the basket of herbs was something to do with calling up the dead. How could he go to the police with a cock-and-bull story like that? He gave Mike a brief outline of events.

Mike shook his head slowly. 'This ghost – did you actually see it yourself?' He didn't smile when Christopher glanced at him sharply.

'I don't know. I suppose for a moment . . .'

'You saw it in the attic, you said?'

Christopher nodded.

'Have you got any of Evie's pictures stored up there?' He saw the sudden suspicion and anger which flashed across Christopher's face. 'Why?'

'Because there seems to be a bit of an issue with Evie's

paintings at the moment.' Mike realised suddenly he didn't want to tell Christopher that he had been right all along and that Lucy did have one of the pictures. 'I have been hearing stories of some kind of ghostly interference going on with one or two of the pictures which are out there in private hands.'

His cousin looked at him sharply. 'There aren't any pictures out there.'

Mike shook his head. 'You mean you have every single one?'

'No. No, that's not what I mean. It's just that I have never heard of any in private hands.'

'Well, there are a few.'

'And I suppose Lucy Standish told you that?'

'Yes, she did.' No harm in admitting that much.

Christopher tightened his lips, but said nothing, so Mike went on, 'There seems to be some kind of malign influence surrounding them.'

'And you are suggesting, what exactly?' Christopher's antagonism seemed to have changed to fear. 'That the ghost has kidnapped my daughter?'

'No, I don't know what I mean except that is it possible something happened to frighten her?'

The two men remained silent for a moment. 'Have you ever thought that this house might be haunted?' Christopher asked suddenly.

Mike shook his head. 'Not for a moment. I suppose I get the feeling that Granny might be keeping an eye on things occasionally, but the atmosphere of this cottage is gentle and benign. I have never felt afraid here. After all, she loved the place. And,' he couldn't resist adding, 'there are none of her pictures here.'

Christopher ignored the jibe. 'You think I should go to the police?'

Mike nodded. 'She's only –' He paused, realising that he didn't even know how old Christopher's children were.

'Fourteen.' For a moment Christopher looked haggard with worry, then he straightened his shoulders. 'I'll go back. If you hear anything . . .'

'I'll let you know at once.' Mike stood up. 'How is Frances coping?'

'She's beside herself.'

After he had gone Mike wandered into the kitchen and stood staring out of the window into the dark. If Hannah had seen anything like the ghost that Maggie and Huw had described the child would be terrified out of her wits. Fourteen. Too young to drive. Half child, half young woman. Probably full of wild certainties and unproved convictions about her own capabilities. He found himself wishing he and Christopher were on better terms so that he could have had the chance to get to know his – he was about to describe them to himself as niece and nephew, but of course they were cousins of some sort.

August 1945

'I will finish the painting when I am ready! I'm too tired to do it now,' Evie shouted. It was weeks now since she had touched the canvas on her easel. She was exhausted and depressed, and Johnny, sensing the atmosphere at the farm, was playing up all the time.

'So, what have you got to be so tired about?' Eddie retorted. 'It's not as though you have a baby to occupy you and that child will be going to nursery school soon.'

'No, I have no baby to exhaust me!' she yelled back at him. 'And whose fault is that?' Her eyes filled with tears.

'Well, luckily I don't have to look to you to give me a son. There are other women who are still capable of bearing my child!' His sneer was delivered with vicious suddenness.

The silence that followed was electric. Evie sat down suddenly. 'What do you mean?' Her voice was dangerously quiet.

Eddie took a step backwards. 'Never mind. Forget it.'

'No. I won't forget it. I am hardly likely to forget a statement like that,' she said. 'What did you mean?'

465

Eventually he told her. What was the point of denying it? Besides, he was proud of his son.

'Lavinia Gresham,' she echoed quietly. Of course, she had known it was still going on but she had chosen to ignore it.

Two days later she drove into Arundel and parked outside the woman's house. There was a pram in the garden. She let herself in through the gate and went to peer inside it. The child was sleeping peacefully, tightly tucked in beneath a warm white blanket.

'So, he told you.' The voice behind her made her jump. She turned. Lavinia was standing on the doorstep, a cigarette in her hand.

'Yes, he told me.'

'I thought he would. I'm sorry. That was cruel of him, but then he is a cruel bastard, isn't he?' Lavinia leaned against the doorpost and took another puff from the cigarette.

Evie was trying to hold back her tears. 'What is he called?'

'Paul.' Lavinia smiled. 'Eddie hates the name.'

Evie gave a wry smile. 'He would hate any name he hadn't chosen himself.'

'Do you want to come in? He'll be all right there for a bit longer.'

The woman led the way back inside and put on the kettle as Evie sat down at the table in the front window. From there she could see the pram. A small pink fist was waving from the blankets. Lavinia put a cup down in front of her and glanced outside. 'He's woken up. He'll be screaming blue murder in a minute. Do you want to go before I bring him in?'

Evie shook her head slowly. 'Can I hold him?'

'You really want to?'

Evie nodded. 'Please. Just this once. Then I'll go. I won't bother you again.'

28

Saturday 14th September, 10.30 p.m.

Lucy was sitting in her bedroom at the vicarage staring into space. What was she going to do now? She had no one to blame but herself for this débâcle with Mike. If all her research fell apart now what would she do? How could she bear not to know what happened next in Evie's life? And how could she bear not to see Mike again?

She frowned. Where had that thought come from? How could she? How could she be so disloyal to Larry's memory? She was chewing miserably on her thumbnail when she heard Huw and Maggie's car turn in on the gravel below.

Five minutes later there was a quiet knock at the door. 'Lucy?' It was Maggie.

'Come in,' she said despondently.

Maggie opened the door and put her head round it. 'Lucy, dear. Mike is with us. He wants to see the portrait.'

Lucy felt a shaft of panic run through her then she sighed. 'Why not?'

'It's up to you.' Maggie walked over and sat down on the

bed beside her. 'He phoned Huw. He is very confused and hurt, but I have a feeling if you can explain to him why you didn't tell him he will understand.'

Lucy gave a grim smile. 'I doubt it.' Standing up, she pushed her hair back behind her ears. 'Come on then. Will we need a screwdriver or something to open the crate?'

They walked down the landing and Maggie opened the door to the little chapel. She let out a small scream. 'Oh my God!'

'What is it?' Lucy peered over her shoulder.

The crate appeared to have been chopped open with an axe. The painting was lying in front of the altar, the canvas ripped.

'Oh, no!' Lucy stood stock-still, aghast. At the sound of Maggie's cry Huw raced up the stairs from the hall, followed closely by Mike.

Huw walked over to the picture and gently picked it up. 'It's the boy's face. Ruined.' He leaned it against the altar and squatted down in front of it.

Mike followed him and peered over his shoulder. 'It's a lovely portrait of Evie. She looks so young and happy.'

'But Tony.' Lucy said sadly. 'Why is it always Tony he attacks?'

'This wasn't a ghost!' Mike said firmly. 'Don't try and tell me that. Someone has been in here.'

Huw was thoughtful. 'That is what we say each time this happens. But how did they get in? Where? The house was locked. We were here. Lucy was here.' He glanced round at his wife helplessly. 'Maggie, can you sense him? Can you sense anybody?'

Maggie had moved away from the others and was standing with her eyes closed, her hands held slightly in front of her as though she were testing the quality of the air. 'I can sense immense anger. If it was a thief they would have taken the picture which, if what you all say is true, is worth a good bit of money. This person has attacked the young man in the picture and been careful not to touch Evie. How, using such force, could he have been so discriminating?' She moved forward and gently ran her fingers over the tears in the painting. She shuddered. 'It's the same person, Huw, as at the gallery. I can almost see him. His fury and –' she hesitated, 'his jealousy are so strong. He is full of hatred.'

Lucy shuddered. 'Who is he?'

'It is Eddie Marston,' Maggie said quietly.

There was a stunned silence. Mike stared at her. 'What on earth makes you say that?'

'Hannah recognised him from a picture in your mother's dining room. She saw his ghost hovering near the paintings in their house in Midhurst.'

'Hannah?' Mike said quickly. 'When did you see Hannah?'

'This afternoon.'

'Christopher came to see me this evening,' Mike said. 'Hannah is missing. They are frantic about her.'

Maggie frowned. 'I understood they knew she was staying with your mother,' she said slowly. She sighed. 'I'll go and ring Juliette now, just to check what is going on.' She turned and left the room, leaving them standing in a semi-circle round the picture.

'I thought it would be safe in here,' Huw said, shaking his head. 'My prayers were not strong enough. I am so sorry. I failed.'

'It's not your fault!' Lucy cried. 'I won't hear of that. It is the fault of this malicious man; and mine for coming here. I shouldn't have brought the picture here.'

'If not here, Lucy, where else?' Huw said sadly.

The room was silent for a moment. 'My grandmother looks so very happy,' Mike said at last. He cleared his throat. 'You think this man was her lover?'

Lucy looked at him almost apologetically. Was there a resemblance there to the face which had been so viciously hacked about in the portrait? Without the photo she wasn't sure. 'Yes, I think he was. His name was Tony Anderson and he was stationed near Box Wood Farm. I don't know where she met him, perhaps through her brother, Ralph. But it didn't work out and later he was killed.'

'And she married my grandfather on the rebound?'

Lucy nodded. 'That's what it looks like. She was devastated when Tony died.'

Mike gently touched the torn margins of the canvas. 'Can this be repaired?'

'I am sure it can. It is just such a shame. The face had been painted out when Larry bought the painting. He was cleaning the canvas when he realised that something had been over-painted.' She looked at him pleadingly. 'The painting wasn't signed. It had no attribution in the auction. It has never been verified.'

'I recognise her,' Mike whispered.

She smiled sadly. 'You knew her. We didn't. Not then.'

'But you guessed. Your husband obviously thought he recognised it,' Mike said harshly.

She nodded again. 'He did, yes. He hoped it was a Lucas. It was looking her up, and trying to find out about her that made me want to write about her. She is one of the great women war artists, but somehow she had slipped out of sight. I submitted a plan for the book and applied for a grant and the acceptance came after Larry died.' There was a long pause. Lucy's face had fallen into an expression of intense sadness.

Mike cleared his throat uncomfortably.

'I still do not see why you chose to keep the fact that you had this picture from me.'

'Maybe I suspected that you would react the way your cousin did. Suspicious and resentful and attributing all kinds of horrible motives to me,' she snapped. 'I wasn't wrong, was I? That was exactly what happened. From the moment you knew it existed you suspected me of all that and more.' She took a deep breath, but it was too late to stop now. 'I am not planning to exploit Evie,' she cried. 'I want her recognised for her talent and her skill and her brilliance. I haven't stolen the painting. We bought it legitimately. I have the receipt!' For a moment she stared wildly from Mike to Huw, then for the second time, unable to confront him, she turned and ran out of the room.

June 1945

Tony was still in Egypt when VE day came. Shortly afterwards he returned to Britain, leaving Port Said for Toulouse and then Dieppe. He stayed a few days in London before heading back to Scotland. While he was in London he went to the National Gallery and there he had stood for a long time in front of a painting entitled *The Madonna of the Blitz*. He found himself lost in the picture, feeling the desolation, the anguish and the love of the mother for her child. He stood there so long, lost in the sadness of his dreams that he did not at first feel the touch of the woman's hand on his arm. He jumped, and looked at her, almost expecting it to be Evie. It wasn't. It was a middle-aged woman in a black suit with a small black velvet hat with a half veil. Her face was pale and tired but very kind.

'I saw the tears in your eyes,' she said gently. 'I am so sorry. You've lost someone you love.'

He nodded. What was the point in correcting her. After all, he had lost someone, and it was someone he had loved almost more than life itself. They walked together out into Trafalgar Square and strolled up the Strand to the Lyons Corner House where they had a cup of tea together. He never knew her name, or why she had been in the gallery. She too had lost someone, that was obvious, and for a couple of hours they kept one another company, then it was time for him to go.

He took the train north, heading back to his parents' farm and from there he was to restart his law studies in Edinburgh, no longer a Squadron Leader, just a student lawyer once again.

He graduated three years later and joined the Faculty of

Advocates as a rising star. If he thought about his times at Westhampnett, and his visit to the National Gallery in London he did not mention it to anyone, not even his parents. Why should he?

Saturday 14th September, midnight

Mike left the vicarage without seeing Lucy again. Sadly he climbed into his car and headed back to Rosebank Cottage. He couldn't get the image of the slashed face of the young pilot out of his head.

He was standing on the back lawn, staring up at the night sky when his phone rang suddenly. He groped for it in his pocket. 'Lucy?' He wasn't sure why he had thought it would be her. Not after the way she had run out of the room. Whatever he said to her it seemed to be the wrong thing, but he hoped he was right and that she was trying to make up for her hasty disappearance. In the chapel they had waited for a while, then Huw had gently placed the painting facing the wall and the two of them had walked slowly downstairs to meet Maggie. Minutes later Mike had made an embarrassed exit from the vicarage.

He paused now, waiting for her to reply, but the moment of silence was followed by a harsh laugh.

'No, sorry, not Lucy. It's Charlotte. I need to talk to you.'

Christmas 1947

Rachel was waiting for Evie in the kitchen at the farm when she came in.

'Hello, Mummy,' She greeted her mother. She gave Johnny a gentle push so that he ran on, heading straight for the biscuit tin on the table. 'What is it?' She had seen Rachel's face, which was pale and drawn. 'How is Daddy?'

'He is all right.' Rachel took a deep breath. 'I'm sorry, Evie, but I don't know how long we can go on like this. Eddie has gone too far this time.'

Evie was taking off her hat. She threw it down on the sideboard and turned to her mother with a sigh. 'What has he done now?'

'He's brought a baby.' Rachel sat down abruptly and ran her fingers through the tight greying curls of her hair. 'He says it is going to live here and that you have agreed.'

Evie stared at her 'A baby?'

'A child.'

For a moment, Evie was speechless for several seconds, then at last she said, 'Where is he?'

'He took it upstairs.'

'Keep Johnny down here.' Evie headed for the door, slamming it behind her before heading for the stairs.

'Come in. Don't say a word.' Eddie looked up at her as she walked into the bedroom.

The baby was lying on the bed asleep.

Evie looked down at him. 'That's Paul, I take it.' Her voice was harsh.

Eddie looked up. 'George. He's called George.'

She frowned. 'It is Lavinia's baby?' Her hands were shaking.

He nodded and she was astonished to see tears in his eyes. 'Lavinia is dying.' He bit his lip hard. 'They took her into hospital three days ago.' He sounded completely helpless. 'Her landlady was looking after George. She rang me and I went to see Lavinia.' There was a tremor in his voice. 'Her heart is failing. They said she only has a few days to live.' He swallowed hard. 'I told her I – we – would take the baby and rear him here. I promised her. She said she trusts you. She said you knew about him and you had been to see her. She said she gives you her blessing; she wants you to be his mother.' Again his voice trembled and then it failed altogether. He stood looking helplessly at the sleeping child on the bed. The little boy was wearing grubby pyjamas with teddy bears on them and he was wrapped tightly in a woollen blanket. He smelled of dirty nappy. 'Please, Evie.'

She stared at Eddie. She had never, in all the years she had known him, seen him so vulnerable.

She took a deep breath. 'Does she not have any relations?'

He shook his head. 'Her parents died before the war. Her brother was killed at Monte Cassino. I was the only one there for her, and I was cruel to her. I bullied her. But I loved him. From the first moment I saw him, I loved him.' His voice was husky.

Evie felt a sharp twinge of resentment. 'You bully me and Johnny,' she whispered. 'I doubt you would cry if I were to die; or give Johnny your love.'

He turned away from her and wandered over to the window. 'Johnny wasn't mine,' he said.

'And Paul is not mine.'

'Please, Evie. I can't make myself love Johnny. He reminds me that you loved his father as you have never loved me, but I will try, I promise I will try to treat him better. He will never know –' he paused and took a deep breath, 'he will never know that George is not his real brother. I will treat them the same.'

'Why do you want to call him George?'

'After my dad.' He held her gaze. 'Our family have never been close to one another. It would please my father so much.'

'And how are you going to explain the sudden arrival of a ready-made grandson?'

'I'll tell them the truth.'

'But no one else?'

He shook his head. 'If anyone asks, he is adopted. People will forget soon enough.'

'And my parents?'

'They will do whatever you want.'

'Will they?' Evie was thinking about Rachel and Johnny downstairs. *Eddie has gone too far this time.* Her mother's words echoed in her ears.

Sunday 15th September, morning

Charlotte was on the doorstep at Rosebank just after nine. Mike greeted her without enthusiasm. 'I don't know why you have come back. You are lucky that I didn't call the police after the stunt you pulled last time.

She pushed her hands into her pockets defiantly. 'Up to you. There are things I can tell you about your precious Evie. If you don't want to know –'

'What can you possibly tell me?'

'Dolly gave me some of her stuff. Her writing case.'

'*Dolly* did?' He stared at her. She was dressed in tight designer jeans and a loose-fitting silk blouse, low at the neck. Round her throat was the crystal necklace he had bought her for her birthday. She looked undeniably sexy. 'When?'

She dropped her gaze. 'A while ago. I was asking about Evie and Dolly told me I could look through her stuff and take anything I wanted.'

Mike narrowed his eyes suspiciously. 'I doubt that very much.'

'I don't frankly care what you doubt,' she said, her voice harsh. 'The fact is, I've got it.'

'So where is it, this case?'

'At home. I wasn't going to bring it here and have you take it off me by force.'

He sighed. 'I have never used force against you, and you know it.'

She smiled and pushed past him. 'So, where is the lovely Lucy?'

'She is not here. Charlotte, if you have something of Evie's I would like you to return it. It could be important.'

'It is important.' She glanced into the sitting room and headed towards the kitchen. 'Are you living here? I have been to the London house several times and there has been no sign of you.'

'You've been in?'

She gave that sweet smile again. 'You gave me a key, darling, remember?'

'Which I took off you. Did you have a copy made?' He let his disgust show in his voice.

She ignored the question. 'I rang the office and they said you were taking some leave and working from home. They seemed astonished that I didn't know. I had to pretend to have a failing memory.'

In the kitchen she looked round critically. 'No tidier than I remember and no cleaner.' She ran a finger over the surface of the table. 'It's time you sacked Dolly. She is completely past it.'

Mike gritted his teeth. 'Charlotte –'

She opened the back door and stepped outside, staring at the studio. 'The damage isn't too bad, is it, considering?' She turned to face him. 'Mike, I think you should consider your next move very carefully. I have the capability to do you and your research worker,' her voice dripped with venom, 'a lot of harm. I have items which probably have a great deal of value, some of which would burn oh so easily, some, jewellery, which I could sell down the Portobello Market for a fortune, some sketches which I gather are irreplaceable. Did you really think I sat around here knitting while you and Miss Lucy were chatting over Evie's pathetic scraps? You thought there was nothing there, didn't you. Had you even bothered to look? There was a mass of stuff lying around in drawers and boxes, clogging up this house. I put a lot of it in the studio and then I thought, why am I doing this? Why don't I take some of it home if it is so valuable? I remember you telling me she had no jewellery. She did. She had a lot of lovely stuff and now, as you didn't even know you had it, and as you could never identify it, it is mine.' She put her hands on her hips and waited for him to say something.

He took a deep breath. 'Charley –'

'Oh, *Charley* is it now? Do I sense a change of tone?' Her eyes narrowed. 'So, where is Lucy?'

'She is not here. That is all you need to know at the moment.'

She eyed him with amusement. 'So, you finally saw through her.'

476

'My relationship with Lucy is none of your business. The important thing is that ours is over, Charley.' His exasperation was obvious in his voice. 'If there was ever a chance of picking it up again after what you did, you have scuppered it now. This attempt at blackmail is pathetic.' He began to walk across the lawn. 'If you have property of mine I would like you to return it. My guess is that you've made all this up.'

She stood and watched him head towards the tool shed at the top of the garden. 'Made it up, have I?' she whispered under her breath. 'I'll show you, Michael Marston.'

He watched as she made her way back into the house in an agony of terror that she might do something else to destroy his home but he managed to force himself to wait ten minutes before strolling back towards the kitchen. She had gone and as far as he could see all was as it should be; to convince himself he opened the front door and, after scanning the lane, actually walked up a little way up it to make sure that her car had gone, then he went back indoors and rang Dolly.

'Are you accusing me of something?' He heard the indignation and hurt in her voice as soon as he explained why he was ringing.

'No,' he said wearily. 'I didn't believe her, but I had to be sure. You might have said something she misinterpreted, or you might have seen her take something which she said I had given her. She has been, is, very manipulative. You were right, Dolly. You were a far better judge of character than I was.'

There was a pause. 'I am glad you recognised the fact,' Dolly said at last, obviously mollified.

He gave a wry smile. 'So, what do I do?'

There was a short silence. 'You believe that she has stolen things from the house?'

Stolen? The word brought him up short. 'I suppose I do, yes,' he said. 'She talked about a writing case. I don't remember a writing case.'

Dolly made a noise which might have been a laugh. 'It used to sit on top of Evie's wardrobe.'

477

'And when did it go, can you remember?'

'A couple of weeks ago. I was going to give it to Lucy if it had papers in and when I went to fetch it down it had gone. I assumed you had already given it to her.'

Mike grimaced. 'If only I had.'

'So you are regretting telling her to go away.' She sounded smug.

'I don't know what I am feeling, Dolly. I don't know what to do.' He found himself wishing suddenly that it was one of Dolly's days, that she would arrive soon and make them both tea and produce some homemade biscuits from her tin on the dresser. He gave a bitter little laugh. 'I am not doing very well with women, am I?'

'Go and see Lucy, Michael,' Dolly said firmly. 'Today. Now.'

29

Sunday 15th September, afternoon

Hannah went home meekly when Christopher arrived to collect her and the expected row had not ensued. He was too relieved to see her safe and well, but as they drove up the drive to Cornstone House everything changed.

'I am not going back in there!' Hannah was sitting in the front seat of her father's car, peering through the windscreen in sudden complete terror. 'You can't make me.'

'Hannah, darling, there is nothing to be afraid of.' Christopher turned off the engine and withdrew the keys, jiggling them up and down in the palm of his hand. 'I am going to be there with you.'

Hannah shook her head. She buried her face in her hands, her hair hanging down over her shoulders. 'I can't go in, I can't!' she whispered.

Christopher sighed. He reached for the handle and pushed his door open. 'I'll go and find your mother. Perhaps she can make you see sense.' He climbed out of the car and ran up the steps into the house.

Hannah closed her eyes. She was trembling.

It was a long time before her mother appeared. Ollie was with her.

'Darling –'

'No!' Hannah cried. 'I can't. I can't go in.' She had clenched her fists so tightly her nails had dug into her palms. 'I don't want to go in there ever again.'

Frances glanced at Ollie helplessly. He pushed past her and crouched by the car window. 'Listen, Hanny. Why don't you and I go back to Granny's at least until Grandfather's funeral? Would that make you feel better? Could we, Mum? She can take us back to school and that will give you and Dad a chance to get the house exorcised or something.'

Hannah still hadn't looked up but he could see by the tense-ness of her shoulders that she was listening.

'Would you like to do that, Hanny?' It was a long time since he had called her by her baby name. 'Mum can pack your stuff. You needn't go back in. You would drive us back to Scotland, wouldn't you, Mum? Or we could go by train –'

'I'll drive you,' Frances broke in. She turned back to the house. 'Wait there with Hannah. I will go and speak to your father.'

Hannah was persuaded to get out of her father's car and agreed to walk down into the village where she waited for them in a coffee shop while the arrangements were made and at last Frances appeared with Ollie beside her. Her car was loaded with all their school gear as well as holiday clothes. Hannah smiled weakly at her mother as she joined them and climbed into the back seat. 'I am sorry to be such a coward.'

'You are not a coward, Hannah,' Frances said firmly. She peered into the mirror, shocked at the paleness of her daughter's face. 'It was very brave of you to do what you did to try and get rid of –' she paused, at a loss for a moment as to how to describe him, 'the man in the attic. I would never have dared do all that. Your father will deal with it. Just look on this as a lovely extension to your holiday.' She paused. 'And a holiday for me too. I think I will stay up north for a while. It is such a long way I might as well take the chance to have a break myself.' Turning on the engine she pretended she didn't see Ollie turn to look at his sister and raise his thumb at her with an expression of relieved triumph.

January 1948

'You are not telling me that you are going to adopt that child?' Rachel stared at her daughter incredulously.

Evie was wiping George's face with a damp flannel after giving him his breakfast. She glanced up at her mother, her face white with exhaustion. 'His mother has died, Mummy. He has no one and he is Eddie's son. What do you expect me to do?'

Johnny was sitting at the table drawing. Every now and then he sent a puzzled look towards the little boy sitting at the other end of the table. 'Is George my brother now?' he asked at last.

'Yes, darling.' Evie bent over him and gave him a kiss. 'Lots of your friends have got brothers. When he is a bit bigger he will be someone to play with.'

'How old is he?' Rachel asked as she hung a dishcloth near the range.

'He's two. I'm not sure when his birthday is. I went to see him when he was a baby. His mother was a nice woman, Mummy. It wasn't her fault that the men in her life had let her down.'

'It is always the woman's fault.' Rachel sniffed. 'If you have an affair with a married man, what can you expect?'

There was no reply.

Rachel sighed. 'Well, I can tell you now, your father is not happy. He does not want that child in this house.'

'Then we'll have to leave.' Evie's temper was rising. 'I think

481

I've made enough sacrifices for Daddy over the years. It is time for him to make one for me. If he can't support me over this, it is better that we move out.'

'Maybe it's better that way anyway,' Rachel said after a long pause. 'You don't seem to realise, Evie, how ill your father is. Having one child careering round the house is almost too much for him. Two children would kill him.'

'I thought Daddy loved Johnny,' Evie said quietly. Her father had been ill for so long she no longer reacted to her mother's threats. If he was at death's door, he had been lingering there for years now. Another shock would not make any difference as far as she could see.

'He does love Johnny. But he is ill,' Rachel protested again, almost automatically. 'He is getting tired.' Her eyes flooded suddenly with tears. 'Just think about it, darling. Look for somewhere else, please.'

Evie broached the subject with Eddie that evening when he came back from London where he was setting up an exhibition of southern artists, one of whom was of course Evie. To her astonishment he greeted the news with alacrity.

'About time. I thought you wanted to stay here forever. It will suit me far better to move to London. I will start looking for somewhere at once.'

'London?' Evie looked at him aghast. 'Not London. I couldn't bear to live in London.'

'It will be good for your career,' was his only reply. 'And it will be good to make a new start for all sorts of reasons.'

One of the reasons, it turned out, was George. On the eve of their eventual move Eddie handed Evie an envelope. In it was a birth certificate for George Edward Marston. She stared at it. 'But the adoption papers?'

'There will be no adoption. Why should we adopt our own child?'

'This is a forgery?'

He smiled. 'Good, isn't it? No one will ever know.'

'I will know.'

His smile faded. 'But you are never going to tell anyone, are you?'

The new house was near Hampstead Heath. It had belonged to another artist and had a glorious studio for Evie. The money came from Eddie's parents, who had sold up their farm after the war and retired to Bexhill.

To Evie's distress only two years after they had moved her father died. Eddie refused to go to the funeral. 'Why should I? The old curmudgeon as good as threw us out of the house.' So, Evie went alone with Johnny, leaving George with his father. It was on the train that Johnny turned to her and asked when George was going back to his own mummy.

Evie froze. 'What do you mean?'

'He's not my brother. I know you said he was, but when I asked her, Grandma told me he wasn't really. I remember when he came to live with us. You said it was to keep me company but I don't like him.'

Evie shrank back into the train seat, overcome with horror. It had never occurred to her that her own mother would betray them. Luckily they were alone in their compartment. She put her arm round him and gave him a hug. 'Grandma made a mistake, Johnny. George is your brother now. He is always going to live with us, darling. Why on earth don't you like him?'

'Daddy loves him much more than me.' The boy's mouth turned down.

Evie sighed. 'It only seems that way because George is younger. Younger brothers and sisters always seem to get more attention but it's usually because they are naughtier. As George grows older Daddy will love you both the same, you'll see.'

Going back to Box Wood Farm was agony for Evie, and for Johnny too, she realised. She shouldn't have brought him. This was her home. The Downs were in her blood. Hampstead might be right in so many ways, but it wasn't home. She said nothing to her mother about her revelations to Johnny; she doubted anyway if her mother would have listened. She was a shadow of herself, drawn and grey-faced, talking incessantly about Ralph, convinced that the report of his death had been a mistake, that one day he would return to the farm and take it over and that she would be there to meet him however long she had to wait.

'But, Mummy,' Evie said, when the last of the mourners had departed and she and her mother were clearing up the table in the living room they had so seldom used in the past. 'You can't run the farm on your own.'

'It's your farm now. Daddy left it in trust for you and Ralph,' Rachel said. There were streaks in her face powder from her tears. 'He said to get in a manager for you so when you came to your senses and left that dreadful man you could come back and keep it going. Please, darling, come home.' Her eyes flooded with tears again.

She couldn't, of course. For one glorious moment Evie thought about doing it. Staying here, cancelling the taxi back to the station, ringing Eddie and telling him she had left him and was never coming back. Her father was dead. Eddie no longer had any hold over him. Then she thought about George. George was Eddie's son in every way as far as looks went, but in other ways he was nothing like him. He was a delicate, sensitive child, easily hurt by his father's shouting, hiding from him whenever he could, following her around with adoring eyes fixed on her face. How could she abandon him? With a sigh she kissed her mother and told her she would consult a local agent to find a manager for the farm and she promised to come back in the summer.

To all intents and purposes they settled down in Hampstead relatively happily. The two boys were sent to school nearby and Evie painted a series of pictures of Hampstead Heath which were exhibited to great acclaim. It was after her third sale of a large expensive painting that the trouble started. 'It is my money,

Eddie. It is only right that I receive it.' She had found the receipt book on his desk.

He snatched it from her, threw it into a drawer and locked it. 'This is nothing to do with you.'

'But it is. It said clearly that it was my picture of Keats House.' She clenched her fists. 'This has gone on long enough. You have pocketed my earnings for years, Eddie, and it has to stop.'

He laughed. 'I don't think so. I think you will find that you signed your earnings over to me as your agent. I have the document, if you don't believe me. Your job, my sweet, is to paint for me. In return I house you and feed you and look after your brat of a son.'

She went white. 'When did I sign such a thing?'

'On the 20th September 1940, the day you had your first commission from the WAAC.'

'But I signed something for them.' She stared at him aghast.

'If you think back you signed two documents. In your excitement you read neither.'

'I was only nineteen.'

'Old enough, I think you'll find.' He walked over to the fireplace and reached onto the mantelpiece for his pipe. 'We have a nice home here, Evie, and two presentable sons. Don't rock the boat.' He reached into his pocket and produced his wallet. Opening it he peeled two fifty-pound notes off the wad of cash and handed them to her. 'There. Buy yourself something pretty with that. You are right. You have worked very hard and you deserve a reward.'

Barely able to contain her fury she snatched the notes from him, tore them in half, threw them at his feet and stormed out of the room.

Monday 16th September, early morning

At the bottom of the last damp cardboard box she had brought over from Rosebank Lucy found another notebook which, as

485

she eagerly extricated it from the surrounding foxed papers and gingerly prised open the pages, proved to be another diary. Evie's writing was cramped now, less exuberant than usual, but she had entered in great detail over several months the happenings of her daily life with her sons. Then came the surprise.

July 1953

'Evie!' Her mother's voice was shrill on the telephone. 'Are you there, darling? Listen. I've seen Ralph!'

Evie sat down, her heart sinking. 'Mummy –'

'No, I know what you are going to say. But I did see him. I was walking across the yard and he flew over. I stood looking up. It was his plane, I know it was. I waved . . .' Her voice died away. 'You think it was someone else, don't you?'

'Mummy, it can't be Ralph, you know it can't.' Evie tried to keep her voice level. At least this time there was a plane. The last time Rachel had rung in the middle of the night she thought she had seen him in the kitchen. 'He was standing there looking at me, Evie, with his lovely smile. He held out his hand and then . . .'

Then she had burst into tears.

'Would you like me to come down and see you, Mummy? It's holidays. I could bring the boys for a few days. You enjoy it when they come down, don't you?'

She waited for the inevitable hesitation and then when it came, the caveat that followed, 'I don't think you should bring George, darling. This is not his real home. He won't feel comfortable here.'

'He loves the farm, Mummy, you know he does.' Usually if she was firm it would be all right. Once or twice her mother had put her foot down and Evie had refused to go without the boy she thought of as her younger son. He would always be her younger son. She loved him absolutely and completely, as much as she loved Johnny. There was always a risk in taking him, of course, that one day her mother would tell George that he had been adopted but somehow it had never happened and usually when they arrived the two boys ran outside and were hardly seen in the house at all. When they were there Rachel treated them both the same with lavish supplies of homemade cakes and biscuits, and Evie suspected she forgot her reservations in the joy of having the house full again.

As she had suspected, Eddie showed no interest at all in where they were going or for how long. Evie had her own car now, a Ford Popular which was all she could afford. Eddie had grudgingly given her a little towards it with a scathing remark about women drivers but other than that he had made no objection to her having a car of her own so she had kept quiet and revelled in her new-found freedom.

She loaded the suitcases, put the two boys in the back and set off one glorious morning. Besides packing their clothes she had smuggled in a selection of paints and sketchbooks. Her old easel was still at the farm in her attic studio. Down there, in the place she still thought of as home, she could paint to her heart's content and any pictures she thought good enough to keep would be secreted away somewhere Eddie would never find them. Or sell them. When she had finally met David Fuller after the war they had become good friends. Without her having to say a word he seemed to understand that any deals he made with her were of no concern to anyone else. She adored the old couple and their gallery and never failed to visit them when she was down at Box Wood Farm. They would provide her with cake and Chichester gossip and when she left David would sometimes slip her an envelope with a wink and then a warm hug. Those holiday visits gave her more money than she had ever dreamed possible and it was her very own.

The boys grew brown and fit running around the fields. It was down here in Sussex that they seemed to get on best together. There was no Eddie to set them up against each other; Johnny forgot that he was the elder. He forgot his resentment of his younger brother and seemed to enjoy his company. They borrowed ponies from a neighbour of Rachel's and rode up on the Downs with picnics strapped to their saddles, leaving Evie to paint and talk to her mother alone.

Rachel was growing very thin. From time to time her wild cries and frenzied excitement terrified Evie, but the boys seemed to take her moods in their stride – it was, after all, the way they remembered her.

It was on a humid day in August, when another neighbour had taken the boys off to a funfair in the next village, Evie was upstairs in the attic, painting a wild thundery sky much like the one she could see outside the attic window. She was enjoying herself, dressed in a cotton shirt and slacks, her hair, short now and curly, at this moment tinged with vivid blue streaks from where she had pushed it back from her face with paint-stained fingers. She was standing back to study the painting when she heard her mother's cries from downstairs. Dropping her brush she turned towards the door.

'Ralph, Ralph, please, darling, wait!' Rachel's voice floated up the stairs as Evie began to run down. 'My darling, wait for me.'

'Mummy?' Evie ran into the kitchen. 'Are you all right?'

'He was here again.' Rachel was standing by the table, tears pouring down her cheeks. 'Oh, Evie, why won't he wait and talk to me?'

Evie put her arms round her mother and hugged her, horrified at how thin she had grown. 'I don't know why,' she whispered.

'He wants to tell me something. I can sense his unhappiness. He can't rest.' Rachel looked up at Evie, her eyes still brimming with tears.

Evie sighed. 'There is nothing we can do, Mummy. We have to let him go.'

'But that's the point!' Rachel pulled away from her angrily. 'Don't you understand? He can't go! Not till he has told us what it is that is making him so unhappy.' She turned and walked out of the kitchen.

Evie stood for a long time lost in thought, then at last she turned towards the door. Ralph was standing near the table looking straight at her.

Lucy read the whole extract again, then she pushed the diary away and sat staring at the wall. So Ralph was haunting Box Wood Farm even then.

Monday 16th September, mid-morning

Lucy had been hard at work for another couple of hours when the doorbell rang. She sat back from the computer and listened. Huw and Maggie had gone out early and she wasn't sure if they were back yet. The bell rang again and she pushed back her chair and stood up.

Mike was standing on the step, his back to the door, staring up into a tree. She was tempted to slam the door before he turned round but it was too late. He swung to face her and she saw the look of astonishment in his face. 'I thought you would have gone back to the gallery by now.'

'Sorry to disappoint you.'

'No, no, Lucy, I'm sorry. That came out wrong. I was hoping to see you, but I wanted to consult Huw and Maggie as how best to do it. Now I'm all unprepared.' He gave her a nervous smile. 'I owe you an apology. A big one.'

She looked surprised. 'No. I was in the wrong. I didn't trust you and that was unforgivable.'

'Can we go back to the beginning?'

She smiled. 'I would like that very much.'

'Good. If I went home without us making up Dolly would

probably kill me. She says I am a lousy judge of character, which brings me to my next problem. Charlotte.'

'Do you believe her?' They were walking round the garden in the soft autumn sunshine as he told her Charlotte's latest threat. 'If I'm honest, I think I do. Dolly remembers the writing case. She thought I had given it to you. I don't remember ever noticing it. What worries me is that if it was in the bedroom, maybe it had particularly important things in it. I can't imagine how Christopher missed it.'

'And it might contain more recent information. I think I have a grip on Evie's life up until she and Eddie moved to London. George told me a bit about it, but I feel there is a huge gap. There are so few paintings from that period. Where did they go? She sold some through David Fuller, I gather, and they presumably disappeared into the open market, but I wonder if when she was back in London she stopped painting altogether. I gather from one or two letters she had never wanted to move from Sussex. The Downs were her muse. And if she was having problems with Eddie and his reluctance to give her any money perhaps she went on strike.'

'She's always been known as a Sussex painter, that is true,' Mike said thoughtfully, 'though she seems to have painted Hampstead when they lived there.'

There was an awkward pause. 'Hannah has gone home, by the way. Did you know?' Lucy said after the silence had drawn out uncomfortably long. 'She ran away from home because she saw a ghost in the attic of their house. It was hanging around some of Evie's paintings that Christopher had stored up there, and, Mike, she recognised who it was. Your mother has a picture of Eddie in her dining room and apparently Hannah completely freaked out when she saw it.' She glanced over her shoulder towards the house and dropped her voice as if she could be overheard. 'She was terrified.'

'The ghost is Eddie? My grandfather? I did wonder when

you mentioned before that he seemed so angry.' He paused for a moment, looking confused. 'I thought you'd said the ghost was Ralph.'

'It is,' she said. 'But the other ghost, the angry ghost, no, I've never seen him. I just feel him. See what he does. I don't think I've seen a clear picture of him. Quite a few old photos but none close up. I want to go and see your mother's portrait. Do you think she would mind? Did Evie paint it?'

'I don't know. I'm not sure I can remember it, to be honest.' He thought for a moment. 'Do you want to go over there and see?'

'Now?'

'If you like. I want to get this sorted, Lucy. The whole thing is getting to me.' He ran his fingers through his hair. 'I've never seen a ghost at Rosebank. I keep telling myself that. It's as if Evie's presence is too strong. She's not a ghost. She died peacefully, as far as I know, but I do sometimes think she is still there, keeping it all safe.'

'Even when the studio caught fire,' Lucy agreed. 'It could have been so much worse.'

They went in his car. Forewarned by a phone call, Juliette was waiting for them and apart from a quick glance at them both as if to reassure herself that they were not about to kill each other, she refrained from saying anything about the last time they had all met in her house. She led the way inside.

'Christopher came and collected Hannah,' she said over her shoulder. 'I phoned them as soon as I realised she hadn't told them where she was.'

'I hope he wasn't too angry with her,' Lucy said with a shiver.

'No. Surprisingly not.'

'Did you show him the picture?'

Juliette nodded. 'He was very shaken by the whole thing. Hannah disappearing like that had really rattled him. He stared at it for a long time. He was very white about the gills and tight-lipped but he didn't say anything. He just turned round and walked out of the room.'

'You didn't ask?' Mike was incredulous.

'Don't forget Hannah was standing there,' Juliette said defen-sively. 'I didn't want to upset her any more than she was already.'

'Can I see the picture?' Lucy asked.

Without a word Juliette walked along the passage and opened the door into her dining room. She stood back and ushered them in. She didn't follow them. Lucy and Mike stood side by side looking at the painting. It wasn't large, about thirty centi-metres by twenty or so, a pen and ink sketch with a sepia wash to shade it.

'That's Evie's work,' Lucy said at once. 'I recognise her style.'

Mike walked over and took it off the wall. He carried it to the window. 'It is very good, isn't it? I do recognise him. I was about thirteen when he died.'

'What do you remember about him?'

'Are you going to take notes?'

Lucy stepped back, surprised by the sharpness of his tone. 'I probably should,' she said as gently as she could. 'It is part of Evie's story.'

'I'm sorry.' He put the picture down on the table and rubbed his hands on the seat of his trousers with a shiver. 'He wasn't a very child-friendly person, as I remember. I avoided him. We hardly saw him because of course he and Evie were divorced long before I was born, but he came to Rosebank once or twice when we were there. It must have been to family parties.' He thought for a moment then shook his head. 'That doesn't sound likely, does it? I don't know, although –' He paused again. 'Once, I remember there was a row going on. He and Evie were shouting at each other. He wanted to go into her studio and she wouldn't let him.' He looked up. 'That was it. He wanted to go and look at her paintings and she said no. They were screaming at each other and Mummy dragged me away. I remember we walked down the lane and we didn't go back until his car had gone. He drove a huge Mercedes, which rather impressed me. I hoped to have a ride in it, but that was, I think, the last time I saw him.'

They stood looking down at the face in the portrait before them. It was Lucy's turn to shiver. His eyes appeared to follow her even when she stepped away from the table. They were a hard brilliant slate colour as far as she could see, all seeing and all knowing.

As they stood there Mike's mobile rang. He pulled it out of his pocket, glanced at it and switched it off. 'Charlotte,' he said. He glanced at Lucy. 'I think it would be a good thing if you avoided seeing her on your own at the moment.'

'I don't intend to see her at all if I can help it,' Lucy retorted.

'Good.' With a sigh he turned away from the table and headed back towards the door. 'So, what am I going to do about this writing case?'

They went into the kitchen where Juliette made a jug of coffee. She produced a plate of flapjacks. 'I never liked that woman,' she said succinctly. 'Of course I could never say anything to you, Mike, but really!'

He gave a surprised laugh. 'Not like you to hold back on your views.'

'No. But with one's son's girlfriends one has to be tactful.' She sat down at the small table in the window and leaned forward on her elbows, pushing her bracelets up her arms with a rattle. The other two sat down opposite each other. Outside the garden was misted with rain. 'So, what do you make of the picture?' Juliette changed the subject.

Mike glanced at Lucy and shook his head. 'Did Dad ever say anything about it?'

'No. He didn't get on with his father very well, as you know. I sometimes used to think Eddie actually hated him. It was so sad. That picture was never hung while Johnny was alive. I found it in a box when I moved in here with Bill. I could see it was a fine portrait and I guessed Evie did it.'

'Do you remember the time at Rosebank Cottage when he came over and wanted Evie to let him into the studio?' Mike said thoughtfully. He picked up a flapjack and took a bite.

Juliette nodded. 'I believe he used to ring her up from time to time and try and browbeat her into giving him any paintings she had done. He claimed he had a right to them. She wouldn't, of course, and I don't think she was frightened of him, I don't think Evie was frightened of anyone, but he used to swear at her terribly, so Johnny told me. He only actually turned up in person once when I was there.'

'I remember it vividly. I think that was the last time I saw him except –' Mike broke off suddenly with an expression of horror on his face. 'At his funeral. Oh my God! I saw him at his funeral. I remember now. We were at the front in the church in Hampstead. Evie had insisted he should be cremated but George and Chris wanted him to have a memorial service first. His coffin was there in front of the altar and it must have been the first funeral I'd been to?' He glanced at his mother for confirmation. 'It gave me the creeps to think of his body there, so near us, and then I looked up and I saw him standing there on the far side of the coffin and he was looking straight at me and Dad. I can remember it clearly now. He had this sort of sardonic smile on his face and he could obviously see us and I nearly freaked out. But I was too afraid of all the people behind us to make a fuss. There were a lot of people at the service, and you didn't seem to see anything, Mum, and nor did Granny.

'I remember thinking, he's not dead. The coffin is empty, and then as I watched he sort of faded away.' He exhaled loudly. 'Oh my God, he was a ghost even then, wasn't he? I don't know if I twigged. I don't think so. We went to the crematorium and I don't think I saw him in there, I was too horrified by the coffin disappearing and imagining it going into the flames and then we went and had tea somewhere and I put it out of my mind.' He shook his head. 'To think, I didn't believe in ghosts until all this happened! What rational person does?' He shook his head and exhaled loudly. 'And now –' He didn't finish the sentence.

July 1956

Evie was staring round her studio. The picture on the easel was half-finished, a bright sketch using acrylic paints, with which she had begun to experiment, of Christ Church, the sun reflecting off its green spire, the women in Church Row wearing gaudy summer dresses, some of them with parasols. She walked over to it and then turned to survey the room. Two or three paintings which had been standing, face to the wall, had gone. She stared at the space where they had been and then looked again to be sure, then she went to find Eddie.

He was sitting at the kitchen table with a copy of *The Times* spread out in front of him as he finished his breakfast coffee. He looked up as she came in and narrowed his eyes, folding the newspaper and pushing it away. 'So? What is it now?'

'My pictures. The two of Hampstead pond, the large one of the dog walkers. They've gone.'

'They fetched good prices. You should be pleased.'

She stared at him with such a wave of dislike and anger she was for a moment unable to speak. 'They weren't ready to go, Eddie. They hadn't had time for the paint to harden.'

'I told the buyer. He was quite happy to make sure they would be hung carefully.'

'And it didn't occur to you to ask me if I wanted them sold?'

He gave an exaggerated sigh. 'We've been through this so often. They are my paintings to dispose of as I see fit, Evie. Your job is to produce them.' Pushing back the chair he stood up, folding his glasses and slipping them into his breast pocket.

She watched him dispassionately. 'One day, Eddie, I will stop painting.'

'And then I will throw out your son. I spend a lot of money on his school fees.'

'My money.'

He gave a sarcastic laugh. 'Would you care to debate that point in court? I have a contract which says that all you paint is to be handled by me. And anyway, you are my wife.'

Walking silently back into her studio she closed the door behind her, then reaching for a tin of red poster paint, left on her table by George, who had been painting something for school, she hurled it across the room. The lid flew off as it hit the wall and the paint ran down the white surface like a streak of curdling blood.

30

Tuesday 17th September

It was ten o'clock at night when Mike rang Charlotte's doorbell. He waited several minutes before he rang it again then he reached into his pocket for her keys; she had obviously forgotten that she had given them to him or she would have demanded them back. He pushed open her front door and peered into the hall. The flat was quiet, the lights off. Of course she could have gone to bed early but the flat felt empty. 'Charlotte?' he called warily. 'Are you there?'

There was no reply.

'Charlotte?' He walked in and closed the door quietly behind him, then he reached for the light switch.

There was no sign of her anywhere; her bedroom felt unused. As he stood in the doorway looking round he noted the bare dressing table top, the faint layer of dust on the shelves, the cupboards slightly open. He moved towards them and looked inside. There were some clothes there but the vast majority had gone. The bathroom was the same, no toothbrush, no cosmetics, only one towel, dry and faintly sweaty. So where was she? He moved into the living room and it was here he began to hunt in earnest for the writing case, going through every cupboard, scrutinising every corner, hunting every possible place it could be. He moved on to the kitchen area, again opening all the cupboards and it was there at last he discovered the small brown leather case in the back of a saucepan drawer draped with a tea towel. He paused for a moment and listened carefully, but the flat was still silent and empty. Lifting it out he put it on the worktop and tried to open it. It was locked. He could just make out the initials E.L. under the handle, between the locks. Evie Lucas. Presumably Charlotte hadn't managed to open it either, and to his relief she had not forced it. Absent-mindedly he dusted it with the teacloth, then he lifted it and gently he shook it. He could feel whatever was inside shifting from side to side. It was quite heavy, so presumably it was full of papers. With a sigh of relief he looked round one last time, wondering where she was. It didn't look as though she had been at home for a while. Perhaps she was staying with her father; his flat in Kensington had always been her bolthole when she was upset or worried or felt herself in need of a little TLC. Her widowed father's uncritical worship of his daughter was, in Mike's opinion, way over the top. She had only to ask for something and Daddy would provide it. Well, if that was where she was, good luck to the man. Mike turned off all the lights and went back to the front door. Locking it behind him he was about to put her keys through the letterbox but he hesitated. If he did that she would know he had been there and how he had got in. He needed to keep the option of prevarication ready for the outraged phone call he would receive as soon as she discovered that the case had gone. With a grim smile he ran down the stairs and let himself out onto the street. There he made his way quickly round the corner and out of sight. Only when he was several streets away did he hail a cab.

He rang Lucy at once. 'I've got it. She wasn't there so I let myself in and found it.'

'What's in it?' She sounded excited.

'It's locked.'

'So, where are your Boy Scout skills? Surely you can pick a lock?'

He laughed. 'I'll wait till I get home. In fact perhaps I'll wait till the weekend and come down. We can do it together.'

He heard the slight hesitation before she replied, 'That would be great. I would like that.' There was a note of caution in her voice. As far as he knew she hadn't been back to Rosebank Cottage since he had seen her in Brighton the week before. She had said she had so much to get on with that she didn't need to go there at the moment, but he couldn't help wondering if, in spite of their new rapprochement, he had scared her away. He squinted out of the cab window. They were nearly back in Bloomsbury.

As the taxi drew up he put the case under his arm, paid the driver and stepped out onto the pavement. It was only as he was walking up the steps to the front door that he realised there was a light on in his front room and someone was standing in the window looking out.

June 1957

Evie's studio in Hampstead had been ransacked. She stood in the doorway and stared at the room in complete shock. The walls were bare, the easel, on which she had left an almost completed picture of the church, was leaning against the wall without a sign of the large canvas which had adorned it. Her sketchbooks and notepads were gone, the table on which they were spread out, empty but for several trays on which had been laid all her paints and chalks and inks.

Behind her the house was silent. Eddie and the boys were out. Dazed, she walked slowly back downstairs. The rest of the house was as it always was, tidy, clean, thanks to the administrations of whoever the latest charwoman was. They never stayed long; Eddie paid the minimum and was not particularly appreciative of their hard work. One after another the women had gone, leaving Evie alone again in the huge house.

She walked slowly round from room to room. Only the boys' bedrooms looked normal, untidy, bright, full of their possessions. She sat down miserably on Johnny's bed and wondered what on earth she could do. Her studio, the one room in the house which was indubitably hers, where she felt at home and safe, was safe no longer. He had not only taken the finished canvasses, he had taken her private notepads, her sketches, her very thoughts from the drawer of her desk. He had taken the last remnants of her private life, the contents of her head and her heart. For one thing she was glad. She had left behind the paintings she had done at Box Wood Farm. They were safe there in her old studio, out of Eddie's reach.

When he returned she was conscious of his hard gaze following her as she prepared the supper, aware that he was waiting for her to explode with anger. It wasn't until the boys had gone up to their rooms that she spoke.

'I am going to leave you, Eddie.'

For a moment he looked astonished then he burst out laughing. 'I don't think so.'

'You can't stop me.'

'I can stop you taking my sons.'

'Johnny isn't your son.'

'And does he know that? Does anyone?' He reached into his pocket for his tobacco pouch. 'Face it, Evie, you will be going nowhere. I suggest that, instead of making these futile threats, you go upstairs and start painting. Your stock seems lamentably low.'

In Box Wood Farm that same evening Rachel slowly climbed the stairs to Evie's studio and stood looking round. This room, in the whole, empty farmhouse felt warm and loved. Evie had left several of her paintings behind, hanging in an uneven line on the attic beams. There were two of Johnny, growing ever taller now, and the image of his handsome father, another of the two boys together and several sketches of George. Rachel studied them carefully. She knew Evie had grown to love the boy and she could see the fact in every stroke of the brush and pencil. There was very little of his father in his face, she noted. He must have taken after his mother. She would of course have been good-looking, otherwise Eddie would never have looked at her.

She wandered slowly round the studio, trailing her fingers over the table, staring out of the high window towards the Downs where the evening light was turning the fields to deep green velvet shadow. It was a long time before she walked slowly down the stairs and, as she did every night, went into Ralph's bedroom. Evie had wanted it for Johnny when they all lived together but Rachel had refused. The room was as it had been the last time her son had walked out of its door, a curious mixture of schoolboy's haven and young man's retreat. She felt closer to him here than anywhere else in the house. She sat on the bed and stretched out her hand to touch the bedspread. 'Are you there, Rafie?' She flinched as the pain in her chest returned. Somehow she had managed to keep it from Evie. It didn't matter. The doctor had told her it was her heart and if it meant she would one of these days drop dead just as Dudley had done, well and good. Then at last she would be with Ralph. She smiled up at him as he appeared before her. 'I knew you would come,' she whispered.

He stood looking down at her, his face full of compassion.

Where did you put the letters?

He had asked her that before. She didn't know what letters he was talking about. *The letter for Evie. The ring.*

It was hard for him to talk but this time she understood him perfectly. 'What ring?'

Tony's ring. For Evie. Where did you put it?

She shook her head wearily. 'I don't know anything about a ring, Rafie.'

501

But he had gone.

She lay back on his pillow and sighed. Sleep would come soon and in the morning another day to be got through.

Tuesday 17th September

The doorbell rang a second time and with a sigh Christopher went to answer it. He pulled open the front door, coming face to face with two men he did not recognise. They pulled out ID cards.

'Christopher Marston?' the elder asked. There was a slightly sinister edge to his tone. 'I am Detective Inspector Pulman and this is Detective Sergeant Wells. I wonder if we could have a word.'

Christopher looked from one to the other coldly. 'Is this about my father?'

'No, sir. This is another matter.' Inspector Pulman took a step forward and Christopher found himself moving backwards. With a loud sigh he turned and led the way into the sitting room. 'How can I help, Inspector?'

The two men stood gazing round the room for a moment, then Bill Pulman smiled. 'I wonder if we could sit down, sir?'

'Please do.' Christopher tried to make the invitatation sound gracious, noticing that the two men had glanced at one another. He perched on the edge of a chair opposite them. 'You haven't told me yet what this is about.'

'I understand you know Professor David Solomon, sir,' the sergeant asked after another silence.

Christopher frowned uneasily. 'I do, yes.'

'And he is one of the acknowledged experts on the paintings of your grandmother Evelyn Lucas?'

'He is, yes. Look, you said this wasn't about my father –'

'All in good time, sir, if you don't mind.' Bill Pulman leaned forward slightly. 'How well do you know Lee Ponting?'

Christopher stared at him in confusion. 'I don't. I don't think I've ever heard of him.'

Again the two men opposite him glanced at each other. 'Are you sure, sir? Think carefully.'

Christopher hesitated. 'No, I don't think I have ever met anyone of that name.'

Pulman leaned back and folded his arms. 'My colleague here and I have been investigating a hit-and-run accident which occurred back in March when a car was run off an unfenced Downland road between here and Chichester. Mr Laurence Standish was killed in the accident.' He paused, his eyes fixed on Christopher's face. 'We have identified the car involved as one belonging to Lee Ponting. On his arrest he gave us a great deal of interesting information.'

Christopher felt himself go cold. His stomach had turned over with fear. He stood up abruptly. 'Are you accusing me of something, Inspector? Should I be calling my solicitor?'

'I am not accusing you of anything, Mr Marston. Not yet.' Bill Pulman smiled. 'Ponting is not what you might call a reliable witness at the best of times, but his accusations regarding yourself are, shall we say, interesting and very specific. He claims that Mr Standish was on his way to visit Professor Solomon with a valuable painting in the back of his car. He claims that you paid him, through an intermediary, to make sure that the painting never reached the professor. He hasn't gone so far as to say that you paid him to murder Laurence Standish; he says that the crash was a mistake and a genuine accident. He claims he was trying to force the car to stop so that he could remove the painting and get rid of it. The painting was by your grandmother, Evelyn Lucas.'

There was a long silence. Christopher was about to speak when the inspector went on. 'You assumed I had come about your father, Mr Marston. Uninitiated as we might be in artistic matters in the force, it did occur to us that it might be more than a coincidence that your father recently died violently, that another of your grandmother's paintings was damaged and that it had been removed from the house in London by you.'

He waited, his head cocked to one side. Christopher steadied his breathing. 'You are barking up the wrong tree, Inspector. That is all nonsense! Complete nonsense. I don't understand –' He swallowed hard. 'For one thing, my father didn't die violently. He had a heart attack –' He stopped abruptly as the inspector shook his head slowly.

'The post mortem has revealed certain anomalies, Mr Marston. I am afraid your father's death is now being treated as suspicious.'

Christopher shook his head violently. 'No. No, it can't be. No one would hurt my father. No one. Unless –' He stopped again. 'Have you questioned Lucy Standish? She had just seen my father that day. She had every reason to be angry with our family.'

'Oh? Why exactly?' The sergeant held his gaze. 'Because she thought you had killed her husband, you mean?'

'No! No, I do not mean that!' Christopher stared icily from one man to the other. 'This is all complete nonsense. How dare you suggest I had anything to do with any of this?'

Pulman stood up slowly and his colleague followed suit. 'We are not suggesting anything beyond telling you what the driver of the car which killed Standish told us, sir,' Pulman said slowly. 'I am sure you have an alibi for the evening your father died, and I am sure we would find it very hard to prove that you were acquainted with Ponting, but we will be looking into both matters. We'll leave you now, but I should warn you we will probably be talking to you again. Sir.' The final Sir was emphasised just enough to make it chilling.

Christopher stood in the doorway watching as the two men climbed back into their car and turned it on the gravel before disappearing down the drive. It was several minutes before he went back into the silent house, closed the front door and, with a nervous glance up the staircase towards the rest of the empty house, proceeded to pour himself a large whisky.

Tuesday 17th September, night

Stashing the incriminating attaché case in a dark corner of the passageway just inside the front door, Mike quietly pushed open the door into his sitting room. The lamp on the table was lit and Charlotte was standing with her back to the fireplace, arms folded as she waited for him. He stared at her, shocked at the sight of her. Her hair was tangled, her face devoid of make-up, her jeans and shirt unironed.

'You've been a long time,' she said.

'I wasn't expecting anyone to be waiting for me.' He kept his voice calm.

'Where were you?'

'I don't think that is any of your business.' He walked over to the bookcase and turned on another light. 'Please, Charlotte. It's late and I am tired. I don't think there is any point in us going over things again, do you?' He could see her hands shaking.

'You love me, Michael,' she said.

He sighed. 'No, Charlotte, I don't. You and I had a lovely time together but it didn't work out. I am sorry. These things happen.'

'You told me we were going to marry.'

'No!' His voice sharpened. 'No, I never said that. I never gave marriage a thought, Charlotte. I am sorry. I am not ready to marry anyone.'

'Except Lucy Standish.'

He shook his head in despair. 'I don't know where you have got this idea from. I have no intention of marrying Lucy. Or of having an affair with her. Or anything, as you would know if you paused to give it half a second's thought. Charlotte, give

505

this up, please, for both our sakes. You're a lovely woman. You will find the right man. I am not marriage material, truly.'

'But you are.' There were tears running down her cheeks.

'No. I'm not. And I don't want to be. Now please. Go home.'

'I bought some things for your house. I was going to make it nice for you.'

'Charlotte, for God's sake. You tried to burn the place down!' Finally he was losing patience. 'Go. Now.'

She gave a miserable little smile. 'I could burn this down.'

'Yes, and I could call the police. I want the key. Now please. I thought you had given it to me.'

She sat down abruptly on the arm of one of the chairs. 'I had copies made. Lots of copies.'

'Very well. I will have to have the locks changed. Please leave, Charlotte.'

'You've got my key.'

He felt a twinge of guilt. 'Yes, true, and I was going to post it back to you.' He had the presence of mind not to pull it out of his pocket. 'I'll find it for you and then I want you to go.' He walked over to the desk and pulled out one of the drawers.

'It's not in there. I looked.' She shivered.

He scanned the desk hurriedly. 'So, have you taken anything?'

'Why would I?'

Because you are a manipulative, devious bitch. He managed to stop himself from saying it. 'Why indeed?'

She staggered to her feet. 'I could call the police. Tell them you have molested me, kept me here against my will.'

He laughed. 'They would find that hard to believe, I suspect, when I beg them on my knees to take you away.'

For a moment he thought she was going to hit him. If she was she changed her mind. 'I'm going, but don't forget I know where Lucy lives. You will never be with her, Michael, I will see to that.' She stood quite still for several seconds, her eyes locked on his face as though memorising every detail, then she walked out of the room.

For several seconds he was incapable of moving, chilled by her expression as much as her words, then he followed her. To his relief she had walked past the case without seeing it. She opened the door and went outside, staring up and down the street.

'Shall I come with you and make sure you get a taxi?' he said.

She glared at him. 'I'll walk.'

'It's late, Charlotte. You need to be careful.'

'Why?' She spun round. 'If I was murdered it would get me out of your hair, wouldn't it? But life is not that easy, Michael. I will never be out of your hair. Never.' She walked away without looking back. He stood on the step watching her until she had turned the corner, then he stepped back inside and closed the door on the night. Even after drawing the bolts he didn't feel safe.

Tuesday 17th September, late

Christopher was packing the smallest and most portable paintings into his car, carefully wedging them with blankets. He had had them secreted in a cupboard in one of the back bedrooms, a cupboard which his nosy daughter had not discovered. Frances had rung him from Scotland to say they had arrived safely and that she would be staying up there for the time being. He didn't argue. To hell with school. If they never went back it wouldn't matter. Let their grandparents organise something in Scotland. It suited him fine to have the house to himself. Or it had until the wretched police had turned up with their news about Lee Ponting. He had never heard of the man. For a while he had been completely confused until they had mentioned Laurence Standish and the car crash. The stupid, insane car crash. His hands shook at the thought of what had happened. A man had been killed, for God's sake, and the stupid picture had escaped. Of all the incompetent, bungling idiots his contacts had had to pick this one. He pushed another picture into the car and saw a flake of soft blue oil paint scrape off and fall on the gravel. Stupid! Careful. He paused and tried to steady himself before carefully pushing the door shut.

There was room for a couple more on the passenger seat. He took the stairs two at a time and headed back down the passage. There were still several large paintings in the room. He would have to hire a van to move them, but at least he would have got the majority out of the house. For the time being he had hired a secure storage unit in Southampton. No one would find them there.

Behind him the door closed quietly in the draught from the hall downstairs. He swung round, his nerves on edge. A shadowy figure was standing near the bed looking down at the picture leaning against the wall.

Christopher froze, the hairs on the back of his neck and along his forearms standing on end. For a moment he was speechless, taking in the man's shape, trying to make sense of what he was seeing. He was paralysed with terror. 'What the hell are you doing here?' he gasped at last. His voice was little more than a whisper. 'Get out!'

The figure didn't move. It was intent on looking at the painting. It was an oil entitled Christ Church, Church Row, Hampstead, dated 1956. The painting had never been finished; there was a small patch in the corner where the charcoal sketch beneath showed through, and the sky had not been filled in.

For several seconds nothing happened, then as the figure faded it turned towards him, the blank eyes appearing to look right through him, and he recognised the gaunt features of his grandfather, Eddie Marston.

Wednesday 18th September

Rosebank Cottage was shut tight when Lucy arrived. She took out her key and put it in the door. It didn't turn, and now that she was looking properly she could see the lock had been changed. Her heart sank. She headed along the path in front of the window and round the corner to the lawn and the studio. That lock too was new. She stood for several seconds undecided what to do then slowly she turned back towards the road. Had he done this to keep her out? Had he changed his mind again about helping her? She had reached the gate when she saw a small figure hobbling down the lane towards her. It was Dolly.

'Come in!' Dolly was puffing by the time she reached the top of the steps. She opened the door and led the way indoors.

Lucy followed without a word.

Dolly stared round in disapproval. 'Look what happens if I'm not here to keep an eye on things. Still, it won't take me two ticks. Let me put the coffee on for you first. Have you been in the studio yet?'

Lucy looked at her in confusion. 'Dolly, the locks have all been changed.'

'Yes and a fine to-do I had getting that done . . .' Dolly broke off suddenly. 'Didn't he tell you?'

Lucy shook her head.

Dolly let out an exasperated sigh. 'Silly man. I can't believe it. Charlotte Thingy, the stupid woman, broke into his place in London. She threatened to set fire to it, and to this cottage. She told him she had made copies of all his keys so he rang me and told me I had to get back here and arrange to have all the locks changed. Can you believe it? What is it? Why are you smiling?'

Lucy shook her head. 'I thought he had changed them to keep me out.'

Dolly was stunned into silence for a moment. 'Why should he do that?'

'Because at one point not that long ago he said he didn't want me to come here any more.'

Dolly turned to the sink to fill the kettle. For several seconds she didn't say anything, then at last she turned to face Lucy. 'It's my opinion,' she said slowly, 'that Mr Michael is quite fond of you. He would never shut you out.' She reached for coffee and mugs. 'You know he is coming down this morning,' she said after a moment.

'No.' Lucy felt a flutter of unease.

'He said he had found Evie's attaché case and he wanted you there when it was opened. He found it in Thingy's flat.'

Lucy's unease turned to suppressed excitement. 'Of course. He told me about it.'

'He stole it back from her.' Dolly beamed approvingly. 'Anyway, here you are. He will be here soon. You drink your coffee while I run round the cottage with a duster. He would be horrified if he saw the state it's in. The lock man with his drills and things made dust everywhere.' She left Lucy sitting in the kitchen.

In less than ten minutes the door opened and Mike looked in. 'I tried to ring you at the vicarage but there was no reply and your mobile was off.' He walked over to her, hesitated and then to her surprise reached out to kiss her cheek. 'I'm so glad you're here. Dolly told me you thought I had changed the locks to keep you out. I am sorry. '

She suppressed a grin. 'Easy mistake to make.'

'Indeed.' He gave her a rueful smile. 'But I told you I had got the case. Come on through and we'll open it. I don't think there is a key so we may have to lever the locks back. I'll just check with Dolly. If there is a key she would know.'

There wasn't. Mike produced a screwdriver and they put the small case on the table. The two women watched while he inserted the blade under the catches. It only took a matter of seconds before the lid was open.

The case was full of papers and sealed envelopes.

1959

The solicitor looked at Evie with genuine sympathy as he showed her into his Chichester office and pulled out a chair for her. Outside the traffic in South Street was very busy.

'I was so sorry to hear of your mother's death. I knew your father and mother for many years, of course, and our firm has dealt with your father's family for many generations.' He smiled.

Evie nodded, fighting her tears. Her mother had been found lying on Ralph's bed. She had looked, so she had been told, completely peaceful with a small smile on her lips. The doctor said it was a heart attack and that he had warned her that her heart was weak, but Evie wondered if that was true. Perhaps Rachel had just chosen to go to Ralph at last. It was what she would have wanted.

'Of course, my job is to read you the will.' The solicitor paused. 'But I am sure you already know it. Your father left the farm to you and your brother.' He glanced up at her. 'Your late brother. Which means that on the death of your mother everything comes to you.' He paused. 'You are a married woman, I believe?'

Evie nodded.

'Your husband is not with you?'

Evie shook her head. 'I don't want him to know about this. I want the farm sold and I want the money.' She sat forward on the edge of her chair. 'There must be a way to keep it from him. He won't give me a divorce. I need that money to leave him. You must help me. I have to buy somewhere to live where he can't find me. Ever.'

31

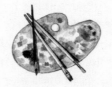

September 20th 1960

George arrived only four months after she and Johnny had settled in to Rosebank. 'You can't leave me with him, Mummy, you can't.' The boy, for all his fifteen years, had tears in his eyes. He was still in school uniform and had only a haversack with him. 'Why did you go without me? I don't understand.'

George had been away at school when Evie had finally plucked up courage to go. She doubted if Eddie would ever rest if his son went too. She took nothing from the house in Hampstead. She had all she needed from her parents' home. The farm had sold quickly and only months later she had moved into Rosebank Cottage, using some of the extra money to build her studio, putting the rest into the bank. For the first time in what seemed a lifetime she was secure and happy, or she would have been, were it not for George. She missed him dreadfully. She felt guilty at leaving him. She wrote to him at school and he wrote back begging her to let him come to her. His father, he said, was so angry he didn't want to go home. Ever.

She should have known that if George came, Eddie would follow.

His fury and his spite were a shock after several months without seeing him.

He pushed the front door open so hard it slammed against the wall and looked into the sitting room. his face twisted with disdain. George stared at his father in terror and fled into the garden.

Evie straightened her shoulders. 'How did you find us?'

'I won't even dignify that remark with an answer,' he retorted. 'I'm taking George back with me.'

Evie folded her arms. To her surprise after the initial shock she found she wasn't afraid of him any more. 'That is up to George,' she said. 'If he wishes to stay I am prepared to look after him. If you insist he goes with you I will have to tell him that I can't fight for him through the courts because I am not his real mother. You never told him that, did you.'

Eddie froze. He held her gaze for several seconds before sitting on the sofa and slumping back against the cushions, visibly deflated. 'That would destroy the boy.'

'Yes, it would.' She tightened her lips.

'And Johnny?' Eddie managed a sneer.

'He is away at university.'

Eddie's gaze sharpened. 'And who is paying for that?'

'My father paid for that,' she said quietly, 'in his will. Don't worry. Johnny will never be a call on your purse again and neither will I. And now I would like you to leave.'

To her astonishment he went. Without another word he turned and walked out of the door, leaving it open behind him. She had no doubt he would be back or that at the very least she would hear from his solicitors but to her surprise there was no further word from him. George fitted seamlessly into the cottage and to her further surprise Johnny didn't object when he found he was sharing his small bedroom. The boys would never be close, she realised, but at least for the time being they seemed to get on well, perhaps cemented in their relationship by their dislike of their father. She sent George to Lancing College and to her joy found she could paint again now she was embedded once more in her beloved Sussex countryside.

Saturday 21st September

'So, that is how she came here.' Mike looked up at Lucy. They had been poring over Evie's diary for 1960. Lucy was overjoyed to find three more diaries in the case as well as several envelopes and packets. The next notebook was a form of diary but not so detailed, and spanned a dozen or so years. Johnny graduated with a law degree from Oxford and joined her parents' former solicitors in Chichester as a trainee. At university he had met another undergraduate, Juliette Phelps, and shortly after he took the position in Chichester they were married, to Evie's delight. George took his A levels and then went to study art, first in Florence then in Rome. The cottage which for a few years was bursting at the seams with the two young men as well as Evie was now a lonely place, or would have been had it not been for Dolly. Evie's affection for her housekeeper was obvious on every page as it was for her daughters-in-law. George and Marjorie were married in Italy in 1967. Christopher was born in 1972 and back in Chichester Johnny and Juliette's son, Michael, was born four years later.

'So, now we are into the present,' Mike said as they reached the end of the book. 'Christopher and me.'

'But nothing about Evie painting again,' Lucy commented. 'She mentioned it that once. She had her lovely studio and enough time and she was happy here. So why no further mention of her pictures?'

'Perhaps she had a separate notebook for that as she did in the early days?' Mike reached into the case for another of the notebooks. He flipped it open and stared at it. 'Oh Lord. Look.'

Eddie had come back into her life.

1989

Evie opened the door to find him standing on her doorstep one rainy day in March. Her hair was grey now but still curling loosely over her shoulders.

He pushed the door open and walked in. 'Where are they?'

'Where are what?' She was alone in the house and completely unprepared for his arrival.

'The paintings.' He seized her wrist and held up her hand. 'I know you have been painting. Look, you can hardly deny it.' Her fingers were stained with oils and the smock she was wearing over her slacks was covered in old paint stains. 'I've seen several of them now in galleries around the country.'

'Probably paintings you sold,' she said bitterly.

'No. I remember every painting I sold.' He walked across the room and pushed open the French doors into the garden. 'That, I take it, is your studio.' Without waiting for her reply he was striding across the grass through the rain. She hadn't locked the door. It hadn't occurred to her. She watched in dumb horror as he pushed open the door and walked in.

There was no point in following him. He had always been taller and stronger than she. Now in his seventies, he had put on weight but he still looked a fit man. He could easily over-power her if he chose. She stood staring out of the window as he carried the paintings out of the studio one by one to his car. There wasn't room for all of them. Some he left, stacked against the wall by the door. He would no doubt return for those and if she called the police he would invoke his supposed contract as her agent. It felt as though she had been raped.

He did not come back into the cottage. After a while she

515

realised he had gone, his car loaded, the door to the studio hanging open, allowing the rain to soak the boards of the floor. She stood looking round in complete misery, noting which of her favourites were missing, then she turned and went back into the house and picked up the phone. Johnny and Juliette were there within an hour. Within a day Johnny's senior partner had initiated divorce proceedings. She and Eddie had been separated so long it was a mere formality. He did not contest it.

For a few months there was no further contact with Eddie. He came once more when Juliette and Johnny happened to be there and then in September 1989 he appeared for the last time.

This time when she said no she threatened him with the police and told him that enough was enough. It was time both boys knew their story. Then he would have no hold over her any more.

He stood looking down at her with an expression of extreme contempt. 'Do you think either of them would care now?' he said at last. 'Johnny is forty-eight years old, for goodness' sake. He wouldn't care if his father was the Archbishop of Canterbury!'

Evie looked at him with real loathing. 'No. But he would be so pleased to know his father was a war hero and not a black marketer who never lifted a finger to fight the enemy.'

Eddie reached into his pocket for his cigarettes. 'War hero, eh? Maybe. But he was a coward as well. He left you without a word so he could save his own skin. I had him killed, you know.' He smiled. 'I tried once when he was stationed here, but later, in Scotland, when his plane crashed, that was my doing.'

Evie felt her face drain of colour. She couldn't move.

'I was sorry I couldn't tell you what I had done, but at the time it seemed better for everyone to keep it quiet. Tony Anderson, DFC, downed by some dissident Commies from Clydeside who didn't need asking twice when we suggested a small stick of gelignite strapped to the engine cowling of his Spitfire might be a fine gesture in the support of the Marxist cause. That and a suitable donation, of course.' He was silent for a moment studying her face. 'You didn't know, did you?'

'Of course I didn't know.'

'It hardly matters. So much for his beloved Evie. Did he even know you were pregnant? No, I don't suppose he did. You were just a passing flirt. Did you really think I was fooled even for a minute by your sudden show of affection for me?' He opened his cigarette case, extracted a cigarette and reached for his lighter. 'You've always played me for a fool, Evie. That was stupid.'

'Get out!' Her voice was very quiet, but its force surprised him.

'I'm going. As soon as I have collected one or two paintings.'

'No. You are not taking any paintings. You are never coming here again.'

He took a long draw on his cigarette, watching her carefully. There was a flicker of amusement in his eyes. 'I will do as I wish, Evie. No one will stop me. There is no point in you telling anyone what I have just told you. No one would believe it. Not in a million years. They will just say you are a dotty old woman with a grudge.' He smiled. 'And I have a legal right to your paintings, don't forget that.' He tossed the end of the cigarette into the fireplace and strode towards the French doors.

The studio was unlocked. He took two small watercolours and an oil portrait of George and strolled back towards his car in the lane. He went back once more and this time he had her painting of Chanctonbury Ring under his arm. He raised the other in her direction in an ironic wave and then he was gone.

For a long time Evie stood still. She realised she was shaking. Tony. Eddie had killed Tony.

These days she drove an MG sports car, chosen for her sixty-eighth birthday present by her two sons. It took less than two hours to reach London. He wasn't expecting her and opened the door at her ring. She pushed past him, just as he had done to her, and ran to the staircase. The house had not changed much in all the years since she had walked out that fine day in May nearly thirty years before, but she was more agile than he now.

Her former studio had been repainted and carpeted and fixed up as a gallery. On the walls hung some two dozen of her works, some taken from Rosebank, some from the old days when she lived here, and several which must have been bought from galleries in the south of England. She glanced round, then turned to face Eddie as he pounded up after her.

'You bastard!' Her anger had not dissipated in the drive from Sussex. If anything it had intensified. 'You utter murdering bastard. I will kill you for this!'

He laughed. 'How nice to see you here, Evie. Well, if you kill me all I can say is that I will haunt you forever. But you've got to do it first! I must say, I've missed your fiery presence, my darling.' His smile vanished and his eyes grew hard again.

'Have you?' She took a step towards him, her face a mask of anger. 'Have you indeed?'

He stepped backwards in spite of himself. 'Yes, I think I have. So, what do you think of the gallery?'

'It proves you are a thief!' She took another step forward. Her hands were balled into fists and suddenly she flew at him. He stepped back out of the room onto the landing, and then once again, missing his footing on the top step of the stairs behind him. For a moment he staggered, grabbing for the banister, then with a shout of fright he fell, heavily and awkwardly down the full flight of stairs, landing at the bottom with an horrific crash.

Evie froze. 'Eddie?' she whispered. 'Eddie, are you all right?'
He didn't reply.

Slowly she walked down the flight of stairs, pausing at the bottom to look down at him. 'I warned you, Eddie,' she said at last. 'I warned you I would kill you.' She could see from the angle of his head that his neck was broken.

She didn't touch him; what was the point. No doctor could help him. Slowly she walked down the next flight of stairs and then along the passage to the front door. Her painting of Chanctonbury Ring was still there, leaning against the wall. Eddie had not had time to bring it in and hang it. She picked it up and it was only as she opened the door and stepped outside clutching the picture that she realised she was still wearing her soft leather driving gloves. She had left no fingerprints; her car was parked several streets away. As far as she knew no one had seen her. It was the perfect murder.

Saturday 21st September

'Jesus!' Mike looked up at Lucy. 'She killed him!'

'And then wrote it all down in her diary?' Lucy said softly.

'And he killed the man who was my grandfather.' He exhaled loudly, rubbing his hands up and down his face several times. They looked at each other in silence for several seconds. 'She didn't actually murder Eddie,' Lucy said at last. 'It sounds as though that was an accident.'

'But she pushed him.'

'Even so. She couldn't have known he would die.' She stood up and walked over to the window, staring out at the studio. 'Did she ever tell anyone, do you think?'

Mike shook his head. 'I don't know. My parents never said anything to me but I was only thirteen when he died so even if they suspected anything they wouldn't mention it to me, would they? But then I saw his ghost.' He shivered.

'And he had already planned his revenge by leaving everything to George and then in turn to Christopher.'

'And now we know why. He obviously didn't realise he was

519

going to die at her hand, but he was determined to cut Dad out. I wonder when he made that will.'

'That's easy to check.' She turned to face him, leaning with her back to the sink. 'The Record Office is just round the corner from me at home. You know, I think we are going to have to tell Huw and Maggie about this.'

He frowned. 'Why?' He stood up and came to stand beside her.

'Because he is a ghost and now we know why. He swore he would haunt Evie, he is still obsessed with Evie's paintings and he is still obsessed with his hatred of Tony Anderson. My God, he killed the man! He got some communists to blow up his plane! Surely that's treason or something. There was a war on, for goodness' sake! It needs professionals like Huw and Maggie to sort out someone so obsessed with hatred.'

'They haven't managed to cope with him yet, Lucy,' Mike said slowly. 'After all, he followed the picture to their house and attacked it again there.'

She was silent for a moment. 'I feel safe with them.'

'I know you do.' He reached out and touched her hand. 'Perhaps now if they know what they're dealing with they will be more successful. You're right. We should tell them. I am sure they would be discreet.'

'Do you think Evie ever saw his ghost?'

They looked at each other. 'Unless she wrote it down, we'll never know.' It was Lucy's turn to shiver.

'You can't write about this, Lucy. You realise that, don't you? None of it.' He paused, still stunned. 'All that stuff about him blowing up the Spitfire. I just can't believe that that could really be true.'

'I don't know.' She glanced at him. 'Do you think she told Dolly?'

'It's possible. Dolly was always her confidante. But I don't think we can ask her.'

'No.' Lucy moved away from him. 'And you're right, I can't

write about this, but the fact that Eddie died as a result of a fall would be part of the historical record. I can put that in.'

Mike moved back to the table and pulled the case to face him. 'There are more things in here.' He glanced at the last remaining notebook. 'This takes her story up to 2000.' He flipped through the pages. Of course she never exhibited again after Eddie died. And although he sold her paintings they were never exhibited by him either. I suppose he couldn't without her say-so.'

'Which is where I came in because I wanted to put her back on the map.' Lucy gave a rueful smile.

'At least I know now why he left nothing to my dad, and why Dad seemed to hate him so much,' Mike said.

'Quite a family history.' Lucy smiled. 'Shall we see what else is in here while we are at it?' She nodded towards the attaché case.

In one of the pockets was a large sealed envelope. Lucy pulled it out and read the scrawled inscription on the front. *Property of Flying Officer Ralph Lucas.* She passed it to Mike.

He tore open the flap. Inside was a small sealed envelope, two sheets of paper and a ring. He glanced at the ring. It was a delicate, filigree gold design set with a sapphire. The first sheet of paper was written in the same hand as the inscription on the front of the envelope. *Dear Mrs Lucas, It is my sad duty to pass on these items to you. They were found at the back of your son's locker after his other belongings had been returned to you. Please accept my apologies for the delay in returning them. Yours sincerely . . .*

The other sheet had some lines of poetry on them. The envelope, inscribed in another hand was simply addressed to *Evie*.

Mike looked at Lucy, then he opened the letter.

My darlingest Evie,
    You know how much I love you. I have been trying to reach you to ask you again to marry me. Please, my love. You are the only one for me and I want so much to make you my wife.

521

I am giving Ralph my grandmother's ring for you. It is the colour of the milkworts we found that day on the Downs. Remember? Wear it for me. We are being posted north at any moment and I will have no more chances to see you for a while but come to my parents farm and we can be married from there. I have told Ralph so that he can help you arrange it.

Until then, my darling you have my love forever,
Tony. xxxxx

PS. If I don't hear from you I will know that you don't want me.

'She never got the letter,' Lucy whispered.

Mike shook his head. 'Look at the date. It was the day before Ralph was killed. He never delivered the letter and Tony must have left thinking she didn't want to marry him.'

'And she was pregnant with his child and loved him so much that one day, nearly fifty years later, she would kill Eddie for killing him. Oh God, Mike, this is like some Shakespearean tragedy.' Lucy had tears in her eyes.

'Is that what Ralph has been trying to tell us all these years?' Mike said. 'Great-granny Rachel was too upset ever to open his things and when Evie inherited all her stuff, she never bothered, she just shoved this in her writing case. If she had opened it she would have known how much Tony loved her.'

Mike put his arm round Lucy's shoulders and pulled her against him and they stood in silence for a long time like that, together, lost in thought, as outside the evening began to draw into night.

As the shadows lengthened the roar of an aircraft engine grew louder in the distance. They both turned to the window. The Spitfire flew low and straight over Rosebank Cottage, then turned and flew off into the darkness.

Monday 23rd September

'I can't go on staying here with you.' Lucy cornered Maggie before she went out of the front door. 'It's not fair. I have to go home.'

Maggie was on her way to what she described as a vicar's wife's meeting, something about which she had been complaining at breakfast. She looked distracted, her arms full of books and ledgers.

Lucy smiled in spite of herself. 'You know, it doesn't suit you.'

'What doesn't suit me?' Maggie tried to brush her hair out of her eyes with her forearm only to succeed in dropping one of the notebooks.

Lucy stooped to pick it up. 'You should be swathed in beads and shawls and hung with lucky charms and on your way to talk to the trees!'

Maggie smiled. 'How do you know I'm not?'

'Because of this.' Lucy glanced at the writing on the book in her hand. It said Budget. She tucked it into Maggie's elbow. 'Trees don't have budgets.'

'So true.' Maggie gave a theatrical sigh. 'Let's talk about what you want to do this evening. Huw is burying someone this morning and taking a class of some sort this afternoon, so we'll foregather about six.' She gave Lucy a fond smile. 'I shall miss you so much when you go.'

They had all talked for a long time the previous night about Eddie Marston and the latest revelations about him. No decisions had been reached. Maggie had sent Mike back to his cottage and despatched Lucy to bed with firm instructions not to worry. 'Eddie's not here now,' was all she would say. 'That is what matters. If you go home tomorrow with the picture I want you to feel safe. I am pretty certain that Eddie has other fish to fry now. I don't know how I know, but I feel I am right. Perhaps this house is too holy for him.' She smiled. 'I almost said too hot! Let things be for a while and we will see what happens.'

Lucy left the next morning, her car loaded with books and papers and her painting, still damaged and no longer crated, leaning against the back seat.

Robin was waiting for her outside the gallery with a huge grin. 'The old place has missed you!' he said giving her a hug.

She walked slowly round the flat upstairs. Robin and Phil had turned the studio into a study for her and the windows were opened onto the September sunshine. They hung Evie's picture, damaged as it was, on the wall. It looked as if it had come home.

'Have you still got a lot of writing to do?' Robin had brought a bottle of wine and they were sharing it in the back garden after the shop was closed that evening, seated at the little wrought-iron table.

Lucy nodded. 'Quite a few loose ends to tie up.'

'But you're not afraid?'

'Afraid?'

'Of the horrible Edward Marston.'

Lucy thought for a minute. 'I suppose I am, yes. I will always be a bit afraid of him, but Maggie's right. I don't sense he has followed me here.'

'So can I leave you here alone?'

She smiled. 'Of course you can. I am newly shriven by my contact with the Church. I can stand up to the worst ghost. For a while anyway.' She resisted the urge to peer into the shadows. If Eddie was going to come for her she would sense his presence, she was sure of it. And he wasn't here. Not at the moment.

And there was something she had to do as soon as she was alone, something she had been meaning to do for a long time. She switched on her laptop and typed in the words, Anthony Anderson.

Evie had been devastated by the news that Tony had been killed all those years ago. She had never mentioned him again until her conversation with Eddie. It was time to look up the official record of Tony's death and the crash which had killed him.

There were, of course, dozens of men with that name. She refined it down by typing in Battle of Britain and there he was. His squadron, his medals, his career. There were pictures of him, pictures she recognised from the young man in the portrait upstairs. She stared at the screen. There was no mention of a crash. He had been posted to Egypt in 1944, had returned to Britain at the end of the war, had resumed his studies at Edinburgh University. He had become a partner in a law practice in Edinburgh and had in 1970 become a Judge. He had retired in 1990. He was unmarried . . .

He was unmarried.

Lucy shook her head sadly.

His address was care of the New Club, Edinburgh.

Tony Anderson, now ninety-five, was still alive.

32

Wednesday 25th September

Christopher pulled his car into the lay-by and switched off the engine. He was shaking violently, pouring with sweat. Opening the window, he closed his eyes and took deep breaths of the cool evening air then he fumbled for the door handle and at last managed to climb out of the car. He stood for a long time leaning on the fence, staring out across the fields. It couldn't be true, of course. In fact it was impossible, but he could not rid himself of the feeling that Eddie was there, with him, in the car. He had become aware of him as he pulled out of the drive at home. Somehow he had overcome his desire to scream to a halt, leap out and leave the car where it was in the middle of the road. He had turned off up this lane only some two miles from home, swerving wildly, ever more conscious of the still, dark presence on the back seat.

Now that he was out of the car he forced himself to turn round and look at it. He could see nothing. The sun was setting in a blaze of deep crimson, slowly being swallowed by dense black cloud and the shadows were creeping down the lane towards him. The interior of the car was invisible, stacked as it was with another load of paintings. Almost unconsciously he put his hand in his pocket to make sure he had the keys to the lock-up. It didn't matter how late he was, the system gave him twenty-four-hour access, but still he had wanted to be there before dark. He took several deep breaths. It was ridiculous to think that the ghost of his grandfather was there in the car with him; that the ghost was malign, vicious even, but that was how it felt, how it had felt from the first moment he had been aware of the presence in his house. Hannah had known. Hannah was sensitive like her mother. In Frances the sensitivity irritated the daylights out of him, but in his daughter it brought out an aching sense of protectiveness. Why else would he have let the family disappear to Scotland, leaving him alone? The kids were at a day school up there now, temporarily, and loving it, apparently.

And he was alone with more than a ghost; there was his conscience to face as well. He folded his arms with a shiver and turned away from the car to stare back across the fields. He had never suffered from conscience before, but ever since his father had died somehow he had felt as if the death had been his fault. How could it have been? He wasn't there. He knew nothing of what had happened that night in Hampstead, so close to Eddie Marston's old home, but it was all connected. Of that he was sure.

It had started with the will.

He had found an expert forger to add the codicil to his grandmother's will, giving him all the paintings, leaving Mike with the cottage; he knew it was not what she would have wanted. He thought she would never know but now he was not so sure about that. She was watching him, he was certain of it, and she was disgusted. No one else knew but the thought of what he had done was for the first time making him uncomfortable. Mike had never suspected and there was no reason for his deception to be discovered by anyone, not even that nosy cow, Lucy Standish.

The name Standish brought him back to the visit from the police. He shuddered. The sun was dropping lower. It was growing darker. They hadn't accused him of anything, but they obviously knew that one of his contacts had sent Lee Ponting on his fatal mission. He had not intended to hurt anyone but something had driven him to act as he did. He couldn't even remember now why he had decided the painting had to be destroyed. Some inner prompting, some instinct that he couldn't allow it to continue to exist had driven him to do everything in his power to think of a way to get rid of the picture. It made no sense. It would be worth a fortune, like all Evie's paintings, so why destroy it? What was it about that picture that had to be hidden forever? Only one person knew the answer to that. He realised it now. It was his grandfather. The thought that his grandfather had pushed him to do what he did filled him with horror.

He turned to face the car again. He knew now why he had felt so panic-stricken, why he had had to climb out of it. He was expecting the car to burst into flames.

It hadn't. Not yet.

It was completely dark when at last he forced himself to walk back and climb into the driver's seat. The presence in the back had disappeared; the car just felt extremely cold and a bit damp. He turned the key, closed the door and pulled out onto the road heading for Southampton.

Wednesday 25th September

Tony Anderson was fairly tall, considering his years. He walked with a stick, but his shock of white hair and his bright blue eyes gave him a youthful appearance which matched his infectious smile. Lucy recognised the smile at once from the portrait.

They had arranged to meet at the RAF Club. Though his home was in Edinburgh he was, it appeared, staying in London for a couple of weeks after taking part in some of the Battle of Britain anniversary celebrations. 'Not many of us left from the old days,' he said with a smile as she and Mike followed him to a corner of a large reception room on the first floor of the club and settled round a low table to wait for the tea he had ordered. 'So, may I ask what this is about?'

Lucy had spoken to him on the telephone and given him her name. Other than that she had been deliberately vague about the reason for the meeting. She wanted to make a judgement about how good this man's memory was and whether she felt he was strong enough to confront a past which seemed to be so full of tragedy. He had assumed, she realised, that she wanted to interview him about the Battle of Britain. Well, in a way, she did.

She glanced at Mike. 'First I must introduce you two properly. This is Michael Marston.' She paused, watching Tony's face. For a moment a shadow seemed to pass across his eyes, but he smiled gamely. 'I see,' was all he said.

'Evie's grandson,' she went on gently.

'So I guessed.' He leaned back in his chair. His hands on the handle of his walking stick were very thin.

Mike had said nothing. He seemed to be struck dumb.

'I have been researching a book about Evie and her painting,' Lucy went on, 'and with Mike's help we have been going through all Evie's old records and notebooks.' She paused. 'And diaries,' she added.

'Ah.' Tony nodded. 'I see.'

A bar steward appeared with a tray bearing a teapot and cups and a plate of biscuits. The three of them sat in silence watching as he set the table for them and then withdrew. The full-length windows in the room, looking out onto a balustrade, were open to the warm afternoon sun. They let in the sound of the rumble of traffic from Piccadilly below. On the far side of the busy road the trees of Green Park rustled gently in the breeze behind the railings. Their leaves were turning a golden brown.

The interlude seemed to have given Tony time to gather his wits. 'Evie and I knew one another a very long time ago. I followed her career, of course, she was famous, but we lost touch.'

Lucy looked at Mike. 'We have found out quite a bit about those early days.' Suddenly she didn't know how to go on. She stopped helplessly.

'Why not pour the tea for us,' Tony said firmly. 'And you, Michael did you say your name was? You tell me what happened.'

Mike took a deep breath. 'From what we gather you gave a letter to Evie's brother, Ralph. I'm afraid we read it.' He hesitated before plunging on. 'Evie never received it. Ralph was killed the next day and the letter and your ring were parcelled up with Ralph's effects and returned to his mother. She was too upset to look at them and they stayed sealed in the original envelope from Ralph's CO until last weekend when Lucy and I found it in an old writing case.'

Tony bowed his head. He sighed. 'So she never knew.'

'No.' Mike took a cup and saucer from Lucy and then put them down on the table. 'I'm not sure how to tell you this.' He paused. 'But I think maybe you would like to know. She was pregnant. She was expecting your child. She didn't know what to do when you flew back to Scotland without saying goodbye. She was devastated and she was under pressure from her parents so she agreed to marry her neighbour's son, Edward Marston, who had been a suitor for a long time.'

Tony nodded slowly. 'Eddie would have been pleased about that.'

'You knew him?' Lucy asked.

'Oh, yes, I knew him.'

'She had a son, Johnny, my father,' Mike said simply.

Tony looked up. 'So you are my grandson?'

Mike nodded. To his embarrassment his eyes filled with tears.

For a moment Tony didn't say anything, then he leaned across and put his hand over Mike's. 'I never had any children of my own; I never married. Evie was the only one for me.

You have no idea how much this means to me.' He gave a beaming smile. Then he sobered again. 'But why did Evie never get in touch? I told her in my letter that if she didn't I would assume she didn't want to marry me, but she didn't know that. All she had to do was telephone.'

'She thought you were dead. Your plane crashed.'

Tony looked perplexed. 'I don't know what gave her that idea.' He shook his head and then he nodded slowly as the memory came back. 'Of course. When I was stationed at Prestwick a plane I often flew did crash out at sea. It was another poor sod who was killed. The base knew someone else was flying it, of course they did. I was on leave when it happened. But someone must have got the news wrong.'

Lucy sighed. 'Eddie gave her the message. Her diary records her misery. She mourned you all her life. She almost wrote to your parents and they would have told her the truth but she was too unhappy to finish the letter. We've seen it. Oh, Tony, I am so sorry.'

Tony's face hardened. 'There was a lot of suspicion at the time that someone was out to get me. I don't know if it was true but I always thought it was Eddie. He was not a man to cross. It would have been like him to tell her I was dead.' For several seconds he was silent, gazing into the distance, then he went on. 'Of course her father hated me as well. Or at least he didn't approve of me, for some reason.' He shook his head wistfully. 'I found out later, or perhaps I guessed,' he paused, staring off into the distance for a moment, 'that he was part of an Auxiliary Unit, a kind of underground army. He caught me once going to see Evie at night,' he paused again. 'I thought he was furious that I was there, but he was angry because I had seen him on his way to some kind of secret exercise.' There was another silence. 'I never quite lost touch – my mother kept everything she saw in the papers about Evie's exhibitions and sent the cuttings to me – but I moved around a lot. I had several postings before being sent to Egypt towards the end of the war. I think my original CO was watching out for me, keeping me out of trouble – he suspected sabotage and knew about my suspicions, but I had seen that Evie was married and had children.' He stopped and cleared his throat. 'I assumed she had made her decision and had forgotten me.' He paused. 'Is Evie still alive?'

Lucy shook her head. 'Oh, Tony, I am so sorry. She died fourteen years ago.'

He nodded. 'I assumed she must have gone. And Eddie?'

Mike and Lucy exchanged glances.

'He died in 1989,' Mike said.

'And Johnny. My son?' Tony hesitated over the words.

'I am afraid he is dead too.'

Tony shook his head. 'But he was young.'

'Sixty. It was cancer.'

'And he had a brother?'

'Uncle George. I am afraid he died only a month ago in an accident.'

'And he was Eddie's son.'

Mike nodded.

Lucy cleared her throat. 'George wasn't Evie's child. He was the son of a woman called Lavinia Gresham. It was in Evie's diary. She wrote it all down. She lost a baby but shortly afterwards she found out that Eddie had a mistress who lived in Arundel and she went to see her and met the little boy. He was called Paul. Sometime later Lavinia died, I suspect of TB, and Eddie brought the child home. He changed his name to George. Evie seems to have doted on him. I don't think he ever knew they had adopted him.'

Mike stood up abruptly. 'It has just occurred to me that Christopher is no blood relation to Evie at all,' he said. He spoke more loudly than he intended and glanced round, embarrassed, realising that the room had grown silent and people at the other tables were staring at him.

'I suppose not.' Lucy nodded.

'And he took all the paintings!'

'I don't suppose he knew he was no relation. I don't think George knew either although he did tell me that Johnny had once said he was adopted. He thought it was Johnny being mean and he didn't really believe it. Or he didn't want to believe it.'

She became aware that Tony had beckoned one of the stewards over. 'I think this needs something stronger than tea,' he said firmly. 'What do you two drink?' He pushed his teacup away. 'My goodness. An hour ago I had no family. Now I seem to have inherited a grandson, a family scandal, one might almost call it a hornets' nest, all sorts of relations, through you, my boy, and by the look of things, a biographer as well!' He smiled at Lucy.

She returned the smile, almost mesmerised. 'I am so pleased we found you. It is weird. This all goes back to your friendship with Ralph. My late husband bought a picture which he thought was a self-portrait of Evie. He started to clean it and there was a portrait of you, standing behind her shoulder in your air force uniform. It had been painted out, presumably by Eddie. Then I saw Ralph's ghost.'

There was a long silence.

Mike cleared his throat. 'There is a lot to catch up on, clearly. I don't want to impose on you, but if you would like to take this further, I would love you to come down to Sussex. I inherited Evie's cottage. It was her refuge from Eddie, the place she and her boys lived for many years.'

Tony had ordered a double malt whisky. He reached for it and took a hefty swig. 'I certainly want to take it further, as you put it. Please don't think I don't want to know you all. This is the best thing that has ever happened to me.' He took another sip. 'I have just one painting by Evie. It is a portrait of me. She did it as a present for my parents in the middle of the Battle of Britain so they would have something to remember me by if I was killed.' He shook his head. 'When I went back home from

Sussex and told them we weren't going to be married after all my mother put it away in case I was upset by seeing it in their house but she treasured it and when my parents died I found it. It has always been a very special thing for me.' Again he paused. 'I would love to come to your cottage, Michael. Thank you.'

Thursday 26th September, the early hours

The banging on the door woke Huw from a deep sleep. He sat up abruptly, reaching for the light switch and groped for his watch.

'What time is it?' Maggie murmured.

'Two thirty.' Huw groaned. 'Don't get up. I'll see who it is.'

Grabbing his dressing gown he turned on the lights and stumbled downstairs, running his fingers through his hair in an attempt to straighten it.

He turned on the porch light before opening the door and peering out. At first he could see no one then he realised there was someone standing in the driveway. As the door opened the man turned to face it, his clothes muddy, his face scarred by a deep scratch. He was trembling visibly.

'Help me, please. I'm Christopher Marston, Frances's husband. You helped her and my daughter. Please, you have to help me! Please, let me in.'

Huw shivered. The ice-cold draught which whistled into the house was nothing to do with the night wind or the driving rain. It was evil. Eddie was back.

'Come in, Christopher,' he said. 'We'll go into the kitchen. It's warm in there.'

He led the way down the hall, reaching for the light switches as he went. The darkness which surrounded this man was chilling. He glanced up and saw Maggie's face peering over the banisters. Imperceptibly he shook his head, but he knew she would come down whatever he said and deep inside he was glad. He was going to need her.

They went into the kitchen and Huw sat Christopher down in a chair by the Rayburn. He found a rug and put it round the man's shoulders and then went to fill the kettle.

Maggie appeared a few moments later. She was fully dressed and to his surprise he saw she was wearing a crucifix around her neck. He wasn't sure he had ever seen her wear a cross before.

'This is my wife,' he said. Christopher looked up but he didn't seem to register her presence. He was still shaking violently.

Maggie went to the dresser and brought down the tea caddy. She glanced across at Huw. 'He's overshadowed,' she whispered. 'Bad stuff. Eddie.'

Huw nodded. 'You did right to come here, my friend,' he said quietly to Christopher. He pushed a cup of tea in front of him. 'Tell me what happened.'

Christopher shook his head. 'I don't know,' he murmured. His voice was husky. 'I went to put some pictures in storage in Southampton. I locked the door and went towards the car then everything went haywire. I couldn't see. I had this pain –' He put his hand on his chest. 'I thought I was having a heart attack. I got to the car and got in and then I knew he was in there with me. I had to get away. I don't know how I drove.' He tried to sip the tea, his hands rattling the cup on the saucer so it slopped over the table. 'I'm sorry. I don't know what's going on.' He took a deep shuddering breath. 'Father, I have sinned. Isn't that what one says –' He broke off again with a sob.

Huw smiled. 'Not to me, my friend. Wrong religion. But it doesn't matter. We'll sort this out. My wife and I will both respect your confidence as though in the confessional and we can help you.'

He sat down opposite Christopher and covered his hands with his own. 'First, where is Frances?'

Christopher shook his head. 'With her parents in Scotland. And the children.' His teeth were chattering audibly. 'They are safe.'

Huw breathed a sigh of relief.

Maggie had moved slightly to face him. She raised her hands in silent blessing and Huw felt the warmth of light coming from her. This was what she was so good at. Her strength was amazing. Now it was his turn.

'Lord, give us your blessing and your help this night,' he said quietly. 'We pray for our brother Christopher in his trouble. Bring him comfort and guard him from whatever evil confronts him here.'

Christopher was not looking at him. He was staring down at his hands. 'These are not mine,' he said. His voice was barely audible. 'They are not my hands. There is blood on them.'

'Whose hands are they, Christopher?' Maggie said firmly.

He didn't seem to hear her. He was staring at his hands, turning them over, tensing his fingers, an expression of disgust on his face. 'I need to get rid of them. To chop them off –'

'Nonsense!' Maggie's voice was sharp. 'If they are another man's hands we will tell him to go away. You are a strong man, Christopher. You can dismiss him. Is this your grandfather?'

Christopher looked up at her at last. His mouth had dropped open. 'How do you know?' His whisper was barely audible.

'Because I can see him! He is a wicked man, a bully and if you say so, it is his hands which are covered in blood. You are strong, Christopher. Tell him to leave you alone.'

Huw was praying quietly. He could feel the atmosphere around them growing thicker.

Christopher went on, stumbling over his words. 'He tried to kill so many people. Anyone who got in his way. He killed my father's mother so he could take George as his own. No one ever found out. He killed Tony so he could keep Granny. He killed my dad. He told me to destroy the portrait in Laurence Standish's car to hide what he had done, so he was responsible for his death

too. And now,' suddenly he was crying, 'he is going to kill me.'
He looked up. 'You have to help me. Don't let me hurt anyone
else!'

'You are not going to hurt anyone else!' Maggie seemed to
have taken charge. 'And nor is he.'

Huw prayed on silently, content to leave this to her. Between
them they were holding the light in the room. The shadow
was wavering.

'He wants me to kill Tony. I don't understand. Tony is dead.
He wants me to go to Rosebank Cottage and kill Tony.' Suddenly
Christopher was tearing at his hair with his fists, shaking his
head in despair. 'Don't let me. Please, don't let me.'

'No one is going to let you do anything,' Huw said firmly.
He stood up and raised his right hand to make the sign of the
cross. 'Edward Marston, in the name of Jesus Christ, I command
you to leave this man alone!' His voice seemed to echo round
the kitchen for several seconds.

The kitchen was desperately cold. The atmosphere was
clogged, hard to breathe and full of electricity. For several
seconds Huw felt his heart straining to beat as though he was
hundreds of feet beneath the water. He wanted to turn away
and run, he wanted to scream, he wanted to turn on God who
had forsaken them. Then slowly he felt the room returning to
normal. He took a deep breath and then another. Christopher's
face was shiny with perspiration, his eyes wide with terror, but
he was slowly sinking back into his chair. The sinews of his
neck were relaxing.

Eddie had gone. Huw could feel the space suddenly, the
lightening of the atmosphere, the soft reassurance in the room.
He tried to hide a smile. Round one to God.

The echo of his voice was still there holding the silence in
place. As it died away the kitchen door opened and the cat
walked in. It looked from one to the other and sat down.

'Has he gone, Roger?' Maggie asked softly. 'I think he has,
don't you? For now.'

The cat began to wash its ears.

Huw nodded cautiously. 'Good. Are you all right, Christopher?' He put his hand on Christopher's head. Christopher looked up, his face dazed. He stared round as if he didn't know where he was. 'I'm going to ring the doctor,' Huw said gently. 'I don't doubt for a minute that you are better, my friend, but I think it might be wise if you were to have a bit of a rest somewhere safe, do you agree?'

Christopher nodded.

Huw headed for the door, then he changed his mind. He nodded at Maggie. 'You go. I'll stay with him. Tell them he's had a psychotic episode,' he said quietly. 'It is over, thank God, but he needs to be kept safe from our friend Eddie. Eddie is the one we have to deal with now and no hospital on earth can fix him. I have no doubt at all that he will be back. I'd like to think that we have banished him for now, but my prayers have never been strong enough before. Even with God's help, I don't think he's finished yet. He's gone somewhere else.'

Saturday 28th September

'Evie loved thunderstorms.' Tony smiled fondly as the sky darkened over the Downs behind the cottage. 'We were caught in one once when I was with her. She adored the drama of the lightning up there on the Downs. I was scared we'd be struck but she was so brave. She revelled in it.'

They were sitting round the lunch table, drinking their coffee as the rain rattled against the windows and poured off the roof, splashing on the terrace outside. Dolly had made them a casserole and left it in the fridge for them after promising to come the next day to meet Tony. Time enough, she said. In the meantime she would stay away to let them get to know him better and let him get to know Evie's home.

Mike had collected Tony from London and Lucy was there

to meet them when they arrived. He walked slowly and stiffly up the front steps and into the sitting room where he stopped and looked round.

'There are no pictures,' he said. His face had fallen.

'No.' Mike helped him into a chair. 'That is a long story.'

'There is one, Lucy added. 'I brought it over this morning. I've hung it in the studio for now.'

He smiled. 'I remember. You said your husband bought it.'

Lucy nodded.

Tony studied her face for a moment. 'How strange. Fate is sometimes very cruel but in this case she seems to have relented at the last moment. I am so pleased. Can we go and see it?'

Lucy glanced at the window. 'It's pouring.'

Tony pushed back his chair and stiffly climbed to his feet. 'Don't you have umbrellas in Sussex?'

The studio was dark as the thunder rolled ever closer. Mike closed the door behind them then reached for the light switches. Lucy had hung the picture opposite the door, where one of the spotlights focussed directly on the canvas. Leaning on his walking stick Tony stood staring at it for a long time. Glancing at his face Lucy saw there were tears in his eyes.

'I remember her doing this. It seems to have been in the wars,' he said at last. He cleared his throat. 'It's been torn.'

Mike looked towards Lucy, not sure what to say. 'It seems to have had a few adventures,' he said at last, his tone guarded. 'As far as Lucy can make out Eddie sold it in about 1942.'

'He took it without Evie's knowledge,' Lucy said. 'According to her diary she found out later he took it to a man called David Fuller and asked him to paint you out.' She scowled. 'I'm sorry. Perhaps you would rather not know all this.'

Tony shook his head. 'On the contrary. I want to know every detail,' he said firmly.

'David Fuller ran an art gallery in Chichester which sold a lot of Evie's early works. Ironically it is the same building that Larry and I bought to run as a gallery ourselves. The whole thing seems to have been destined in some strange way.' She took a deep breath and went on, 'Eddie seems to have asked David Fuller to paint you out and you stayed out until my husband Larry, started to clean the painting seventy-odd years later.'

'Then I owe your husband a debt of gratitude. Without him you would never have found me and given me back my grandson.' Tony gave a grim laugh. 'Eddie would not be happy about any of this. He didn't like being thwarted.'

A flash of lightning cut through the room followed by a loud crash of thunder. The lights flickered uncertainly and went out.

Lucy stepped closer to Mike. 'That is truer than you know,' she murmured.

Tony had stepped nearer the painting. 'So, how did it get torn like this?'

'Eddie did it,' Lucy whispered.

Tony turned and fixed her with a stern look. 'Tell me how.'

She opened her mouth but no sound came out.

'It sounds mad,' Mike put in. 'And you probably won't believe it, but it's Eddie's ghost. He seems not to be resting in peace. Far from it.'

They both watched Tony. He had stepped forward again and was peering closely at the canvas. 'In which case this storm seems rather apt. Clichéd even,' he said dryly. 'Are we about to receive a visit from the demon king, do you think?'

Lucy shivered and felt Mike's arm round her shoulders. 'It's not a joke. He's real. A real ghost. I shouldn't have brought the picture here. He haunts the picture. I'm such an idiot. I didn't think.' She reached into her pocket for her phone. 'Oh my God, this is awful! I'm going to ring Huw, he seems to be able to hold him at bay. Please, let's go back into the cottage,' she said nervously.

'You two go, Lucy,' Tony said. 'I myself would rather enjoy the opportunity to tell Eddie Marston what I think of him. I have waited a long time for this. The man was a bounder; he was a bully and a cheat then and it seems to me he still is. Besides which he tried to murder me.'

Another low rumble of thunder reverberated round the shadowy studio.

'I can smell oil paint,' Lucy murmured. The room was suddenly full of the cloying scent of turpentine.

Mike pulled her close. 'Please, Tony. He's dangerous. I think we should leave this to the professionals.'

Tony swung round. 'And you think I'm not a professional? Not a ghostbuster, maybe, but this man is mine! You say he made my Evie's life a misery, he was unkind to your father, Mike, and he tried to kill me! If anyone is going to rid the world of his wraith it will be me. If he's got the nerve to show himself.'

Another flash of lightning sliced through the studio. Lucy gave a little whimper.

'Come on, Eddie!' Tony called. 'Are you too afraid to appear now you know I'm not afraid of you? I'll come after you if I have to. That's the great thing about being my age. I'm not afraid of ghosts; I'm not afraid of dying!'

'Tony!' Mike cried. 'There is something we haven't told you.' He glanced down at Lucy, who was huddling in his arms. 'Evie killed him.'

'What?' Tony turned round to face him.

'Not on purpose – at least, I don't think so – but she pushed him down the stairs.'

Tony let out a shout of laughter. 'That's my girl! Can you smell her paints? Her hair always used to smell like that. Turpentine and linseed oil. I loved it. Even on the farm when she was working with the animals she smelled of the paint; she used to get it under her fingernails.' He turned round slowly. 'Well, Eddie? Where are you? Let's see you.' He rapped his walking stick on the floor.

'We've never seen him here,' Lucy said. Her voice was husky. 'We thought it was so completely Evie's he would never haunt it. He wouldn't dare.'

'Is she here?' Mike whispered. 'If you can both smell her paint. Perhaps she has come to see you, Tony –' He broke off as another lightning flash illuminated the studio. It was followed instantaneously by a huge crash of thunder.

They all saw the figure standing near them as more lightning flickered on the walls.

It was Evie.

Saturday 28th September, afternoon

'Something is happening at Rosebank Cottage.' Maggie greeted Huw as he opened the front door and shook his jacket free of rain. 'Lucy rang me. That's where Eddie went. Come on. We have to get there!'

Huw allowed himself to be pushed back into the rain. He had only just driven in and behind him the car bonnet was steaming gently under the force of the downpour.

She dived into the driving seat. 'Get IN!'

Huw ran round and let himself in beside her as she was already reversing out of the drive. 'How was Christopher?' she asked curtly as she pulled away. 'Come on!' There was another car in front of them, making its way cautiously up to the crossroads.

'They have kept him in for the time being.' Huw had gone to the mental health unit with Christopher and their doctor, where Christopher had voluntarily admitted himself. 'He seems a defeated man. I spoke to Frances on the telephone. She and the children are safe in Scotland. It is terrible. It seems the police had been to see him. They think he paid the man who ran Laurence Standish off the road. He wanted the portrait of Evie and Tony destroyed. He doesn't seem to know why himself, but Frances says it was Eddie bullying him, making him act out of character. Watch out!' He clutched at the dashboard as Maggie braked and swerved past the car in front. 'Did Lucy say what was happening at Rosebank?'

'No, but she sounded desperate.' She slowed the car and turned onto the main road. It was awash with rain. The sky in the west was zigzagged with lightning.

'Christopher has admitted forging the codicil to Evie's will, leaving all the paintings to him. He has promised to return them to Mike. He's stashed them all in a lock up somewhere,' Huw went on. He was hanging on the hand hold.

Maggie frowned, leaning forward to try to see better through the streaming windscreen. 'Hold them in your prayers, Huw.' She indicated right and slowed, trying to see a gap in the traffic.

Huw was groping in the pocket of his wet waterproof, trying to get hold of his mobile phone. He extricated it at last and stabbed at the buttons. 'I'll try Lucy again. And Michael. Find out what is happening. One of them must pick up.'

But the numbers rang and rang unanswered.

Maggie pulled in right beside the gate and threw herself out into the rain. 'This way. They're in the studio.'

Huw followed her and he could feel it now: an ice-cold stillness in the heart of the storm. He felt for his crucifix, as usual worn discreetly under his jumper. It was warm and solid and reassuring.

He pushed open the studio door and stood there staring into the darkness, aware of Maggie beside him holding her breath. For several seconds they were unable to see, then another flash of lightning lit the space. Eddie Marston was there, and in front of him they could see a tall elderly man who appeared to be brandishing a walking stick. There was another figure there too, shadowy, near the wall where the portrait hung. It was a woman. It was Evie.

Maggie and Huw stared from one figure to the other. Lucy and Mike appeared to be clinging together near the doorway but they were outside the drama being enacted in the centre of the studio in front of the torn portrait on the wall. Every second Evie was becoming more solid. The three figures were locked in some kind of duel.

'My God, it's Tony,' Huw murmured. He had seen the old man's face as he moved towards Eddie. It was the face of the young pilot in the picture, seamed with seventy years of memories.

'May God blast you to hell and keep you there forever!' Tony's voice was still strong. 'You failed, Edward Marston. As you were always destined to fail. Slicing my face out of an oil painting is not going to help you. I am here. And I am still alive and now everyone knows the truth you were so anxious to hide.'

He stabbed at Eddie with his stick. The stick passed right through the figure. Tony laughed. 'Didn't feel it, eh? I am sure God can arrange something you can feel. I've been a judge in my lifetime, Eddie, and I've sent a good many rogues down for what they've done but if the time has come to refer you to a higher court, so be it!'

Huw stepped forward and cleared his throat. 'That is probably where I come in.' He raised a hand and made the sign of the cross. 'I still don't know if you believed in God in your lifetime, Eddie, but now will be a good time to find out the truth of our Lord's mercy. You seem determined to haunt everyone you ever wronged and to be regarded as evil personified. It is for God to judge that. May God bless you, Eddie, and take you to himself so that you can release your attachment to this world. May you be forgiven for the harm you have done to your family. Leave your grandson Christopher and his family alone; leave Mike and Lucy alone. Step back and allow Tony here the memories of his love. Allow Evie her freedom at last.' He paused, summoning a strength to his voice which he didn't know he possessed. 'Leave now, in the name of God the Father, God the Son and God the Holy Spirit!'

For a long time nothing happened. Eddie seemed frozen. Immobile, he was staring now at Evie, devouring her with his eyes.

'Go, Eddie,' Huw said quietly. 'She is not yours and never was. You know it. We all know it.'

For a moment Eddie reached out towards Evie. She didn't

appear to see him. Her eyes were fixed on Tony. Eddie's hands clawed at her, pleading, trying to catch at her, to hold her. She ignored him.

He stood for a while gazing at her and then at last he turned away. He stared for a moment at the portrait and raised his hand as though to strike it but his hand brushed though it without touching the paint. The shadowy figure that was Eddie was wavering, growing less distinct. His face was dissolving as they watched.

'He's going.' Maggie mouthed the words silently.

Oblivious now of what was happening to Eddie, Tony's eyes were only for Evie as she stepped towards him and held out her arms. Dropping his walking stick he gave a small cry, and reached out for her. For several seconds they hugged one another, desperately clinging to each other, then slowly she began to fade and Tony was left alone. He staggered forward and almost fell, tears pouring down his face.

Huw and Mike reached him together.

'It's all right,' he said. 'I'm all right. She'll wait for me. I'll see her again. She knows I have to have time to get to know you, my boy.' He clung to Mike for a moment then painfully slowly he straightened and looked round for his stick. Lucy stooped and retrieved it for him, gently folding his hands over the handle. No one spoke for a long time.

As a rumble of thunder in the east signalled the departure of the storm, the lights came back on. Tony managed a grin. 'Life with my new family is obviously never going to be dull,' he said. He wiped his eyes with the back of his hand.

Back in the cottage Mike lit the fire. As the storm had tracked away across the Downs the sky had cleared and the sun appeared out of the bank of cloud, sending shafts of warm light over the countryside. Lucy brought in the attaché case and opened it for Tony, putting it on a low table beside him near the fire. He picked up his letter to Evie with shaking hands and turned the envelope over and over.

'I can't believe she never got it. It never occurred to me. I suppose I was so afraid she was going to turn me down that when I didn't hear from her that was what I assumed.' He stroked the envelope sadly.

In the kitchen Huw and Maggie were making a pot of tea. Lucy heard the sounds of washing up in the background but she couldn't drag her eyes away from Tony's face as he reached into the case and brought out the ring. Mike too was watching him. No one said anything for a long time. At last Tony looked up.

'You should have this, Michael. If it had been your grandmother's it would have been what she wanted. When you find the right girl you can give it to her.' He glanced at Lucy and winked. She froze, feeling her cheeks colour with embarrassment, remembering all too clearly how she had clung to Mike out there in the studio, how right it had felt as he put his arms round her. It was several seconds before she dared to look at him. She found he was watching her in amusement.

Tony chuckled. He reached for one of the diaries then he pushed it back into the case. 'I think I will save these for tonight on my own. Do you mind?' He climbed to his feet. 'I need to speak to those two good souls in the kitchen. Excuse me for a minute or two, will you?'

He disappeared into the kitchen closing the door behind him. Mike laughed. 'The crafty old devil is leaving us alone.'

Lucy nodded. She didn't know what to say.

'I suppose it makes sense for us to get together one day, perhaps go out and have a meal?' he said.

'I would like that.' She hesitated a moment. 'What about Charlotte?'

'Charlotte is no longer in my life. She threatened all sorts of mayhem when I last saw her but my spies tell me she has a new man in her sights. Whatever she said, I don't think we need to worry about her.' He leaned forward and took her hand. 'It felt right, out there, with my arms round you.'

She nodded again. 'Yes.'

'Have you tried on the ring?' His eyes were teasing.

She laughed. 'Of course. What woman wouldn't when she finds a sapphire lying around in an old suitcase?'

'Did it fit?'

'It did actually, but, Mike –'

'No, wait.' He held up his hand. 'I know we mustn't rush things. But we haven't any need to delay either. Just leave it like that.' He moved forward and, putting his hands on either side of her face, kissed her on the lips. He grinned. 'Shall we let them come back in now?'

She nodded.

It was Maggie, carrying in the tea tray, who noticed the young man in RAF uniform standing by the window, watching them. He was smiling. As the others turned to see what she was looking at he raised his hand and gave a thumbs up.

'Ralph?' Lucy said.

But he had gone.

A few minutes later they heard the throaty roar of the Spitfire engine in the distance. Throwing open the French windows Mike led them out into the garden. They were in time to see the plane perform a victory roll overhead before disappearing into the sunset.

Epilogue

Two years later
Press Release

The launch party for *Evie: The Story of a Legend* was held in a hangar at Goodwood aerodrome last night. In its former incarnation as RAF Westhampnett during World War Two the airfield was the subject of many of Evelyn Lucas's paintings and the setting for some of the most dramatic scenes in her biography. Lucy Standish, author of this outstanding biography, winner of the Samuel Johnson Prize, was present, together with Michael Marston, Evelyn Lucas's grandson and various other members of her family and Evie's former fiancé, Squadron Leader Tony Anderson, ninety-seven-year-old subject of many of her pictures, the only surviving member of 911 Squadron, which was stationed at Westhampnett for the duration of the Battle of Britain.

Postscript

The book made no mention of murder.

Author's Note

The chronology for Tony's story and the framework for his career in the Battle of Britain come from my father's experiences. He (a.k.a. Squadron Leader Nigel Rose) joined a Scottish auxiliary Spitfire squadron as a pilot officer in mid-1940. Briefly stationed at Drem, near Edinburgh, his squadron, 602, (City of Glasgow) was then sent to Westhampnett in West Sussex as the Battle of Britain was getting under way.

I have been privileged to have the use of his log books and letters to form the frame for Tony's time line, but of course the story itself is pure fiction. My dad did meet my mother only a week or so after arriving in Sussex. He is rumoured to have performed victory rolls over her parents' garden after returning from successful sorties (legend has it that the gardener would throw himself down on the grass when dive bombed by my mother's suitor with the laconic words, 'Mr Nigel has made it back then').

I have also managed to extricate many stories of the kind not usually heard by the aficionados of the Battle of Britain from him over the last few months – the stories of everyday life, of sadness and of hardship as well as the tales of derring-do.

The squadron was posted back to Scotland on December 13th and Daddy had already decided he had found his future wife. Luckily for me (born a few years later) she said yes. Many of the background storylines are taken from events that he was involved in, including his voyage to Egypt as security officer on the *Britannic* and the discovery of explosive strapped to the exhaust of his Spitfire, an action which was attributed to the fifth column at work on Clydeside. It was thought that one or two planes which had disappeared without any obvious reason on sorties over the sea might have been similarly sabotaged. My dad was lucky.

I have met many of his colleagues from the war in the course of my life, but one especially, the late Sandy Johnstone (Air Vice Marshall A.V.R. Johnstone) became a close friend. From my days at university when he was AOC Scotland and took pity on a student obviously in need of a few square meals by sending an official car to drive me in state back over the Forth Bridge to lunch at his HQ, to the days of his retirement near us in Suffolk, we saw quite a bit of Sandy and I listened spellbound to the stories with which he regaled us when he and my dad 'opened the hangar doors' as they called it, often, of course, accompanied by a wee dram (it was a Scots squadron).

Apart from that, my father, like so many of the men and women who fought in the last war, was reticent for many years about his exploits, and it has only been relatively recently with the various anniversaries of the Battle of Britain that he and some of his surviving comrades have been persuaded to talk about their experiences. It was as I began to hear more about them, and accompany him on his visits to the memorial events, and grow to recognise that inimitable roar of the Merlin engine for myself, that I began to think what a wonderful backdrop all that would make to a novel, and how it would be almost a sin to waste such an opportunity to write about it.

Thank you to everyone who helped me with advice and memories and generous encouragement. There are so many but I would particularly like to mention Ronnie Lamont, committee member of the 602 Squadron Museum in Glasgow, who invented Tony's and Ralph's squadrons and was the source of much extra information, and Group Captain Patrick Tootal, honorary secretary of the Battle of Britain Fighter Association and the Battle of Britain Memorial Trust, who first suggested I write a novel about the B. of B. and then asked several times if I had done it yet – always a good lever to inspiration!

Any mistakes and adjustments to fact (especially weather) are mine – sometimes I found it hard to fit the actual time line of the battle into the complications of my plot without a little tweaking of the dates. I hope this can be forgiven in the context of a novel. To write about such a thoroughly documented period is a challenge but I hope I have recreated the atmosphere and feel of the 1940s with sufficient accuracy to convince.

A special mention also goes to my son, Jon, for his sterling work in the office and on my website, and for his last minute all-night read-through of the manuscript, which showed him to be a proofreader born and bred.

Thanks as well, as always, are due to my agent, Carole Blake, and to my editors Kim Young, Susan Opie and Lucy Ferguson, and to all the wonderful people at HarperCollins. Their enthusiasm and support never ceases to be a huge bonus.